VALE'S SPEED

VALE'S SPEED

DY51V SERIES BOOK THREE

BY D.G. PEARSE

ALSO BY D.G. PEARSE

DY51v Series

Orphans of Avalon – Book One
The Red Thread – Book Two

Book Design: Tinytooth Publishing
Cover Design: TTP
Editor: Amanda Bidnall

For more information, visit www.dgpearse.com

DEDICATION

To all the genetic engineers and all the different scientific communities.

AUTHOR'S NOTE

For an author, putting a story together is much like sewing a jacket. If you don't put all the sections of fabric in their appropriate places—sleeves, chest, back, collar and lapels—balancing the character's age and backstory with the timeline and plot, you'll be dead in the water. I cannot count how many times I reread this series, while keeping handwritten and typed notes, double checking descriptions, weapons, names, places, seasons, and whether it was day or night. And even when it came time to publish, I still found the odd error. It just goes to show, no matter how diligent or how much of a stickler I am, nothing is perfect.

PROLOGUE

Do you think we're friends due to circumstance?

Are we friends, doll? I thought our relationship is more like a master and commander. You tell me what to do; I am your commander.

Maybe. The parasite giggled softly in his ear; a unique personality and voice he'd come to accept as part of his life.

Sauntering through ancient rubble in District S, Sloan broke with unrestrained laughter. Her presence was strange, almost as if he had a dual personality, nonetheless she was essential to his physical survival, as he was essential to hers. That's the way symbiotic beings worked. Although two different organisms, they could never be separated. And he believed that the longer they remained entwined, the more indelible their union.

Thus far, she'd assimilated to his emotions and personality, making them her own, but she'd also developed her own identity quirks. Basically, she was part him, part herself, while also the opposite of him, because it was the only way she knew how to adapt. She had no one else to reference. If needed, she could mimic him or she could oppose him. Emotions were tricky to gauge. Should she respond? Or should she just react? Every situation elicited thoughts, then comprehension and an answer.

As far as Sloan and *Medicus* knew, those he'd turned didn't share the same intimate relationship with their parasites.

ONE

LITTLE LUCY

**SUMMER
THIRTEEN YEARS LATER**

Days turned into weeks, then months and finally, years. During that time, the North American Continental Bloc became the fastest developing bloc in the world, and as a result, Avalon flourished. The federal panel officially stated such prosperity was due to a strong military presence and sound laws, but most believed it was the Independents, especially their auspicious leader. The Irishman's reputation had far surpassed all expectations. His legend had spread to the four corners of the earth.

For thirteen years, he'd kept his oath after General Morgan Griffin had died. He'd protected Avalon, enforced the laws, and helped restructure the military. He'd placed respectable people in charge of the units, and with Vincent's assistance, he'd gutted the black market of its worst criminal element—the human traffickers—re-establishing a fair barter system and auction house. The salvage shops, food bins and open-air markets were booming, and more were opening every year.

Even the island saw an upsurge in population. What had originally started with only five hundred people had almost tripled in growth. The feds continuously heard rumours about the inhabited island just off the northeastern seaboard, but they decided to leave well enough alone. As long as Doctor Avolare made regular trips to the mainland and visited them as promised, whatever the general did in private wasn't any of their business. If he was happy and productive, they remained satisfied.

Invasions from the South American Bloc had dwindled to the odd renegade gang or scavenger group. The fewer disturbances were attributed to improved precautionary measures and new safeguards that were put in place, including regular patrols into the wilds and deadlands. And, if a problem did arise, there were rules. The Avalon Police Force was far better trained and equipped than in the past. However, depending on the circumstance, they could be classified as a secondary line of defence. Sloan refused to send healthy young men into battle unless it was absolutely necessary. But that didn't stop the daily training exercises and rounds of policing in the city. The APF were busy twenty-four hours a day, seven days a week.

Sloan arrived at the island by midmorning, and the heat and humidity were already at a suffocating high. Rueben, Benny, Star and Ingalill greeted him on the shore: four out of the first ten young people he'd saved years before. Rueben had married Ingalill, and they had three sons, ranging in age from six to pre-teen. Benny and Star had two girls, eight and ten years old. Akira had left the island with Jens in search of his younger brothers, who'd fled with their grandfather to the Central Asian Bloc. While Ulvaeus and Chase were long deceased.

Thanks to Stephanie Shiro's astute eavesdropping, Sloan had gotten a reliable tip through the black market. Akira's grandfather and siblings had indeed worked at an auction house in Manzanillo. But once they'd saved enough money, they'd bought boarding passes. Whether the pirate ship had made it to the Central Asian Bloc was unknown, but they hoped for the best for their absentee friends. As for Jade, she had taken in Algar's blind baby and raised him on her own. But three years before, during a summer heat wave, she'd developed pneumonia after lying on the floor in her cottage to cool herself, and as a result she had died. The boy now lived with the village baker's sister, a spinster who taught the local children how to read and write.

Sloan jumped off the bow and landed in mushy sand to the gentle slap of the waves. Benny helped him moor the yacht. Star hugged him, as did Ingalill. Rueben, after a moment of vacillation, also gave him a rough hug.

"You all look great. How's everyone?" Sloan said.

The small group walked together in the direction of the forest.

"Everyone's doing well, Sloan, and you?" Benny asked.

"Good."

"We're glad you could make it," Rueben said.

"I wouldn't miss her birthday for the world." Sloan grinned, unwrapping a stick of gum. "How is she?"

"She's… great, real great." Rueben looked to the others for encouragement, and they looked back at him with eager anticipation. "Actually, Sloan, there's something you need to know."

He glanced at each of their faces, but he couldn't determine whether they were happy or concerned. "Okay… Wait, don't tell me: she's got a boyfriend!" he chuckled.

"You could *kind of* say that." Ingalill smiled brightly.

"That's one way of putting it." Benny smirked, shoving his hands in his front hip pockets.

Star frowned and elbowed him. "Don't start, Ben."

"Wait till he finds out, then we'll see how well things go."

"What does that mean?" Sloan chewed, briefly narrowing his eyes.

"Nothing, Sloan." Rueben glared at his brother. "I think it'd be best if we let Lucy tell you."

The cottage appeared the same as it always did—the cobalt-blue gate, door, and window frame were cheerful and added pizzazz to the otherwise ancient structure. The flowers were blooming, and the garden pruned. Lucy had been staying at Sloan's family home since her fourteenth birthday, when she'd requested to live there instead of with her adoptive parents. She'd grown into a strong, independent young woman, and Sloan didn't have the heart to deny her. On her fifteenth birthday, she'd asked him for a sewing machine, a set of encyclopedias, books on gardening and anything he could find on cursive writing. He wondered what she'd ask for this year.

The cottage door swung open, and little Lucy was on the stoop. "Sloan!"

"Happy birthday, doll." He bent over somewhat, embraced her and kissed the top of her head. "I can't believe you're sixteen already."

"Me neither." She kissed his cheek and searched his face. "I'm so glad you came."

"Me too."

She grabbed his hand and dragged him inside the cottage. "I've made a cake, sandwiches and punch."

"Sounds fantastic. But someone else should've prepared the food for you. It is *your* birthday."

The others followed them inside.

The party lasted several hours, filling the wee cottage with laughter and chatter. Sloan wandered around in the garden to catch a breath of fresh air. The rose bushes, hydrangea, rhododendrons, and heather were beautifully colourful and flourishing. He was thankful Lucy had taken such good care of his family home. He ducked back inside, closing the door to the rattle of the knocker. Lucy was opening her gifts, each one handcrafted: scarves, a quilt and even a new cloak. He sat at the kitchen table and watched with fondness as she kissed the women and hugged the men. They all sang "Happy Birthday," and she blew out the candles before cutting the cake.

Sloan speared the thick, fluffy piece of apple spice cake drenched in cinnamon drizzle with his fork. Birthdays were an important celebration, especially for the orphans, a symbol of triumph over the odds. He sighed and set the fork down on the edge of the plate. "What would you like, doll?" He propped his head on a tight fist with a tender, handsome smile. "If it's in my power, I'll get you whatever your heart desires."

Everyone, including Lucy, stopped talking. The women's smiles were hopeful, whereas the men seemed apprehensive.

"I want to see Wade." She slowly got up from the sofa but kept her fingers on the armrest, as if it were a brace. She nervously picked at the worn chenille.

Glancing at the others, Sloan chuckled in disbelief. "What kind of birthday present is that? Be serious, Lucy."

"I am. Take me to him," she pleaded.

Sloan knew she was sincere because she was a serious creature by nature. But he couldn't fathom the attraction. "He's a hermit and a packrat, doll, and he lives in this gigantic building full of junk. And he's really, really old," he said placidly. "I don't think you'd be hap—"

"*Please*, Sloan." She was suddenly down on her knees, pressing her face to his chest, hugging him. "You're the only way I can get to the mainland."

"Give me one good reason."

Lucy tugged on his jacket until he bent down. Then she whispered in his ear. "Because I really like him."

Why, that dirty old dog. He respired a lengthy sigh, searched her expression, then straightened as she giggled and hugged him again. "Thank you, Sloan."

"Yeah, yeah. I think I *am* too bloody soft."

The others laughed, and Rueben winked at him, apparently pleased with his answer.

While the women helped Lucy clean the mess, Rueben and Benny strolled with him around the village. He always inspected the place and spoke to the locals whenever he was on the island. Most would give him lists of items they needed, or they'd share the latest gossip. Not only was he their benefactor, importer/exporter and guardian, but he was also their key link to the outside world. Usually, he made bi-weekly trips. Wade and Raphael had taken turns with the monthly medical visits, until Raphael made the island her full-time residence with Krista. The feds disapproved of her choice, but they accepted Wade's growing expertise as fair trade. Sloan had offered Raphael his family cottage, but she'd refused and chosen a vacant cottage to the west, outside of town, stating she preferred the isolation.

And with the subsequent upsurge in the population, another village had grown seemingly overnight, two kilometres past the extensive property where Doctor Avolare lived.

Sloan slipped out of the local food bin and waved goodbye to the owner. "That guy's always chipper."

"So how are *you* doing, Sloan?" Rueben's tone was cheerful.

"Great." Sloan offered him a stick of gum, and he took it.

"How's everyone back on the mainland?" Benny ambled on Sloan's left, squinting against the burning sunlight with his hands once again in his hip pockets.

"Okay. Tristan and Peaches are going strong. Elyse has become an amazing sniper—chip off the old block," he grinned with pride. "And Warrick is an outstanding soldier. I'm thinking about appointing him to general when I'm ready to retire. The Independents are fine."

"What about Petrov?" Benny looked at his brother, his sharp hazel-blue gaze urging him to say something.

"Petrov's fine. He and Mona are doing well."

"They're still together, then." Rueben chewed his gum. "That's great."

Sloan stopped in the middle of the road and huffed a weary sigh. Both men had moved to block his route. "Okay. I know you've got something to fecking say."

"Hey, don't look at me, old man." Benny shrugged and motioned to Rueben with a tilt of his head. "He's the one who's worried. Me, I like to *not* stick my nose in."

"Thanks, Benjamin." Rueben focused on Sloan. "We don't mean any harm."

"I told you this was a bad idea," Benny whispered from the side of his mouth.

Sloan glared. "Just spit it the feck out already!"

"All right. You saved us all," Rueben attested evenly. "Now it's your turn to be happy."

"What he said," Benny added in a matter-of-fact way. "And we think Raphael is the perfect candidate. Even though she's a recluse and way too much into her scientific experiments, we know it's you she's in love with."

"Bloody hell, Ben." Rueben stared at him with disgust, and Benny shied away a few feet. "What my knucklehead brother meant was… you don't have to be alone. You deserve a relationship and love, Sloan."

Perturbed, Sloan eyed the pair. He'd rescued a lot of children—several hundred, in fact—and most were now adults, living together in peace on the island. Thanks to Wade's genius and the inventions he'd salvaged from the ancients, they'd learned to cultivate the land for gardening and crops, even medicine, and raise livestock. Now many of the orphaned children had families of their own. They were safe from the government, slave traders, and scavengers.

"I am happy. Look at you." Sloan gently gripped Rueben's shoulder and smiled warmly. "I have both of you and everyone else I brought to this island, and my family too. What more could any man want?"

"What about someone for you?"

He tried to maintain his artificial smile, but every time love and relationships were mentioned, he thought about Amanda, and he'd feel an asphyxiating pang. "When you get to my age, you learn to accept the cards you've been dealt… and love isn't in them."

"Amanda would cry if she heard you talking like this," Rueben said.

Sloan's chest literally ached; it had been well over a decade since her passing, but the grief felt as fresh as if she'd died that day. "It's fine. Honest. If I ever meet someone who might interest me, then maybe…"

"Promise me." Rueben grabbed his arms. "No, that's wrong. Promise *us* that if you do meet somebody, you won't think twice. You'll just seize the moment."

After a somewhat tense, drawn-out silence, Sloan gave in with a perturbed grunt. "Fine. I promise."

"And we're gonna hold you to that, Mr. Whelan." Benny grinned, pointing a large finger at his nose. "So don't you fecking forget it." He winked.

Bright and early the next morning, Lucy was on the bow of the yacht, bouncing on the balls of her feet and frantically waving goodbye to the others. Her enthusiasm was infectious, and Sloan couldn't help but chuckle.

The Atlantic waves were rough and made the journey less than ideal, but the old boat had sailed the route many times. Sloan kept his hands on the wheel while Lucy stood beside him.

Briny gusts of wind blew her soft strawberry-blonde curls everywhere. She pulled a strand from her mouth. "I can't wait to see him."

"*Yeah*, you and me both," he said with a sarcastic drawl.

Once they reached the small harbour, Sloan dropped anchor, and they started the nine-kilometre hike to the truck. Lucy didn't seem fazed. She adjusted the knapsack and trailed behind him, climbing the ancient hills of rubble.

"I can carry you on my shoulders," Sloan called back.

"No. I'm quite all right." She pulled herself up onto a huge barnacle-covered rock.

He sighed, bent down, and extended his hand to her. "Let me help you, doll."

"It isn't necessary," she gasped, patting her brow with her sleeve.

"True. But it's fecking hot, and I can't stand the extreme heat. The faster we get to the truck, the better."

Finally, Lucy swallowed her pride and conceded to his prudent advice. Her throat was parched with thirst, and her stamina inadequate. Getting up and over the busted sections of concrete and stone wasn't easy for someone of her diminutive stature. She grasped his large, rough hands with her tiny, delicate ones. The warm strength of his grip reminded her of when she was still a child, and how he'd made her feel safe.

Sloan crouched in front of her. "Hop on."

Next, he was running and jumping. She bounced, hugging his thick neck tighter. The movement seemed to wake the memories from dormancy deep inside her subconscious. "I remember the cabin, and how you saved me and the others."

"But you were only three." He kept a gentle but firm grip on her legs.

"Actually, I was older… just underdeveloped for my age like Chase."

"Then you aren't sixteen."

"No. More like eighteen, possibly nineteen." She pressed her thoughtful expression against his shoulder, and her eyes grew glassy. "You always held me, and I remember how protected I felt. I thought you were my father, and I was heartbroken when you left me on the island. But eventually, I came to understand."

The truck came into view a couple of yards away. Sloan stopped, dropping to squat, and she slid to the ground.

"Why did you save us, Sloan?" She adjusted her knapsack, then pants.

"To make amends… at first. Then I fell in love with this awesome group of kids." He handsomely smiled, digging a key fob from his hip pocket.

TWO

BUILDING RELATIONSHIPS

"Is this the place?" She peered out the grimy truck window, smudging it with the side of her fist.

"Yep, that's it: paradise." Sloan put the truck in park and shut down the engine. "I'm really busy, doll, so—"

"I know. You won't be returning to the island for at least a month."

"Yeah, and that means you're stuck with the old fart until then."

"Oh, I don't mind." She smiled sweetly at him and grabbed her knapsack.

"Wait. I'll help you with that." Sloan got out, shut the drivers-side door, and rushed around to the passenger's side. He lifted Lucy from the truck cab and set her on the ground. He handed over her knapsack. "If there's a problem, let me know."

"I promise."

They walked to the building to find the front double doors unlocked. Lucy looked around, committing everything to memory. The clinic was an amazing building: partially split-level with two storeys constructed of solid concrete and brick, with a huge lobby entrance and vaulted ceilings punctured by skylights.

"Hey, what brings you here, Irish? I thought you were still on the island."

"I was, but I've got a personal delivery for you." Sloan grinned stupidly and scratched the back of his scalp.

Lucy peeked out from behind the Irishman, her complexion flushed.

"*Lucy...*" Wade said in astonishment, staring at the young woman. "Why's she here?"

"Her birthday request was a month with you." Sloan didn't sense any deception on his friend's part, so he figured Wade's surprise was genuine, but he also sensed something else. Wade's pulse started to rise the instant Lucy got closer to him, and he suspected his childhood friend felt something for the young woman. *Maybe their feelings are mutual?* "Okay, well, I'd better take off." Sloan pointed back over his shoulder in the general direction of the lobby.

"This is crazy." Wade frowned. "You can't stay here, Lucy."

"But why?" She clutched her knapsack.

"Oi, where do you think you're going?" Wade grabbed Sloan's arm and dragged him into a dark aisle between the shelves of preserved body parts and a strange array of packaged organic materials. "She has to leave."

Sloan eyeballed a snake suspended in a jar of formaldehyde, and he grimaced. "But she's crazy about you."

"I know she is." Wade frowned, leaning on a shelving unit. "And that's what I'm afraid of."

"Why? Because she's young?" he said in an absent-minded tone, turning the jar so the snake wasn't gawking at him.

"That's part of it…"

"What you fail to see is that she's a highly intelligent young woman. If I were you, I wouldn't waste time debating the semantics—*I'm too old for her* or *will she love me forever*—and I'd make the girl mine."

"Would you really?" Wade's expression remained deadpan.

Sloan's tone was firm. "I would."

"Are you trying to tell me that's what you did with Amanda?"

"Yep. Pretty much. The moment I saw her, I knew, irrespective of the age difference, I had to have her. I just told her how beautiful she was, romanced her, and then I married her."

"And it was that simple."

"Not long ago, you were bellyaching again about how *lonely* you are. Now you've got this pretty young thing standing in your shop who promises to take all that away, and you're not willing to even give it a shot?" Sloan frowned, searching his friend's hazel-blues. "What are you, a fecking eejit?"

"I like my privacy, and I've never lived with anyone other than my mam… well, after my da died." Wade sighed, resting

23

his forehead on his arm, and staring at the polished concrete floor.

Sloan cuffed his arm. "Shite, you really *are* an eejit. It's called compromise and setting boundaries. Aside from love, sex, and companionship, that is what relationships are all about. You learn about each other and learn to enjoy that union."

Wade looked at him in disbelief.

"Since you can't seem to make a decision to save your life, I'm making it for you." Sloan glared at him before walking away. "Stubborn arse."

"Hey, wait a minute!" Wade slid out from the aisle.

"Nope. This conversation is terminated." Sloan skirted the steel table and strode into the cafeteria, where Lucy was already preparing a meal. "I'm leaving, doll."

"Oh, okay." Lucy apprehensively smiled, wiping her hands on a tea towel. "Is everything all right?"

"Sure." He bent down and kissed her cheek. "Good luck."

Lucy frowned, watching him leave, when she noticed Wade standing in the shadows of the clinic as Sloan exited the building, and he didn't look thrilled. In fact, he looked somewhat despondent. She smiled weakly at him, then turned to face the industrial sized cooker. "I guess I shouldn't have come," she said quietly. "I think I misunderstood."

"It isn't like that, Lucy." Wade stood in the open doorway.

"It's okay. You don't have to lie." She folded the tea towel and set it neatly on the counter. "I'll leave as soon as I can, and I'll stay out of your way." She dashed past him with tears in her eyes.

"Crap." He cursed and swung around, giving the nearest object a kick, a garbage can.

Sunlight illuminated the dirty window, and Wade woke with a stretch. He pushed away the blanket and sat up. He had a shower, dressed, and knocked on an examination room door opposite his. When no answer came, he carefully turned the knob and peered inside. To his regret, Lucy was gone. "Shite." He turned and flew for the stairs, snatching his jacket dumped over the handrail. Even though the city was considerably safer than in the past, it still wasn't a place for a young woman to be wandering the streets alone, especially when the populace was mainly comprised of sexually deprived men.

Sloan scratched his scalp with an enormous yawn and wandered out of the master bedroom. He tarried in the hallway, shocked. "Lucy. What the feck are you doing here?"

"Elyse offered to share her room last night. Don't worry, I won't get in your way."

"That's got nothing to do with it. You'd never be in the way. What happened with Wade? You were so determined yesterday…"

She burst into tears. He exhaled a grievous sigh and gave his head another rub. He had no idea what to do. Elyse touched her back, and Lucy suddenly clung to her, bawling. Elyse hugged her and stared questioningly at her father, as if he were to blame.

"If it'll help, I can talk to him, doll."

"No, *please*. This whole situation is embarrassing enough." Lucy released Elyse, hastily wiping her cheeks. "Coming here was a mistake."

Someone knocked on the apartment door.

"All right, I won't say a word. Just wait a second. Let me get that." He strode through the hallway, and when he flung the door open, he was stunned to see Wade with his fist in the air, primed to knock a second time.

He grabbed his childhood friend's jacket and shoved him into the corridor, closing the door behind them. "What the feck is going on? Right now, Lucy's inside my apartment, crying her eyes out. What did you do?"

"Hey, do you mind." Wade scowled, pushing his grip away. "I didn't do anything. *That's* the problem."

"Okay. Now I'm confused."

"I don't care if you're confused. This is none of your business, Irish. So would you let me handle it?"

Sloan grimaced and reopened the door. "Fine. Be my guest."

Not fifty seconds later, Sloan watched as Wade led Lucy out of the apartment by her hand. Her eyes were glassy, and her complexion kissed pink, but she was also shyly smiling when she passed him.

Sloan smirked and shook his head. He shut and locked the door, then met his giddy daughter in the living room. "I know you're dying to tell me. What did I miss?"

"That's extremely rude, Dad—but you'd never believe it! Wade said he loved her, and she was to come home with him immediately. Then he dragged her away." Elyse beamed from ear to ear, clasping her hips, leaning toward him. "*Very romantic.*"

"Yeah, that's fecking romantic, all right. That's about as romantic as a kick in the arse from a frozen mukluk."

"A frozen *what*?" Elyse's smile wilted into a disconcerted frown, and her forehead rumpled. "Tell me again... How did Mom ever fall in love with you?"

"Honestly, I haven't a clue." Sloan ambled into the kitchen.

"Well, it couldn't have been your rapier wit or seductive charms. You must've brainwashed her. Or maybe you bit her."

"Smartarse. I only bit her when she begged." Sloan chuckled to himself as he opened the fridge.

"Eww. Come on, Dad. I don't want to hear how my parents got it on."

He bent over the door, hemming and hawing over what little produce sat on the racks. "You're an adult. How do you think you got here? Sex: that's how." Sloan took a couple of eggs from a bowl and examined them for a moment. "We saw each other, and that was it. We were head over heels."

Elyse planted her hand on her hip and shot him a *"you expect me to believe that BS"* look. "You're so full of it."

"Nope. That's the fecking truth. It was love at first sight." He bumped the fridge door shut with his knee, set the eggs on a tea towel on the counter and began hunting through the cupboards. "Where the hell are the frying pans?"

"Here." Elyse passed him a small frying pan. "Actually, Mom said you were so handsome, she couldn't tear her eyes away."

He flashed a broad, smug grin and whistled, cracking the eggs in the pan.

"Oh, *please*. I'm going to vomit." She rolled her eyes, crossing her arms.

"Where's your brother?"

"Dunno. He's been working a lot for Uncle Vince and Colonel Vargas. Last time I saw him, he was exhausted and slept for two days straight." She flopped out in a chair at the kitchen table. "But it's been the same for me. Uncle Vince is a slave driver. I can't even see Ry—" She quickly bit back her words. "We've just been really busy. You know how it is."

"Are you dating Ryouichi?"

"Don't start, Dad. I'm an adult, and I am entitled to date whoever I want."

Sloan finished cooking the eggs and scraped them on a plate. *He's an old fecking man compared to you*, is what he wanted to say. But he had to respect his daughter's choices, whether he agreed with them or not. "Don't lecture. It's my right as your father, baby doll. I've got decades on you."

"Yeah, all right, Dad." She groaned, resting her chin on her palm, leaning on the table.

"When did you last see him?"

"Ryouichi or my turd of a brother?"

"Your turd of a brother." Sloan sat at the table, tucking his chair in.

She thought about it for a second. "Maybe a week ago. Why?"

"I've got something important to discuss with him."

***

"I'm a little jealous." Lucy snuggled into his chest. "Sloan gave you everlasting life. You'll always look this good, while I continue to age."

Wade had never considered their genetic differences, and it scared him for a moment. He kissed her forehead. "Just because I carry his parasite doesn't mean I won't age or die. There are no guarantees, pet."

He touched her face, and she kissed his palm. They'd had so much sex, he thought they'd wither away to nothing. But she was young and hot, and he couldn't resist. *You were right, Irish. I can't help myself.* Suddenly, she jumped up and straddled his pelvis like riding a horse bareback. She giggled, leaned down and kissed his bare chest. He groaned, staring at the ceiling. *I can't take much more...*

***

Sloan wandered through the main floor of the clinic, the lobby, then into Wade's sanctuary beside the cafeteria. As per normal, he was fully armed, ready for any given situation. The sword was a weighty nuisance, but indispensable to his survival. Whereas he only brought out his sniper rifle when required.

Wade had his forehead planted on the stainless-steel table, and his arms were dangling.

"Hey. Are you, all right?" He approached the table with a little more urgency. "You look like shite."

"Yeah, and it's all thanks to you, arsehole."

"Pardon?" He rolled a stool over and sat on it.

"Is Lucy a vampire?"

"No." Sloan pinched his eyebrows in a comical way, as if he were about to laugh.

"Are you sure?" Wade pressed his hands flat on the tabletop and pushed himself into an upright position.

"Of course, I'm sure. What the feck is wrong?"

"I did what you said. But now I can't keep up." Wade cupped his face, peering through his stiff fingers. "She's like this sex-starved machine, and if I don't comply, she just jumps on me. My dick is getting worn out—hell, it might fall off yet."

Sloan snorted, hugging his stomach and doubled over with mirth.

"Oh, that's it. Laugh it up, arsehole. I blame you for my inability to function."

"It's okay."

"No, it isn't."

"That's not what I meant. Would you relax, man? She loves you, that's all, and it's new. Eventually she'll come to her senses. Don't complain." Sloan smirked to himself, unwrapping a stick of gum, his own memories were stirred. "Or maybe it'll get worse, who knows?" He stuffed the gum in his mouth. "Amanda was the same. So were Peaches and Tris. Love is love, and the laws of attraction… Who can say?"

"You're a real fecking jerk." Wade whipped a rubber glove at him.

Sloan ducked, shoulders hunched, chuckling. "You sure upset easily."

"Anyway, why are you here?" Wade watched him savour the gum.

"For over a decade, there's been nothing. Now, all of a sudden, reports are coming in. A few people have gone missing again, and these recent cases resemble those in the past. How many creatures are there? Where have they been hiding all this time? Why come out of the woodwork now after so long? Are they the parents of the mutant vampires, MVs or more MV children?" Sloan scratched his head. "Do you think there's any way to find out?"

"I understood Snickers and Roddy tried to hunt down said creatures years ago."

"Yeah. They spent three years probing the wilds. But it was like the creatures vanished without a trace."

"Creepy, and odd." Wade sat back, his hands clasped together in his lap, chair creaking. "Well, there's only one place to start… I need facts. Can you get me those diaries, and any other research material you have?"

"Consider it done." Sloan rose from the stool, adjusting his belt. "Oh, and I'm guessing you'd like a live specimen too."

"Wow. You just read my mind." Wade grinned sardonically. "Yeah, a parent if possible. Raphael said it would be a hybrid-human similar to you."

"Right. Leave it to me."

"I don't think that'd be wise, Irish." Wade pitched forward and rested his forearms on the table. "Get Petrov to do it."

"You just said you need a specimen."

"I do. But Avalon needs you in one piece."

Peaches bashed through the clinic entrance out of breath, and both men jumped. "I've been looking everywhere for you, big man. We've got a serious problem. *Hurry.*"

Sloan frowned. "Well, don't leave me hanging."

"Mona and her entire unit have gone missing."

"Aw, feck. We'll talk later, Wade." Sloan strode out of the medical building directly behind Peaches. "When? Where?"

THREE

RE-EMERGENCE

"Two hours ago. Bunting." Peaches entered the scorching sunlight, hopped in the Jeep, and started the engine. "The unit was just south of the district, searching for evidence of a missing herd."

Sloan nodded. Normally, white-tail deer inundated the area every year, but not this summer. And because the locals relied on the extra meat, they'd asked Mona to investigate.

"Stoner's unit has gone to search the site."

"Great." Sloan slammed the passenger door.

Peaches was no stranger to driving, and the Jeep took off like a pebble from a slingshot. If the vehicle had a functioning engine, she could drive it. She knew every clear, passable road in Avalon, and she had Sloan in District B in less than forty-five minutes, a miracle considering the distance, traffic, and terrain.

Sloan took a double-barrelled flare gun out of the glove compartment: standard issued equipment in all military vehicles. He stuffed both his front jacket pockets with flares, shut the Jeep door, and approached Stoner, who was standing on a moss-covered section of concrete. "Anything?" he inquired.

"Not yet, General," Stoner answered.

He sighed, watching the forest. "It's been quiet for years, and now this. Why?"

"Maybe the MVs have been around all along, but they didn't care until Mona crossed into their territory."

"The deer herd."

"Not even a vamp can survive indefinitely without some type of sustenance. Hunting people would mean entering the city, an unfamiliar environment. Remember, even though it was an age ago, Petrov killed one, and that marked the city as our territory."

He appreciated Stoner's insight. The European was a brilliant, soft-spoken man and a natural problem solver with a knack for stating the overlooked but most logical answers.

Petrov with little effort swiftly zigzag-climbed the steep grade of boulders in front of them. "I have checked the outlying forest, and there is nothing."

"My unit and I combed the deadlands in a twenty-kilometre radius, and it's like they just disappeared," Stoner said. "Nothing."

"Stay here, and that's an order." Sloan watched the APF back away while Petrov, Stoner and Peaches stood as sentinels in a row at the forefront. "Do not—I repeat, *do not*—follow me."

Petrov gripped his rifle with a deepening frown.

Sloan knew he was worried, but if anything happened to any of them, his conscience would haunt him for the rest of his days. "Watch for my flares," he called back.

He descended the boulders to the rocky ground below and hiked a gentle, grassy slope. At the summit, the forest began. He pressed the side of his palm to the rough, crinkled bark of an eastern cedar, carefully stepping into the shadows. The trees were old growth and extremely tall, with wide trunks, and patches of rich soil spread like webbing between their gnarled roots. He craned his neck. Darkness solidified the canopy, and when the wind pushed, the trees knocked and creaked. It was a weird sensation, standing below such height. He felt insignificant. But he continued his trek, sinking deeper and deeper in the woods.

Pulling back his cuff, he checked his wristwatch. He was fifteen minutes in, and still nothing. "No birds, no animals and no unit," he murmured. Then he caught a whiff—the faint odour of decomposing flesh. *This is a little too familiar.* Instantly, the same gut feeling he'd experienced at the secret lab returned like PTSD, amplifying his senses, and he knew he was about to walk from the frying pan into the fire.

After an additional kilometre, there was a noticeable drop in temperature, and without a shred of sunlight, he was swallowed by the gloom. He glanced back in the direction he'd come, and all he could see was a barricade of trees. *No bodies, not even a drop of blood.* He was seriously beginning to wonder if Stoner had made a mistake, and maybe Mona and her unit had returned to the barracks. But she would've checked in, and that didn't explain the pungent smell of rotten flesh, which had grown significantly stronger. He stopped, loaded his flare gun, and aimed it skyward.

Peaches adjusted her binoculars. "There!" She pointed westward.

Everyone watched the distant neon green plume arc the sky. Flares were position locators, but it was the colour that mattered. Green meant everything was status quo, neon orange was an alert—not necessarily life threatening, but a sign he'd encountered something—while red meant he was in trouble and neon blue denoted an incursion of some kind.

"He has gone in deep," Petrov said.

"Too deep," Stoner added.

"Why did he go so far?" Peaches lowered her binoculars. "There's no way the unit went in that deep… is there?"

Petrov gritted his teeth, tempted to chase after him, but Sloan's orders kept his boots lag bolted. If he showed any insubordination in front of the others, it would undermine Sloan's authority as the general. In the beginning, the APF had been a fragile, rundown machine, and the restoration process had been trickier than they'd initially expected. Morgan Griffin had done a psychological number on the men who'd quit, and they weren't willing to trust another genetic freak. Those who joined were wary, and Sloan made a point to meet each man to demonstrate he was nothing like his predecessor. Progress had been slow, but as time passed, the recruitment campaign gained momentum.

The Irishman's reputation for honesty and sound unbiased judgment, and protecting military personnel became renowned, and Petrov was proud to assist in any way he could.

Another flare blazed, crossing the sky, but this time it was red. A mix of concern and trepidation broke out in the ranks as the soldiers talked amongst themselves.

Petrov's heart pounded, and he removed the rifle strap from his shoulder. If Sloan shot an additional red flare, he'd need help.

"I'll go with you." Peaches watched the sky.

"All right, comrade." Petrov anxiously awaited the second flare.

"We'll stay here," Stoner said.

Niklas Schulze, a thirty-three-year-old with an aptitude for investigative tracking, stood quivering in a small fir grove. He was aiming in opposing directions, and the guns were rattling in his white-knuckled grip. Large beads of perspiration rolled down the sides of his flushed cheeks. His blood-bathed unit littered the ground around him, and some of them lay motionless. And Mona was nowhere to be seen. Sloan cautiously stepped into the lieutenant's line of sight.

Schulze was instantly misty-eyed, and his forehead peaked, as if he were relieved. "They're everywhere, General," he said in a soft stammer. "Don't make any sudden movements…"

"Everything will be okay, son," Sloan whispered. He sensed some men were deceased, while others were gravely injured. *Great.* He rested his spine against a gigantic American basswood and stared at a pair of red eyes, a couple hundred metres directly behind the lieutenant. He slowly turned his head to the right. Two more sets of eyes. And when he peered to the far left, there was an additional set. He did not know if there was anything behind him and the tree, but he had to assume the worst.

Shite. Keeping his attention on the enemy, he carefully took a red flare from his pocket and slid it into a chamber. He switched the gun from his left-hand to his right, dug in the opposite pocket and placed a neon blue flare into the secondary chamber. Then he waited, breathing shallow, the scent of decomposition now nauseatingly strong. Sloan figured the moment he shot the flare gun, it was game over, and he'd be in a battle for their lives. The first MV he'd fought years earlier had exhibited agility, strength, and speed, and if he multiplied those capabilities by four, he was in a problematic situation.

He looked at Lieutenant Schulze; it was apparent the guy had been guarding the grove for hours. His entire body was trembling with fatigue, and occasionally, he'd lose strength in his arms and lower his guns. "If my memory serves me correct, you were born in Newberg?"

"Ah… yes, sir," Niklas said.

"Good agricultural land. Were you raised on a farm?"

The lieutenant nodded, shivering violently. "They're getting closer, sir."

"Don't look at them," Sloan ordered quietly; he couldn't let anyone else die. "Focus on *me*."

Niklas gulped, nodding again.

"Where's the colonel?"

The lieutenant's expression instantly sank to pallid uncertainty. "I-I don't know. One minute we were fighting beside each other, and the next she was…"

He waited. "*Lieutenant*," he said sharply.

"She screamed, and all I saw was blood, sir. She was gone."

Sloan didn't care for his explanation, but he stayed calm. "As soon as I shoot the flares, hit the deck and bury yourself with the dead."

The flares exploded, a far-off pop echoed faintly, and a twisting fusion of red and neon blue streaked the heavens. Peaches and Petrov bolted. Darting through the trees a short span apart, they watched for Sloan and whatever else might be in the woods with him. They were running into the unknown.

"Spread out and take aim!" Stoner barked, then climbed to the highest boulder he could find, drawing both his platinum Glock 19s.

The deafening screeches went straight through Niklas as he scrambled to get underneath the bodies. He wanted to help the general, but his nerves were shot, and as a soldier's partially missing arm fell and bumped his face, he retched. The stomach-churning scent of death had permeated everywhere. He lacked the courage, and he couldn't believe it when the general took on all four of the MVs that bullets wouldn't stop. In those hazy moments, pinioned under the soldier, he realized the APF was nothing more than a glorified clean-up crew. They were meant to fight other humans, not genetic freaks. They were solely reliant on the Independents.

Drawing his Irish longsword, Sloan sprang high in the air. He caught a mutant vampire's neck. Blood, black and slick as oil, spewed, and its head flew, disintegrating into a cloud of ash. The body detonated, blanketing the unit in dust. Niklas hacked, covering his nose and mouth.

Sloan landed with a thud near the unit, his eyes gleaming. "Come on!" He held out his arms as the other three mutant vampires crept closer, screeching and growling. "What? Are you scared?" He couldn't seem to ignore the urge. The thirst drove him, feeding his rage, and vice versa; he wanted a damned good fight. Besides, he refused to let anyone under his command get eaten. He sheathed the sword and dashed, hollering, "Catch me if you can!"

Each mutant turned and took off, a racehorse from the starting gate. On all fours, they galloped after him, manoeuvring the uneven terrain and vegetation with ease.

Sloan flew without looking back. He covered metres per second. A branch nicked his cheek. He blinked. Another scraped his leather sleeve with a whiplash snap. Then, from the right, he noticed one gaining on him. The mutant vampire leaped around clusters of saplings.

Suddenly, the forest thinned. Sloan glanced down. The ground was spongy and his boots squishing. Only two locations near Avalon's borders retained their water level in the summer, even when other areas didn't; the Avalon River, a fast-moving tributary north of the city that emptied into the Atlantic and a bog. The bog was thick with vegetation, a turbid maze filled with insects, amphibians, and reptiles—everything that made Sloan's skin crawl. He sprinted in a huge curve to avoid the vast area.

Breathing hard, he examined the terrain ahead. He trusted Mona was still alive and not anywhere near the fecking bog. He just needed a breadcrumb. Anything. *Come on, doll, give me a sign.*

The sun's sweltering heat beat down. Mona sucked in the stifling air, holding out her makeshift spear, her clammy chest heaving. Gripping the steel pipe with an old bayonet shoved in the end, she gradually turned. She was surrounded. Five mutant vampires, the likes of which she'd never seen, were waiting for her to cross the invisible line. The only thing between her and death was the length of her spear. She'd killed one, but it had taken every ounce of her strength, and now it was sheer will that kept her fighting. *At least we know where the deer went.* She smirked, then her chin quivered slightly. *What am I thinking? If I die out here, no one will ever know.* Her eyes welled up, and she lifted her arm, brushing her damp, grimy cheek against it. She wished Petrov or Sloan or even Snickers were with her.

Coming to an immediate stop, Petrov was relieved to find Mona's stranded unit, and a shaken Lieutenant Schulze helping the wounded. But his best friend and girlfriend weren't in sight. Peaches slowed down and walked in on the other side of the fir grove.

Schulze noticed both of them and he stood at attention with a salute. "Colonel…"

"At ease, Lieutenant." Peaches patted the air, gesturing for him to relax. "We saw the flares, and we're here to help. What happened?"

Petrov scanned the outlying forest and helped a soldier to his feet. The man shambled away to lean against a tree. But he also noted how many were deceased; a third of the unit would have to be shipped for cremation. The situation wasn't good no matter how they sliced it. He checked another man's injuries.

"We were searching the area with Colonel Mona Lisa, and instead of finding the deer herd, we crossed paths with these *things*. They attacked us without warning, and during the frenzy, the colonel went missing. Then sometime later, the general appeared. He told me to stay here, and he set off the flares." Niklas wiped his hand on a pant leg. "After that, he killed one of those *things* and led the rest of them away, deeper into the forest."

"What direction did he take?" Petrov asked.

"That way." Niklas pointed northwest.

"How many creatures followed him?"

"Three, that I saw."

Petrov looked at Leona. "Can you handle this?"

Peaches had dumped the contents of her knapsack and was bandaging a man's leg. She glanced at the Russian. "Of course. Just be careful. We don't need any more casualties."

"I am always careful, comrade."

A high-pitched scream in the far distance frightened everyone in the grove. Petrov's gut lurched, and he vanished, running at top speed.

Sloan heard his friend's cries, and he took a sharp left. The mutant vampires, crashing into one another, switched direction, tearing the ground, giving chase.

Mona screamed, holding the pipe lengthwise above her chest as a MV leaned on it, viciously snapping at her face. She abruptly jerked, sliding through the grass, and wailed at the top of her lungs; another was gnawing on her leg. Frantically, she screamed again, kicking.

Trees whizzed past. Sloan entered the small meadow like a speeding tank. *Fecking hell.* Mona's hysterical screams were dry and hoarse. Half her leg was gone, and she was losing a ton of blood. He grimaced, whipped out his sword and yelled, careening into the MVs. The one eating her leg looked up, and it was already dead, its body halved. Sloan shoved the other mutant vampire off her, dropped the sword and snatched the spear. Twirling the spear around, he drove it through the mutant behind him. He and Mona were both hit with a second wave of ash.

Mona coughed, clutching at her thigh. "It burns!"

"Hold on, doll." Sloan stepped over her, driving the spear into another MV's skull. The creature screeched, tugging wildly to get away. He slashed out its windpipe and crushed it in a fist. Blood spattered his face followed by a *tsunami* of ash. That is when he noticed the vampires that were chasing him had joined Mona's remaining two, which were ominously bigger. But before he could process, the remaining MVs attacked at once, and he unintentionally let go of the spear.

He groaned, shielding his face and chest as they tore through his clothes into his flesh, back and front, in a feeding frenzy. No part of his body was safe. Mona screamed again, and he knew they were finished if he didn't take control.

Feck. He was fast, but not supersonic. *These things are unbelievable.* He'd held off on ingesting their blood because he feared it might do something abhorrent to him, but now he knew the alternative would be far worse. Doctor Raphael had been correct all those years ago: he had to get a handle on his apprehensions and fears.

44

Okay, that's fecking it. Sloan sniffed the putrid plasma on his hands. *I can do this.* He grimaced, but licked. The bee's sting was sharp, intense, and lasting as it numbed his tongue. He wheezed, and his throat began swelling. Similar to when he'd absorbed Red's genetics, the mutant vampires' attack seemed to happen at a distance, while he was inside a glass bubble, looking out. The pain, too, was situated beyond the same mental barrier.

The pins and needles came next, a burning heat from deep within, while the genetic editing that he was beginning to understand and tolerate took over. For those fleeting moments, he was safe and filled with tranquility. But it was the end result that mattered, and the genetic consolidation came in a flash.

Freed from the temporary paralysis, he exploded, driving his hand through a mutant's chest. The creature screeched and collapsed into a pile of ash; he held its black, crumbling heart.

"Sloan, look out!"

Another mutant vampire came at him, but he was able to dodge and counter its chaotic attack. Punching with lightning speed, he beat it into submission. Then he grabbed and twirled the spear and plunged it, bayonet side down, deep into the creature's gut. "Five down and three to go." He whipped the spear around above his head, stepping toward the last three mutants. "Don't be shy."

Mona licked her parched lips and dropped her head in the grass, holding her thigh, watching Sloan obliterate the last three mutants. The bleeding had lessened, but her leg wasn't healing as it normally would, and she refrained from moving, even though the pain was unbearable. "Sloan, help me," she wept.

He approached, tousling the ash from his hair and brushing it from his body. "Bloody disgusting." He shook his head. "I'm coming."

"My leg won't heal!"

"All right. Stay calm." He hurriedly removed the scabbard, his shredded jacket, and his ripped shirt, and he dropped to his knees. Biting and tearing the dirty, pale-blue cotton into lengthy strips, he gently bound Mona's leg. She flinched. "Sorry. I know it hurts."

"I should be healing. What's wrong with me?"

He examined her overall appearance. She was sweating profusely, her complexion was abnormally pasty, and he could smell decomp. "You need to see the doc."

"Something's wrong," Mona cried. "I just know it!"

"Shh. Calm down, doll." Sloan put on his jacket and strung the sword over his back. "I think you might have an infection. But I don't know for sure. Doctor Avolare's the expert."

Her dark eyebrows pinched. "I don't wanna die."

He scooped her into his arms, getting up. "Everything will be fine. Don't cry."

"Sloan! Mona!"

They both looked toward the booming voice. Petrov raced from the timberline, accompanied by a hot wind that bent the grasses and rustled Sloan's jacket and dirty hair.

"Here he comes, your knight in shining armour," Sloan quipped.

Mona sputtered a teary laugh, smacking his chest. "Be nice."

"Took you long enough." Sloan held Mona out to him like a peace offering. "Hurry up, take her. I don't want anyone to get the wrong idea."

"Oh, would you stop!" Mona winced, glaring daggers at him as she was passed to the Russian like a basket of dirty laundry.

Petrov frowned, cradling her against his chest. "I searched everywhere, comrade." He smiled fondly at her and kissed her forehead. "But I am glad you are both alive."

"Well, I'd be dead if it weren't for General Smartass here. You should've seen him. He killed them all within minutes."

"What about your leg?"

Sloan sighed and unwrapped a stick of gum. "Enough chit-chat. We've got to get her to Raphael."

When they reached District B, Peaches drove Petrov and Mona to the medical building in Limerick, taking a short detour along the way to pick up Doctor Avolare, who was at the library visiting the federal panel with Krista. Sloan stayed behind with Stoner's unit to get Lieutenant Niklas and his men out of the forest. Claire's unit arrived shortly after and assisted with shipping the dead to the old naval base that had served as Avalon's primary military base for centuries. The deceased next of kin had to be notified, and the bodies were prepared for cremation.

Mona lay on the gurney in Wade's clinic, and Doctor Avolare sat on a red-leather stool in a beam of brilliant sunshine, arms crossed, rubbing her lips with her finger. Seated behind the steel table, Wade was reading from a volume on infections. Raphael had cut and thrown away the strips of blue cotton, exposing Mona's injury—a bloody stump. She'd also cleaned the wound and applied a strong antiseptic. The proactive measures had helped, but Mona still wasn't healing at a normal rate.

"She's got all the hallmarks of septicaemia," she said at last. "Red lines running up her leg and a puffy redness around the damaged tissue."

Wade paused his reading. "That's impossible with her genetics."

"I said *hallmarks*. It could very well be something else disguised as such an infection."

Petrov, observing from a nearby stool, said, "What does that mean?"

"Technically, it means blood poisoning. Which is impossible, considering her genetic editing." She looked at Mona. "Did you get bitten or cut prior to your leg injury?"

"Nothing."

"I think the mutant vampire gave you a contagion—something that hinders the healing process and therefore gives it a predatory advantage. If you can't heal, then your odds of survival plummet." Raphael patted her arm. "But don't worry. You are on the mend."

"How much longer, doc?"

"Probably another two to three hours." Raphael lit a slim cigar and placed her lighter on the trolley. "What about Sloan?"

"What about him?" Mona asked.

"Was he injured in any way during the fight?"

"Sure, at first. The MVs tore him apart both back and front, and I seriously thought he was going to die. But then something odd happened."

Although Raphael believed Sloan was more or less indestructible, he and his parasite still had a long way to go when it came to complete cellular harmonization, and of course, adapting to any future genetic modifications. Since Morgan's death, she'd continued to study him, and when the opportunity arose, she hoped to get another fresh blood sample from him. "Odd. How so?"

Mona tucked her arm behind her head. "Well, he just stood there covering his face and chest, and a minute later he was like a different man. He was able to match the mutant vampires' speed and viciousness." She glanced back at Petrov. "And just before the change, maybe for twenty seconds, his eyes turned completely black. Then he was back to normal."

"You mean his irises?"

"No, doc." Mona looked at Raphael. "I mean… even the whites were solid black. It frightened the hell out of me, but I tried not to react."

Fiddling with her cigar, Raphael pondered this new information. Genetic editing was dangerous, and the results were largely unpredictable. She'd conducted thousands of experiments throughout her career, and it wasn't uncommon to observe physical changes, fleeting or permanent mutations. But she worried the eyes were a sign of a greater shift, something irreversible inside Sloan's body. She trusted that the parasite, with its high IQ, would make only "safe" and "satisfactory" modifications. But what if the parasite believed the genetic code to be benign when it actually wasn't? She sucked on the cigar and exhaled a trailing cloud of smoke. She patted Mona's hand. "May I leave her here with you?" she asked Wade.

"Sure," he said.

"If anything changes, Mona, or if you start to feel sick, notify me or Wade immediately. Do you understand?"

"Yeah, sure." She nervously smiled.

"Petrov, do you mind giving me a ride?"

Startled from his thoughts, Petrov cleared his throat. "Where would you like to go, doctor?"

She approached him. "First, I need to speak with the general. Then, if you can, the library."

"I believe Sloan is at the military base."

They bid Wade and Mona goodbye and exited the clinic. The ride into District S, on the eastern side of the sprawling city, was relatively smooth for a change. At one time, huge potholes and fissures riddled the main road. But it was another one of Sloan's rehabilitation projects. Each unit took turns repairing the road. Since it was the only way in and out of the larger of the two military bases that housed the most personnel, it had to be in proper working order.

"He's done so much in such a short time, even fixed this road. It used to be so horrible." Raphael watched the moving topography, an architectural merger of space-age and antediluvian. "I'm truly impressed."

"I read once that Virgos are perfectionists," Petrov said. "Sloan is a Virgo, and he comes by it honestly. He believes everything should look and function a certain way; otherwise, he complains."

She giggled. "I bet that drives his subordinates crazy."

"It does." Petrov grinned. "Back when we first joined the Independent Initiative, his quirk was especially noticeable. He never went into battle without analyzing the field first. The rest of us would be trigger-happy and charge in, but never Sloan. He would wait on the sidelines, observing us. And once he figured out the simplest solution, he would end the fight. But he has softened with age. It is not so important to have everything perfect."

Raphael found his statement perplexing. Sloan never talked about his stint in the military or the Independent Initiative. She knew he'd won several medals for bravery, and he certainly wasn't the trigger-happy type. But to stand there and observe? That sounded more of a solicitous nature to her.

Petrov pressed on the brake, and the truck came to a bouncy halt. "We're here."

"The building's been cleaned and repaired."

"His quirk."

She got out of the truck and shut the door, then she followed him, passing through a pair of reinforced steel gates that the guards opened for them. The interior was tidy, the soldiers were in clean uniforms, and the atmosphere was abuzz. Everybody she came across seemed to have a specific job.

Petrov gestured to the meeting room. "He is in there. I will wait for you in the lobby."

She cautiously wandered into the spacious room full of chairs and desks. The exterior wall housed a window with a crack. "Sorry to intrude, Sloan. Can we talk for a minute?"

"Sure. One sec, doc." Sloan finished his conversation with Snickers and Roddy before turning his focus on her. "What can I help you with?"

"I'd like you to come see me tonight so I can do a physical exam and run some tests."

He furrowed his eyebrows, flashing a diffident smile. "A physical and tests? What for? I've never felt better. If you want the affection, you can just ask. I won't bite," he jibed.

"You ingested some of the MV blood, didn't you?"

The authoritative tone of her voice silenced him for a minute, and he contemplated what she'd said. "That's what I do, doc. You told me it was my latent ability: stealing genetics."

"I know what I told you, but this is imperative. I'll expect you later this evening."

"Sure. Later." He sighed, giving his head a scratch as she exited the room.

FOUR

EROTIC EXPECTATIONS

"Strip down to your underwear and sit here, please." Doctor Avolare patted an examination bed the guards had brought into the library lab. The piece of furniture was ancient, and she'd given its exterior a wipe-down with hot sudsy water. "I won't be a second." She disappeared into the adjacent, equally well-lit room.

Sloan sighed, draping his clothes on a stack of boxes. He sat and leaned forward, gripping the edge of the cracked-leather mattress.

When she returned, she stopped dead and blushed scarlet up to her ears, fumbling with a tray of medical instruments.

"Is something wrong, doll?" He wore a cheeky smirk, brows raised.

She swiftly set the tray on the nearby island with a clatter. "I said you could keep on your underwear."

"I don't always wear it."

"There are seamstresses in the city, and clothing hampers."

"True. But I'm so fecking busy most days, I never get a chance to do anything for myself. Running the military and city doesn't allow for a lot of personal time. And, unfortunately, I need to do laundry," he confessed. "But my clothes are clean, and I did take a bath before I came."

She had caught a whiff of soap in his damp hair. Her heart was pounding, and she groaned softly under her breath, swallowing a knot of saliva. *Why does he have to be so damn attractive?*

"I can put my clothes back on."

"No. It's fine." She made a fist and pushed off the counter to face him. "I'm a professional. You just shocked me, that's all."

"You're a doctor. What's a little flesh?"

Ignoring his sarcastic wit, she put the stethoscope earpieces in and pressed the resonator to his chest. As she'd noted in the past, his heartbeat was slightly slower than the average human's, a normal anomaly for a hybrid. The parasite, for unknown reasons, favoured lower pulsations. She tested his reflexes and checked his ears, nose, and throat. After which she carefully felt all his glands. "How do you feel?"

"Great."

She grabbed her notepad and pen. "Mona mentioned something out of the ordinary."

"Ah, so *that's* why you asked to examine me," he said with aggravation. "I knew this wasn't your idea. What did she say?"

"She said that after you were attacked by the MVs, your eyes turned black. She didn't want to say anything to you for fear of reprisal."

"Huh. Okay. If that's what she claims, then I guess they did."

"Did you ingest some of the MV blood?"

"Yeah, but only after I'd run out of options."

"Can you remember what happened after you ingested it?"

He watched her write in shorthand. "It's pretty much the same every time I steal genetics. First, my tongue tingles, and that's followed by pins and needles, and at that point, I zone out. It's like the world is beyond my reach; it's very peaceful. Then I can feel this burn from deep within, like every cell in my body is on fire. When the burn starts, I feel a euphoric high. Then I come back to earth, and it's over."

"How long does the whole process take?"

"It sounds like it takes a substantial amount of time, but in actuality, it lasts less than a minute."

"What happens if you're attacked while the genetic splicing occurs?"

"There's no pain. It's as if I'm nestled comfortably inside a glass bubble, but also standing outside myself, looking in. I think it's the parasite's way of protecting me."

"Can you fight back?"

"No. The parasite won't let me."

"Interesting…" She quickly reread her scribbles and set the notepad and pen on the counter. "Did this genetic splice differ from any previous incidents?"

"No." As soon as he saw the hypodermic needle and vacuum tubes in her hand, he looked away. "Why did my eyes change colour?"

"That's what I'm trying to figure out. Can you stop your blood from coagulating, please?"

"I'm trying." He kept looking away. "Do it quick."

She slid the needle into the thick, protruding, median cubital vein in his right arm, and then the first vacutainer blood bottle began to fill. "Please keep this between us, but Mona is still not fully recovered."

He frowned. "What?"

"Her leg has grown back, but she's exhibiting flu-like symptoms again. She's had a fever since yesterday. She gets the chills, sweats profusely, and she feels weak. I suspect the MV gave her some type of genetically modified virus, instead of a bacterial infection… something that her genetics are finding difficult to combat." Raphael finished filling all the bottles, set them aside, then removed the needle and placed it on the same tray. "I'm concerned, Sloan."

"So that's why she's been absent from work. She said she needed a break because she wasn't feeling one hundred percent."

"Oh, it's much worse than that. When she came to me, I quarantined her here in the basement where Krista used to live. Don't worry though. She's under twenty-four hour surveillance." She looked at him with trepidation; her heart was pounding again. "I'm concerned you may be infected too. If anything changes, you must tell me immediately."

He lightly touched her cheek with his fingertips, and she nuzzled his hand, kissing his palm. "I can't lose you, Sloan. You're my Arthur."

"I enjoy teasing you because you're adorable when you get flustered, doll." He wore a handsome smile, gently taking a hold of her face and tenderly kissing her lips. "Once we're done here, I could kiss you all night?"

She clasped his warm hands as she searched the flicker of desire in his eyes. He was serious, and it was that sincerity that made her heart pitter-patter with excitement. No man had ever found her attractive. They'd all thought she was weird. They'd accused her of being more interested in her experiments than life. "Do you think I'm attractive?" she whispered shyly.

His hot breath caressed her cheek. "I wouldn't make the offer to kiss you all night if I thought otherwise."

"Thank you so much. That makes me feel special."

Sloan searched her glassy gaze for a moment. "Whoever he was and whatever he said, he was an insecure arsehole. You are extremely attractive, doll."

She pursed her lower lip, pink-eyed and lachrymose, and sank into him. And there they remained, together, wrapped in each other's arms. His porcelain skin exuded a wonderful earthy scent, and she wanted to make love... until she came to her senses and forced herself to ease away from his embrace. "You're a good man."

"That's debatable. I'm just too old to give a shite."

She giggled with a nod. "Nevertheless, thank you, Sloan."

"Sure. Now… Are we done? I don't mean to rush you, but I've got a meeting this evening with my commanders."

"We're done."

He slipped the T-shirt down over his head.

Petrov ducked back into the corridor, pressing his spine into the wall. He'd seen and overheard enough. Though Sloan and Raphael weren't having sex, it was evident the genetic engineer had genuine feelings for Sloan. *Is he in love with her?* Surprised, he tittered. But his happiness soon faded when he thought about Mona's diagnosis. Just as he'd suspected, she was still ill, and he feared the worst. *I can't lose her.* He grabbed his own head and dropped to a squat. His mind raced like the wind. And he wondered what he could do for her, if anything.

"Let me know what the test results are." Sloan clicked the door shut and stopped short in his tracks. His best friend was muttering incoherently to himself while almost kneeling on the floor. "Headache? Or…"

Petrov sprang to his feet with flushed cheeks. "Comrade!"

Sloan stuffed a stick of gum in his mouth, unperturbed as ever. "Everything okay?"

"Yes, just fine." Petrov tried to smile, and he haphazardly saluted. "I need to speak with Doctor Avolare."

"Sure." Sloan stepped out of his way. "It's none of my business, but are you sick?"

"Not me. I am worried about Mona."

"Understood." Sloan gave his shoulder a reassuring pat. "I'm sure she'll get better soon. See you later."

Petrov felt horrible for lying, but he'd been caught off guard. He did want to talk to the genetic engineer; however, the problem was personal.

***

As soon as the meeting ended, Sloan returned to the Red Geisha. He felt worn to the bone, not so much physically as mentally drained. There'd been too much to process, so after kissing his daughter's cheek and bidding her good night, he quickly disappeared inside the master bedroom. He tore off his jacket and boots, then collapsed, still wearing his holstered FN Five-seveNs, and the instant he hit the king-sized bed, he slipped into his dreams.

He sensed a loving presence. Amanda was standing to his right on a grassy hill. They were watching the sunrise together, as it sparkled in a dance of white on the ocean swells. He caught a whiff of the soft, floral scent in her hair and saw the red thread, broken but flowing between them, and he nearly burst into tears. She was dead.

Once again, he'd entered that transcendental realm, a lucid dream, that strange, unnerving place wedged somewhere between his subconscious and conscious mind. It angered him to know this was the only way he could communicate with her. His ability to converse with the dead was seemingly limited at present; a fleeting exchange of words after the loved one had passed on or, as in his wife's case, lucid dreams. Additional manifestations outside sleep just didn't occur. But he wondered if that would change in the future. Perhaps his supernatural ability needed time and honing to improve.

"Everyone's fine. Don't worry." She tucked a sable lock behind her ear.

"Right. Not that I asked."

"But I know you, and you're a horrible liar, sweetie. You always worry about what others think, and you're terrified to fail anyone's expectations." She faced him and clasped his hand to her chest. "But that's no way to live. You're only one man, after all."

"What do you suggest?" He sniffed, fighting the stinging ridge of moisture rising in his eyes.

She kissed his fingers, and a gust of salty air ruffled their hair and clothes. "Do what your heart tells you."

"Even if it goes against everything I swore never to do?"

The environment changed, and they were encapsulated in the white void. The red thread was everywhere, multiple strands trailing from his pinky.

She slowly released his hand, fading. "Even if everyone disagrees."

Sloan woke to someone shoving his shoulder. He blinked, twisting backward to focus on the Russian.

"Comrade, we have a problem."

"Okay, okay. I'm awake." Sloan rubbed his eyes and sat on the edge of the bed.

Petrov unbent his posture. "Forgive me. You were sleeping peacefully."

"No biggie. What's wrong?"

"Stoner and Yasmine spotted an MV outside of Bunting."

"Shite, not Bunting again. It's like that area is cursed. You sure it wasn't a shapeshifter? Those fecking things can look like anyone, and they're shifty—no pun intended."

"Positive."

He hastily retrieved his jacket and boots off the floor and dressed, arming himself with the sword, rifle, and ammunition belt. "I assume you've got a vehicle to drive us there," he asked as they left the bedroom.

"Of course, General."

"Can the 'general' crap. We're alone, Mikhael."

Petrov took the lead, digging out the truck fob from his hip pocket. "Forgive me. We have spent so little time together lately, I forget."

"No problem." Sloan shouted goodbye to Elyse, who was in the bathroom, as he shut and locked the apartment door. "It's nice we can talk like this. I've missed your company."

Petrov blushed, ducking inside the elevator. He knew Sloan had spoken those kind words out of friendship, but they were embarrassing, nonetheless. "Thanks."

"How's Mona Lisa?"

"She is fine, I guess." He watched the numbers drop. "Would you like to have dinner with me?"

"Dinner? What about Mona?"

"We do not spend every waking minute together, and you are my best friend." He frowned.

"Tell me you're not going to cook."

Petrov gave him a sharp sideways glance. "Are you saying there is something wrong with my culinary skills?"

"That's *exactly* what I'm saying." Sloan remained poker-faced. "Your cooking sucks, Mikhael. No offence. But if you're planning to kill me, then be my guest."

"Asshole." Petrov gave him a hard nudge and strode out of the elevator. "I know it is bad, but you did not have to say it."

Sloan groaned, hugging his ribs. "Come on, I was only kidding," he called with laughter, exiting the tenement block. "It's not that bad. I don't mind my eggs super crispy... like bacon."

Putting his back to the wind, Petrov got in on the driver's side and shut the door. Sloan barely got in the passenger's side when the truck took off. He was flung backward in the seat like water sloshing around in a bucket. Grabbing the dash with both hands, he steadied himself and glanced awkwardly at the Russian. "Sorry. I love your cooking. Yum!"

"Do not treat me like an imbecile." Petrov scowled, his attention glued to the bumpy road ahead.

"You're right. That was a bit much. Forgive me."

"I try my best. But it is like the food hates me." Petrov sighed, tensely squeezing the steering wheel. "I do not mean to make you ill. And you are so tolerant—you always eat every morsel, even though I can see it in your face that you want to puke."

"Don't get upset. I exaggerate... it's my humour."

"That is what I like best about you: you will do whatever necessary to make the people you care about happy." Petrov shook with mirth and shoved him in the shoulder. "No one will eat my cooking except you. See? It is fate—you truly are my bestie!"

Sloan rolled his eyes. "*Great.*"

Bunting crept up on the asphalt horizon like a derelict spaceship out of a science fiction novel, an amalgamation of disparate shapes and structures: dark, hollow, tall, squat, tapered, plumb, irregular. Petrov cranked left, and the truck trundled onto a patch of dead grass and came to a creaky stop, putting the shifter in park. The other Independents, armed and waiting, stood not a hundred metres away.

"What's going on?" Sloan shut the door.

"We figured it'd be best if we hunted this thing down ourselves," Stoner replied, "since we really don't know what we're up against."

"And Vargas?" Sloan pulled out a stick of gum as Petrov stood behind him.

"Don't worry, papa bear—he and the other commanders have been notified. The city isn't under lockdown yet, but patrols have been doubled. He's just awaiting the order."

He acknowledged Claire with a nod, chewing. "Okay. Who spotted what where?"

"The herd returned, and I offered to help Mona kill a few," Yasmine said, her recurve bow in hand. Arrows, the fletchings striped like bumblebees, plugged her suede hip quiver. "But as soon as we took our first shot, this mutant vamp came out of nowhere and started screeching like a lunatic."

"It was deafening." Mona's hands were on her waist and her hair was braided in a tight ponytail. "It freaked us both out, so we carefully retreated from the woods."

"What the hell is she doing here?" Petrov growled quietly behind Sloan.

"I have no idea," Sloan muttered from the side of his mouth. He wasn't pleased to see her in their midst, either. The tiny woman had lost weight, and she appeared a bit peaked.

"What should we do?" Snickers sucked on a lollipop with Roddy beside him.

"One sec, Snickers. Where did you see it?"

"Almost in the same area where my unit was attacked before."

Sloan frowned. "You were in that deep again? Alone?"

"Sorry." Mona gauchely looked away.

"Didn't I tell you to stay out of there?" he barked, glaring daggers. "Hey, don't ignore me when I'm speaking to you!"

"There's no need to yell," she griped. "Yeah, you did, and, yeah, we went in there unaided."

He was tempted to chew her out even more, but decided it would be a waste of his breath. "Okay. We need to find the MV before nightfall, which means we'll split up into three groups. That way we can cover more terrain at once. Snickers, Roddy, and Claire will head into the northern portion. Stoner, Yasmine, and Petrov will take the southern portion." He pointed in each direction. "That leaves me and Mona to search the middle. We'll call it west."

"But that is the most dangerous area!" Petrov protested.

"Your point?" Sloan's dark gaze pierced his.

"It's all right, big fella. I'll accompany him." With a lit cigarette stuck between her cracked lips, Peaches patted the Russian's lower back. "Good afternoon, General Grumpy."

Quiet laughter broke between the others, a welcome tension breaker.

"Where the feck did you come from?" Sloan demanded, staring holes through her.

"You need to settle down, or you're gonna blow a gasket. I took a potty break."

"Sorry, General, I forgot to mention she drove us all here," said Stoner.

Sloan chewed furiously for a moment, then spat out the gum. "Where's Tris?"

"Helping Warrick with his new unit. I bet you forgot your son graduated from lieutenant to lieutenant-colonel."

"I didn't forget, since I'm the one who promoted him, smartarse, and would you stop fecking badgering me? We need to get a move on." Sloan continued to grumble as he descended the boulders. "You nag me non-stop."

Peaches grinned and followed his lead while Mona trailed close behind. "That's my job, since you refuse to date anyone," she countered brusquely. "Find someone, and I'll shut my mouth."

The others departed in their designated groups toward the forested belt. But Petrov lagged at the rear, his trepidation mounting as Mona disappeared among the trees. He had a bad feeling of déjà vu. The conversation, even their designated groups, seemed somehow vaguely familiar. But what really bothered him was his separation from Sloan and Mona. Slinging the AK-5000 over his shoulder, he tramped into the woodland, yards away from Yasmine and Stoner.

Not far into their journey, Sloan caught a fetid whiff of decaying flesh, and he paused to sniff the cool air, hoping the nauseating stench might lead him to the MV.

Per their genetics, hybrid human vampires, even himself and the other Independents, secreted gender-specific scents. These unique smells also included pheromones brought on by heightened emotions.

That was the parasite. Once its genetics fused with those of the host, the pair created a unique fragrance identifier. Because of their testosterone, the men always seemed to emanate either musk-or plant-based. Claire, Yasmine, and Mona, thanks to their estrogen, gave off a floral, fruity or spicy scent. But the mutant vampires stank. The genetic engineer believed it was the parasite Morgan had given the laboratory to work with: perhaps a mutated prototype of the *warrior*, since he'd stolen it after injecting himself with the *shield*.

Sloan wandered deeper and deeper into the forest with Mona and Peaches at his heels. He tramped through a shallow stream and climbed an embankment onto spongy grass pitted with rocks. The bushes were ablaze with fire-engine red leaves. The weather had begun to shift once again, and it wasn't quite as hot as in the weeks past. Autumn was fast approaching. He rounded some deadfall—a huge pine bleached a ghostly greyish-white—toward a dell. And all the while, Mona laboured to breathe as if she had pneumonia.

"You shouldn't be here," he remarked with a cool stare.

"I'm fine," she wheezed.

"You're far from fine, doll. We've been hiking for an hour, and you're on the verge of collapse. That's not normal. So don't tell me you're not sick."

"It isn't that bad."

"I could take her back, big man," Peaches offered from the rear.

Sloan came to a standstill in front of them, and his foolish optimism spontaneously evaporated. "Somehow, I think it's too late for that," he said in a distracted tone.

"He means I'm a liability." Mona grabbed Sloan's arm, looking up at him. "That's it, isn't it?"

He raked the entire circumference of the dell inch by inch, calculating their odds. *Great, several hundred to one. Shite. This really isn't good.*

"That's it, isn't?" Mona's protesting died, and she slowly released his jacket sleeve.

Peaches realized Sloan's concentration was on something else, and she stood abreast from the pair. "Crap." She drew both her sidearms. "Now what?"

Sloan didn't want to hurt Mona's pride, because she was a very capable soldier. But she wasn't in any condition to fight adequately enough to survive. The mutant vamps were just too agile and fast. He looked at Leona. "Get her out of here."

Peaches's face drained whiter than normal. "You can't be serious."

"I am."

"I was afraid you'd say that. Your kids will kill me."

"Get her back to the truck then bring the others here. We have to stop them before they reach the city." Sloan loaded his flare gun with both red and blue flares, aimed high above his head, and squeezed the trigger.

The flares whooshed skyward, circling one another.

"No, Sloan!" Mona grabbed his jacket. "No—this is my fault. You were right: I'm a liability, and I shouldn't have come. But you can't fight them alone!"

Sloan gently touched her panic-stricken face. "Please don't disobey me, doll. Go with Leona."

"Don't worry. We're outta here." Peaches holstered both Magnums and got a hold of Mona's arms, yanking her backward. Mona struggled, but Peaches's eyes flashed metallic, and she forcibly moved the tiny woman.

"I'll keep them distracted for as long as I can." Sloan ditched the flare gun and removed the scabbard, then rifle strap and the aviator jacket. Then he brought the rifle to eye level and switched off the safety. "Go!"

Mona stared at him with powerless regret as Peaches expeditiously dragged her from the glade. Her eyes swelling with tears. *Papa bear...* A thunderous gunshot resonated all around them. Screeches followed.

Her heart couldn't do it. She couldn't leave the man behind to fight alone. She clutched Peaches's hand, begging, "He's my friend, and I owe him for everything."

Peaches's eyebrows drew to a fearful peak. "He'll kill me."

This is suicide, Sloan, the parasite beseeched.

Yeah, if I run. The way I see it, we have a better chance if I stand my ground.

All right. She sighed tremulously.

"Flares." Snickers peered skyward, shading his eyes. The twisting red-and-blue trail of smoke got his heart banging.

Next, they heard gunfire.

"That can't be good," he said.

"When is it ever?" Roddy thrust him to run. "Come on, buddy."

"Hurry, they need our help!" Claire was already racing in the direction of the flares.

Another gunshot echoed in the distance. Gripping the AK-5000 strap at his chest, Petrov was gone like a rocket, zooming between the trees with his heart on fire. Stoner and Yasmine had difficulty keeping up; they'd never known the man to move so fast.

Caught in a hurricane of confusion, falling ash and bodies, Sloan swung around, knocking an MV in the jaw with the butt of his rifle. He punched another in the head and booted a third. They swarmed in a blur of movement, and he could hardly keep up. Then he glimpsed Mona and Peaches in his peripheral. *They should be long gone.* Wondering if something had gone wrong, he blanked for a split second and his skin softened. That was all it took.

He suffered deep gashes to his throat, chest, nape, skull, back, buttocks, arms, and legs. He groaned, trying to heal and harden simultaneously, but the assault overwhelmed. Fearing for his friends' lives, he lost focus. "Get out of here!" he hollered, pushing with brute force through the MVs, whipping the rifle around like a baseball bat.

FIVE

CHOPPY WATERS

Skidding to the edge of a squat, rocky ridge, Petrov hovered above the dell. "*Mona!*"

Her ghastly scream hammered his soul. She jerked violently as her heart tore from her chest and her head came away from her neck. Enraged, he bellowed at the top of his lungs and flew down the long, rugged slope. At the bottom, he yelled again, running for the mass of writhing bodies, unleashing a barrage of gunfire.

No. Sloan watched in a state of delayed shock as Mona vanished in a crumbling pillar of ash right before him. He immediately felt a sharp twinge in his chest, and his eyes filled with hot tears. The intense sorrow seeped upward, a burn from the base of his skull, and he roared, lifting the sword.

Claire came to a weary stop in the grass; Snickers and Roddy arrived seconds later. Sloan blew through the mutant vampires like they were tissue paper. Blood saturated the grass and darkened the sky, and ash rose in massive, thick, chalky clouds.

No one could beat him when he went on a rampage, and Claire made sure to steer clear. His copper eyes were alight, his fangs huge, and his long claws dipped in black paint. He disembowelled and dismembered and beheaded, feasting on his own savagery. The whole scene was grotesque, but it was impossible for her to look away. Instead, she gagged, pressing a fist to her mouth.

Stoner and Yasmine reached the ridge completely winded, but they hastily descended the slope. They ran to aid Peaches, who was semi-conscious; she'd been flung away from the chaos.

Petrov rushed to Claire's side, but his attention was fixated on Sloan butchering the remaining mutant vampires. He was angry and hurting, and a slew of vile, hateful words came to his mind, but he didn't dare breathe a syllable—not with Sloan in his current state. He had to tread with care.

Then, all of a sudden, it was quiet. The battle had been won, and the victor stood amidst the gore, bathed in death from head to toe, sovereign of his grisly domain. Sloan gasped loudly with his eyes closed.

Claire moved to approach him, but Petrov grabbed her arm and held her steadfast. "What are you doing?" She slapped at his steely grip. "It's papa bear. He'd never hurt me."

Petrov refused to let her go even as she struggled, and that is when he noticed Sloan staring at him with wet, dull eyes, his arms slack at his sides. He abruptly released Claire, but it was too late. The Irishman's miserable expression had disappeared. Petrov hastened into the ashy haze, searching, but Sloan was nowhere to be found. Something crunched beneath his feet; he lifted his boot to find Mona's bent dog tags, the new ones issued after Sloan's promotion to general, along with her clothes. "Crap," he mumbled, crouching. Watery-eyed, he put the small, tarnished pieces of oval metal to his lips, and he sniffed.

"Where did he go?" Claire laid her hand on his arm. "What happened?"

"I don't know," he lied, hurriedly wiping either side of his face.

Over the next month, five additional mutant vampire nests were discovered outside Districts A, B, C and E. Doctor Avolare hypothesized, such an elevated increase in numbers meant the MVs were successfully interbreeding, because it was physically impossible for the original hybrid-human parents to produce that many offspring in such a short time span. Unless the genetic engineer in charge of the project had genetically altered the female parents' reproductive organs. Even then, she believed they'd have to lay eggs like a bird. But then, maybe that was the exact reason there'd been a thirteen-year gap between the very first kill and the present.

Sloan didn't care how they were multiplying. But he did care that they'd aptly positioned their nests beside the most densely populated districts in the city.

Before each extermination, the general and Independents met with the APF commanders at the Dalhousie Hotel military base and barracks to discuss a plan of action. Sloan led these meetings, voicing his strategy, and then he departed without a word to anyone. At best, he was taciturn and unsociable. Everyone, the human personnel included, noticed the drastic change in his personality, and they traced the cause to Mona's death.

But Claire knew the truth wasn't as simple as Mona's passing, and she feared if Petrov didn't own up to his part in their rift, their family would fall apart, and that is what worried her the most. Sloan was the foundation—the rock upon which they'd built their hierarchy, friendship, and trust. He'd held them together through thick and thin, even when they'd argued. She watched the Russian leave the meeting hall. He'd been abnormally withdrawn as of late, and it was only getting worse.

"I found this in one of the salvage shops, and I thought you might appreciate it." Stoner waited for a minute, then his enthusiasm vanished. "Claire, did you hear me?"

She glanced with absent-mindedness at him before noticing the ornately carved wooden jewellery box in his hand. "Oh, sorry, Stoner. It's beautiful, thank you." She smiled with genuine gratitude, opening the lid. The lid bore ancient Roman script and a textile-type square pattern around the edges. It reminded her of a dowry chest, just in miniature. She gently rubbed the letters and giggled. "It says 'do not open, lest you unleash the sorrows of the world.' You've given me Pandora's box."

"Ha, ha, I have." He grinned with pink cheeks, adjusting his top hat. "I thought you'd get a kick out of it. It's ancient, but an ancient gag gift that would fit in with your collection of peculiar artifacts."

"I love it." She hugged the box.

"What happened between Sloan and Petrov?"

Her happiness waned to disenchantment. "I really don't know."

"Well, whatever it was, I wish they'd sort it out." He sighed. "I get a sense that the moment this is all over with, Sloan's going to disappear for good."

"Whatcha talkin' about?" Yasmine asked, putting on her lightweight flak jacket.

"The internal struggle," Stoner said.

"Oh, that. They're both stubborn, so there's not much we can do." She flipped up the collar. "For someone who is supposedly Sloan's bestie, the Russki sure doesn't act like it."

***

The following afternoon, they fought as a unit and destroyed another nest. And they repeated the same in the subsequent weeks until they were down to the final two nests located outside District G.

Everyone ate and slept at the barracks. Sloan went home only to visit his daughter and Vince; otherwise, he was stuck at the smaller military base like everybody else.

They'd just returned to the barracks from their second to last nest extermination. He thanked everyone for their hard work and parted company. Sloan wandered past the second-floor offices that had been converted into comfortable, one-person living units. He leaned against the fourth open doorway and said, "Thanks for everything you did today. You were great. I know you're tired... but the last nest is the biggest, so I could really use your help again when the time comes."

Coated in filth, Petrov lifted his bloodshot, watery gaze. He stank and he was dog-tired. "You can shove your good Samaritan cause up your ass. I do not care what you want." He glowered with tears streaming his face. "Fuck off," he yelled, white-knuckling Mona's dog tags. "Leave me alone! I never want to see you again! Do you hear me, Irishman? I never want to see you again—*ever!*"

Sloan's expression sank to wounded, and he stared for a moment, then he acknowledged his friend's choice by quietly shutting the door. The Russian's incensed rejection didn't hurt nearly as much as his distrust had in the weeks prior, but it was scathing nonetheless, and it cut deep. Everybody handled loss differently, and Petrov was no exception. He was mad at the world, and Sloan more than understood—he could empathize. But no one said he had to accept the verbal beatings.

77

He marched the length of corridor, entered his own private unit, slammed the door, and drew to a hesitant stop. Partially veiled by the shadows was Mona Lisa, her semitransparent gaze pleading for leniency. Sloan continued to stare reticently as he removed his jacket, tossed it and sunk into a worn loveseat. He didn't want company, especially anyone of the ghostly variety, invading his private space.

She hovered closer. "I know he's been awful. But please forgive him."

"Why didn't you listen? Huh?" He anchored his head, gripping the armrests, and tears stained the sides of his grimy face.

"I wanted to help you because you helped me... all those years ago. If it wasn't for you, I never would have survived."

He looked at her through clouded vision and said in an unsteady baritone, "You owed me nothing, doll. I did what any decent human being would've done."

"Tell Petrov I love him and I'm okay, now."

"Sure, sure." He watched her tender smile fade.

***

Stoner and Vargas burst inside the meeting hall, startling everyone. "Has anybody seen Sloan?" Stoner asked.

"No. Why?" Peaches put a cigarette to her lips.

"The last nest. It's been wiped out, and he's gone."

Peaches was on her feet. "He fought them on his own?"

"Apparently, it seems. The nest and surrounding areas are coated in a ton of dust," Vargas said. "And there wasn't an MV in sight."

Claire hurled a frosty glower at Petrov, who remained impassive in the corner of the large room with his arms bent over his chest. She had figured out what had transpired between the pair, and she was getting sick and tired of his petulant attitude.

Roddy shrugged, giving his nose a rub. "He wouldn't just leave, would he? He's the general."

"No idea." Snickers munched on a banana-yellow lollipop.

"Maybe we should ask his kids or brother," Yasmine suggested.

"I already did, and they're very worried." Stoner lit a cigar. "They haven't seen him either."

"Where is he?"

The entire group turned their attention to Claire and Petrov.

"I asked you a question, Russki," Claire growled.

Petrov tilted his chair back, clasping his hands atop his head and staring at the ceiling. "I do not know."

"Bullshit. You must have an idea."

"Why would he know?" Snickers asked, munching.

"Because he's the one who told Sloan to f-off and never come back." She watched the Russian with indifference, waiting for his response.

"What are you talking about?" said Peaches.

"He blames Sloan for Mona's death."

"Pardon?" Peaches frowned. "You egotistical prick!"

"She died during a fight. How is that Sloan's fault?" Stoner puffed harder on his cigar.

"He promised to watch over her," Petrov retorted venomously without acknowledging them. "He let me down, and now she is gone."

"Okay, I know I'm not the sharpest tack in the box but…" Snickers scratched his head. "You laid the responsibility on Sloan, and because he failed to protect her against, like, a thousand friggin' MVs, you told him to hit the road. Just who do you think you are, Russki?" He jumped to the ground from his perch on a desk and whipped out his *nunchakus*. "*You* were her man, not Sloan. You're just angry because *you* let her down."

"You're a spoiled rotten brat," Peaches sneered.

Claire eyed the Russian with cool disdain, setting her sniper rifle on the table. She knew why he'd told Sloan to hit the road, and it had nothing to do with Mona's death. "You're so full of crap your eyes should be brown."

Petrov sprang to his feet and glared with bleary, tear-soaked eyes. "I may have been her lover, but he broke his promise—a promise to both of us. He let us down!" He boomed, "You do not know a fucking thing! Nothing!"

"Sloan isn't a god. He's just a man, no different than you," Claire remarked collectedly.

"Wrong. Sloan told her to leave. But she wouldn't listen." Incensed, Peaches drew both Magnums, flicking the safeties.

"So, screw you, Russki." She booted a desk out of her way. "You'll never be good enough for him. *Ever!*"

The room became a football field when the men tackled Peaches, confiscated her guns, and pinned her over a table.

"You've got some nerve."

The confusion died down, and the bickering stopped.

Yasmine's distaste for Petrov manifested in her emotionless gaze that picked him apart, piece by piece, until he was standing there with all his sins completely exposed. "Sloan met Mona long before you were a part of this unit. He spent countless nights training her in private. They were inseparable. How do you think he felt when she died?"

Petrov gawked at her for a split second, then Peaches and, as if hit by a bolt from the blue, his eyes widened and he bashed through the doors, leaving the room. He jogged the long hallways, zigzagging past APF personnel, until he was out the front doors.

People packed the streets. The APF was reinforcing sections of fence and fortifying the southern main gates while the citizens were boarding the windows and doors to the food bins, salvage shops and restaurants. The city was still under lockdown, preparing for the forthcoming invasion— an invasion that wouldn't come since Sloan had destroyed the last nest.

For hours, he jogged the city, checking every place he figured Sloan might go. He talked to countless people, even Elyse, Warrick, Tristan, and Wade, but no one had seen or heard from the general in almost a week. Before he left the clinic, Lucy stopped him with her sweet voice.

"The cathedral is his favourite building in the city."

Petrov acknowledged her with a grateful smile. "Thanks."

He departed from Wade's clinic and strode till he reached the extensive flagstone walkway outside the gothic Anglican Cathedral. Wiping his damp brow, he craned his neck. A soaring sixty-nine metres high, the bell tower offered a seamless bird's-eye view of Limerick.

He strode between the colossal solid-fir doors, took a right inside the antechamber, and climbed over thirty flights of steep, spiralling stairs to rise through a hatch in the floor. The rusted hinges creaked. The older man was leaning on a stone ledge, looking through a medieval porthole.

Swallowing a knot of apprehension, Petrov mustered the courage and let the hatch go and stood tall behind the general. No matter what, he had to be forthright; Sloan wouldn't accept any less. "I broke your trust, and I blamed you. My behaviour was horrible. I am very sorry." He hesitated just briefly, but when he got no immediate response, he said, "I know I do not have a right to ask, but I hope you will find it in your heart to eventually forgive me."

Sloan got up from the stone ledge and faced him. "No problem." And he brushed past without batting an eye.

"Everyone is worried." Petrov followed him, quickly descending back into the darkness.

"Sure, they are." Sloan's heavy boots clunked the steps, sending tremors upward.

"They want to discuss the mutants with you."

"There's nothing to discuss. The biggest nest was demolished. If anything else crops up, I'll deal with it."

"What?" Petrov frowned, clipping at his heels; the tight corkscrew of steps was disorientating.

"It's simple. Every time some creature threatens this city, someone gets killed. So, it's best if I deal with it on my own. Morgan was my friend and therefore my problem, not yours."

"Then you *are* still angry with me."

"Nope." Sloan looked at him from the bottom of the stairwell. "But you and the others deserve a life beyond the shite we've been forced to endure all these years."

"And what about you?" Petrov raced to catch up, then walked beside him, crunching the gravel on the flagstones.

"What I want doesn't matter," Sloan replied sharply. "It never has."

"What is that supposed to mean?" He remained perfectly synced with Sloan's lengthy strides.

Sloan stopped on a dime and looked at him again. "The minute Raphael injected me, I accepted this lousy job and all the fecking bullshite that came along with it."

"We all did, comrade."

"Not really. You and the others were test subjects."

"Do not give me that crap." Petrov grabbed his jacket, yanked him close and searched his dark copper threads. "Whether or not the doctor picked you, the injection was still a gamble. So do not make yourself out to be the chosen one.

83

We all agreed." He shoved Sloan away, and his chin quivered. "I cared for Mona, and I hate she is gone. But I do not want to lose my best friend too. Do not do anything reckless."

"Right. Reckless." Sloan cast his watery gaze skyward. "It's okay if you hate me, Mikhael. I can handle it."

Petrov took a stab at the air. "Shut your mouth, or I will shut it for you!" He backed away, making a fist, debating whether to punch him, but he reined in his anger. "Sometimes you are the most tactless person. How could I ever hate you—you belligerent fool? I was looking for someone to blame. You did your best. I should have been there to help. And Mona… she was stubborn."

Sloan dug inside his pocket to reveal yet another stick of gum. "Did you know there are still millions of these? That's why I'll never run out." He peeled the wrapper like a banana and held the gum out to Petrov. "Take it."

After a moment's contemplation, Petrov snatched it from his fingers. The sweet, effervescent spearmint filled his mouth as he chewed, awakening his taste buds. He and their unit would be lost if Sloan were to abandon them. They needed the man—his experience, knowledge, guidance, and strength, but also his indispensable friendship. As the alternative would inevitably be death. He pressed a fist to his mouth, smothering a chuckle. "You really *are* the papa bear."

Sloan scowled and punched the younger man's arm hard and strode ahead. "Thanks a lot, arsehole. No more treats for you."

"What about porridge?" Petrov faltered behind, holding his gut.

"It's Goldilocks and the *three* bears, not seven bears. Bite me."

Petrov's laughter died. "I have waited long enough. But now I am tired of your lack of trust. We are friends, comrade. You need to rely on me more—allow me to share whatever burdens you are carrying. All we have left is one another."

Sloan came to an unsteady halt a few yards away, and his heart fluttered. He knew eventually the Russian would demand genuine friendship, a deeper connection, something tangible to hang on to. They'd periodically lived together, slept in the same bed, ate, and breathed together, worked together. But that didn't mean things were equal. Sloan was too prideful to admit, there were many times he felt uncertain, scared, or lost, and that he needed help. He'd dragged Petrov along for nurturing and comfort, but he gave nothing in return and pushed him away when it suited him. His actions were cruel and selfish, and he knew it.

Petrov's honesty was all he needed to hear. Even so, he couldn't bear to face the man and conceded he was wrong. *Shite, my emotions are compromised. I can't believe it.* He chuckled softly to himself. It was exactly like Doctor Avolare had claimed. Now that he'd cleared the air, he felt liberated. Petrov *was* a good man.

"Did you hear me?"

"Yeah, I heard you." He said quietly and quickly, "I apologize for acting like a prideful, know-it-all, arsehole." He shoved his hands in his hip pockets and glanced back, teasing with a crooked grin.

In a panic, Petrov rushed ahead and blocked him with his arms outstretched. "What did you just say? I could not hear you."

"I *said* I heard you."

"No, no! After that. You said something else. An apology perhaps?"

"Nope. I didn't say anything."

Nearly in tears, Petrov squeezed Sloan's arms and shook him. "You are lying!"

"Hey, you need to relax." Sloan gave his cheek a gentle slap. "I may be cheap, but that doesn't mean I'm easy. After what you did, you're going to have to earn it, big fella."

Baffled, Petrov's brows furrowed, and he watched him cross the road. "What does that mean? Sloan, you Irish bastard!" He tackled Sloan from behind, putting him in a headlock. "Do not mock me! I know you said something important!"

Sloan gripped his huge, bulging forearm, choking and laughing. "Watch it, or I'll have to teach you a lesson."

That night, after a long soak in the tub, Sloan had to contend with a houseful for dinner. Warrick sat beside him. Elyse had invited Ryouichi and, of course, he had to listen to Peaches's cheeky banter. Tristan had prepared beefsteaks, potatoes, and fresh vegetables. Even though his eldest son had invited Petrov to dine with them, Petrov had turned the offer down. And he wondered why.

"You okay, big man?"

Sloan kept gawking at his food, holding his fork.

"I'm sorry if it doesn't taste good," Tristan said.

"Dad?" Elyse touched his wrist.

"Sorry, Tris. It isn't the food. It smells delicious." Sloan set his fork down. "I just don't seem to have much of an appetite."

"No problem. I can get you something else."

He lifted his gaze to meet theirs. "I'm really worried about Petrov."

Peaches rested her head on a tight fist, and her freckled countenance filled with a concerned frown. "I thought you guys talked things out."

"We did. But we didn't. We joked and I apologized in a roundabout way. I know he's hurting and depressed, I can sense it."

"You mean Mona. Well, everyone grieves differently, big man."

Sloan leaned back with a sigh, locking his fingers over top his head; he searched their bemused expressions. "I know, and that's my point. What if I lose him?"

"All you do is live in the past and think the frickin' worst. Would you give it up, already?" Peaches clicked her tongue in disgust and opened her tin of cigarettes, glancing at everyone else. "You need to tell your father to be tolerant."

"Patience, Dad," Elyse said. "Everything will work out. Petrov just needs time."

"Yeah. And you can babysit. Finally, you'll be out of our hair." Warrick grinned cheekily.

Sloan rolled his eyes and uncurled, slapping his hands on his knees. "Okay. That's my cue. I'm out of here."

"I was only joking, Dad."

"I know, son." He checked his wristwatch. "Oops, it's time to leave. If the general is late, everyone else will slack off."

Warrick, Peaches, and Tristan leaped into action, each scrambling for their footwear and jackets. They'd forgotten about the meeting.

"Sorry, sis. You'll have to do the dishes." Tristan grabbed his boots from under the kitchen table and sat in the living room to put them on.

"Don't worry, it's fine."

"Damn." Peaches quickly mashed the cigarette she'd just lit in the ashtray. "We'll meet you there, Sloan!"

"Uh-huh." Sloan flipped on his mangled aviator bomber and strode toward the apartment entrance with Warrick in tow, jangling a set of keys with a key fob. "See you shortly, then."

"I'll drive you over, Dad." Warrick shut the apartment door behind them. "What's really going on between you and Mikhael?"

"Mona didn't listen to me, and she died as a result. Mikhael was furious and he told me exactly what he thought of me. Which, he had every right. But it was more than that…"

Warrick stepped inside the elevator at the same time as his father. "Dare I ask?"

"He hurt my feelings. I don't know what to think right now."

Whatever Petrov had done, Warrick knew it must have been very upsetting for his father to blurt his innermost thoughts. Sloan was a very private person, and he rarely conveyed his genuine emotions—aside from rage, of course, but that had more to do with the vampiric thirst. Warrick wondered what his mother would say. She'd been a sensible woman. "I think you need to have a serious heart-to-heart with him. Get everything out in the open. Then you'll know where you both stand."

They got inside the Jeep and shut the doors, making loud, clapping echoes in the Red Geisha underground parking level.

"Is that your best advice?"

Warrick pressed the start button; the electric engine idled almost silently. "It's simple, Dad. Do you want the friendship or not? If you do, get on with it. If you don't, you'd better cut ties with him once and for all."

"Then I might lose my best friend."

"I hate to say this, but Petrov broke the friendship rules. And when someone breaks the rules, there are consequences."

Sloan smiled, slowly folding his arms and shook his head in disbelief. "Bloody hell, you're one sensible young man. I wonder where the feck you got all that awesomeness?"

"Mom." Warrick sputtered with laughter.

"Thanks," Sloan said, giving him a playful shove.

SIX

THE HIERARCHAL SHIFT

The arrangement of the chairs and tables formed neat crescent moons, facing a large metal desk at the front of the meeting room closest to the entryway. The large, cracked window provided a panoramic view, drenching the room in the dreamy light of dusk. The Independents and Peaches and Tristan were the only military personnel present.

Sloan gazed out the window. "I don't want anyone else to die," he said evenly.

Momentarily dumbfounded, Stoner hesitated. "You're relieving us of duty."

"Yes," Sloan said in a solemn voice. "We've been Independents for twenty-three years. I think that's long enough, don't you?"

"What if a war breaks out?" Snickers asked.

"Then the choice will be yours. I don't want you to act out of obligation." Sloan watched a raccoon waddle through the grass. *He's a fat little bugger.* Nocturnal scavengers—raccoons, opossums, badgers, mice, and rats—were common, especially around the military bases.

Yasmine stared at him for an extended period. "What if we don't want to leave the APF?"

"That's fine. It's your choice."

"What about you, papa bear?" Claire studied him with concern. "What will you do?"

"Sit around and drink all day. Read a book. Learn to crochet." He burst with miserable laughter and pressed his hand flat against the cool pane. "I haven't a clue, doll. I've been in the military for so long now—almost five decades of unwavering service—I don't know any fecking different. I'm like a machine."

"Who will take your place?" asked Stoner.

"Warrick. He's desperate to fill his father's boots. I told him it wasn't necessary—there's more to life—but you know how bloody defiant kids are. He's determined to protect the city with or without my seal of approval." Sloan hung his head with a grave sigh, then turned around. "Of course, his father will always have his back if he's needed."

"He's tough. He'll do just fine." Claire smiled softly. "Don't worry."

Petrov remained deadpan, and Sloan found his unreadable expression somewhat annoying. He sensed his best friend would more than likely get mad and chew him out. But to his astonishment, it didn't happen. Instead, the Russian's mouth filled with the most handsomely serene smile he'd ever seen on any person's face. It was as if Petrov were falling into a deep, peaceful slumber.

"I am glad. You deserve a change." Petrov rose from his slouched position against the wall. He looked Sloan in the eyes and placed his fist on his chest. "But wherever you go, I will follow."

Sloan could feel his cheeks burn through every shade of embarrassment, and the spot on his chest where Petrov touched him felt numb with heat. The guy was *still* too touchy-feelie at times.

Petrov glanced over at the others, who were as quiet as mice. "Do not act so surprised. We have been together since the beginning. And now that we are both alone, we can help one another even more."

"You've got a lot of fecking nerve, talking like that. What are you, a poet?" Sloan glowered as Petrov headed for the exit. "And where do you think you're going? This meeting isn't done yet."

"To get a haircut. Elyse offered." He paused at the doors. "But if you insist, comrade, the haircut can wait."

"Yeah, I do insist—and what's wrong with your hair?"

Petrov sported a dry grin, refolding his arms over his chest. "If you prefer it long, you can just tell me."

"What are we—a pair of women? I don't care. Cut it if you want! I'd just like to finish our discussion."

"Of course. Continue." Petrov gestured with a hand.

Everyone quietly sniggered.

Sloan grimaced. No one else on the planet could get him agitated, like the Russian did with his nonchalant, smooth-as-ice attitude. *Calm down, eejit. He's just trying to wind you up.* "Anyway, you're no longer obligated to serve the APF, the feds or me. Whatever happens in the future, it'll be your decision."

"Thanks, papa bear." Claire sighed, slumping, elbows bent over her chair backrest. "But personally, I like what we do now: fighting for the right reasons. I'm staying put."

"I'm with her." Snickers grinned like the Cheshire cat with a lollipop stick jutting from the corner of his mouth. "We get paid, and I enjoy kicking ass."

"Me too." Roddy patted Snickers's shoulder.

Yasmine scratched her head. "I just took over Mona's unit, and they need more training..."

"You can just say you want to stay." Stoner laughed, and she frowned in ashamed dismay, then he said to Sloan, "I have to admit, the offer is tempting: to dump and run. However, I've grown accustomed to my life. So, thanks but, no thanks, Sloan."

"Sure. No biggie." He chuckled. "Okay then, I guess it's settled. The deal was that as soon as someone was available to take my place, I'd leave. Thus, I'll resign as general. That means you'll have to listen to my son."

Within days of notifying the feds and receiving their reluctant blessing, the transition of control promptly switched to Warrick. He was every inch as powerful and physically intimidating as his father, though in his own way. But he had his mother's serious, gentler disposition, which made him more approachable. The Independents didn't mind, and the human soldiers really didn't notice much of a change: father and son were so much alike.

"It's been a month since I took over. Have I met with your approval?" Warrick arranged the papers on his desk at the head of the meeting room.

"Approval? Of course, son," Sloan said. "That's not why I hang around. I know you're more than capable of handling the job."

"Okay, Dad. What's on your mind? And don't bother lying. I know you too well."

"We've yet to meet the parents of the MVs. I've decided to hunt them down."

Warrick was astounded. He'd honestly thought his father would retire. But then he realized he'd been duped. He laughed derisively. "You're serious, aren't you? You planned this. You wanted the freedom to do what you love best, and you knew I'd follow in your footsteps. I don't know if I'm mad or disillusioned."

"Hey, I didn't force you to take the job." Sloan slouched against the desk edge with a sigh. "It hurts to know you think I tricked you."

"Oh, come on, Dad. Where's your sense of humour? I know it was my choice. Lately, you've been excessively sensitive." Warrick watched him for a minute. His father was strangely upset and more restless than normal. "Where's Petrov?"

Sloan shrugged, fiddling with a tinfoil gum wrapper. "Supposedly, he went to one of the salvage pits."

"Did you guys have an argument?"

"Nope."

"Dad, look at me." Warrick frowned, searching Sloan's dull copper eyes. "What's wrong?"

"Nothing. I'm good."

Now he knew for certain something *was* amiss. When his father spoke in terse sentences, he was definitely holding back. "All right. Well, I've got to get moving—duty calls."

"Sure. Have a good evening." Sloan patted his shoulder.

Warrick glanced back from the meeting room exit with apprehension. "Where will you go?"

"Vincent has a shipment ready for the island. I'll probably stay there for a couple weeks. Catch up with Rueben and everyone and see Raphael."

"And after that?" Warrick asked quietly.

"The wilds. I've got a lot of ground to cover, starting with Morgan's secret laboratory."

"I hope we can see each other regularly."

"Shite, do you ever sound like your mam." Sloan heaved a sigh and stood in front of the open doorway, facing his mirror image. "You're my son, Warrick. Of course, I'll visit you."

"You'd better. And be careful."

***

Panicked, Petrov banged on the apartment door. No one answered, and he banged again, this time sending tremors through the corridor walls. He couldn't believe what was happening. He felt like his entire life was about to fall apart. The door opened, and a miffed, dopey Peaches clad in grey track pants and a puffy shirt met him. "Crap, man, do you know what time it is?" Peaches scratched her butt, squinting against the glare of the outer corridor lighting.

"Sorry, Leona." He stepped inside the apartment, quietly shutting the door behind him.

"Everyone's sleeping, and I've got to get up in a few hours." Peaches wandered into the living room and flopped out on the sofa, gnarled in blankets. "What do you want?"

"Is Sloan here?"

"Nope. As far as I know, he left for the island yesterday." Peaches sifted through the layers of magazines, books, and other junk on the coffee table. "Why?"

Dumbstruck, Petrov collapsed into the loveseat across from her, springs squeaking. He stared, in a state of incredulous shock. He couldn't believe Sloan had left without saying a word to him.

Peaches put a cigarette to her mouth. The match sparked with a sizzle, and she puffed until the cigarette tip burned bright saffron. She leaned back, arms draped over the sofa, contentedly puffing. "I know it's hard, but you've got to have patience."

Petrov lifted his head. "Why would he not tell me he was leaving? I do not understand."

"I dunno. Maybe he wanted to go alone. Maybe he thought he'd be pushing you to do something you don't want to do."

"That is not true—I would do whatever he wants. I have told him."

"Then tell him again. Keep telling him until it sinks through his thick skull." Peaches leaned forward and tapped the glowing end against the ashtray. "He's obstinate and grumpy, but he'd do anything for you."

"I do not know if I believe that anymore."

"Trust me, Petrov. He'd go to hell and back for you. He's worried about you and the whole Mona thing. He knows you've been depressed. Maybe he decided it'd be best to back off—you know, give you some breathing space."

This time Petrov stared in bewilderment. "I admit there are moments I… find it difficult. But I do not blame him."

"Then *talk* to him," she emphasized, mashed the cigarette, and got up from the sofa. "Sorry, but I've got work in a few hours. You can sleep in the master bedroom if you want."

"Thanks, but I will leave. When will he return?"

"Not sure. Maybe a couple of weeks."

***

The early morning sun ascended as a beautiful goddess, veiled in rippling gold, spreading her enchantment across the ocean swells to wake the world. Sloan shaded his eyes from the goddess as the yacht bumped against the oncoming waves. The island was dead ahead. No one knew about his visit, so there wasn't anyone to greet him at the mooring boulder. But lately he desired the solitude, and the silence came as a bonus. He found the isolation made it much easier to think.

He killed the engine, allowing the yacht to drift. Then he jumped the bow with the rope, landing in chest-high water. He slowly guided the boat to a gentle, crunching stop on the gravelly shore. Once he'd tied off the line, he boarded again, retrieved his duffel bag, and retraced his wet boot prints back to the bow.

He landed with a splash and waded to the beach. From there, he trudged the lush grass toward the forest. Dripping and sodden, he sniffed, shaking the excess ocean water from his hair, appreciating the warm sunshine.

The village was a twelve-kilometre hike, about two hours at a normal gait from the coastline, and it was a journey filled with memories. Most were from his childhood, but he also remembered Petrov and the countless times they'd travelled back and forth to the island. He frowned, adjusting his grip on the duffel bag straps. The whole point of leaving Avalon was to escape the emotional upheaval, but it seemed to have followed him, digging its claws in. He grumbled under his breath, passing the orange-painted rock, the halfway marker. He didn't get far before he sensed another presence, and he stopped on the trail.

"Well, if it ain't the legendary Sloan Whelan. It's been a while." Benny rested a high-powered rifle on his shoulder, wearing the biggest grin. "What brings you to our neck of the woods?"

Sloan chuckled. "Lilith's shop. And I had hoped to savour the peace and solitude."

Benny shifted sideways to rest his weight on his left hip, his hazel-blue gaze analytical. "Peace and solitude... That doesn't sound like you at all, old man. You love to live by the hair of your balls."

"Not anymore."

"Maybe you need a little bit of adult entertainment? There're a lot of pretty women on the island who would snap you up in a heartbeat."

"Ah, thanks but no thanks, Ben." Sloan put a hand up. "I've got enough to deal with."

Benny lowered his rifle. "Well, at least have a drink with me and the boys tonight. Everyone's missed you."

"Sure." Sloan watched him retreat to the footpath. "I'll see you later." He retightened his grip on the duffel bag straps and continued on his way. The compacted path wound through the forest and eventually straightened and expanded, sloping away from the canopy of soaring evergreens. At the verge of the path, he saw the village, nestled in rolling hummocks, a carpet of verdant greens dotted with wildflowers. It was a hotbed of activity. A new secondary street ran parallel to the central thoroughfare, and people were everywhere.

Soon he joined the bustling confusion. A group of children were laughing and chasing one another around the village square. The baker was wiping his hands on his apron, talking to them, and the local blacksmith was fitting a horse with shoes. The butcher's assistant was chatting to a farmer at the rear of the building, no doubt making a sale for livestock. There were a wide variety of unique shops that lined the ancient street, even a bookstore and clinic, and Sloan knew every single one. He also knew the people who ran them.

The brewmaster tipped his hat, and Sloan grinned, ducking inside a small shop with leaded stained-glass windows. The entrance door creaked, and tiny bells jingled. Sunlight streamed through the dusty air, illuminating shelves of fabric and bins stuffed to overflowing with skeins of wool. There was a spinning wheel, a loom, and a manual sewing machine. In the back corner, hidden in the shadows, was a table strewn with dressmaker's shears, needles and pins, a measuring tape, tailor's chalk, ruler, pencil, and various shades of delicate pink linen.

"Lilith," he called, shutting the door, jingling the bells once more. "It's me, Sloan."

A curtain that separated a private suite from the shopfront lifted, and a slender woman in her late fifties drifted into the room. Her auburn hair, streaked with white, was loosely swept up in a bun. She was wearing a baggy fawn long-sleeved sweater over a pleated, floor-length black peasant skirt and brown suede boots. "I'd know your deep voice anywhere, Sloan." Her cocoa eyes sparkled with amusement. "It's good to see you."

"You too." He set the duffel bag on the floor. "How have you been?"

"Busy, mostly with knitting booties and such. We are expecting several dozen newborns this fall. It's our two midwives, Doris and Star, I feel sorry for, not to mention your lovely doctor friend Raphael. She's been a godsend." She smiled affably. "But you didn't come here to listen to me prattle on."

He was stunned. The population *was* really growing. "You can talk all you want, doll. I don't mind." He squatted and unzipped the duffel bag. "I wondered if you'd have time to repair my jacket."

"My goodness, I can't believe you're still wearing this ancient scrap of leather." She put her glasses on as he handed her the aviator bomber. She held up a patched sleeve, every gesture graceful. "Honestly, Sloan, this poor thing should be recycled."

"Sorry, I can't do it. She's been with me since I joined the military." He gripped his nape, watching her meticulously examine the jacket inside and out.

"I could make you a brand-new one in less time than it would take to repair this. I need strips of leather, and some of the wool has been singed on the lapels…"

"I don't care what it takes."

She folded the heavy jacket and draped it over a bin filled with zippers. "Give me a week." She peered over the upper rim of her glasses. "But it's going to cost you."

"Okay. How much?"

"Well, with the materials and my sweet tooth…"

"Let me guess. One large box of Swiss chocolate and…?"

"Twenty in silver coins."

"Shite, you drive a hard fecking bargain, Lilith! The chocolate is one thing, but *twenty*?"

"I could've said forty." She smirked and gave his hard gut a slap with the back of her hand. "You've got the money. Don't be stingy."

He sighed. He'd always had a soft spot for women, whether they were in tears, yelling at him or demanding his affection. He blamed his mother, who had always pampered him. Though, oddly enough, she was the one who'd had the dark sense of humour while his father had been a laid-back, serious man. "Twenty it is. How's your daughter?"

"Getting married this Christmas." She grinned with pride. "He's a bit older, but he treats her well. Everyone in the village has been working hard to restore the old stone chapel in time."

"She wants an actual wedding ceremony?"

"She always had her head in books, dreaming about marrying a prince and living in a castle. You know that."

"True." He slung the duffel bag over his shoulder, adjusting the weight. "Well, pass on my felicitations to Laura. I'll return in a week." He backed out of the shop, and a little boy bumped into him. The boy fell and scraped his knees on the weather-beaten cobblestones. "Are you okay?"

Snivelling, the little boy nodded, getting back up.

"Sorry, Sloan. He's just too rambunctious."

"No problem." Sloan turned around, and the woman's stunning beauty took his breath away. Ingalill was bent over, hugging the child, wiping his runny nose with a kerchief. She was such an attractive woman with her flaxen tresses, big blue eyes, and supple, pouty lips. *Her hair is almost the colour of Mikhael's.* He wondered why he was comparing Ingalill to Mikhael.

"Sloan, are you okay?"

He flinched slightly. "Sorry, I blanked there for a second."

She grabbed the boy's arm, and he tugged, whining. "It's great to see you. Does Rueben know you're here?"

"No. But Benny was in the forest."

"It's his patrol day. Are you staying at the cottage?"

"Yep."

"Good. I'll let him know you're here." She smiled. "I have to run. We'll talk again soon!" She waved.

Sloan curled his fingers and dropped his hand. *What am I doing here alone? I should've brought him with me. I bet he's miffed and confused.* He heaved a dismal sigh. He really was acting like an idiot again, keeping his friendship at a trouble-free distance. *I bet he could use the company. You are such a fecking eejit.* He sauntered to the other end of the village, the same way he'd come. His family home was located at the village outskirts, the first on the cobblestone street nearest the forest.

Unlocking and pushing on the cobalt-blue garden gate, he paused to examine the cottage exterior. Grime coated the windows, and overgrown flowering bushes surrounded the cottage, but the structure remained in decent condition.

He worked the entire afternoon; washed the windows, mowed the lawn, weeded, trimmed the bushes, and clipped the shrubbery until early evening rolled around. Then he had a bath and retreated to the back porch with the dense paperback novel *Atlas Shrugged* in hand. The cover had a tiny hole that burrowed deep through the pages. He'd acquired the book along with a bunch of paperbacks from the book depository: a thriving environment for Psocoptera. Lying outstretched on a dilapidated lawn chair, he read and consumed glass after glass of whiskey.

A couple hours later, the sunlight was growing hazy, and dusk began settling. He shut the book and set it on the porch under the lawn chair. But just as he was about to close his eyes, he angled his head sideways, his attention on the tree-lined border around the backyard. The operation of his abnormally acute senses defied explanation. But the first indicator was that discomfited sensation of being watched. Sloan knew for certain somebody was hiding amid the leafy darkness, although he couldn't pinpoint their exact location. He didn't care for the infringement of his privacy, but he didn't feel any dread. He felt annoyed more than anything.

"Hey, old man!" Rueben's voice rang from inside the cottage.

Shite. He rolled his eyes, drawing to a pause. "I'm out here," he called back.

Weighty footfalls shook the cottage, and Rueben and Benny appeared at the rear door, each sporting a wide smile and a bottle of wine.

"Why don't you come inside?" Rueben wiggled his bottle.

"Oh, is that supposed to entice me or something?" Sloan chuckled, picking up the book.

"You bet!"

"We've got a surprise for you," Benny said.

"All right, I'm coming."

"Do you need help? You're moving awfully slow." Benny held out his hand.

"Smartarse." Sloan cuffed his hand.

Benny laughed, patting and pushing his brother's shoulders until he tripped inside the house. Sloan followed their lead. Once he reached the door, he paused and glanced behind at the now blackened woods; the trees were so big they blocked the moonlight. Whoever had been spying was gone. He shut and locked the door.

Before he could exit the long, narrow hallway that led from the back door to the central living areas, Benny told him to close his eyes. Then he guided Sloan to the armchair and got him to sit.

"Not yet, old man," Benny ordered, holding his shoulders.

"What's going on?" Sloan listened to the upheaval of noise: moving furniture and dish-ware and footsteps in a rush.

"Never you mind," Rueben said from the direction of the kitchen.

There were more than just the brothers in the room. By smell alone, he knew there were at least four other men. *Interesting. I wonder what this is all about.*

"Okay, you can open your eyes now." Benny released his shoulders.

The first person he saw was an Asian man with muted, straw-brown hair seated on a kitchen chair directly across from him. His soulful hematite eyes were glassy.

"Holy shite… Akira?"

"Yeah, it's me."

"And Jens!" Sloan said in surprise when he noticed the dirty-blond beside Akira.

"Ha, ha, I knew you'd look exactly the same." Jens grinned. "It's good to see."

Sloan hugged them both, thrilled to see them too. He'd also noticed two strangers, a pair of younger Asian men, seated on the sofa beside Jens, but he didn't want to come off as rude, so he belted Benny in the gut. "Hey, eejit, aren't you going to introduce them?"

Benny doubled over with a groan. The other men laughed as he struggled to regain his composure. "Bastard," he managed to whisper through his teeth.

Rueben set seven glasses on the coffee table. "Be nice, Sloan."

"Do you remember that tip you got me from the black market?" Akira poured himself a glass of wine.

"Of course," Sloan replied.

"Well, thanks to that tip, I found them," Akira gestured. "These are my brothers, Sloan. Rin and Yukio."

"It's nice to meet you, Mr. Whelan." Rin, the smaller of the pair, gripped his knees and bowed. "Thank you for helping my brother find us."

"Sloan's fine. And I really didn't do anything. But I think it's great that you're a family again."

Akira, his brothers and Jens stayed until late evening, only departing after they'd polished off six bottles of wine. Sloan shut the front door behind them and wandered into the kitchen, stretching. Benny had cozied in at the far end of the sofa with one arm draping the backrest and holding a tankard of beer to his mouth. Sprawled like a throw on the armchair, Rueben snored with his head tilted back.

Benny eyed his brother with a smirk and downed the last mouthful of his beer. "He never could handle his booze."

"Nope. Evidently, not." Sloan flopped out in the twin armchair opposite Rueben and crossed his bare ankles on the coffee table. "What's up, Ben?"

He sighed, bent forward, and set the tankard on the table with a dull clunk. "How the hell do you always know? Eh?"

"It's written across your face that's something's wrong and, you handle all the island security. Besides, a lot has happened on the mainland, and I'm worried it may have spread here." Then he mumbled, "Bad things usually do."

"So that's the reason for your unscheduled visit. I had wondered." Benny stared at Rueben and said gravely, "It started three weeks ago... the unsettling feeling that I was being watched while out on patrol. At first, I thought it was my overactive imagination. But then it rained hard for six days in a row, and I discovered footprints in the mud. Larger than a normal human." He looked at Sloan, and his expression revealed his stress; prominent lines marred his forehead like battle scars. "I haven't told Rueben yet. Star knows, and so do the younger guys who help with patrols. I mean, as a safety precaution, I had to warn them. But I didn't want to upset my brother. He's got enough responsibility on his plate with the construction of the new road behind the village and updates to the infrastructure."

"The village council has to be informed, Ben," Sloan said.

"I know. But how can we even discuss it if we don't know what we're up against?"

"Just before you and Rueben entered the house, I was lying on the back porch, reading, and someone was watching me."

Ben's face drained of colour. "Then I'm not losing my mind."

"My senses have yet to make a mistake. We'll have a meeting here tomorrow after I've done a quick search of the village."

SEVEN

UNTIMELY DEATH

The top commanders of the APF—Antonio Vargas, Niklas Schulze, the Independents and Tristan, who was working as liaison in Peaches's stead—crowded the conference room at the military base in District S. Vincent had requested Peaches investigate the shapeshifters coming up from the South American Bloc. So, the redhead had snuck across the border, on the hunt for information, in particular anything to do with the government's genetic projects. If shapeshifters were to become commonplace, the feds and APF needed data: numbers, weapons, habits, et cetera.

The stale, dead air made the conference room stuffy. Warrick carefully pressed his fingertips to the only operational section of the broken window and slid the pane open. It grated along the track. His shirt puffed as a lukewarm breeze circulated, shifting the papers around on his desk; he slapped his hands down to stop the paper from gliding to the floor.

Those he'd called to the meeting took their seats. Petrov at the rear, and Tristan sat abreast of him, several chairs away. Once it had quieted down and the commanders were focused, Colonel Vargas shut the door.

"Everyone's here, sir," Vargas said, pulling out his own chair.

Warrick organized the papers before acknowledging his subordinates. "Thanks for coming. I'll get straight to the point. It seems that we're a long way from exterminating our pest problem. Several men from a salvage crew, in Bunting, disappeared at approximately twenty-three hundred hours last night during a deep recovery operation. Early this morning, their mutilated bodies were discovered at the forest edge." He propped his head on his fist and concentrated on his silent audience; he thought for certain one of them would've offered their insight, but they remained respectfully quiet. *Huh.* "Past intel tells me that their deaths were not caused by MVs. The men were not consumed. Instead, they were torn to shreds. Of course, the bodies had been exposed to animal degradation."

Tristan raised his hand. "You mean something else killed them."

"Something I suspect we haven't seen yet. My father has often talked about the genetic parents of the mutant vampires, a completely different type of human-vampire hybrid. He was referring to the specimens in the footage taken at the secret laboratory—which I suggest you watch in the computer room, if you haven't already."

"Well, whoever it was, they didn't kill for food," Stoner said.

"No. They killed for sport."

Petrov scowled. "Sport?" he remarked gruffly. "What does that mean, General?"

Warrick wandered away from the desk toward the window; he lightly dragged his fingertips through the dusty grit on the ledge. "Whoever killed the men, put their bodies on display like a hunter would mount an elk's head on his lodge wall: as a trophy for everyone to see. Wade was with me when I examined the bodies, and he agreed with me: the killings were planned."

Everyone murmured. But as soon as he turned to face them, they were quiet once again. "This time, there can't be any mistakes. These creatures exhibit a high level of intelligence and cunning. So, no matter what happens, from here on in, no one," he said sternly, "not even the Independents, are to go anywhere beyond the city perimeter alone. You must always work in pairs, minimum."

"Bro— Sorry. General," Tristan said. "If we can't go alone, who's going to run the units?"

Warrick sighed, just like his father. "I'm getting to that, Tristan."

"Ah, s-sorry." Tristan blushed.

The room rumbled with soft laughter.

"Everybody will have to designate someone in their chain of command to help run their unit. You're the best soldiers I have, and I need you. Make certain you find a decent replacement. I refuse to deal with problems here when I'm out in the field. If anything goes wrong, it'll be your responsibility, so choose wisely." Warrick noticed Petrov was itching to say something, but he continued. "Give me a moment to finish, and then you can share your thoughts. I know what most of you are thinking. And, yes, I will talk to my father when he returns. I hate to ask since he's just retired, but his help will be essential."

He walked over to the large map screwed to the rear wall under a protective acrylic plate, and he placed his index finger on a forested section that ran from Chartreuse down to the bottom of Bunting. "This entire area seems to be the hot zone. I want everyone to concentrate their efforts here, unless new evidence should suggest otherwise. We will start the day after tomorrow. We'll meet at the library by zero-five hundred hours. Then I will decide on pairs, and we'll move accordingly. Make sure to find your replacement before then." He dropped his hand. "Now, if anyone wants to speak, they can."

After a brief stretch of silence, Claire said, "I think we're good. Thanks, General."

Everybody began to file from the room.

"We've gotta find replacements, and it's getting late." Snickers exited with Roddy at his heels.

Soon the noise died down and the room was empty except for Petrov and Tristan, who had purposely stayed behind.

Warrick sat on the desk. "Well, that went crappy. I don't know if I should be ecstatic or sad," he grumbled, tightly folding his arms.

Tristan laughed, gesturing with his hands. "Do you want everyone to argue with you?"

"Not especially, but I thought they'd at least say something. I mean, anything would've been nice. They always talked to Dad."

"They do not know you well enough yet." Petrov smiled, giving his shoulder a firm pat. "You did well, General."

"You're more soft-spoken than Dad—more laid-back, if that's even possible," Tristan offered with a bountiful encouraging smile. "Maybe they don't know quite how to handle you yet."

Tristan's innate enthusiasm always lightened the mood, and it was that personality trait Warrick loved the most. "Maybe you're right. If you're both free, I could use your help tonight."

"I'm free. What about you?" Tristan gave Petrov's back a slap.

"It is my duty to accompany the general wherever he wishes to go, since I am his personal bodyguard. So, I am free." Petrov grinned sassily, giving Tristan an extra-hard slap on his back. Tristan choked, flying forward a few steps.

"You're such a freakin' brute!" Tristan griped at the hulking blond, pressing on his lower lumbar while realigning his posture.

Petrov and Warrick laughed.

***

The late summer evening came with tepid zephyrs and the sun sinking in the western sky, draping a pall of ruddy light over the treetops. Chartreuse was peaceful. The only people about were the scheduled military patrols. Warrick unfurled the small, crudely drawn map of the forested belt behind the library, that pinpointed the location of the secret laboratory. According to other ancient maps, there was supposed to be a town south of the lab. He quickly pocketed the map as Petrov came around from the rear of the truck with Tristan in tow. Both men were heavily armed, and Tristan was toting a supply knapsack in case they stayed out overnight.

"Ready to go?" Warrick asked.

"Ready," Petrov replied.

"Ready." Tristan held the knapsack straps. "Where is the town again?"

"Approximately four kilometres south of the secret laboratory." Warrick took the lead.

Tristan didn't care for the answer, but he bit his tongue. The lab gave him the creeps, and for good reason. And from Petrov's pasty expression, the Russian wasn't keen on the idea either. Both were experiencing mild PTSD—flashbacks they'd rather forget.

Repairs to the perimeter fence were complete, and now Chartreuse, like all the other districts, had a reinforced gate and gatehouse. They passed through the gate.

Last in line, Tristan glanced over his shoulder to see the posted guards shut and lock the towering, steel-reinforced gate behind them. Now they were outside and travelling farther away from their lifeline. He caught up to Petrov. "W-we aren't going to the lab, are we?" Tristan stared at his brother's wide shoulders.

"Not inside. Don't worry, Tris. I only want to establish direction and location," Warrick said, traipsing into the woods. "But you know how reliable the old maps are."

"As long as we aren't going inside, then it's fine."

"I'm sorry for doing this to you. I know neither of you are fond of the place, which is understandable. But Morgan's secret facility is the only solid clue we have. Everything began there." He peered back at both men. "We won't stay long, I promise."

Petrov chuckled, holding the AK-5000 at his waist, and a moment later Tristan joined him, shaking with mirth.

Puzzled, Warrick turned to face them, stopping dead. "Okay. I know I'm not stupid, but I fail to see the humour in what I just said."

"Sorry, Warrick." Petrov cleared his throat. "We were expecting you to make some sick joke about our traumatic experience."

"Yeah. Dad would've ribbed us over something like this, but you didn't." Tristan wiped under each eye. "It was just funny—you're much calmer and more thoughtful."

"You may look like your father, but your personalities are opposite."

Warrick stared at them for a moment. "I guess I am more like Mom. She hardly ever laughed, and always hit Dad when he thought he was being hilarious."

They reached the laboratory in almost complete darkness under a full strawberry moon. Crickets chirped, and the brittle grass came up to their knees and rustled in the evening breeze. Petrov wiped his brow, and Tristan swigged a mouthful of water while Warrick did a quick perusal of the building interior. Less than five minutes later, he'd rejoined the two men, and they followed his compass south.

The town was actually five and a half kilometres from the laboratory. A spread-out grid of eighteen avenues crossing fifteen streets and three roads, with an overgrown railroad line that vanished at the town limits, and a downtown core several blocks deep with businesses. The buildings were six storeys tall at most, sketched in moonlight down to every architectural detail: windows, entranceways, storefronts, lighting, signage, and even the grooves and pits in the masonry.

Petrov, Tristan, and Warrick wandered apart but remained vigilant, aiming their guns at whatever they investigated. The buildings were obscure voids, hollowed-out husks, and there were a few that slumped like wet laundry. Rusted lampposts lay broken on the main street. Decaying vehicles of every description and era besieged the curbs and laneways, and grass burst like knotted hair from cracks in the asphalt. The local grocery store hosted a gathering of shopping carts and a circle of saplings in the middle of the parking lot. It appeared as though Bridesville's heart had ceased to beat during the lull between the third and fourth world wars, the most chaotic period in history.

Warrick peered into a storefront through one of a few windows still intact. The words *Maria's Bridal Boutique* coloured the frail pane in an elegant, sun-bleached script. Although fleeting, he felt as if someone were watching. He backed away from the bridal shop, casting his gaze skyward.

"Do not go in there!"

Warrick quickly peered to his left as the Russian took off at a sprint. "Hey!" he called, chasing after the enormous man. When he reached the spot where the Russian had been, he stopped short and caught a glimpse as Petrov vanished down a laneway. "Mikhael!" He dashed through the laneway and at the next block over, found Petrov wandering in a circle. "What's going on?" He rushed to him. "Where's Tris?"

"He saw something and went in pursuit—the fool." Petrov cursed in his native tongue. "I told him to wait, that I would help."

They both froze as a series of gunshots echoed from streets away to their right. Then they raced in the sound's direction. But the gut-wrenching wail that followed sent a chill up Warrick's spine.

Petrov tore ahead, flying over debris. Warrick followed. He wasn't blessed with the night vision Petrov had, but he flew regardless, the fear catapulting him onward. More gunshots went off in a flurry, and another cry from Tristan resonated off the buildings.

Then it was dead still.

Warrick came around the corner of a stout tenement building and almost collided with Petrov.

"Shh… It is here." Petrov aimed, advancing into the darkness.

Warrick felt something slick under his boots, and he nervously looked down. A dark patch of blood trailed off, as if someone had dragged a body along the cement in the opposite direction. Numbed, he hurried after the Russian, who had darted deeper into the night.

But even as they searched the blackness far and wide, they both knew they'd never find the creature; it was long gone. Instead, they were left with the path of blood. That eventually led them to a ramshackle barn with a low, bonnet-style roof just outside the town limits. One of the boarded-over double doors banged shut, and chains rattled against the other.

Petrov saw Tristan's sniper rifle on the gravel drive leading to the barn. He continued to aim straight and stepped over it. "Tristan," he called with tentative softness. "Tristan, are you in there?" Metres away from the rifle, he found the knapsack grated like cheese, and he stepped over it too.

"Why won't he answer?" Warrick walked around the rifle behind the Russian. "Tris!"

The door wobbled on the evening breeze and whacked the frame hard, hinges creaking. The nauseating scent of blood wafted over, and Petrov knew for certain whoever was on the other side of the doors was deceased. His heart sped up and thudded in his ears as he reached out; he didn't want to look. Finally, he gripped the loose door and pulled it open. His breath escaped in a groan, and he faltered a few steps backward, his vision growing hazy. Pressing a fist to his mouth, the gastric acid shot into his throat. Confused, he searched the surrounding moonlit darkness, trying to keep from puking.

Warrick stared at the dismembered corpse, and hot moisture filled his eyes. "My brother," he cried. "My brother!"

***

Knock, knock.

Sloan wearily lifted his head from the pillow; he'd fallen asleep naked on his stomach, and the position wasn't comfortable, considering the age of the mattress and its elderly support. He paused; a disconcerted sensation seized his chest with a flutter. He didn't know where it had come from or why, but it filled him with uneasiness. He pinched the sleep from the corners of his eyes and tried to focus on the alarm clock. *Six in the morning.* Someone knocked on the front door again: frantic small taps. *Who the hell...* He glanced back, twisting around. "Yeah, I'm coming, for feck's sake," he grumbled, rising on all fours before sitting on the edge of the bed. He needed clothes. *Shite, where are they?* Bending over, he swiped his underwear, pants, and shirt from the floor. While slipping the T-shirt on, he ambled through the main living area.

He opened the door to a blast of sunshine and birds chirping. "Feck, Rueben, do you know what time it is?" He squinted, shielding his eyes.

Rueben followed him back inside the cottage. "I apologize, Sloan. But it's an emergency."

"Uh-huh."

"I'm serious. I could've been a total dick and walked right in."

Sloan grabbed his belt off the sofa. "Then you would've seen me naked."

"I'd like to keep my breakfast down." Rueben sighed, watching him fiddle with the belt, then his boots and his tolerance vanished. "Okay, enough of this!" He grabbed Sloan's wrist and yanked him toward the door. "We've got to go now."

"Whoa!" Sloan barely ducked the lintel, leaving the cottage front door wide open and lagging behind the lanky brunet like an obstinate child. "You do realize I could flick you away like a bug."

"Of course. But I also know you care about me, so I can get away with certain things."

"All right. You've made your point. Let go now."

"No way!" Rueben kept walking.

"*Now.*" Sloan's authoritative baritone startled Rueben, and he released his wrist. They stared at one another, and he sighed. "What's got you so upset?"

"It's old man Phelan's cattle. Six were killed last night out in the field... mutilated. Everyone knows his cattle are imperative to get the village through the winter. We need you to take a look."

"Right. Lead on." Sloan gestured, and Rueben strode through the village.

By the time they reached the fenced and cross-fenced cattle field, half the village residents, including the town council, were behind them. Rueben gripped the fence top rail. Sloan nodded to the butcher, Mr. Phelan, as he approached. They stood beside each other at the metal gate and Sloan leaned on it, placing his boot on the lowest rung, staring out at the grassy field and the dead cattle.

"Mornin', Sloan." Mr. Phelan hooked his thumbs in his belt loops.

The man had a slight potbelly, a thinning hairline, and rosacea-kissed cheeks, but he was tall and sturdy for his age—certainly sturdy enough to take on whoever killed his cows, Sloan figured.

"Good morning, Cid. Is that the rest of your herd in the adjoining field?"

"Yessiree." He motioned with a nod. "I rotate them, that way they get the best grass."

Everyone behind them was extra quiet, straining to listen in on the conversation.

"Any ideas?"

"Well, the biggest predator we've got on the island is a small black bear—they get up to no more than three hundred pounds for the females and five hundred for the males," Mr. Phelan said. "But we keep a food run at the back near the forest. That's where we dump scrap vegetables and fruit. It keeps the deer and bears happy and out of our livestock, gardens, and orchards. Not that a bear would normally go after a cow."

"True. But if it's starving or injured..." Sloan stepped away from the gate, studying the field. "Mind if I take a look?"

"Be my guest." Mr. Phelan unlatched the gate and pushed it open with a creak.

Sloan strode the field, and everyone else rushed to the fence to watch. Hoof prints and manure the size of landmines littered the compacted ground in spots. He noted the tightly knitted arch of trees a short distance from the west fence. The field was three-quarters hemmed in by woodland and certainly secluded.

He squatted beside a cow and lifted its head by the lower jaw. Someone or something had slashed its throat. *No other injuries.* He purposely lengthened his own claws, noting that he could've inflicted the wound. *Huh.* He waved the flies away. It quickly became apparent, at least to him, that the predator was in all likelihood a vampire. The cattle deaths were eerily similar to the MV attack on the deer herd. However, MVs were messy, and they devoured their prey, even the bones, leaving only scraps of a carcass behind. The cattle had been killed with precision—one solid, powerful hit that had severed the jugular and windpipe. Rising to stand, he scanned the entire length of fence before he walked back to the gate.

"What do ya think?" Mr. Phelan asked, eyeing him carefully.

"I think… we need to have a village meeting." Sloan ran a hand through his mop, giving a subtle nod toward all the children. "Without little ears around."

"Of course. Right away, Sloan." Richard, the village mayor, adjusted his straw hat. "Myself and the rest of the council will meet you at the village hall."

Rueben watched the mayor, a stout cup of fiery-red hair with ruddy freckles and striking, sky-blue eyes, stride past. He waited until Sloan finished talking with Mr. Phelan, and then he joined Sloan to saunter back toward the village square. "It's bad, isn't it?"

"If my hunch is correct, very."

"Speculate away."

"I don't know how, but I think a hybrid-vampire has gotten onto the island."

"You're joking." Rueben gawked at him.

"The cow's neck was slashed. There were claw marks." Sloan held up his own to indicate the accuracy of his claim. "Just the jugular and windpipe—a very clean and deep wound."

"Great. So that means Benny *was* being watched."

"More than likely. Right after the meeting, I'm heading back to the mainland."

"But…"

"Reinforcements, Rueben." Sloan paused and gripped his shoulder. "I need help. The island's too big for me to patrol on my own."

Rueben grudgingly nodded. "I get it. Just don't be gone too long."

"Never." Sloan smiled with reassurance.

***

As the sun peeked over the rooftops, Warrick staggered out of the ramshackle barn and slumped his shoulder against a tree. Petrov listened to his ragged sobs. His nose burned, his throat hardened, and tears streaked his face once again. He snuffled against his short sleeve. Tristan had been killed swiftly and without a sound. One minute they were together, and the next, he was gone. But while Petrov was trying to understand what had happened, there was another ear-piercing wail. He jumped. Warrick's eyes were a raging storm of sapphire-blue, and his fangs had grown long. The Russian knew what was to come.

The general tore the entire town apart, cursing like a madman, threatening whoever had murdered his brother. Tumultuous and violent, he moved with the destructive force of a hurricane, demolishing each man-made structure in his path. He booted doors in, smashed walls down, kicked and flung huge sections of Gyproc and concrete and brick. Buildings collapsed in an earth-shattering medley of thunderous crashes, as Warrick stood in the middle of the town, gasping for breath, his knuckles bleeding.

"Peaches will kill me." Warrick turned to him with tears sliding down his quivering features. "And what do I tell Dad?"

Petrov rested a hand atop his head and shrugged. His heart was aching, and he shed a few more tears of his own.

"This is entirely my fault. I ordered everyone not to go beyond the perimeter, and what do I do?" Warrick watched the sunrise. "I was so hell-bent on finding the creature…" He wept, pressing his dusty jacket sleeve to his face. "Leave."

Petrov frowned. "What?"

"We need something to carry him home in."

"I will not leave you alone—not in the present situation with that thing still out there! You are the General and my highest priority."

"Don't worry, Mikhael," Warrick murmured. "Your top running speed is faster than mine. You'll be back in no time."

"But—"

"No buts!" Warrick glared at him. "And bring back one of those tablet-adaptable cameras with you as well. It makes me sick just thinking about it, but we have to document his death for Wade to see."

Petrov knew there was no point in trying to reason with the man. Warrick was as formidable an opponent as Sloan when it came to a battle of wills. Without a word, he ran back the way they'd come, racing north toward Morgan's secret facility.

EIGHT

LOST FOR WORDS

"Hey, where have you been?" Claire grabbed Petrov's arm before he could get past her. "And where's the general? Is he with you?"

The hotel was a hive of unusual activity, and Petrov wondered if something had gone wrong in their absence. He paused and looked back at her with sore eyes. "Why do you ask?"

"Sloan's just returned from the island. Some of the farmer's cattle were killed, and he figures it was the handiwork of another vampire—not a mutant but something else. Can you believe it?" She searched his sullen expression. "I mean, how did it get on the island? Anyway, the islanders are scared. Sloan's looking for Warrick. He needs backup."

"Where is Sloan?" Petrov asked with a heavy heart and absolutely no ambition.

"He was in the meeting hall last I saw him. No offence, but you don't look so good. Are you okay?"

"No." He excused himself and strode toward the meeting hall, and when he reached it, the door was ajar, and he could hear Sloan's distinctive baritone. He was wrapped in conversation with Stoner. Petrov swallowed, but the lump in his throat wouldn't dislodge. Placing his tremulous hand on the doorframe, he circumspectly poked his head inside the room, unwilling to face the music. Perhaps he could soften the blow.

"Hey, bestie," Sloan said with a wry smile. "We were just talking about you. There's a problem on the island, and I could really use your assistance."

Petrov stared glassy-eyed at his best friend for a period. Sugar-coating the news would just make the situation worse. "There's no easy way to say this…"

Stoner looked at Petrov, who was shaking like a leaf.

Sloan's eyes immediately lost their spark, turning dark and dead. "Just say it."

"Tristan is dead."

Dumbstruck, Sloan's expression teetered between doubt and alarm until the words sank in. "You're lying," he thundered in a raw voice, hands clenched. He moved toward him, as if to threaten the truth out of him, but Petrov stood his ground, unflinching. "You're fecking lying!"

"When have I ever lied to you, comrade?"

Sloan searched the man's weary, tear-streaked features, and without another syllable, he blew from the room, vanishing before their eyes.

Petrov instantly collapsed, planting his hands on the nearest tabletop. He inhaled deeply over and over.

"*Crap.* Poor Sloan." Stoner sighed tremulously, wiping the moisture from his cheeks. "I'm sorry about Tristan. He was a great kid."

"He was." Petrov paused and said with fondness, "He did not like me in the beginning. But eventually, we grew to respect one another." He glanced at Stoner. "If Sloan returns, please tell him I am sorry. I did not mean to speak so thoughtlessly."

"I will. Can I get you something? A cold beer? You look worn out."

"That would be nice. But I really need a tablet-compatible camera and a body bag." Petrov eyed him. "Can you sign them out of supply for me?"

"Sure." Stoner patted his back. "Give me fifteen, and I'll be right back."

Good as his word, Stoner returned to the meeting room fifteen minutes later with a heavy-duty body bag, a tablet-compatible camera, and a chilled bottle of beer. Petrov gulped the beer as if it were his last.

"Sloan's still gone. Look, it's none of my business, but is Warrick, okay?"

"Far as I know. But I must get back to him ASAP. He's alone in Bridesville, guarding Tristan's body, and that… thing that killed Tristan is still out there." Petrov set the empty bottle on the table, and he grabbed the body bag, rolling it tight and binding it with the attached strapping. "I want to get back to the base before nightfall."

"Don't forget this." Stoner passed him the camera, which was inside a small, zippered canvas bag. "If you don't return, Vargas will send out a unit."

Petrov put the camera strap and body bag over his neck and shoulder. He locked his loaded AK-5000 and checked his wristwatch. "The general is slower than me. Give us until nineteen-hundred hours."

"All right. Be careful."

No sooner had Petrov exited the building than he was racing for District C. He had to reach Bridesville and return to Avalon before sundown. One death was too many in his books, and no matter what anyone said, he was duty-bound to protect the general at all costs. As he ran from District C into the outlying forest, he sensed another presence. He came to an abrupt halt and spun around. Sloan emerged like a ghost from the shadows at the mouth of the forest.

"I'm going with you."

"I do not think that would be wise."

"He's, my son. I don't care what you think."

Petrov touched his chest before he could get past, and he held him at bay. "No disrespect was intended, my friend. I just want to spare you any more pain."

Sloan cast his watery gaze to the right, and his chin quivered. He knocked the Russian's arm away. "I have a right to know how he died, Mikhael."

Petrov knew he'd never convince the man to wait at home—not with one son dead and the other possibly in danger. "As you wish. But we must hurry." He took the lead and ran, flying through the forest with Sloan at his heels.

They didn't stop, not even for a drink. It would have taken the average person five hours, especially with the uneven terrain, but since Petrov could move fast and Sloan was able to maintain similar speed, they reached the town in a little over two.

As the decaying Bridesville came into view, Sloan gasped deeply, slowing down, kicking up a dust storm. During their run, Petrov had explained the chain of events leading to Tristan's death. Sloan's heart ached like crazy, but he'd suspected something awful had happened. He just didn't know what. He stood beside the big Russian, hands on his hips, trying to catch his breath. "The parasite... I think she tried to tell me early this morning before I left for the mainland," he said, staring at the town. "She'd sensed something."

"You always refer to your parasite as female. Is it female?" Petrov asked with curiosity.

"Yeah, I think so... A nurturing female physician. At least her voice sounds feminine," Sloan replied vaguely, walking along the main street.

"Her *voice*?" Petrov looked inquisitively at him, holding the AK 5000 at his chest. "You mean, the parasite actually talks to you?"

"Yeah, crazy as it sounds. I'm not sure exactly how the science works, but because we're symbiotic beings, her intelligence was created by but is also infused with my

131

brain—that's how she talks to me, inside my head." Sloan glanced at him. "Where's Warrick?"

"Probably at the barn." Petrov pointed and took the lead once again.

The closer they got to the barn, the more rancid the smell became, and he knew they were in the correct location. He noticed a darkened pool of blood underfoot, and he knew Tristan had initially been attacked in that spot before being dragged away, leaving a trail of blood behind. He continued to follow Petrov and the trail.

The tightly packed buildings went on for several blocks, gradually thinning along with the blood trail until nothing but droplets appeared on a bare gravel road. They'd exited the town to see a sprawling farm. Hectares of hayfields were cordoned off by split-rail fence, and a dirt road stitched up the middle like the hem of a skirt. The tumble-down barn was at the end of the dirt road, looking lonesome beneath the shade of huge leafy trees.

Sloan jogged onward, taking the lead from Petrov.

Surprised at the sight of his father, Warrick shot to his feet, almost accusing. "Why are you here?"

"He was at the base," Petrov explained. "And I had to tell him."

"What does it matter? He told me everything."

"It matters. I had wanted to spare you."

"Well, it's too fecking late for that. I want to see him. *Now.*"

Warrick blocked the barn entrance, arms spread. "You don't want to go in."

"Move."

"No," Warrick demanded sternly, standing tall like a brick wall in front of his father. "I'm the general now, and I'm in charge."

"I'm ex-military—so don't pull that shite with me!"

"This is not about who is in charge," Petrov pleaded, trying to get in between the two men.

"Don't push me, son." Sloan glared.

Warrick hedged, and his eyes welled. "It's awful," he sputtered, squeezing a fist. "I just don't want this to be your last memory of him."

Petrov courteously retreated to give the men their space.

Sloan stared at his son for an extended period; he knew the young man was dying of guilt. He felt like a hapless fool. He believed he'd made the correct call by investigating the town, but it had backfired. Sloan rolled his watery eyes, sighed, and hugged his son's head. Their damp cheeks touched. "This isn't your fault. Do you hear me?" he whispered and held his head tighter. "*Do you hear me?*"

Warrick swallowed. "I do."

"Good. And don't forget it." Sloan kissed his cheek.

The general, with great reluctance, ultimately stepped aside.

Sloan didn't want to see what was beyond the door, but for his own understanding, he had to know. Pushing with his fingers, the door creaked open, and he was instantly assaulted by the putrid scent of rotting, organic matter. His nostrils flared. Suspended on the threshold, unable to move another millimetre, he stared at his adopted son's remains. Dusty sunlight illuminated Tristan's head on a stake. Mutilated beyond recognition, the rest of his body, organs and limbs, was strewn across the floor and walls like someone had tossed him about during a feast. Flies walked over his eyes and swollen tongue. Dried mucus and blood were everywhere. The whole barn was swarming with flies and drowning in the rancid scent of death.

He forced himself to concentrate on Tristan's wounds. *Slash marks again.* Another second more, and he'd retch. He stumbled out into the fresh air and roasting sunlight, tilted his head back and inhaled deeply, filling his lungs as tears streaked his cheeks. After he'd lost Chase, Tristan became his reason for continuing to save other orphaned children. "Burn it," he said before walking away.

The flames rose high, and embers floated heavenward. Sloan's throat hardened, and he tried to swallow. The ache in his chest was so bad he could barely scrape a breath. He traipsed through the wheat fields, far from the inferno. Then he doubled over and bawled, shoulders heaving. His emotions were all over the map, ranging from bitter fury to utter anguish.

Sniffing, he clutched his shirt and gradually slumped to the ground. He searched the blond wheat stalks compressed under his knees. "God, what do I tell Peaches?" He wiped his upper lip and nose with the back of his hand. "I don't know what to do anymore."

The claw marks. Tristan's wounds were similar to the cattle. *But that's impossible.* And then Sloan realized. *There's got to be more than one of these fecking things.* He sat back on his ankles, mopping his face. He felt a tad calmer, better able to focus. The wheat crunched like dead leaves behind him, but there was no need to look; the Russian followed him wherever he went. "Don't worry. I'll be okay," he said.

Petrov stood behind him. "I am not worried, comrade. But it is getting late."

"Whoever killed Tris did it on purpose. They were sending a message." Sloan glanced back at him. "Which is a sign of higher-than-average intelligence."

"Another trophy?" Petrov bent over and held out his hand.

"No. The murdered salvage crew was the bait. *This*—what happened *here*—was personal. It was meant for me." Sloan grabbed Petrov's hand and got up.

"Not that I do not believe you," Petrov held his hand steady, "but how do the cattle come into the equation?"

"Fecked if I know yet. A distraction, maybe. Or deliberate confusion. We have to get Warrick back to the base. Pronto."

They strode through the field to the smouldering ruins to find Warrick slouched against a broken-down tractor. Weeds sprouted from the flat, cracked tires, and the metal body was rusted through in patches, with just a hint of chipped blue paint around the fenders.

"It's time to go, son," Sloan said.

"But I need to search the town for evidence." Warrick moved away from the tractor.

"We have all the evidence we need, General." Petrov motioned. "You, first."

Suspicious, Warrick loured at them, speaking slowly. "I'm the one in charge."

"Of course, you are," Sloan gently chided with a smile, patting his back. "But we haven't seen one another in so long. Are you going to deny your father quality time? I have important news from the island."

Warrick knew his father was up to something. His exceedingly congenial attitude was the obvious hint.

"I'm aging here, son."

"Okay, okay." Warrick frowned. He hated how he always reverted to a little boy in front of his father, especially when Sloan played on his feelings. He walked between the two men toward Avalon. "What's happened on the island?"

***

EIGHTEEN DAYS LATER

Peaches entered the penthouse suite of the Red Geisha with a bounce in her step, expecting to find Tristan and Vincent waiting for her. Instead, she found Sloan standing at the penthouse window as the late-afternoon sunlight illuminated the dust particles in the air. Petrov, Vincent, and Warrick occupied seats around the Queen Anne desk.

Vincent tapped ash in the antique crystal bowl. "I'm glad you made it home safe, Leona. Masaki mentioned you had arrived this morning. How are you?"

"Great. Sorry I'm a week overdue—and late for this meeting. I needed a shower and bite to eat." She dug inside her jacket and placed a blue matte flash drive on the desk in front of Mr. Shiro. "Everything about the SA Bloc government's genetic program is on that." She paused. "Where's Tristan?"

As soon as she asked, a heavy miasma engulfed the atmosphere. Peaches held an unlit cigarette a centimetre from her mouth, scanning each man's face. Then she wandered over to stand alongside Sloan at the panoramic window, an automatic reaction, since she trusted him the most. She looked up at him. "Where is he?"

Sloan gazed out the window. "I'm sorry," he said calmly.

"Pardon?"

"Dad, this is my responsibility." Warrick got up from his chair. "Peaches—"

"Not you," Peaches barked viciously at Warrick, crushing the cigarette in her fist. "He started this." She turned on Sloan. "I asked you a question, Sloan Whelan, and I want a straight answer. Where's my man?"

"He's dead."

Peaches searched the surrounding space, gulped, and croaked, "No! There's been a mistake!"

Sloan looked down at her with sad fondness. "He ran after an MV on his own."

"You're full of shit," she spat, throwing her cigarette and lighter at him.

"We cremated his body inside a barn in Bridesville. What was left of him."

Peaches exploded with fiery indignation. She hit Sloan in the arm, slapped his face and walloped his chest. "I asked you to do one fucking thing—*one thing!* And you couldn't even do that. What kind of a useless asshole are you? Huh?"

Sloan eyed the men, a subtle warning to stay where they were and not get involved; Leona was about to fall apart, and it was his job, as her long-time friend, to hold her tight.

Peaches's face scrunched and she fell forward, pressing her forehead to Sloan's chest, feebly hitting him. "I love him… I really, really love him."

Sloan embraced her snug. "I know. I love him too," he confessed with fogged vision and kissed her head.

"Tristan's gone," she cried, hugging him tight, gripping his jacket. "What do I do without him?"

I don't know. Sloan closed his eyes, giving her a warm, powerful hug. *I haven't got a fecking clue.*

NINE

THE HUNTING PARTY

Stunning sunset hues drenched the clinic in Limerick. But the air was still somewhat sour, a sharp contrast to how oddly striking the building appeared. Every single thing in Avalon was ugly or beautiful, with no in between.

"You can't leave the city." Sloan could read his son like a book, and Warrick's hard grimace said he was hopping mad.

"Why?" Warrick demanded in a strained voice.

"We've been through this, son."

"You and your theories. What if you're wrong?" Warrick gestured brusquely to his father. "Tell him, would you?"

"Ah, no thanks." Wade continued to peer through his microscope. "Don't involve me."

"But what if I'm correct?" Sloan, composed as ever, chewed on his gum while perched on the red cracked-leather stool like a gigantic buzzard.

"Now you're just mocking my authority." Warrick folded his arms.

Sloan sighed. "I am not mocking your authority, son. You're the General. Do as you see fit. I just don't want you hunting any more vampires, shifters or whatever. Leave it to me."

"You seem to think you're invincible, Dad. But you're not, and there's strength in numbers."

"True. However, I've never claimed to be invincible." Sloan leaned forward, elbows on his knees. "Okay... How about this?" he offered in a pacifying tone. "You give me the Independents, just for a couple of weeks, and we'll try to find the creature. You'd still have the APF."

"What about the island?"

"Petrov's willing to go, and it's only temporary until we catch the bastard who killed Tristan."

Warrick heaved a grim sigh. He didn't want his father's participation at all, but that was a pipe dream. Sloan was headstrong, and he'd never relinquish until he'd avenged his son's death. "Fine. I'll tell the Independents, but you've got to promise you won't do anything rash. And you've only got forty-eight hours."

"What?" Sloan exclaimed, rising from the stool, sending it rolling across the semi-polished concrete. "Why the time constraint?"

"Because that's what I'm giving you. I need the Independents, and the island needs your help. Petrov can't do it alone. You place too much responsibility on his shoulders. He'll go with you and the other Independents. After that he can go to the island." Warrick pointed at him, brows furrowed. "Got me?" he snapped. "*Forty-eight hours.*"

"Yeah, I heard you." Sloan frowned, switching attention to the far wall. "Forty-eight."

"The moment you take them, the clock starts ticking." Warrick briefly eyed him, then strode from the clinic. The doors swung shut behind him.

"I can't believe the nerve—my own son!" Sloan ran his hand through his mop of sooty-black hair.

"Oh, yes. He's nothing like you at all. More like his mother, he is." Wade adjusted the microscope, wearing a sharp, sagacious grin.

Sloan turned on him. "Aw, shut the feck up!"

***

By sunrise, the Independents were on the move, racing south through patches of deadlands and forest to reach Bridesville. Before entering the town, they did an in-depth search of the surrounding area. There wasn't much to find. But Sloan refused to leave until they'd exhausted all possibilities, and the town was secondary. They separated, and Petrov followed Sloan, who had decided to investigate the town hall with Stoner.

After a few minutes, Sloan was about to leave.

"There's a reason it killed Tristan," Stoner said out of the blue.

"Oh, yeah?" Sloan wandered around inside the building, looking through the gaping upper floors to the partial rafters and non-existent roof; the unpleasant smell of wood rot was nauseating. "And what's that?"

"You killed the mutants. In return, the creature killed your son. Tit for tat."

Sloan was truly astonished their thoughts were along the same wavelength. "Okay. Let's say you're correct. That means everyone's lives are at risk."

"Not exactly." Stoner stopped searching and faced him. "I didn't want to say anything in front of the others."

Crossing his arms, Sloan sighed. "All right, I'll bite."

Stoner holstered his sidearms as the Russian, who'd been the Irishman's constant shadow for a very long time, snooped nearby. He examined both men with grave concern, sensing a major change in their friendship. Ever since Mona's death, he'd noticed their dynamic had evolved into a closer bond. In fact, they stank of it. "How long have you two been together?"

"What's it to you? Are you writing a book?"

"I wasn't asking you, Irishman." His sparkling obsidians shot to Petrov. "In order for us to fully trust one another, we all need to be honest. So, I'm asking one more time, Russki. How long have you been with Sloan?"

The huge man lowered his rifle a couple of centimetres, glancing at Sloan, his complexion sour. "Years—since I joined the Independents. I was twenty-six then. You know this."

"That's not what I meant."

"If you mean living together... Off and on since Mona died. And before that, for a while."

"I know. And do you know how I know? Because I can smell Sloan all over you."

"Hey, *come on.*" Sloan frowned, and his shoulders dropped just as his arms did; he was on the verge of being blinded by rage. "That's enough," he growled. "I'm really sick and tired of the crude accusations!"

"Even if it were true, so what?" Petrov scowled, gripping the rifle at his side, muzzle end down. "It is not a crime, and I do not care if you or anyone else believes us or not."

"Not *sex*. These creatures can sense our weaknesses, and it will surely sense yours."

"I am not weak," Petrov barked. "I will protect Sloan and myself."

"I wasn't talking to you, Petrov. I was talking to your best friend." Stoner's focus switched to Sloan. "You may be the alpha in private, Russki, but he's the alpha in public, and if those creatures so much as get a whiff of his weakness, they *will* come after you."

Petrov stared blankly at Sloan, lowering the gun completely; the discouragement was written all over his face.

"Whether any of us want to admit it or not, we are all weaker and slower."

"You mean inferior," Petrov sniped with resentful ire in his eyes.

"How many times do I have to say it? Wrong choice of words. Not weak or inferior, just *different*. I received a *different* fecking injection." Sloan sighed, running a hand

143

through his hair, giving his head a scratch. "Listen, it doesn't matter. What matters is we're toge—"

"I have always known you are superior." Petrov smiled, although his minty greens were drowning in humiliation. He slung the rifle over his shoulder. "It was obvious when you killed Red on your own. All of us knew then, and we exploited you. But I can defend myself."

Sloan watched the Russian exit the building, and his watery eyes were enough to break his heart. He turned on Stoner, glaring holes through the man. "What the feck was that?" he accused under his breath. "Did you enjoy trampling his pride?"

"I just stated the facts. He is a liability for *you*, Irishman. Which puts you both at risk. These creatures chose their prey partly based on their limitations and weaknesses."

"You know that for a fact, huh?"

"I do. That commander's diaries, shed light on a lot of things. Not only will they pick up on your scent all over him and vice versa, just like us, they can sense emotional bonds—when we care about someone. For lack of better terminology, they'll believe he's either *your* mate or *your* child—not the other way around—and then they *will* hunt him down. No different than Tristan."

"Fine. I get it. But you didn't have to fecking say it like that." Sloan belted Stoner hard in the chest and walked away. "It's called *tact*."

"I understand you're angry, and I apologize for hurting his feelings, but it had to be said." Stoner hesitated for a split second and then blurted, "Because I'm in a similar boat."

Sloan stood near the exit—no doors, just a gaping entryway with rusted hinges screwed into the rotting door jamb. He thought about how long everyone in their unit had known one another: the years of training and working together, and the strife. No one else, not even his wife, had understood what he'd gone through.

Although they'd spent the majority of their time working alone, the Independents also revolved around partnerships. Petrov had been Sloan's partner right from the beginning; they'd done absolutely everything together, seen each other at their worst, protected one another, argued with one another. The circumstance had been no different for the rest of the Independents. Claire had worked tirelessly alongside Red. Mona had paired with Duke. Snickers and Roddy.

"We were on watch one night, and one thing led to another. The sex was amazing, and after that, I had to have her constantly. I knew it went against regulations, and it was risky as hell, so I did everything possible to hide it from Morgan," Stoner confessed in a quiet voice. "Yasmine means the world to me, Irishman. We have to pay extra close attention."

Sloan glanced back over his shoulder before walking through the opening. "I appreciate the heads-up."

They continued their exploration from Bridesville, backtracking to the secret laboratory. Then they did a thorough sweep of Bunting and Chartreuse before calling it a night and returning to the smaller military base. As soon as everyone got to the hotel, they separated once again to retire for the evening.

Sloan accompanied Petrov to his private quarters on the fourth floor, and ten minutes later he was waiting for him to shower. "Would you do me a favour?" he said extra loud through the bathroom door, then it clicked open to a hazy soap infused steam.

"Of course, comrade, if it is within my power." Petrov wrapped a towel around his waist.

"You always answer too quickly. What if I asked you to do something unethical?"

"You would never do that." Petrov chuckled, walking from the closet-sized bathroom into the adjoining bedroom. "What would you like me to do?"

Sloan watched him pull up a pair of black jeans, but his mind was elsewhere. His intuition told him that the cattle attack and Tristan's murder were definitely linked. Both incidents occurred around the same time. Which meant not the same vampire, but two. *Shite, I'm an idiot. Of course, there's more than one, and that means... Double feck.*

"Are you all right, Sloan?" Petrov pulled down a soft grey T-shirt over his head.

He snapped back to reality. "Uh, yeah, sorry. What were we talking about?"

"The favour?"

"Right. Would you mind going to the island ahead of me?"

"The cattle."

"I'd feel better if you were there to help Benny and monitor things."

"No problem. I will go, provided you come soon as you are done here." Petrov stood in front of him and held out another towel. "Here."

"What's this for?"

"No offence, my friend, but you could use a shower too."

"Do I stink that bad?" Sloan took the towel.

"It is not pretty." Petrov rummaged through a long chest of drawers. "Have a shower, and I will take you out for a bite to eat. I believe I have a clean change of extra clothes here. I am embarrassed to say, I forgot about the laundry pickup this week."

"Don't tell Warrick though."

"Okay."

After Sloan showered, they ate and drank at the military recreational bar and lounge on the ground floor. By dawn, they parted company. While Vincent sailed Petrov to the island, Sloan rejoined the other Independents for the final chapter of their investigation.

***

Petrov had stayed with Sloan at the cottage on numerous occasions, therefore the setting and inhabitants were familiar. He'd thoroughly enjoyed the time they'd spent visiting everyone: the card games, drinking, and light-hearted conversations were things he always looked forward to. But this time, the usual inviting atmosphere was non-existent. There were no children playing on the street, and all the shop doors were closed without a soul in sight.

He wandered away from the main street into a narrow alley, tucked behind the shops, that faced a row of Irish stone cottages. He unlocked the third gate on his right. Each cottage had a brass nameplate, and a brightly coloured gate with window frames and a front door to match. Painted a striking canary yellow, the quaint cottage in front of him had subsequently been labelled Canary Cottage. He tapped the brass knocker. Shortly after, he heard movement, and the door opened from within. Ingalill greeted him with a radiant smile. *Sloan is right. She is a beautiful woman.*

"Petrov, it's wonderful to see you." She stood aside with a welcoming gesture. "Please come in. Rueben will be back any minute."

"Thanks." He ducked under the lintel and continued to walk with a stoop until he took a seat at the kitchen table. "How are you?"

Canary Cottage was the oldest, and it had the lowest ceilings. He set his rifle and knapsack on the area carpet that abutted a table leg.

"Good. The boys are watching farmer Phelan's cattle." She filled a kettle with water in the sink. "I'm sure that's why you're here."

"It is. I agreed to patrol the village until Sloan arrives. Have any more cattle been killed?"

"No. It's been reasonably quiet since Sloan left." She set the kettle on the stovetop and turned on the element. "Where is he, anyway?"

"He stayed in Avalon."

The door opened.

Rueben brushed his boots on the outside welcome mat and stepped inside the cottage. "Oh, hey, Petrov!"

"Rueben." He smiled.

The Norseman removed his boots and gave the Russian a pat on the shoulder as he pulled out a chair to sit. "It's good to see you. Where's the old man?" He set a large ring of skeleton keys on the table.

"Sorry, it is just me for now."

"No need to apologize." Rueben grinned and gave him another pat. "Everyone appreciates the help."

He nervously frowned as Ingalill filled the teapot in the centre of the table with boiling water; immediately, there was a strong smell of peppermint. "There are a few things I must tell you both…"

He paused and looked at Rueben. "Tristan is dead."

Ingalill practically dropped the kettle, and Rueben helped her grab it before the hot water spilled. Her eyes were brimming, and she rushed to set the kettle on the stovetop with a clatter. Rueben slowly took a seat, his glassy stare attentively focused on Petrov. Although they'd shared a convoluted history, Rueben still regarded Tristan as a friend, and he'd been happy for him when he'd met Leona.

"I am sorry," Petrov said.

"When? Where?" Ingalill dabbed her eyes dry on the tea towel. "How?"

He exhaled a shaky sigh and explained, in as non-visceral terms as possible, what had happened to Tristan. "That is why Sloan sent me here. He believes the cattle attack and Tristan's death are linked. He said it is a vampire we have not seen yet—an intelligent being compared to the MVs."

"He thinks there are two, one here on the island and another on the mainland?" Rueben asked. "Both the same species of vampire?"

"Yes. Right now, he is attempting to track down the one who killed Tristan, and when he is done, he will come to the island. In the meantime, I will do my best to fill his shoes." Petrov leaned on the table, forearms folded. "Have any humans been attacked?"

"Thankfully, no." Rueben slid the ring of skeleton keys over to him. "The cottage is clean and stocked."

"Perfect. Where is Benny?"

"Out on patrol. He's been on edge lately. He said he constantly feels like he's being watched. And now that you've told me this, I'm really worried for his safety."

"Do not fret, comrade." Petrov gave Rueben's back a firm smack. "I will help him."

Rueben finally smiled, but his eyes were still clouded with sorrow. "Tristan was my friend. However, Benjamin is my blood and the only family I have left."

Petrov rose from the chair, taking the keys, knapsack, and rifle with him. "I will see him now. Thank you for the tea, Ingalill."

Standing beside the stove, she nodded, fiddling with the tea towel.

Rueben got up as well and followed him out of the cottage and through the small front garden onto the road. "The old man must be devastated," he remarked.

"He remains strong for his children." Petrov slipped on the knapsack and shouldered the rifle strap. "In truth, he did not want me to come here alone. But I felt compelled when he asked. I will do whatever necessary for him and his children—they're my family."

Rueben slipped his fingers inside his hip pockets, his red gaze glassy. "Don't worry, Mikhael. Things will get better. Both of you will eventually heal."

Petrov glanced back from the other side of the street with an artificial smile. "We will talk again soon."

At the Whelan family cottage, he ate, showered, and prepped his gear in anticipation of a lengthy night. Benny needed assistance with the patrols, and he needed to investigate the vast expanse surrounding the village. It was mainly the farms but included forest. Petrov also planned to discuss a few things with Doctor Avolare.

Evening fell, light and airy over the village, like a mantle of aureate-brown transparent silk, as Petrov began his search. He met with Benny, and together with the other men on patrol, they walked the usual route through the forest and near the shoreline. They made a huge loop, covering some thirty kilometres before returning to the village.

TEN

FRAOCHÁN VILLAGE

By the break of dawn, Petrov restarted the perambulation route. Taking no chances, he was heavily armed as he conducted a thorough off-grid search. However, after hours of combing the forest and beyond, he discovered nothing out of the ordinary except that the island was teeming with wildlife. He ventured past trees covered in butterflies, plus birds, squirrels and chipmunks, a weasel, skunk family, possum, and a black bear gorging on berries near a stream. He even encountered a small herd of white-tailed deer. If anything, the excursion was enjoyably peaceful. He emerged from the forest just as Benny stepped on the path. "Good morning," he said.

"Mornin', Petrov," Benny answered with surprise, holding his rifle lengthwise at his side. "Did you just finish a patrol?"

"I did."

"Damn. What time did you leave?"

"Sunrise. Do not worry. Everything was fine."

"I'm not worried. But did you get *any* sleep?"

"Enough. I do not require a lot."

"Okay. Well, I can handle things for the rest of the day."

"Thanks, comrade." Petrov smiled gratefully and departed with a wave. "See you later."

Instead of returning to Sloan's family cottage, Petrov trekked the main street north, through the heart of the village. The same street continued out of the village and led to a private property. Doctor Avolare's cottage was situated approximately a kilometre from Blueberry, or Fraochán Village, as the elders called it. During their first spring on the island, the settlers discovered many types of wild berries that grew in abundance: blackberry, raspberry, cloudberry, black currant, and gooseberry but predominantly blueberries. The name Fraochán stuck as the berries became the most popular dietary staple.

The genetic engineer's private residence had once belonged to Sloan's maternal fourth great-grandfather, a historical landmark that had been passed down through the family. But before anyone could live in it, it had required significant repairs. In exchange for her medical expertise, the locals repaired the cottage so she could live in isolation. Sloan wasn't keen on the idea of her living outside the village on her own, and whenever he visited, he made a point to check on her.

Petrov's brief journey ended as the dirt road tapered to meet with the entrance to Avolare's property. With a pair of stone columns, a black metal gate and an Irish dry-stone wall crawling in vines, the grand ingress had been a sign of wealth back in the day. Beyond the ancient barrier, the road continued, although barely visible underneath overgrown grass. He pushed on the gate, and then stood at the edge of a sprawling meadow completely hemmed in by more dry-stone wall and forest.

During childhood, his allergies to pollen had nearly killed him, but now he could breathe with ease, and enjoy the moment. He smiled, shading his eyes, feeling a sense of wonder. The meadow was ripe with wildflowers, and cottonwood seeds floated ubiquitously. Everything from the pale-yellow grass and the trees shimmered with light, as if imbued with a mystical beauty. Now he understood why faeries were prominent in Irish folklore.

Perspiration trickled down his sideburns. He loved the summer, just not baking in the direct sun. The grass flattened under his hefty steps, leaving a trail of prints behind.

When he approached the Irish stone cottage, Doctor Avolare was barefoot on the veranda, her airy turquoise cotton skirt and matching blouse puffing out in the sultry breeze. She was snuggling a tiny black bunny into her chest. Her spidery fingers raked the bunny's fluffy ears in contentment.

"Well, well. If it isn't my second-favourite hybrid-human," she said in jest. "What brings you out here, Mikhael?"

"I always knew Sloan was the apple of your eye." He smiled, ascending the short flight of rickety front steps. He put a noticeable strain on the aged wood, and the entire cottage seemed to groan with the shift of his tremendous mass.

"I'm only teasing. You're both special to me." She gave his waist a hug with her free arm. "Actually, all of you are. Come in. I've got a jug of chilled blueberry tea and blackberry scones."

"Sounds delicious." He stroked the bunny's head with his fingertip. "Where did the rabbit come from?"

"I caught him pilfering from my garden several weeks ago. But he's just a baby, and he was starving. I coaxed him with a carrot, and he's been coming back every day ever since." She wandered through the living area and into the kitchen. "One moment."

Petrov shut the screen and front doors, as Raphael set the bunny on the rear porch. He wrinkled his nose and hopped over to a bowl of water.

Petrov wandered into the kitchen seating area, a bulky square table notched toward a padded, L-shaped nook. He sat in the nook. "There is a children's book called *Doctor Dolittle*, and I think you have become like the main character. Every time I visit, you have more animals living with you."

"Now that's an exaggeration." She laughed, closing the wood-framed slider. "I've only got three sheep—which are on loan to mow my backyard—two goats and a dozen chickens. The bunny is new, but he probably won't stay. And since the men from the village rebuilt the pigsty, I purchased two piglets."

"What about that family of ravens I saw last time perched on your clothesline? They looked pretty comfortable here."

"Them too." She opened the fridge.

"And the doe and her babies?"

"That was during the spring. Her fawns are juveniles now, but she still stops by once in a while to nibble on my rose bushes." Raphael set a jug on the table along with a pair of glasses. "Point taken, though." She uncovered a platter of scones and put it down near the jug. "Would you like butter? Mr. Phelan's cows produce the best tasting milk, cheese, and butter."

"That would be nice. Thanks."

After she'd handed him a plate and knife, she tucked herself in on the other side of the table. She eyed him with curiosity for a moment while tearing a scone. "I know you didn't come to sightsee... and you're unusually quiet, Mikhael."

He finished smothering both halves of his scone with the rich creamy butter, and a corrosive sigh escaped his lips. "I just wish circumstances were different. I enjoy our visits, but lately I bring nothing but bad news; or worse, I am picking your brains for information."

"It's fine. As I've told Sloan repeatedly, that's what I'm here for. I'm not just a pretty face, you know." She grinned and put a piece of scone in her mouth. "Don't be shy."

"All right." Petrov held half the scone to his lips and before taking a bite, he said, "Tristan was murdered."

She chewed much slower, searching his morose expression. "That's why you're depressed. My condolences, Mikhael. He seemed like such a nice young man."

He swallowed with an audible gulp and said in an uncharacteristically soft voice, "He was. And I cannot help but feel partly responsible. Perhaps, if I had reached him in time…"

"What happened?"

After he'd explained about the incident in Bridesville, Raphael placed her hand on his and gave his huge fingers a gentle squeeze. "There's no way you could've anticipated such an outcome."

"But that is my job. I am a well-seasoned soldier. I should have paid closer attention. Tristan was young and not nearly as experienced. And I just know I have disappointed and hurt Sloan." Petrov hung his head. "What if he pushes me away?"

"Pushes you away?"

He looked at her with a tear sliding down his cheek. "What if he hates me now? I can handle anything but that."

"Oh, you know that would never happen." She passed him a cloth serviette and rose from the table. "Now dry those beautiful eyes of yours and tell me everything from the very beginning."

"Beautiful eyes?" He blushed, chuckling, and blew his nose. "I am not a woman."

"That's how Sloan described them. He has a thing for your eyes." She shot him an all-knowing smile chock-full of a woman's intuition. So, naturally, Petrov believed her. "Come on, bare your soul."

They talked for hours about the MVs and the chain of events leading to Tristan's death. Once Doctor Avolare had been brought up to speed, they began sorting the evidence, debating who or what might have killed Tristan and the cattle.

She poured him another glass of chilled blueberry tea and set down the jug. "Well, I can certainly see why Sloan would perceive Tristan's death as evidence of a personal vendetta. However, I believe these creatures are more instinctual than intellectual." She meshed her fingers under her chin, keeping her head propped and her elbows on the tabletop. "A perfect example is Krista here."

They both looked at the tiny vampire, who had joined them midway through their conversation and was nibbling on a scone.

"She certainly isn't stupid, but her reasoning is limited. If I claimed otherwise, it would be a gross underestimation on my part, but she isn't a rocket scientist either. That doesn't mean she couldn't be taught or learn on her own. If I'm correct, she's the genetic offspring of an MV—and the reason Sloan was attacked outside the secret lab."

"Now I get it. We disturbed its nest."

"Why else would a lone MV be hiding at the lab?"

"To protect its' child." Petrov took a sip of his tea. "That does make sense."

"I find the correct answer is usually the least expected but the most logical." Raphael stared at Krista in deepening thought for a moment. "Ah, now I see," she said absent-mindedly.

Footfalls and the creaking screen door caught their attention.

Knock, knock.

They both turned to the front door on the far side of the cottage. Raphael went to get up, but Petrov stopped her. He grabbed his rifle from the corner behind the nook, turned the safety off, and took aim, cautiously approaching the door. Krista ducked under the table with her scone.

"Doc, are you in there?"

At the sound of Sloan's muffled baritone, Petrov heaved a relieved sigh. Even the genetic engineer smiled.

He lowered the AK-5000, unlocked the deadbolt, and opened the door. "You scared the shit out of us, comrade."

"Sorry about that." Sloan brushed his shoes on the welcome mat and entered the cool interior of the cottage. "Hey, I didn't interrupt, did I?" He shot them a sassy grin, poking his friend in the gut. "If you want me to leave, I can."

Both Raphael and Petrov frowned.

"Honestly, Sloan Whelan, you're the worst," she remarked with bitterness.

Petrov shut the door. "Do not be a smartass. We were only talking."

"Seriously, if you want me to leave, I will." Sloan stared at him, jerking his thumb back toward the door.

"Oh, will you stop?" Raphael placed her hands on her hips and studied the sparkle of his dark copper gaze. "We're both thrilled to see you. So, there's no way you're leaving. Mikhael is only concerned. Has something else happened?"

"I take it he told you about Tris."

"He did."

"Not particularly. I just couldn't stay there. I needed a change of scenery, and I didn't want to leave everything to him." He nodded to Petrov, sliding his hands into the hip pockets of his jeans. "I'm always dumping too much responsibility on him when it isn't his burden to bear."

"I have told you time and time again," Petrov retorted in a peevish tone, "I will do whatever you ask of me. It is never a burden."

"Thanks."

Raphael touched Sloan's damp cheek. His eyes were, all of a sudden, clouded over with pain. "I'm sorry about Tristan."

Sloan rolled his watery eyes and said softly, "Thanks, doll." He wiped the moisture from his upper lip.

"Come eat something." She dried the tears from his cheek with a serviette. "Now that you're here, we have lots more to discuss."

Krista peeked out from under the table, holding her scone. Sloan patted her head, and she hissed, darting out of the kitchen to vanish at the other end of the house.

"I'm sorry, Sloan. I don't know why, but she's still scared of you."

"It's okay, doc. She's got several legitimate reasons to dislike me. I'm the one who fed her the tranquilizers, I've killed many of her kind, and in her eyes, I'm this huge scary-looking male vampire." Sloan got comfortable beside Petrov in the nook, and the hulking Russian smiled with fondness. He sighed. "What's that look for?"

"I am just glad you are here. And I smile this way at everyone I care about."

"Apparently, you missed me."

"Always."

Raphael observed both men with an impish grin, pulling her chair snugly to the table. "Perhaps the *third wheel* should leave instead," she offered, brows arched.

Sloan and Petrov glanced at one another and burst with riotous laughter. The wonderful noise filled the cottage to overflowing. After a bit, they were quiet again, but much more relaxed.

"That will not be necessary." Petrov leaned back, draping his arms on the nook.

"Nah, it's fine, doll."

"What happened with the search?" she asked.

"Not much. We went over every square inch of land from Bridesville to the secret lab, and there was nothing... not a trace. After that, Warrick put the city on high alert, doubled patrols and locked all the gates. No one can get in or out of Avalon."

She put a scone on a plate and set it in front of him. "You didn't sneak out of the city, did you?"

"No. Warrick and Vince know Mikhael needs the backup." Sloan chuckled at her overprotective response. He sliced the scone in half as the hottest part of the day beat against the stone walls of the cottage. He tried very hard to forget about Tristan, if just for a moment, because if he didn't, he felt like he was going to lose his mind. "So, I'm it: the only reinforcements the island's going to get, at least for the time being."

"That is fine, comrade. We can do this together." Petrov shifted sideways and rested his head on his fist. "I already completed one extensive patrol this morning."

"Let me guess… you found zilch." Sloan took a bite of the scone.

"Other than a ton of wildlife, you are correct. I found nothing—not even a footprint."

"These vampires differ from the mutants. They know enough to hide their tracks, and they are diligent enough to watch and learn. I believe the one on the island and the one on the mainland are part of the same family unit."

"The vampires in the CCTV footage?"

"Yeah, doc." He swallowed the last of his scone and licked his fingers. "I believe those four vampires we saw in the footage—the three females and one male—have been hiding in the shadows this entire time."

"Your personal revenge theory." She sipped at her glass of blueberry tea as if it were steaming hot.

"The moment they killed Tris, my theory became reality. What parent wouldn't be enraged if their children were killed? Stop and think about the chain of events." He pushed the plate away. "Petrov kills the first MV. More than likely, it was at the facility to protect Krista. Whether she's the offspring of that MV or not is irrelevant—they're definitely related. We go back to the facility, find Krista, and take her in. Then nothing happens for years. Not a peep."

He flopped back and folded his arms over his solid chest. "Of course, during that time, hundreds of MVs are bred and they're hungry. They start to follow the migrating deer, and they kill some, and then they kill some more. Mona picks up on this, and she tries to stop them from wiping out the entire herd. She kills one and sets off a chain reaction. As a consequence, some of her men die. I get pissed, I kill more MVs and save her life. But that single incident is like a fecking warning flare. It sends a signal, and more MVs emerge from the woodwork. People go missing. Then we are thrust into this war of sorts, and I end up killing every MV I find. Next thing, the cattle are dead and... Tris is killed." Sloan bit back a shaky breath and swallowed. "These things know about me and the people I care for..."

"The alpha male," she said with quiet restraint.

Both men looked quizzically at her.

"Pardon?" Petrov asked.

"Once, I hypothesized vampires are more animal than human. And in the animal kingdom, no matter the genus, there are leaders. They're the healthiest and strongest of their species. Wolves live in a pack, a family unit. But only the alpha male and alpha female can breed, and they lead the pack. It's nature's way of culling the undesirables, the weak, and ensuring the best possible genetics will be passed on." She set down her knife and moved her plate aside to fold her forearms on the tabletop. "Unfortunately, Sloan, I think you've come to the correct conclusion. You were the general, the pack leader, and most if not all the killings were conducted by you. Now you fear there may be no way to get off this roller-coaster ride."

"Yeah, I'm scared, doc, not for me but my family and friends." Sloan looked at Petrov briefly, then shifted his gaze back to her. "What I need from you are suggestions."

"Suggestions?"

"How to hunt down these things and kill them."

"I see," she said with gravity. She got up from the table. "Well, I don't know, Sloan. Maybe if you take a new approach. 'Think outside the box,' as they used to say in my time."

"Unconventional methods."

"Exactly." She set a pair of pots and a pan on the kitchen island. "You'll both be staying for dinner."

"That is unnecessary," Petrov said.

"I realize you could both survive a century on air alone, but I've invited you, so you're staying."

"Then I will help." Petrov squeezed out from behind the table.

Raphael opened the pantry door, brought out a bowl of potatoes, and set it on the island. She grinned, grabbed his hand, and slapped a peeler onto his palm. "Okay. Then you're my official potato peeler."

"I'd be careful if I were you—handing him a weapon like that." Sloan gave a nod and gestured to the peeler.

"Why on earth should I be careful?" she asked with genuine astonishment.

"He doesn't know a fecking thing about cooking, doc. He's liable to maim you or himself."

Petrov shot him a perturbed glare, whipping a potato at him. "Asshole!"

He couldn't contain it. He roared with laughter, fumbling with the potato at his chest.

"I don't like your condescending attitude, Sloan Whelan." She pointed to the patio. "You're banned from my kitchen."

"Okay, okay!" He shrunk with his hands up as Petrov threatened to throw another potato at him. But before he walked through the rear patio slider, he leaned in and said behind the Russian, "It's okay, sweetie. I'm rooting for you."

Petrov scowled, turned, and booted his rump, propelling him out of the cottage. Sloan tripped onto the patio and swung around, but his best friend had already shut and locked the sliding glass door. He sighed, then smiled, uncurling his posture.

While Raphael and Petrov prepared dinner, Sloan slept on a lawn chair. He wasn't particularly hungry, but he didn't want to insult Doctor Avolare. Hours later, the two men were waving goodbye to her. The sun had faded past the tree line, and the whole meadow was alive with the song of crickets as they made their way to the village.

"The potatoes were good." Sloan smirked, strolling ahead.

The warm evening wind rushed at them.

"Thanks." Petrov frowned. "I will take that with a grain of salt."

At daybreak, they were up to patrol the island with Benny and his men. They split into two sizeable groups, and after an extensive search, they returned to meet on the main road to discuss their findings. Sloan wasn't surprised when they had no new information to report. It seemed the vampire that had killed Mr. Phelan's cattle was part magician.

"Right. That's it!" Sloan shouted, bashing open the front gate to his family cottage.

"What is it?" Petrov asked, bemused by his sudden infantile outburst.

"Everything. Traditional methods haven't worked. Now we have to do the unconventional." As soon as he was inside the cottage, he kicked off his hiking boots beside his fur-lined winter boots, the pair printed with skulls. "I'm fed up with the games. I know they're out there, Mikhael."

"Agreed." Petrov shut the door and removed his boots. "But what can we do until it makes a move?"

"The cattle were attacked at night. Tris was attacked at night."

"It is nocturnal like little Krista."

"Exactly." Sloan tapped his own head, then pointed at him. "Now you're thinking like the vamp."

"You want to go out tonight?"

"It's the only way we're going to know for certain."

Petrov wandered into the cozy living area. He studied the shelves of books and picked a faded, mustard-yellow, linen-bound volume. "*The Diary of a Nobody*... Is this any good?"

"It's an amusing, quick read." Sloan set bottles of beer for each of them on the coffee table.

"Okay. Sounds perfect." Petrov flopped out in the overstuffed armchair and began flipping the pages.

Sloan got comfortable on the sofa with *The Hobbit*. A fierce wind howled against the old stone cottage, rattling the shutters. An Atlantic storm had travelled inland. He listened to gusts of hard rain pelt the windows and roof, and when he peered back over his shoulder, the overcast sky was growing darker. He set *The Hobbit* on the coffee table and wandered about the cottage, turning on the lamps. The temperature dropped considerably, so he swept the grate clean, lit a fire, stoked it to a raging inferno and closed the insert doors.

Then he returned to the sofa and picked up the book again. He read the first page, but eventually his thoughts strayed, and he was staring blankly at his friend. Every once in a while, Petrov chuckled quietly to himself. Evidently, he found the book entertaining. They were alone, and it was quiet. Since such opportunities had been few and far between as of late, Sloan felt a desperate urge to talk about Mona. But he'd been leery of broaching the subject because it invited emotional conflict.

"You have been staring at me for three minutes straight. Whatever is on your mind, you can speak it, Sloan." Petrov flipped a page, continuing to read.

Sloan closed *The Hobbit* and held it crosswise on his lap. If he didn't get the uncertainty off his chest, he'd never move on. But his heart was pounding. "I can say whatever I want...?"

"That is what I said, comrade."

"All right. When Mona died, Claire tried to speak to me in the field, but you held her back. Why?"

Petrov lowered his book, leaned forward, and set it carefully on the coffee table. "Mona died, and you went berserk. I thought you might unintentionally hurt her."

"Unintentionally, huh?" He stared at the roaring fire. "Are you scared of me, Mikhael?"

"No."

"Do you trust me?"

"Unreservedly," Petrov said in a firm tone.

"Then why did you stop her?"

"I have already explai—"

"I don't want you to tell me what you *think* I should hear. I want the truth."

Petrov sighed grievously. "What I said is the truth. But I was also angry... because I thought you let Mona die to get back at me."

Sloan couldn't speak; his throat hardened. He quickly grabbed his bottle of beer and slugged back the entire contents, after which he hastily wiped his mouth. "I ordered her to leave, and she wouldn't fecking listen. She was sick and incapable of fighting, but she did what she wanted." He stared glassy-eyed at Petrov. "Do you have any idea how much that hurt? To know you distrusted me. The way you looked at me."

"It is no excuse, but I was angry, confused, and upset, Sloan."

"Maybe you still don't trust me," he barked. "Maybe you never did."

"And you are perfect?" Petrov snapped back. "Your emotions never get the better of you?"

"I never said that!"

"You might as well have! Do you think I just stopped caring about you?" Petrov accused, searching his expression. "If that is what you think, then you are wrong."

"Right. You had Mona." Even as the words left his lips, Sloan knew he'd said something dreadfully hurtful and manipulative. But he couldn't seem to bite his tongue. "If you care about someone, you're supposed to support and trust them, not throw them to the wolves when things don't go your way!"

Petrov slammed his beer bottle on the table and stood. "Just because you were not there to save Amanda. Do not get mad at me."

"This has nothing to do with my dead wife."

"Actually, it does have everything to do with her, and your lack of emotional control." He loomed over him, his gaze cooling faster than the Arctic Circle. "At the time, I was happy because I believed you needed me. I even pushed Mona aside to help you. Then you shut me out. How could you do that, especially after everything we have been through?" He roared, "So do not play the victim, Sloan. I was the one who got fucking hurt, not the other way around."

The door slammed, and the Russian was gone. The cottage was deathly quiet, a hollow shell of painful silence. Sloan wanted to go after him, but he felt he lacked the right. His legs were suddenly heavy, unable to move, anchored and numb. He remained on the sofa, watching the fire, and a tear trickled down his face.

Hours had passed when the entrance door clicked open and shut to the gust of damp wind. The Atlantic storm was still raging, and that meant fall was just around the corner. Sloan was still seated on the sofa, his burning eyes fixated on the fire. He could hear Petrov remove his jacket, and he could feel slight tremors rise through the floor with his movement. Petrov lumbered past him and sat in the armchair next to the sofa, rubbing his wet head with a tea towel.

Petrov sighed, depositing the towel on the armrest. "Forgive me. I should not have said that. I did willingly go to Mona, but it was not out of love. She was a convenience and, sadly, she knew it. And it had always been that way... even

171

after years together. Then I pressured you to protect her, because I knew you would not deny a friend. I had no desire to take responsibility and like always, she would not listen… I hurt you both." He put his fingertips together and flexed his hands, his expression contrite. "No matter what happens, you will always be my best friend, Sloan, and I love you for that."

Sloan's crooked smile quivered. "Thanks." He cleared his throat. "You were correct about me—correct about everything." He sniffed and wiped his warm, damp cheek, continuing to stare at the fire. "When it comes to people problems, I get scared, and then I made a fecking mess out of everything. Raphael had told me Mona was sick. But I still let her sway my judgment. When we entered that field, we were outnumbered…" He crossed his arms. "But she just wouldn't listen—even when Peaches tried to get her to leave. After that… it was too late."

Petrov frowned, falling backward into the armchair.

"She was just as much to blame in all this, forcing me to make a decision I didn't want to make. I cared about her. She was my friend, and you're my best friend. But then I just let her have her way." Sloan looked at Petrov. "You know what?"

"Tell me."

"What's done is done. And I'm sorry too, Mikhael. I'm sorry that you're stuck with a fecking old fool like me. But I promise from this moment on, I will be more open and honest."

"That is the spirit!" Petrov grinned and rose from the chair, pushing up his sweater sleeves. "I bet you are hungry. We should eat before we go on patrol."

Shite. He's testing my resilience already. Sloan quickly bounced to his feet and closely tailed him into the kitchen. "It's okay. I can do it," he offered as politely as possible. "You don't have to make anything."

"I know I am the worst cook, comrade. But the only way I am ever going to improve is practice."

Sloan rolled his eyes. "Don't tell me. I'm going to be your guinea pig, again."

"That *was* very honest." Petrov chuckled. "And yes, you will be."

"Sorry, I didn't mean—"

He slapped Sloan's back. "Do not worry. You do not have to walk on eggshells around me anymore. We made up, and we are friends. I just want to prepare a meal for you like you always do for me. Is that all right?"

"Sure."

"If it makes you feel better, I will allow you to supervise."

It was Sloan's turn to laugh; he pulled out a kitchen chair. "Nope. It's fine. You do whatever your little heart desires, and I'll just sit here like a good boy and keep you company." He sat, folding his arms. "Fair?"

"Sounds fair to me."

"Excellent. What do you plan to make?"

"Sandwiches."

ELEVEN

HEARTBREAK

"I'll return as soon as I can."

"Do I have a choice?"

"Sorry, no." Sloan set the last empty crate on the boat deck. "The village needs supplies, and I promised Warrick. It's been two months since I last checked in."

Petrov flipped up his jacket collar and stood with his back to the wind. He didn't want Sloan to leave; he'd felt uneasy for days. But the man had obligations. "I dislike it when you travel back and forth alone. The weather has been bad. What if the yacht sinks?"

"Thanks." Sloan chuckled. "I won't die, remember. And it's still too risky to leave the island unattended."

"Whatever you say, comrade." Petrov sighed. "You know I will not abandon my post."

"I appreciate it." Sloan motioned to the rope wrapped around the boulder that kept the yacht anchored. "Be extra careful."

Petrov smirked, tossing him the wet rope. "Yes, Father."

"Not funny, Mikhael." Sloan frowned.

"But that is what you sound like: an overprotective father. Do not worry, my friend, I am a big boy. I will be just fine."

"Famous last words. Look, don't be a smartarse." Sloan pointed an accusatory finger. "If you need Benny and the guys to help, ask. I don't want you running into the woods alone, playing the hero."

"You are one to talk. You can leave now." He scowled, folding his arms over his massive chest. Not surprisingly, if there was even a whiff of danger, Sloan treated him like his child. Maybe it was their age difference, not that he cared. But it was irksome.

"See you soon." Sloan wore a cheeky grin as the engine started with a bubbling rumble.

Petrov wandered alongside the shoreline, but the Irishman had already drifted out of sight, swallowed by the dense layer of fog. "You had better come back," he shouted. "Sarcastic bastard."

As promised, Sloan returned just shy of a fortnight with the supplies. But he didn't expect the large reception waiting for him. Usually, Rueben and Benny would be ready with carts to haul the goods. This time, however, Petrov, along with Rueben's two oldest sons, who were bracing themselves against the torrid wind on the bank above the shoreline, had joined Benny and Rueben. They looked like they hadn't slept a wink in days, and they were all armed with swords and their guns.

Petrov greeted him with a big smile, grabbing the rope when he tossed the line. "It is good to see you, my friend."

"Same to you." Sloan jumped onto the gravelly beach as the Russian hauled the yacht inland, scraping the underside, and tied the rope to the mooring boulder. "It's great to see everyone. But I have a feeling you aren't here for my benefit."

"Sorry. We aren't. We've got an even bigger problem," Rueben said.

"Nice. I thought everyone missed me."

"You wish," Benny chided dryly.

"Well, if it is any consolation, I missed you," Petrov joked extra softly, close to his ear.

"Thanks, a lot." Sloan flashed the Russian a perturbed stare. "What's the problem?"

Rueben's sons loaded the carts to brimming with crates and hauled them back toward the village, while the men and Sloan walked behind. Once they'd delivered the supplies, they crammed themselves inside Canary Cottage.

The aromatic scent of peppermint tea, and the mouth-watering smell of fresh-baked bread, mingled in the air. Ingalill set out plates and teacups. Sloan glanced at the fire, removing his mended aviator before taking a seat at the table.

"Three children have gone missing."

Sloan noticed the worry etched into Rueben's features. "Murder?"

"I know what you're thinking, but the typical foul play wasn't evident. They were taken in the middle of the night—snatched out of their beds." Rueben waited a moment as

Ingalill poured them each a tea. "No, I'm not delirious. We've talked to the families."

"And no one saw or heard anything?"

"Not a peep," Petrov answered. "I have already tracked the areas surrounding the houses, and I found no trace except scratch marks on the windowsills. Whatever it was crawled in through the bedroom windows."

"You said *what*, not *who*. Are you trying to tell me these children were abducted by our mystery creature?"

"That is exactly what I am saying." Petrov cradled the teacup in his large hands, making the delicate piece of porcelain look like a baby bird in a gargantuan nest.

"Right. Then this is going to sound facetious, but… did you find any other clues?"

"No. My guess. It is large and agile with the ability to camouflage itself."

"Great. That narrows it down." Sloan sighed morosely, but more to himself.

Ingalill placed a suede-bound, antediluvian book on the kitchen table, and Rueben slid it toward the two men. "It may sound far-fetched, but we think maybe it's one of these."

Sloan read the faded font: *Vampires in the Modern Age.* He chuckled at first, then bit back his mirth when Rueben's gaze turned resentfully cold. He wasn't sure how to respond. "Okay. You're not joking."

"She isn't," Benny added.

"We're not talking about someone like you," said Rueben. "We're talking about something evil—abnormal—

177

supernatural even." He nursed his cup of tea, the liquid a beautiful pistachio green with an amber hue in the centre. "I'm certain—well, all of us are certain—that your hypothesis was correct. One of General Griffin's genetic experiments has somehow got on the island, and it's taken the children. Just like Mr. Phelan's cows, it has now attacked us." He swallowed his tea. "I'd appreciate it if you'd do a thorough search of the island again. Not that we don't trust Petrov's judgment. He's done a great job."

"Fine, Rueben. I get it."

"If it's still out there, the population is in danger," Benny said.

"Agreed. I'll go. I'm better equipped."

"I'm sorry if it sounds like I'm dumping the responsibility on you, Sloan. I—"

"Stop. Don't worry, Rueben. This is exactly what I'm built for." Sloan rose from the table and said to Petrov, "Show me what you found."

Petrov said goodbye and ducked the low lintel, exiting the small cottage. "I want to know how the creature got across from the mainland," he murmured to Sloan.

Sloan shut the door, rattling the brass knocker, and strolled on to the laneway behind him. "Low tide."

They sauntered side by side.

"Please explain."

"At the northernmost tip of the island, when the tide drops, spiky bits of rock appear. It's kind of like broken bits of reef. The bits are a distance apart, and it wouldn't be easy, but if you were fast enough and strong enough, you might cross from the island to the mainland." Sloan rested his hands inside his jacket pockets. "At one time, Vincent and I discussed destroying them. But we feared the repercussions."

"Just in case the villagers needed to use them."

"Yeah, an emergency."

Petrov showed him where each abduction took place—the children's homes and their bedrooms. Afterward, they scoured the southern tip of the island. Then they moved furtively deeper inland until the village disappeared completely from sight, and they stood in a gently sloping field surrounded by dense woods.

Petrov confessed that something strange had happened to him, only a couple of nights before Sloan's return, something he hadn't shared with Rueben. But he felt Sloan should be made aware of the incident's importance. "The creature was in that forested area over there." Petrov touched Sloan's shoulder and pointed to the dark diffuse tree line half a kilometre away.

"Are you sure?" Sloan was familiar with this valley; Doctor Avolare's cottage was only eight or nine kilometres from the tree line. Too close for comfort.

"I am positive, my friend. The creature was invisible, but I sensed its presence. I felt as if someone were watching me… studying me. But when I looked in its direction and demanded it confront me… nothing." Petrov paused and said in earnest, "As soon as the words left my mouth, I knew I had made a mistake. The experience was unnerving."

Sloan observed his profile. In the moonlight, his blond lashes glistened an icy white, and his long hair hung in an icy wave. "The tiny hairs on your arms stood on end."

"Exactly." An appreciative smile widened Petrov's face; someone believed him. "With goosebumps."

"Just before the cattle incident, Benny said the same thing. And some of the other men who help with the patrols have mentioned feeling unsettled, like someone or something was watching them." Sloan held out a stick of gum. "And if you're collaborating their statements, then it's got to be true."

The Russian gawked at him, nonplussed, but took the gum.

"You heard. I'm taking your word for it. Now look where we are. What's the one major problem with this location?"

Petrov slowly turned, carefully examining the field and trees, then he stopped to face slightly northwest. He chewed, slipping his hands inside his jacket pockets. "The village is east of us, and Doctor Avolare's cottage is west. This field is like a straightaway between the two locations and it is probably the quickest route to travel back and forth unnoticed."

"Precisely." Sloan chewed. "Now that we know how its moving around. We need to find clues."

"Agreed. Which side do you prefer to investigate, southeast or northwest, comrade?" Petrov gestured with a bow toward either side of the field. "Age before beauty."

"Discourteous, smartarse." Sloan shot him a petulant scowl, pointing sharply. "I prefer left over right. So, left. Northwest."

They parted company, each sauntering in their respective directions to search.

Petrov snickered, twisting the gold necklace Mona had given him around his finger. "And you tell me I act like a child? You should see your face, comrade."

"Are you going to search or what?" Sloan growled, eyeing him. "We haven't got all night."

Petrov laughed again, backing farther away from him. "Grumpy much?" he joked. "Elyse is correct, one of these days you will blow a gasket. You need sex—and I know just the woman."

Dirty bastard. He chuckled, folding his arms. "I should've known. No thanks." He sighed. "Whatever. I'm good with how things are at present."

"Are you serious?" Petrov rolled his eyes with disillusionment. "Amanda has been gone for many, many years, my friend."

"Yeah, I'm dead serious. It's not like I have time to dedicate to a relationship."

Astonished, the blond shook his head with his hand on his hip. "I am stunned. For a man who has no problem telling me and everyone else they need companionship. You never take your own advice."

"Oh, for feck's sake, Mikhael, enough."

"What about Claire? Please, just hear me out." Petrov raised his hands, wandering backward, dragging his boots. "I know it is a strange suggestion, considering what she did. But she is an attractive woman, she is single, she understands your line of work, and it is not like you would have to spend time getting to know one another."

Sloan couldn't believe his ears. "Nothing against Claire. She's a fox. But, for the last time, I'm just not interested in anything remotely emotionally taxing right now."

Petrov wandered away into the murky shadows and faced the tree line. "You always say that. Elyse is correct, it is unhealthy the way you live with your lousy diet, then working day and night. You need a good woman, Sloan." There was the faintest swishing noise; he stopped and wavered slightly. "I care that is all," he gasped, then he glanced back, trembling, and a large tear rolled down his pained face. "I am going to miss you…"

"Mikhael?" Sloan's forehead furrowed.

The second time, the strange noise—like metallic slashing—was louder.

Something's got him, the parasite said. *Hurry!*

Sloan raced toward him, trying to hone in on the problem. Petrov went stiff, frozen to the spot, and expelled a gut-wrenching cry. An invisible meat hook seemed to snag him, and his chest jolted violently as he struggled. Then something ripped his heart out in a splash of black paint against the moonlit sky and at the same time, his head flew, landing in the tall grass. His body slumped into a kneeling position and pitched sideways.

"*Mikhael! No!*" The assault had happened pell-mell, and Sloan couldn't calculate. He didn't know what had attacked his friend. He stared at the bloody mess in bewildered distress. *Shite... No, no, no.* The entity knew exactly how to kill him and had acted with precision.

"Come get me!" Sloan bellowed, arms outstretched, walking around the corpse. "Come on, you *fecking piece of shite!*"

The wind picked up, a murmur rustling the leaves, and the grass bowed, brushing his calves. Then the field was blanketed in silence. The ring of forest, an abyss. And the assailant, gone.

Numb, his gaze dropped. "God, help me... not again." His legs buckled, and he sank to the ground as Petrov began to deteriorate. With tears falling off his face, he carefully lifted the man's skull from the grass and cradled it to his chest until it crumbled to ash. "Don't go," he begged with hoarse sobs. "*Please...*"

Sloan steadily collapsed beside the grave, his mouth and cheek dusted with the remains of the Russian. His chest ached, and the flood of tears wouldn't stop. *Why him?* He exhaled a miserable groan, closing his eyes, wishing it all away. *I should've never brought him with me.* He pressed the heels of his palms to his eyes and hollered in aguish.

***

Minutes lapsed, becoming hours.

***

And hours lapsed to days.

***

For a week, Sloan stayed beside the grave like a faithful dog unwilling to leave his dead master. He lay on his stomach with an arm under his face as he touched the ash. He closed his sore eyes. Nothing mattered anymore.

This isn't your fault, she whispered. *Pull yourself together.*

Why didn't it kill me, then? Sloan said from his mind. *I was right here with him. There must be something…*

Perhaps the creature had been stalking him.

No… it's the other way around. He knew the truth. Petrov had been targeted, thanks to his egotistical thoughtlessness.

I don't understand.

The nagging feeling that he'd missed something wouldn't stop. Everything his senses had picked up on was crisp and palpable. He squeezed the Russian's necklace against his throbbing chest. If he didn't find whoever or whatever had killed Mikhael, he'd never forgive himself.

"Warrick was right. I relied on you too much," he sputtered into the cool evening air. "What the hell's wrong with me? I should've said it more often—every damn day."

He paused, then suddenly remembered: there had been an odour in the air just before Petrov received the first slash. Sickly-sweet, on the verge of nauseating. *That's it.*

He opened his eyes and focused on the ebony sky, and his heartbreak steadily developed into wrath. Turning his head to the side, he touched the spot where Petrov had died and said ever so quietly, "Forgive me for not saying it enough… Thank you for always being there."

Sloan put the necklace inside his hip pocket and crouched, digging his claws into the dirt, his copper gaze seething. He sniffed at the breeze, this way and that, moving further afield until he caught a whiff. Then he was gone, cutting the grass, following the scent trail.

On and on he raced.

Westward.

Kilometres upon kilometres.

The odour intensified.

Finally, he pinpointed the location and swung around, coming to a grinding halt, the soles of his boots scoring hard dirt. Stars dotted the sky, as he examined the topography.

Whatever the creature, it was close, lurking in the darkness. "I know you're there," he growled, taking a step. "Your stink is everywhere."

Directly in front of him, a pair of red orbs pierced the black amid the trees and vegetation, needles poking through thick fabric.

"You killed him." He hunched his shoulders, spreading his arms, and snarled, "You killed *my best friend* and *my son*! You killed those innocent children!"

Slinking from the hidden depth of forest, the creature's spindly, sharp digits pulled the darkness away like a black curtain, revealing transparent, whitish flesh crawling with veins; the texture and pigment of which seemed to continuously evolve to match the surrounding environment. Inky fur covered its' lozenge skull, and its' tight mouth was crammed with razor teeth. No eyebrows, but pointed ears that traced the smooth sides of its head, and a flat mushroom cap nose. Whereas the rest of its' body was hairless with pert breasts, a reddish vulva and elongated limbs.

It was a *she*, and *she* wasn't alone; a pair of female vampires joined from the darkness. They were smaller than the one taunting him.

Big, lean and sleek, she dominated the scene, stalking like a cat toward him.

Sloan nearly gagged; he'd seen a lot of disturbing things in his life but never something this hideous. "Feck it. I don't care how many of you there are." His eyes pulsated, and his fangs and claws lengthened. "I'm going to kill you all!"

TWELVE

WORTHY ADVERSARY

The female vampire was a worthy adversary, strong in every sense of the word and fast, not that he could see much. He had to rely on his original abilities, because whatever genetics he'd stolen from the MV, weren't entirely compatible with his human DNA. Doctor Avolare had determined, via testing, that the MV genetics had actually made him sick. His black eyes were the side effect. The parasite had only allowed him temporary usage of the MVs genetics as a last resort, when he'd needed to save Mona. So, he no longer had supersonic speed. Instead, he had to depend on the shield for extra defence.

As for victory, it didn't come, and even the stalemate had a price. The vampire had mutilated his entire left side, broken his ribcage, collapsed his lung, crushed his arm, torn the tendons and muscles in his leg, and gouged his eye. In the end, the vampire had retreated to lick her wounds, and Sloan had dragged himself to shelter under a fallen petrified tree, drifting in and out of consciousness, the pain excruciating, as the parasite worked feverishly to repair him.

Ah, your kidney is pulverized—your bones are shattered— oh your lung and the internal hemorrhaging, the parasite whispered agitatedly. She felt as if she was trying to plug a sieve. The wounds were so severe she didn't have enough control to stop the leakage. But if she gave up now, she'd fail him and their creator.

His breathing slowed to dangerously shallow. "It's okay," he mumbled through blood-soaked lips, and his right eye began to close, "if you can't… heal me."

Hold on, Sloan! She knew the trauma was too much for any normal human to withstand, but she had to keep him awake, otherwise he'd die. Not only had the female vampire destroyed his flesh, organs, and bones, but she'd also passed on her contaminated blood. Similar to Mona, Sloan had contracted a lethal virus and with his injuries, his body now had to fight twice as hard to stay alive. She hit him with more epinephrine, and he woke with a gut-wrenching wail. *Stay with me!*

A dampness clung to the cool morning mist, and the rising sunlight struggled to pierce the fog, its brightness dispersed and muted. While Fraochán Village was a cluster of obscured silhouettes. Once word had reached the mainland that Sloan and Petrov had gone missing, Wade, Elyse and Vincent made a joint decision to return to the island. But even after performing their own patrols, they found nothing.

"What's it been... two weeks or more?" Wade scanned the misty landscape around the main street, holstering his pistol. "That's what Benny guessed."

"It doesn't matter, they've been gone too long." Elyse stood, veiled in mist, a sniper rifle slung over her shoulder. "This isn't normal. I just know something's gone wrong."

Vincent lit a cigarette as rays of sun blasted through the haze. "I understand, but you must stay here."

"There's no way I'm waiting another second. I want to help you search." Elyse respected her uncle for her father's sake, more than anything else, but she also reviled his unemotional, "business first" attitude. "He's your brother. Aren't you worried?"

"Let me reiterate. I empathize with your feelings, but I also know how my brother thinks. He'll string me up if anything happens to you. Do us both a favour and don't move."

She watched him smoke contentedly. "What crap. I will not sit here and wait to see if my dad dies."

Sloan wheezed, every inhalation a struggle as he hobbled in the direction of the village, dragging his leg and holding his arm. Unfortunately, the female vampire's genetics were equally toxic as the MV's and, subsequently, the cellular destruction was extensive. But he wasn't worried; the physician just needed a little more time to repair him, then control the offending DNA. He remembered little of the journey back, but when he heard his daughter's and brother's voices, he felt a great sense of relief. "You're fecking annoying…"

"Dad!" Elyse stared as his wraithlike figure materialized in the fog.

Vincent dropped his cigarette. *"Niisan…"*

Both Elyse and Vincent stared, horrified, and Wade rushed to his aid. Wade lifted Sloan's good arm over his shoulder, and Vincent did the same on Sloan's injured side.

Back at the family cottage, Vincent stood in the living room behind Sloan, and Sloan sat on the sofa, gawking at the crackling flames inside the fireplace. Elyse placed a mug of tea on the coffee table in front of him, and Wade sat in the overstuffed armchair to his right.

"We were in the field, and he walked away from me…" His lower lip and chin quivered as he tried to control the swelling emotion; his chest felt like a volcano ready to erupt. "He…he was lecturing me about finding a woman. He was happy…" His rich baritone turned ugly. "Then something came out of nowhere and struck him down!"

Elyse sat beside him and touched his knee, her expression forlorn; his watery eyes had a vacantness to them, and moisture streaked his grimy face.

He made a fist, suffocating the gold necklace. "I became fecking furious…this irrepressible rage I've never felt before."

Wade listened attentively. "That's understandable."

"After it killed Mikhael, I eventually hunted it down and fought it."

"What was it?"

"It's hard to describe. Humanoid, maybe. Female. Grotesque." Sloan looked at him. "Everyone on this island is in serious danger."

"How do you know that, *niisan*?"

Sloan glanced back. "The missing children... Don't ask me how, I know. But I know it killed them first."

"We need to talk to Doctor Avolare," Wade said. "She'll know what to do."

"No. I know what to do."

The following morning, Sloan assembled all the members of the town council and warned them about the three female vampires. He also educated them on what to expect and how to protect themselves. As anticipated, the villagers were terrified, disputes arose, and he had to arbitrate. But there was nothing else he could do. Short of conducting a mass evacuation, for which there weren't the resources, the villagers had to stay put and weather the storm. Benny and Rueben gathered as many able-bodied men as they could, armed them, and doubled the patrols.

***

MID-NOVEMBER
THIRTY-FIVE DAYS AFTER PETROV'S DEATH

"It took you long enough to get here." Benny held his rifle at his chest, legs spread, and a sour frown painted his face.

Peaches dropped her smouldering butt and stepped on it, grinding with her boot. "I had to wait for the latest storm to pass."

Despite the fact sunlight sparkled through the dense foliage, sections of the forested island footpath remained well shaded, and it was cold in the shade. Peaches took a step back into a narrow ray of sunlight—anything to keep herself warm. She noticed that the brothers, even Rueben, were armed to the gills, which said something. Clearly, Petrov's death had had a substantial far-reaching effect, more than she or anyone else realized.

"We've never seen him like this," said Rueben. "It's worse than when Amanda died."

A gust of cool autumn air rushed past. Peaches shivered with the damp chill and pulled up her bulky navy scarf around her ears. The last time she'd seen Sloan was before he returned to the island with supplies, just prior to Petrov's passing, at the tail end of the summer. Later, Elyse, Vincent, and Wade returned to the mainland without him. Everyone had argued as to the best plan of action, but no one dared to confront Sloan, not even his children. Ultimately, Peaches accepted the grim task of bringing the Irishman home. "Have there been any more attacks? Missing children? Dead livestock?" she asked.

"Thankfully, no," Rueben answered. "It's been quiet. I think the vampires are leery to make a move since Sloan's been stomping about in the bushes everywhere."

Landing on a spindly lilac branch, a chickadee twittered, cocking its head. The front garden was dead and dull. But the cobalt paint was as bright as Peaches remembered and just as cracked. She placed her hand on the garden gate with an unenthusiastic sigh. *How long do you plan to hide in there, big man?* "Has anyone talked to him?"

"We've all tried, even Ingalill, but he snapped at her too. He's become unreasonable and short-fused."

"Is that all?"

Rueben frowned, his gloved hand resting on his sidearm. "What do you mean, 'is that all'?"

"He's always been crabby. He's just ten times worse right now because the loss is still fresh. Let me handle this."

"I wouldn't advise it, Leona," Benny said.

"He's, my friend. He won't hurt me—or anyone else, for that matter." Peaches walked the length of stone-laid garden path. "He's just lost his heart, and we have to help him find it again."

Sloan rarely left the master bedroom. He lifted a crimson T-shirt from the floor, held it in his lap and smoothed the cotton with his thumbs. Then he hung his head. The hollow emptiness of the house was unbearable. Every room resounded with Petrov's laughter and voice. Tears slid down his cheeks as he brought the shirt to his face. He sensed another presence, and he knew by the calming floral scent it was Leona.

Peaches stood inside the bedroom doorway. After a moment, she rested her shoulder against the jamb, arms stiff and hands rammed deep inside her back-hip pockets. "Is there anything you need? Tea, or…?"

"I'm good, thanks," Sloan mumbled, "unless you can bring back the dead. Because I'd take an order of that."

She shed a few tears and quickly brushed her upper lip with the back of her hand. "Sorry." She sniffed. "Why is this happening to us?"

He sighed and tossed the shirt onto his mother's rocking chair in the corner. "I don't know."

She sat beside him on the bed. "Whoever—or whatever—did this has to be stopped."

They both lay back on the bed and looked at one another. Then Peaches curled in a ball with her cheek on a pillow, and Sloan lay on his stomach, hugging a pillow under his head.

"Do you want to stay the night?" he asked.

"Sure."

"Are you warm enough?"

"Yep. This place is like an oven. And it must be your body heat because the fireplace is stone cold."

He chuckled and shifted to get comfortable on his side. "Do you remember when we first met?"

"Yeah, of course." Peaches smiled, curling her eyebrows. "I wanted you so bad. But I was too young, and you knew it."

"True. You *were* just a kid."

"I was one messed-up brat. I still don't know why you helped me."

"I thought that was obvious. Because I care, Leona."

Her heart almost stopped, and she just about burst into tears. But she shoved her face into the pillow instead. She knew the Irishman's declaration wasn't a romantic one, but that of a true friend. If it weren't for him, she would've died long ago. "You've changed," she muttered in embarrassment.

"That bad, huh?"

"Nope. Just different." She peeked sideways, scrunching the pillow, getting lost for a moment in his thoughtful, attractive stare. "You're more shameless than ever. You just blurt out this incredibly considerate shit."

"I've always said whatever's on my mind."

"True, but never your emotions—never what you feel deep down. You're always a blank slate. It's impossible to get an accurate read." She smiled. "But now I can see you for the man you really are, and I like it."

"Huh. You like it?" He tucked the pillow more snugly under his head.

"A lot."

"Thanks, sexpot." He let out a shaky sigh, and quietly confessed, "I can't stay here any longer. It hurts too much. Besides, nothing's happened. Maybe the vampires are gone."

"Then we'll leave in the morning."

Sloan was quiet for a long while, and then he said out of the blue, "Nothing will ever be the same."

Peaches read the sadness in his glassy stare. "No. I'm afraid it won't."

"I can feel the rage building inside me, Leona, and I'm scared whoever is near me will get caught in the crossfire... But I promised him."

"Then you have to keep your promise."

The morning was bright. The sunlight streaming into the bedroom through the small, square, leaded-glass window.

Sloan exhaled a tremulous sigh. *Get a grip.* He pinched the damp corners of his eyes. It felt like he hadn't slept in days, and the knotted ache in his chest wouldn't go away. But he figured it probably never would, not entirely, and he hated that feeling of hopelessness. "I want you back," he murmured.

"Breakfast, big man!"

Sloan blinked. For a moment, he'd forgotten Leona had stayed the night. He got up and rested his bare feet on the warm floor. *She's turned on the heat.* The delectable aroma of eggs and bacon got his stomach rumbling. *She's made breakfast too. Maybe she'll do my laundry.* He grinned, amusingly. "Coming, Jeeves!" he called back, taking a cautious step through the open doorway.

"What was that?" Peaches barked, squinting at him, holding a frying pan and spatula. "I'm not your personal servant. Cocky jerk! Get your ass out here before the food goes cold."

Sloan softly chuckled, slouching against the doorframe and putting on his socks. "Hey. I was only teasing." He wandered into the kitchen, adjusting his belt. "Shite, you made flapjacks too. Now, I am touched. I haven't had them in an age."

"I'm glad you approve." Peaches dumped a plate stacked high with eggs, bacon, and steaming flapjacks drenched in butter and raspberry syrup on the table in front of him. She pulled out a chair. "Enjoy."

"This is a family-sized portion of food." Sloan pointed at the plate.

"Well, you're gonna eat it if it's the last thing you do. I know you haven't had anything nourishment wise in weeks. Vampire or not, it's unhealthy. You're still partly human." Peaches cut her flapjacks into small pieces. "Don't argue. Eat."

"*Itadakimasu.*" Knife and fork in hand, Sloan grudgingly hunkered down to consume a year's worth of food. He started on the six soft-poached eggs, and he managed to eat two before someone knocked on the front door.

Peaches leaped to her feet first and pointed at him. "*Eat.* I'll get it." She opened the front door to find Benny loitering on the stoop. "I should've known. You're ruddy impatient."

"Yeah, and you're uncouth." Benny brushed past the scowling, slender redhead. "How are you this fine morning, Sloan?"

"Better." Sloan patted the chair beside him. "Want some breakfast?"

"Don't mind if I do. It smells delicious."

Sloan grabbed another plate from the nearby open hutch and scooped eggs, bacon, and flapjacks onto it.

"Hey, you need to eat," Peaches scolded, shutting the door. "I can make more for him."

"I am eating. But you gave me way too much." Sloan set the plate on Benny's placemat. "Besides, it's rude to dine in front of company."

Stunned, Benny gawped at the heaping amount of food. "I appreciate the meal, Sloan, but I can't possibly eat all this."

"See? Told you." Sloan eyed Peaches, holding out cutlery. "Too much is *too much*. Do the best you can, Ben."

Benny took the cutlery and tucked in for the long haul. "Star never makes pancakes."

"Bad cook, is she?" Peaches grinned with conceit.

"My wife's a superb cook, actually. But she says flapjacks are too fattening. So, this is a treat for me. How's everything around here, Sloan?"

"Okay." Sloan put another piece of flapjack in his mouth and chewed.

"Just okay, huh?" Benny rested his forearms on the table edge. "With all that's happened lately, I never got a chance to say this, but… thanks for everything."

Sloan sighed with contentment, pushing the plate away; he couldn't handle another morsel. "That's what I'm here for."

"It's not, really, but it isn't like you're going to take my word for it. I want you to know you're not just our bodyguard. You're our friend, mentor, and father."

Sloan self-consciously glanced at them both. He didn't know how to respond to Benny's kindness, and he could feel a stinging, itchy burn filling his eyes.

"Whatever you need—and I mean *whatever* it is—all you have to do is ask." Benny touched his shoulder. "But, more importantly, I want you to be careful when you reach the mainland."

"Careful's my middle name." Sloan blew off his worry with an artificial smile, smudging the wetness from his cheek. "I can handle anything."

"You're so full of crap, old man. The pain is written across your face, plain as day. But if you think getting yourself killed is going to somehow make it all better, you're wrong. I can't tell you if or when you'll come to terms with the grief, but eventually you'll have to accept what's happened. And there's no way in hell Petrov would want you to suffer. He'd want you to carry on."

Peaches watched Benny eat for a second, and then her attention darted to Sloan. She'd half expected the Irishman to blow his fuse, but he remained withdrawn, as if his mother had just admonished him. His depression was soaking through the atmosphere and tainting the mood. Now she understood why Rueben had been worried, and she wondered if Sloan would ever completely snap back. He seemed to be drifting further and further out of reach.

"Well, I'm off." Benny got up from the table. "Sorry to dine and dash, but the men are waiting for me to join them on patrol. Thanks for the meal, Leona."

"Sure," Peaches said.

"Take care, Sloan." Benny closed the door.

"The faster we get out of here," Sloan quickly stacked the dishes, "the better off I'll be."

"Okay." Peaches downed her tea and wiped her mouth on a serviette. "I can do the dishes if you want to start packing."

However, before their departure for the mainland, Sloan took a gamble. He left the cottage to take a walk. He hiked the gently rising incline of field, moving westward away from the village until he'd returned to the spot where Petrov had died.

Standing with his arms outstretched, he hollered at the circumference of densely packed woodland, "No more games!" His voice echoed, and he deliberately turned, studying every centimetre of timber. "Do you hear me? No more games!" He waited for his echo to fade. "I'm returning to the mainland right now, and when I get there, I'm going to hunt down your male. I'm going to tear him to shreds!"

He didn't know if he'd got his point across. Had the vampires heard him? Were they even able to comprehend? Sloan lowered his arms and eyed the forest one more time before ambling back to the village.

THIRTEEN
A BITTER PILL TO SWALLOW

During the trip, Sloan remained withdrawn. He didn't want to talk because if he talked, his mind would stray to Petrov. For over two decades, they'd fought side by side as brothers and best friends, and in the last few years, their relationship had grown even stronger. Sloan couldn't bear to relive the pain, although it preoccupied his every waking thought and haunted his dreams. Instead, he pushed the loss aside and concentrated on the rage. The rage would get him through, because it always did.

The moment they'd moored the yacht in the inlet, he jumped the bow and separated from Peaches without a word, taking the lead in navigating the maze of architectural debris. An hour later, when the city perimeter fence appeared, Sloan's determination grew.

Panting, Peaches caught up to him as the guards cranked open the high, steel-mesh gate. "Where are you running to?"

"If you need me, I'll be at the cathedral."

"Hey, Sloan, wait!" Peaches rushed to follow him past the gatehouse. "Aren't you gonna see your kids?"

"Maybe."

"But I've got a truck parked here. I can give you a lift." Peaches's pace slackened to a halt as the Irishman hiked for the old highway, completely ignoring the offer. She rushed to the truck parked behind the gatehouse, and moments later, the truck flew sideways onto the cracked highway. It started to rain, an initial hard spattering that quickly turned into a monsoon. The window wipers swished as she surveyed the roadsides for any sign of the Irishman. She could hardly see through the partially fogged windshield and kept smudging it with her sleeve. But there wasn't a soul around. So, she drove to the ancient naval base to give Warrick an update and then drove to the Red Geisha.

"I'm warning you. His behaviour isn't normal." Sitting on the desktop, legs swinging, Peaches lit a cigarette and dumped the match in the crystal bowl.

Mr. Shiro wandered over to the picture window, trailing smoke. He brought the cigarette to his lips and gazed out the pane at the decaying District E. "Where is he now?"

"The cathedral."

"Thank you for bringing my brother home. I'll take it from here."

"Sure thing." Peaches snuffed her cigarette and hopped off the desk. "Seriously, he's in rough emotional shape."

Vincent glanced at the redhead as she exited his office area into the lobby and the elevator doors slid shut. Then he turned back to watch the rain hit the window. Haru quietly awaited his orders near the double dragon doors.

"Let the other Independents know where my brother's hiding," he said without looking away from the window. "Perhaps they can talk some sense into him."

***

Stoner shone his flashlight over the pews, slicing the dank, dripping, pitch-black cathedral interior into strips of hazy illumination. At the far end, beyond the main altar, wood creaked. Lightning struck outside, flooding the nave with brilliance for a split second. Thunder followed, and lightning struck again.

Yasmine clung like a monkey to Stoner's back as they cautiously explored the cathedral interior. They knew Sloan was somewhere inside. They sensed his presence, but they just couldn't pinpoint his location.

She nodded, and they entered a tower with a dark spiral staircase. They ascended into the black. At the top, they found an archway with the door propped open. The mezzanine floor had a gaping hole, and there was a row of grimy windows to their right. In the middle, they could just make out a shape under the sills.

"You were right," Sloan whispered hoarsely.

Startled, Stoner peered into the uneven shadows and the traces of a bulky silhouette appeared near the windows. "I was right?" he said, momentarily disconcerted.

"We were standing metres apart, and it… chose him. He never had a chance." Sloan grabbed his own head and curled forward, rocking. "Mikhael's dead."

Stoner ignited his emergency military torch; the Irishman was crouched under two windows, crying like a baby, with rainwater dripping onto his back. This entire section of the building was a massive sieve, rotting from the foundation up. He glanced back at Yasmine and shook his head slightly. She immediately retreated in silence toward the staircase. "I'm very sorry." He paused and crouched closer. "Whatever killed Petrov is going to get all of us eventually. I'm not scared of dying—I'll lay down my life. But I am scared of what will happen to this city after we're gone."

"Since when have you ever given a shite about anyone other than yourself?" Sloan glared at him. "*Huh*?"

"Since I met you!" Stoner glared disgustedly back at him. "Don't you get it, Irishman? Outrageous as it sounds, this unit has become an unconventional family thanks to you. We may not always agree, but we are *together*, a group of people linked to one another through unconventional circumstance."

Sloan hid from his piercing gaze by shifting to face the damp wall. "Right."

"Right, *nothing*. You were the father Petrov never had, *and* you were his mentor and comrade in arms. He literally worshipped you *and* the ground you walked on." Stoner grimaced, rose, and walked away. "What kind of a man watches his best friend die and does nothing?"

Sloan moved even faster than Stoner had predicted, driving him through the mezzanine handrail, startling Yasmine, to sail high above the apse and then fall multiple storeys, crashing through the flooring. And at the bottom, a sub-basement of cement, stone and debris, Sloan seized him by his throat. His dark orange eyes were on fire. "Don't you dare!" he growled. "Don't you fecking lecture me!"

"Then wake up! We can't do this alone," Stoner yelled in his face, grasping his dense wrists. "Do it for Petrov for all I care but just *help us* find the male vampire!"

After a lengthy stretch, Sloan's scowl finally softened, as did his grip, and he gradually let him go and stood. Without looking, he held out his hand. "Come on."

Stoner slapped his hand into Sloan's and Sloan hoisted him to his feet.

"I'm sorry." Sloan grabbed his head and gave him a hug. "Let's do this."

***

EIGHT MONTHS LATER

"I take it you had no luck hunting down the male vampire or his harem," said Doctor Avolare.

"None. Eight months and not a fecking footprint," Sloan bitched. "It's like the damn things vanish when it suits them, and we're left standing around with our fecking thumbs up our arses."

"It's been quiet here too, ever since…" She set a plate of sandwiches on the small circular aluminum table. And the black rabbit hopped through the velvety grass not far from the rear cottage patio.

"It's okay, doc. You can say his name."

"I don't want to upset you."

"My heart's about as damaged as it can get. Saying 'Petrov' is fine."

The heat was just bearable. The sun peeked in a fluttering sparkle through the leaves, and tufts of cottonseeds floated in the air. The backyard contained a small, dry-stone walled orchard that was a hotbed of activity. Bees zipped from one flowering bush and berry blossom to the next, and the birds were singing. A deep green carpet of grass spread throughout the yard, and maturing fruit hung heavy in the trees.

"You've been busy, doc. The orchard looks incredible."

"Doesn't it?" Raphael sat across from him, admiring the literal fruits of her labour. "I pruned everything back in the spring and now look. I've got apples, pears, cherries, and plums. And even the one peach tree is laden." She pointed to a knobby, stunted tree at the corner of the orchard. "The men from the village brought the sheep to help keep the grass down. Did you know fruit tree wood is great for building furniture? Centuries ago, fine handcrafted items like Cherrywood armoires fetched big money. And I've started a small herb garden in a greenhouse at the side of the cottage."

Sloan clasped his hands behind his head. "I think the country bumpkin life suits you."

"Well," she blushed, "I still dabble in genetics. I converted the second bedroom into a mini lab."

He chuckled. "You couldn't resist, eh?"

"No, I couldn't. Krista loves the fruit, but I love what I do best."

"How is the pipsqueak? I didn't notice her anywhere."

"She's just fine, no need to worry. It's too hot right now, so she's in the cellar, trying to keep cool."

"Do you mind if I stay the night?" Sloan squinted as the sun warmed his face. "It's so peaceful here I don't feel like leaving... and I thought we could talk more."

"Of course. You're welcome to stay forever if you like."

Dumbfounded, Sloan stared at her. If that wasn't an open invitation, he didn't know what was. Before she'd turned him down on so many occasions, he wondered if he'd heard her correctly.

Sipping at a glass of chilled apple cider, she continued to gaze at the orchard. "I know it's presumptuous of me, and you can tell me to go to hell... But I've never been with a man, and just once I'd like to experience the throes of passion." She went bright red, shyly turning away from him. "So, you're welcome to stay the night, Sloan. But if you do, I want you to spend it in my bed."

Her unabashed attitude was nice for a change—and it was a major turn-on. He grinned. "You seem pretty certain that I'll agree."

Shoulders bunched up around her neck, she purposely avoided visual contact. "That *was* pushy. I'm sorry. Forget what I said."

"Never." He gazed at her with mounting desire and said in an affectionate rumble, "Don't worry, doll, I'll give you throes of passion. It'll be so fecking good, you'll be begging for it the second time round."

FOURTEEN

MUTUAL COMFORT

He disrobed and Raphael bit the inside of her lower lip, clutching the sheet to her chest. It felt as if she were unwrapping a gift—a rare, valuable and highly sought after gem—something she believed she was unworthy to receive. And what made the situation even more nerve-wracking was the fact he didn't embarrass easily; he was confident in his own skin, unhampered by emotions, unlike her. And he disliked pretence with a passion—any false display of feelings, attitudes or intentions. What you saw was what you got, and she couldn't wait to get him. He simply dropped his clothes on the chair and walked toward the bed, sending tremors through the floor. He was huge, and for a split second, she wondered if she'd made a mistake. Her skin burned from her cheeks up to her ears.

Sloan sat beside her, leaned in, and tenderly kissed her lips. She eased away and searched his expression. His eyes sparkled a lusty, dark orange in the gloomy light, and she couldn't resist. She touched his smooth face with the back of her fingers. He was such an attractive man, and her heart wouldn't stop pounding. "Is it okay if I have feelings for you?" She dropped her gaze, cinching the sheet tighter to her chest.

"Sure. It isn't like I don't care about you." He grinned, nuzzling her flushed cheek with another soft kiss. "We can do whatever you want, doll."

She wanted to tell him she loved him, but she knew he was in no condition to accept such powerful feelings. They were strictly there to comfort one another. She abruptly let go of the sheet, grabbed his head, and kissed him.

He drew her into a strong embrace and passionately caressed her lips. Then he whispered, scorching hot in her ear, "Tell me how much you want me."

She shivered; her cheeks were burning again, and her groin ached with wetness. *This man is an animal.* But she lay back on the bed and got comfortable, searching his bedroom gaze. "I want you so badly it hurts," she murmured coyly.

The foreplay was long and drawn out, and he brought her to climax several times. But as for the actual intercourse, she was ill prepared. He was gentle when need be but also rough, and he drove her crazy. By the end, perspiration dappled her flesh. Her throat was sore, and her groin was throbbing, as she studied his moonlight tinted features. She was a content mess.

Sloan searched her half-lidded gaze, smoothing her cheeks, and then he got close and warmed her lips with another kiss. "How are you feeling, doll?"

"Pleasantly tired."

"That's a good thing," he said with a touch of breathlessness. He shifted to lie next to her.

"Can I tell you a secret?"

He turned his head, and they looked at one another. "Sure."

She blinked, and a tear ran over the side of her face. "I wanted you from the start. That's why I picked you," she confessed with ardent longing in her watery eyes. "But I felt so ashamed. I'd put my lust before a rational scientific choice."

"It's okay. You're human, doc." He kissed her forehead. "I'll be right back. I need a drink." The moment he got out of the bed, she fell fast asleep. He chuckled, pulling up and zipping his jeans. Then he covered her with the sheet and quilt.

Padding barefoot through the hallway to the bathroom, Sloan winced, grabbing his shoulder as he peered in the bathroom mirror. Scratches covered his entire back, but the bloody grooves were healing. He splashed water over his face, then patted his face and throat dry. But as he hung the towel and exited the bathroom, he nearly stepped on Krista. She was staring at him. It was a tad unsettling to have her beady red eyes sizing him up.

"Hey, little one." He went to touch her head, but she lashed out, hissing. "Right. We aren't friends yet." He wandered past her to the kitchen, and she glided behind like a creepy apparition. "Sorry. The doctor can't spend time with you tonight because she's sleeping. She's a bit worn out." He opened the fridge, removed a pottery jug, and poured a large glass of chilled water. As he did, he thought about all the odd jobs Raphael had asked him to help with: cleaning and checking the solar panels, the septic and well, and moving stones for a new retaining wall.

Sloan looked down at Krista, who was suddenly hugging his leg for dear life—a total one-eighty from her actions in the hallway not a minute earlier. Genuinely surprised, he set the glass and jug on the counter. "What's wrong?" There was a weighty thud somewhere outside that rattled the stemware in the ancient China cabinet. "What the feck was that?"

Krista released his leg and hid behind the refrigerator door. Sloan strode into the living room, slid the Irish longsword from the scabbard, and silently crept outside onto the back patio, leaving the door open. Now he understood Krista's agitated behaviour. She'd sensed something before he did.

Once his pupils adjusted, he scrutinized every inch of the moon lit darkness. Silvery-blue light outlined the orchard, stone wall, every wildflower and blade of grass, and the forested backdrop kilometres beyond the acreage. The navy sky twinkled, a pincushion of stars and beautiful celestial bodies.

"Stay inside," he warned softly, and the tiny vampire shut the sliding door. *Huh. She does understand.* Slinking along the wall, he peered around the exterior corner of the cottage, but the greenhouse partially obstructed his view. He moved swiftly, circumnavigating the steel and glass structure.

Silence was key. Keeping alert and controlling his breathing at the same time was the difficult part.

After conducting an exhaustive search of the property and even backtracking into the wilds and glade, Sloan didn't find an intruder—if there'd ever actually been one. However, he did discover an area of flattened grass under a huge eastern white pine, as if someone had been standing in the same spot for a long period. And he couldn't shake the feeling that someone had been watching him at one point. *I wonder if the females are back.* He paused to contemplate, then scanned the surrounding area again. *No, this is different.* His intuition was tingling.

He returned via the back door and slipped inside the cottage. Krista was hiding under the kitchen table and when she saw him, she scrambled across the tiles and hugged his leg. "I bet this isn't the first time something like this has happened, is it? And I bet Doctor Avolare doesn't have a clue."

She just looked up at him, hugging tighter.

"I really wish you could talk, little one." He sighed and patted her head. He suspected Krista patrolled the house at night, wary of the slightest disturbance outside. *Aside from the sunlight, no wonder she sleeps all day.* "Well, don't worry. You can bunk with me and Raphael tonight."

She nodded, releasing his leg. He chuckled. Strange as she was, the tiny vampire was growing on him. *I must be getting soft in my old age.*

Sloan sheathed his sword, checked every window, made sure all the doors were double-locked and shut the curtains. Then padded barefoot to the rear bedroom with his tiny companion in tow. He sat, making the mattress droop and the bed frame rasp. He settled on top of the quilt and set his sword on the floor under the bed. Krista climbed into a fancy wooden box in front of the closet door, cuddling a beige, two-tone teddy bear that was as big as her.

Sloan stayed the weekend to help get the cottage and grounds in proper running order. He repaired the roof, switched out a damaged solar panel for a new one, and built the retaining wall. At night, he played the devoted lover. Peculiar as the situation may have seemed to anyone else, he didn't mind. After many, many years of loneliness, the warmth of another human being felt nice and nourished his own broken emotions.

As for the incident, if he insisted they return to the village, she'd start asking questions he didn't want to answer. She lived alone, and it would only scare her. But he also knew he couldn't keep such information from her for too long. What if the prowler came back?

"Here's your lunch." Raphael set a plate beside him on the circular steel patio table, then she brought out a bottle of vintage cognac with two glasses.

"What's this?" He skimmed the label.

"I can't thank you enough for everything you've done." She blushed slightly, opening the bottle of fine French wine. "You're an amazing man, Sloan."

"Keep talking like that, and I'll have my way with you again, doll."

"That too…" She cleared her throat, glancing shyly at him and poured him a glass. "The sex has been wonderful. I can't thank you enough."

He confiscated the bottle and glass from her and set both on the table. Then he grabbed her wrist and dragged her close. She clumsily skirted the table and fell into his lap. "Don't cry." He smoothed her damp cheek, and she rested her head on his shoulder. "There's no need to thank me. We comforted one another, and I enjoyed you immensely."

"I know I shouldn't say this but… I'm going to miss you terribly." She looked into his eyes. "I'm sorry, Sloan."

"Don't apologize. I said it the other night. You're human." He held her head and tenderly kissed her lips. "How about you return with me, both you and Krista? It isn't like I'm on a schedule." He thought about Peaches, who was waiting at the cottage, but figured a tiny white lie wouldn't hurt. "We can spend a few days together in the village. You can stay at my cottage. I can help you with your shopping— whatever you need."

"I suppose a change of scenery wouldn't hurt. And I do need butter and whatnot…"

"Get ready."

She packed a change of clothes and stuffed the book she was reading, along with a few toiletries, inside a small knapsack. Leaving the country cottage for a day or two wasn't a problem. She had taken care of feeding and watering the animals; they'd survive until she returned.

Sloan had stridden ahead of her, mowing a path through the tall flaxen grass, and Krista was beside him. Raphael had noticed a drastic change in the tiny vampire's behaviour since he'd come to stay. Krista was considerably more tolerant and certainly more trusting than usual. But Sloan was depressed. Although he acted normal, she knew it was just a charade. His eyes gave him away: they'd lost that beautiful copper spark.

Raphael held the top of her hat against the hot wind, shearing her clammy cheeks. "I know it's difficult, but you've got to let the pain go, Sloan."

He glanced in her direction, continuing to plod the dry grass. "What are you talking about, doc?"

"Everything you're holding inside... all that sorrow. You've closed off your heart. They wouldn't want you to give up on life."

"Life is a prison sentence, and I'm just biding my time." He squinted and smiled at Krista, who was holding his hand and an umbrella. "Love doesn't suit me."

His comment filled her with profound sadness. After Petrov died, he had emotionally shut down. He wouldn't express his feelings, and no one could get in. She feared for him and his future, what lay ahead, because if he didn't learn to accept the past, it could very well lead to his downfall, even death. "Part of being a symbiotic organism, is learning to share, even the most harrowing of circumstances. Your parasite can't do it all alone… and if you continue to shut her out, it will have an adverse effect on you in the end."

He looked at her with lifeless eyes. "Everyone has to die one day, doll."

Now she knew for certain he was on a self-destructive course. He wanted to die, and it broke her heart, filling her with an anxious panic she didn't know how to combat. She suddenly felt like the man she thought she'd known wasn't that man at all. Raphael sniffed, fighting back the urge to cry, and she didn't say another word.

Doctor Avolare and Krista remained at the Whelan family cottage for three days, then Sloan escorted them home. Raphael's shopping and visiting was done, and she was antsy to return to her routine. Sloan, still concerned, made sure to check up on her every other day, and more often if he could manage it.

FIFTEEN

SURVEILLANCE

"I watched the cottage every night for a week just like you asked, big man. Either the creature knew I was there, or there wasn't anyone to begin with." Peaches kept her hands inside the front hip pockets of her baggy jeans—navy-blue and stonewashed soft to the eyes. "Now I'm not saying what happened wasn't real. But maybe you scared off whatever it was."

"I hate that she's all the way out there on her own."

"Then tell her. Be honest. Force her to see things your way. But, setting the prowler issue aside, there's something you oughta see." Peaches walked and gestured to a thicket at the far side of the meadow, near the fenced property line and road where Doctor Avolare lived. "At the end of my observation stint last night, I decided to take a thorough look around."

"What did you find?" Sloan strolled beside her.

"I'm not sure, really. But it's definitely odd."

The thicket was a combination of robust, leafy trees and clusters of prickly bushes disconnected from the forest by a meandering creek. Dormant skunk cabbage and jewelweed, the showy orange flowers plump and in full bloom, dotted the dark, mucky ground.

"It's on the other side of the creek."

They heard the gentle trickle of water and bees buzzing, and they saw a cyclone of teeny-tiny flies whirling in the sunlight.

Sloan was careful not to crush the flowers as he followed Leona's path in the mud. But after only a few steps toward the forest edge, he wrinkled his nose; the smell of decomposition was overpowering. "Feck, not again." He waved his hand in front of his face.

"I know it's bad. When we fought those MVs, they stank like this but way more putrid. If the MVs are dead, whose blood is this?"

Dark spatter marked the leaves and bark. Sloan dabbed his index and middle fingers in a big, dripping patch of the blackish-red oily substance. He rubbed his thumb and fingers together; the consistency was slimy thick. He brought it to his nose, sniffed, and gagged. There was a smell of death like the MVs, but also something else: a pungent, sickly-sweet floral scent. "It's blood from the female."

"The one you fought?"

"Yep." Sloan wiped his fingers clean on the soggy grass.

"Okay. What does this mean then?"

"It means she was here, and somehow she got injured." He paused. "But that doesn't make sense."

"I thought *you* found it difficult to fight her."

"I did. She was blindingly fast and powerful. Not the type of female you'd want to bring home to mama." Sloan chuckled, shaking with mirth.

Peaches stared blankly at him and pointed to her own face. "Did you notice? I'm not laughing."

Sloan rolled his eyes, giving his head a disenchanted shake. Wandering into the shade, he snooped around the vicinity. A dense, broken branch lay there; several small trees had been knocked down, and claw marks scored the dirt. He was certain one or more of the female vampires, MV's parents, had got into a fight. Whether they had survived was speculation. But what bothered him was the location. And who had the females been up against? "She can't stay here."

"I figured you'd say that." Peaches lit a cigarette.

"Whatever the feck went on here poses a threat."

"Like I said, don't give her an option. Make her move."

"I'll meet you in the village shortly." Sloan headed to the creek. "Get Benny and his men together. Thanks."

"No worries, big man."

Determined, Sloan was out of the creek and across the meadow in minutes. He jogged the short flight of rickety steps and entered the cottage, letting both doors slam behind him. He brushed his boots off on the matt. Krista was in the ancient rocking chair with her teddy bear. Sloan touched the top of her head, and this time, the tiny vampire didn't hiss.

"I thought you'd left already." Raphael nervously smiled, entering the living room.

"I changed my mind. We need to talk, doll." Sloan sat on the sofa and patted the spot beside him.

"Is something wrong, Sloan?"

"You could say that." He grasped her hand and held it securely. "The last time I stayed here, something or someone was outside the cottage. I spent a good hour that night searching the property. But I didn't find anything other than a pair of indents, similar to large footprints, in the grass under a tree."

Raphael looked at Krista as if for affirmation, and the little vampire nodded in agreement.

"See? Even she knows, and I suspect she's known all along," he continued. "Krista alerted me to the danger before I left the cottage to check. And, gathering by her behaviour, this wasn't the first incident of this nature."

"But I enjoy living here, Sloan."

"I know you do. However, your safety is paramount."

"What about my animals?"

"My family cottage and property aren't nearly as big. But the backyard is fenced with a small greenhouse, and there's a pigsty and a chicken coop. I can certainly fix them for your livestock. I'll even build a hutch for the bunny. It's that or I will return you to the mainland."

Her eyes widened. "No, never. I don't mind helping Wade occasionally, but I refuse to live in the city again. The island's my home and I love it here."

"All right, then. What's it going to be, doc?"

She sighed and whinged, "Oh, Sloan, do I have to go?"

"Yes, and I won't take no for an answer. There's safety in numbers, and you'd be living in the village."

She nodded, although he knew it was an unwilling compliance on her part.

"Good." He leaned sideways and kissed her temple. "I'll try to be back before dark. That gives you the rest of the afternoon to pack. And don't worry. If we can't move it all tonight, I'll borrow a horse and cart from someone in the village and finish up tomorrow." He patted her knee and rose from the sofa, leaving a noticeable depression in the cushion. "It's more important we get you out of here first."

"Will I make dinner for us?"

"That sounds great, doll." He grinned handsomely and shut the front door.

"Well." Raphael gripped her knees, looking at the tiny vampire. "I guess we have no choice, Krista."

On the main road, Sloan met with Peaches, Benny and the other men who assisted in patrolling the island. Their numbers were substantial. Following a brief discussion, they began traversing the forest, progressively moving away from the village. The men walked in two long lines, four metres apart. Keeping their conversation to a minimum, they carefully searched until dusk, and that was when Sloan called it quits. The men were tired and hungry, and since they'd found nothing, he sent them all home.

"Well, that's everything." Raphael placed her hands on her hips; she'd just finished packing her knapsack. "It isn't much, but then again, we won't need much where we're going."

Krista nodded, holding up her satchel.

"Okay. Sloan will be here soon, and I have to make dinner. I'd better take a bath now."

Krista watched Raphael vanish in the hallway, and just as the bathroom door clicked shut, the tiny vampire turned sharply to the right and stared at the fireplace set in the southern interior wall. Something bumped the same wall, and everything in the entire house clanked and vibrated. She hissed, her eyes following the sound as it was slowly scraping the exterior siding lengthwise.

Clutching her satchel to her chest, she edged cautiously toward the screen door. The interior one was wide open, but the screen door was closed with the latch locked. With all the excitement, Raphael had forgotten to secure the door. She got close to the screen and peered through the mesh. A dusky ginger brushed the sky, and all was silent. But she knew something was there, a creature that wasn't supposed to be there. She quickly dropped the satchel, slammed the interior door, and strained to reach the deadbolt.

"What's wrong, Krista?" Raphael buttoned her blouse. "Did I forget to shut the door?"

The tiny vampire promptly turned around and leaned her weight against the door. She wanted to tell the genetic engineer what was wrong. But she was incapable of speech. She sniffed at the air around the front window.

Sloan said goodbye to the other men. "I'll meet you at the cottage later."

"Uh-huh. How's the sex?" Peaches lit her cigarette, giving him a cool, all-knowing once-over.

"What are we, kids?" Sloan chuckled, eyeing the redhead with dismay. "You think I'm going to tell you whether or not we had sex?"

"You don't have to. She was moaning so loud the women in the village were blushing." Peaches grinned, flicking ash into the wind.

"What are you, a fecking inspector?"

"Oh, come on. I'm only joking."

"Okay. Yeah, we had sex. But she asked." Sloan smirked, motioning to himself before walking away. "You're just jealous because she had all this."

"I don't think so, big man. See you later." Peaches laughed, shaking her head as he opened the garden gate.

Thud.

The entire house quaked.

Krista snarled, staring at the ceiling.

"No, Krista!" Raphael called out, but the little vampire was gone like a bullet, leaving the interior door open and the screen door banging shut behind her. A deafening silence filled the cottage. Fearfully, Raphael edged through the gloom toward the front door. "No," she gasped. To her consternation and distress, the tiny vampire had taken it upon herself to protect her and the cottage. "Come back!"

High-pitched screeches and low growls filled the air; then, something slammed into an outer wall of the cottage. Raphael flinched. Her breathing extremely elevated as she cautiously approached the doors. The only vampiric battle she'd ever witnessed was when Sloan had confronted his co-workers in Chartreuse outside the library. The savagery had been a frightening eye-opener, but at least the Independents had been somewhat evenly matched. However, now, she sensed something far worse was happening beyond her line of sight.

Sneaking closer, she peered through the screen door. A gigantic revolting vampire, the likes of which Raphael couldn't have imagined in her wildest nightmare, tore Krista apart. The tiny vampire screeched.

Raphael held her mouth tight to keep herself from screaming and tremulously backed through the front entrance. She shut the screen and the interior doors and anxiously fiddled with all the latches and deadbolt. Suddenly, there was scuttling on the porch, followed by a loud bang, and the doors shuddered along with the front of the cottage.

Terrified, Raphael tripped backward, shifting the rocking chair. There was another shuddering bang, and she jumped. Another, and the wood split. She wedged herself back between the fridge and the large dining room slider at the rear of the cottage. The doors caved, and the creature snarled, biting ravenously, shoving its arm, then head through the gaping splinters. The wraithlike, grotesque vampire frenziedly rammed the barrier over and over, and finally broke free, wriggling inside the cottage. Raphael shrieked, throwing whatever was nearest to her grasp.

Sloan paused at the gated entrance to the property. Burgeoning moonlight partially enveloped the cottage on the far side of the sloping meadow. He knew immediately something was wrong, and he bolted.

As he approached the cottage, he slowed to a walk. A hundred yards from the front porch, a small body was lying in the grass. "Shite, little one…" Krista's head was missing, and his heart fluttered with dread. He stepped around the body and tore for the porch, ascending the front steps to find a gaping hole of ragged, fragmented wood and the doors pressed inward like flower petals.

"Doc…" The floorboards were sticky underfoot, as he moved further inside the house; the pungency of blood made him gag, and he feared the worst, enough not to turn on the lights. But with moonlight pouring in from the kitchen windows, it didn't matter. "Doc," he whispered in desperation for a second time. "*Doc!*"

From somewhere within the brittle shards of darkness, Raphael murmured, "Get the children… get everyone off the island."

He zeroed in on her uncharacteristically weak voice as she appeared in the hallway. With her shoulder drooped, sliding laterally against the interior wall, she shuffled. The wall divided the hallway from the living room. "Not until you tell me what's happened." He gently took hold of her upper arms as she fell into his chest. "Are you okay?" He gave her a subtle shake. "What happened?"

She touched his brow ridge, cheekbones and nose, her hands trembling over his entire facial structure as if she were blind. He lifted her chin, angling her face toward the beams of silvery moonlight. The beautiful turquoise was gone— even the whites of her eyes were black, and her lids secreted teary blood. Her lips were split and chalky. Stunned, he gently held her face and smeared the fluid from her high cheekbones with his thumbs. "*Please* tell me. Who hurt you, doll?" Then he felt something damp near her hip; she'd been torn open.

"Krista tried to save me… She was such a brave girl." She dug into his shirt with the stranglehold of a petrified cat. "A monster with eyes of mustard-yellow." Her lips quivered against his. "The monster did this. I should've left with you… like you wanted…"

Sloan wrapped her in a strong embrace and tried to think of a way to save her. "You're not making sense, doll. What monster? Mustard eyes? Do you mean it was a vampire with yellow eyes?"

"Yes." She gulped. "I'm scared for you," she mumbled feverishly. "I failed you. My arrogance failed you. I don't know if you're powerful enough… Beware of his speed.

227

Strong… so strong." She gently pawed at his mouth. "He was something I've never seen… advanced… a different gene…"

"The genetics are new. Is that what you're trying to tell me?" She slackened in his arms. "Hey." He brushed some hair away from her face, cradling her skull. "Don't die on me—not now. I still need you." A ridge of hot moisture distorted his vision, but he held in the sorrow, shifted her weight, and picked her up as if he were about to carry her across the threshold into their matrimonial boudoir; her free arm swung. He backed carefully through the gaping hole onto the front porch, and the wooden steps creaked.

When Sloan stopped walking, he was a considerable distance from the cottage, waist-deep in grass. He hesitated, then looked back. The tall, dry grass swished in the evening breeze. This time, he was certain that something was watching from the surrounding darkness. He could feel its presence—an overwhelming hostility—enraged and chaotic. Regardless, whatever it was, he knew it wanted the genetic engineer. He kissed Raphael's head. "It's okay, doll. I won't let him get to you." He didn't know why, but his instinct seemed to drive him, and he felt a primal urge to set a boundary line. Predators were territorial, and he had to mark his. By showing affection for the doctor, he would send a clear warning: he wasn't intimidated, and the doctor belonged to him.

SIXTEEN

BEREAVEMENT

Carrying both bodies, Sloan trod greensward, and then moss-traced cobblestones through the sleeping village. The whole time, he'd sensed it was there—Raphael's monster—observing from the edge of the surrounding woods. But there weren't mustard eyes or even a whiff of decomposition. Just the same, he knew it was present, and he knew it definitely wasn't one of the females. The previous day, something had happened in the meadow, and he was beginning to think the male was also on the island. But why would the male attack his mates? And why hadn't anyone else been attacked? Was Raphael's death purely coincidence because she lived outside the village boundary, or was it calculated? But she'd definitely called the monster a male.

By the time he had reached his family cottage, the weight of Sloan's anger had quashed his grief. He was teetering on the edge, his thought pattern manic. And he wondered how much longer he could feign normalcy, especially in light of what was happening to his friends. He was slowly becoming unhinged.

He gave the cobalt-blue door to the cottage a kick with his boot, and Peaches answered. Her smile instantaneously drained to horrified shock at the sight of the deceased doctor and tiny vampire in Sloan's arms.

She shut and locked the door only to gawk in lingering disbelief, as Sloan gently laid the bodies on the sofa. "What the hell?" she whispered. "Are they really—"

"Yeah." He stood away from the sofa, slightly winded and his brow damp. "We're leaving for the mainland now."

"What happ—"

"*Now*, Leona. If the village gets wind of this, we'll have a full-scale panic on our hands. We need reinforcements."

"They're bound to find out soon enough. And, besides that, they need to be warned." She shakily lit a cigarette. "You've got to calm down and really think this through rationally."

He slumped in the armchair. Covering either side of his nose, he leaned forward and stared at the cold fireplace. Without warning, his eyes swelled to overflow. He gripped the top of his head and wept, ragged sobs that filled the room with despair. Tears slid down to fall off the tip of his nose.

She sat in the armchair opposite, her glassy eyes focused on her smouldering cigarette and croaked, "I'm so sorry, for your loss."

Sloan woke with a crimped neck and dry mouth. He groaned, massaging his nape as he tried to swallow. The last thing he remembered was Peaches saying something, and then he'd crashed. But when he saw the two bodies on the sofa, wrapped tightly in blankets, the previous twenty-four hours came rushing back. And he was just as upset and confused as he'd been before.

"Peaches...?" He rose from the armchair, looking at the kitchen. However, the cottage was vacant, its front door unlocked, and his friend's shoes missing. He wondered if he should search when he heard voices in the front garden. Hooking the curtain, he stooped to peek out the window. Peaches was talking to Benny and Rueben, their voices muffled but still audible.

"I can't believe this." Rueben was pacing the small garden.

Benny eyed his brother with annoyance. "You need to calm down."

"Calm down?" Rueben turned to him. "If this thing kills anyone else, we'll have to evacuate the island. That's over twelve hundred people who have never had contact with the outside world, Ben! That type of contact could kill them! Either way, the people—even our own families—are at risk."

"I know. I'm not a complete idiot," Benny grumbled matter-of-factly.

"Then what do we do?"

Peaches opened her cigarette tin. "Relax. We all know the consequences. But right now, it's Sloan I'm worried about. He's lost his wife, son, co-worker, best friend and now his mentor." She paused to light her cigarette, and her hard, stony gaze landed on Rueben. "He's riding the edge. I saw it last night."

"That's why you stayed." Benny tapped his rifle muzzle against his shoulder.

Sloan let the curtain fall back into place, but continued to eavesdrop.

"He wasn't thinking straight, and he was extremely distraught," Peaches said. "He was wound up tighter than a top, so when he passed out, I let him sleep."

"We can't fight this thing alone. If we lose him now, we're done," Rueben said in a worried tone.

The men and Peaches stopped talking, and their footfalls approached the cottage. Sloan darted away from the curtain to return to the armchair. He gripped the armrests as the door opened, forcing himself to relax. *Come on, get it together. Get it together!*

"Oh, hey, big man. You're awake." Peaches flashed a good-natured smile, removing her shoes.

Sloan stared at his three unwelcome guests. *How can you act so nonchalant? Relax.* "Yeah, I just woke up."

Peaches leaned on the other armchair. "Listen, Sloan, I know you didn't want to, but I spoke to the village council this morning. They're worried, but they understand, and they'll take measures to fortify the two communities."

"Great."

Rueben glanced at the bodies wrapped on the sofa. "We're very sorry about Raphael and Krista."

"Sure." Sloan stared at him next.

Benny set his rifle on the kitchen table and stood behind the sofa, hands inside his jacket pockets. He sighed. "We know you're hurting."

Sloan clenched his jaw, digging his fingers in, gripping the armrests tighter.

"For crumb's sake, Benny," Rueben scolded, glaring daggers at his younger brother.

"You don't think he heard us talking just now?" Benny smirked in a pithy way, looking Sloan in the eyes. "The curtain moved. You were listening in the whole time, and that's why you're miffed—aside from the fact you've lost your friend and lover."

"She wasn't my lover," Sloan barked. "And what the feck do you know? What the hell do any of you know about me? Ungrateful fecking bunch of kids! I never should've saved you—I should have let you all die!"

Peaches gawped in pallid disbelief, as did Rueben. But Benny seemed to take it all in stride. He sighed once again, but a touch louder.

"Wow, you really are a rude and cruel old coot. Life doesn't go your way, and you really let loose, huh?" Benny glowered, bending down toward him. "You think you're the only one to suffer a loss? You think it's your privilege alone? My daughter would've died of pneumonia last winter if it weren't for Raphael. Tristan was my brother's best friend. Petrov ate dinner with our families and protected us in your stead." Suddenly, he bellowed: "So if you think we're

233

immune to the pain and loss, you're more of a selfish asshole than I thought!"

Sloan sprang to his feet with tears running down his face, and the armchair toppled backward. "*Leave!*" he croaked, slicing the air. "Get the feck out of my house!"

"Or what? You're going to kill me?" Benny stood his ground like an iron post in front of him, then, surprising everyone, he slapped his own chest. "Well, then, do it. Come on, old man, do it!"

"Just get out, stupid mouthy eejit!" Sloan put his arm up and he slowly got down in the corner like a frightened child, pressing his face to the bookshelves. "Leave me alone."

"Hey, that's enough," Peaches demanded softly.

Benny reached behind and signalled with his hand, keeping them away. He crouched, setting his knee on the floor, and he hugged Sloan's head to his chest, listening to him bawl. "Hear me out," he said. "You're a good man and none of this is your fault." He paused and glanced back at Peaches and Rueben. "Give us some privacy, okay?"

"Sure thing." Peaches grabbed Rueben by the scruff of his neck and pushed him out the front door.

Once the house was quiet, Benny felt like he could finally speak his mind. He held the Irishman snugly and angled himself until he could see Sloan's puffy, bloodshot eyes and despondent features. "Will you listen to me?"

Sloan eased away from him and sat with his back against the shelves, wiping his nose. "What choice do I have?"

Benny sat beside him. "I can't imagine what you've experienced in your life… the constant violence and upheaval, and I won't pretend to understand. But I do know you're a better man for it. You genuinely care. If you didn't, you wouldn't have helped us. You wouldn't have protected your unit or this island. And whether or not you believe me, I am grateful that you saved my life, even though I didn't deserve it at the time."

"You definitely put me through my paces." Sloan sniffed, mopping his cheeks.

"I'm sorry about that."

Sloan exhaled a shaky sigh. "It's okay. Here I was, this know-it-all stranger, telling you and the others what to do. Of course, you'd be suspicious."

"Whatever. You're not a stranger anymore. You're my friend, and as much as it pains me to say this…" Benny looked away with reddening cheeks. "You're also like my adoptive father. I admire you, but I'm also jealous."

Sloan sniffed and stared awestruck at the man for a moment. Then he pitched sideways, cupping his ear, wearing a rascally grin. "Pardon? I'm sorry, but I didn't hear you."

Benny grimaced, elbowing him. "Asshole. You heard."

Sloan smiled faintly, falling back against the shelves. "You're a little envious, huh?"

"What guy wouldn't be? I know you don't see it, but you've got everything I wish I had."

"You mean my devilish good looks and witty charm?"

"Seriously. I'm going to puke." Benny couldn't help it, and he exhaled a disheartened laugh. "Yeah, yeah, that too."

"Ah. You mean the power and immortality." Sloan looked at him with affection. "It is cool, but sometimes I loathe it."

"Well, if you ever want to pass it on, let me know." Benny grasped his shoulder. "Truth is, I know you're better than these other vampires, and I know you can do whatever you set your mind to. And I understand it's difficult and painful but, for your sake and ours, please try not to let what's happened get you down. I'll do whatever I can to help."

They stood and lifted the armchair back to its usual spot in the living room.

"I'm going to take the bodies to Wade's clinic," Sloan said. "The females didn't kill Doctor Avolare. It was a different vampire. She called it a monster, and she said she was scared that it was too strong even for me to defeat." He put a hand on Benny's shoulder. "I'll try to bring back reinforcements. But if I can't, we may have to evacuate the island."

Benny sighed in a dispirited manner, but he nodded. "Understood."

"If I could do it any other way—"

"I know, Sloan. And it's fine. Everyone will just have to accept the decision if it comes to that."

"Can you explain to Rueben and the village council? We have to get moving. The bodies are degrading as we speak."

"Consider it done." Benny glanced at him with his hand on the doorknob. "I meant what I said. I do care about you, Sloan."

Sloan felt his cheeks flush and said extra gruffly, "Okay. Would you get the feck out of here, already? Bloody nuisance."

Benny guffawed, opening the door, and Rueben and Peaches almost toppled onto him. Rueben blushed, taking a quick step back, while Peaches grinned like a fool.

"Do you know what the word 'privacy' means?" Benny frowned, staring aloofly at his elder brother.

"We weren't trying to listen in," Rueben said.

"Actually, we were," Peaches admitted.

"Get in here," Sloan snapped. "We're leaving."

"See ya later." Peaches squeezed past the brothers and slammed the door.

"We need to talk." Benny grabbed Rueben's jacket and dragged him through the front garden gate onto the street.

***

Wade put on a pair of magnifying glasses and spread the baby vampire's fragile digits on his palm under the lamplight. "She's got some defensive wounds on her forearms and upper chest. Which tells me she put up a fight before losing her head—no matter how short-lived." He used a scalpel and carefully scraped under her teeny sharp nails, wiping the dirt on a glass slide. "I'll run tests."

Sloan held Raphael's icy hand between both of his and tenderly kissed her knuckles, closing his eyes. Then he nuzzled her hand to his cheek. He couldn't stop the overwhelming flood of tears. The woman had been his guiding light and greatest confidante. Now he had no one to confide in, no one to tell him when he was wrong, and no one to raise his spirits. The loss was as great as that of Petrov. "I don't understand why she's dead."

"Her parasite was intelligent and granted her longevity, but it wasn't created to heal such aggressive wounds." Wade gently dabbed Krista's mouth, and the damp cloth turned a splotchy, dark red.

Sloan's voice trailed off with his thoughts. "She couldn't regenerate."

"She could, but not like you do, Mr. Freak of Nature. Her words: you're the exception to the rule." Wade rinsed and squeezed the cloth and wiped under each of Krista's beady eyes. "Raphael was just a normal human being. Her liver was diced, and she suffered from exsanguination. Her parasite tried. Unfortunately, it was incapable of healing the damaged tissue and inducing such extensive blood replication at the same time." He paused. "Her parasite fought her cancer and won, but that's because it had time."

"Many ancients died from cancer."

"That's why she injected herself in the first place."

"What kind of cancer?"

"Lung. She called it adenocarcinoma. The parasite was able to combat the disease because it was a less aggressive form."

"She got sick and used the parasite to heal herself, and then she continued to smoke?" Sloan felt disappointed somehow, though he wasn't surprised. "The addiction must've been bad."

"She found smoking too pleasurable."

"I did too. But my parasite rejected it."

"Oh, so that's what happened." Wade fell backward into his chair, rocking it, and clasped his hands behind his head, stretching. "I always wondered why you just quit."

"During the trial, Raphael said that some of us might experience 'supplementary rejections,' aside from the parasite rejecting the host entirely, which meant death. There were other things we ingested the parasite might deem incompatible." Sloan unwrapped a stick of gum. "She said something about the molecular structure of our cells. If the parasite knew the ingested substance didn't jive with our bodies, it would make us sick. And lucky me, I got sick." He stuffed the gum in his mouth and chewed. "Not that it really mattered. The only reason I smoked was because of the war. The stress got to me."

Once Wade had examined the bodies and acquired samples, Sloan laid Krista and Doctor Avolare to rest inside the same casket. Then he had the casket buried in the largest of several Irish cemeteries in Limerick. When the funeral was over, he tried to get plastered, but as usual, his effort was in vain.

Back at the Red Geisha, he lay on the king-sized bed in the master bedroom, hugging a pillow with a tear-soaked face. How many more loved ones would he lose? He couldn't curb the horrid thoughts—even after almost a year—that he desperately missed Petrov.

SEVENTEEN

TRAPPED

Sloan wandered around, inspecting everything, as everyone else filtered inside the spacious room. He took mental note... *No windows. One heavy-duty door. Piping. Electrical sockets. Storage.* The place was like a refurbished meat locker without the chill. He thought it strange that his son had changed their conference venue, from the usual large meeting room at the small military base, to a windowless, World-War-III bomb shelter. The partly underground bunker adjoined the base. A sophisticated ventilation system fed in fresh air while blocking everything from disease to biological and chemical agents. The room was adequately lit and arranged with the general's desk, a whiteboard, maps, and tables and chairs. But there was no echo, no reverberation of sound, and it felt like he'd entered a padded tomb.

"I don't know why you called for a meeting, son. But I'm doing this alone."

Warrick sat behind the bulky desk directly across from his father. He tilted his chair back against the wall and interlocked his fingers atop his head. "Things have changed."

Sloan glanced at each Independent, then back at his son. "What aren't you telling me?"

Everyone hesitated to share the latest intel until Warrick gave the go-ahead with a nod.

"While you were on the island, a herd was migrating north, and we tracked it," Stoner said. "The hunch paid off. It turns out, the MVs' parents like venison, because the male vampire killed a doe on the third night."

"We believe we've found his nest." Claire placed a "living atlas" or self-constructing cartography globe on a small stand on the table in front of Sloan. Such items were rare, specifically such a compact version, and they worked a charm if the natural geography needed continual updating. The globe took perpetually looping images with a laser scanner and automatically calculated all known forms of measurements—like distance and longitude and latitude—to create precise 3D maps. With its rechargeable solar plasma cells, the globe could be pre-programmed to scout alone for an indefinite period. She activated the globe, and it expanded to twice the size, sliding open at its base. A tiny lens projected a brightly coloured 3D map that appeared both solid and transparent as it moved.

"We tracked him to a cave approximately sixty-three kilometres northwest of here." She pointed to a green ridge of mountains alongside a secondary dark taupe ridge: a canyon. The map responded to her touch, adjusting the angle.

He got close and examined the mountains and nearby canyon. "Are you sure?"

"Positive. We observed his movements for weeks. He's nocturnal like Krista was, hunts at night, but he always returns to the cave by dawn."

"We don't know what killed Doctor Avolare, Sloan, but it wasn't this male," Stoner added.

"Then what the feck is going on?" He gave his head an aggravated scratch.

"What about the female that killed Petrov? Couldn't it have been her?" Yasmine asked.

"Not possible. Raphael was an intelligent woman. What she described was something entirely different." Sloan fell back in his chair and anchored his head over the backrest, slouching down. He stared at the ceiling, threading his hands over his chest. "She was terrified…" He thought back to their conversation seconds before she died.

"Krista tried to save me… She was such a brave girl." Raphael dug into his shirt with the stranglehold of a petrified cat. *"A monster with eyes of mustard-yellow."* Her lips quivered against his. *"The monster did this. I should've left with you… like you wanted…"*

As everyone debated a plan of action, his thoughts drifted to a point further in the past. "Mustard-yellow," he said under his breath. *Where have I heard or seen that before?*

Sloan's chest jolted as if snagged on an invisible hook, and he gradually turned his head to the far right. *I know this sensation. I've been here before.* He abruptly sat up and stared at the rear wall; the room faded to pure white, and there, as if it were real, was an unsightly, massive vampire with phosphorescent, owl-like, mustard-yellow eyes and curved horns jutting from its forehead. *Shite, I have seen you before. You're attached to my red thread.*

Staring back at him, the demonic vamp let off a deafening screech and charged.

"Bastard!" he yelled, springing into the air.

Sloan blinked. He was sprawled on the floor with his son, Stoner, and Claire, holding his arms. The chair was on its side. He nervously poked his head between their legs to get a better look. The white void was gone, as was the vampire. *That was trippy*, he smirked.

"Dad?" Warrick demanded, his features stern. "What the feck's wrong with you?"

"You are acting a tad weird, papa bear."

"Sorry about that." He grabbed the table and got up.

"What gives, big man?" Peaches studied his expression with concern.

Everybody in the room was waiting for his answer.

He chuckled, giving his head another rub. "You'd never believe me in a million years."

"Try us," Snickers said point-blank.

"It really isn't that interesting..." he confessed with a rueful sigh. "I can see people and things beyond the world of the living."

"Like second sight?" said Claire.

Genuine surprise filled him. He'd honestly thought they'd laugh at him. "Sometimes. Most are those who have passed on, but every once in a while, I see snippets of the future—people or things I haven't met yet—and those from my future are usually faceless. I know if the being's a man, woman or otherwise, but that's it."

"Can you talk to them?" Peaches asked.

"Yes." Sloan picked up his chair and sat.

"Then they can see you too?" Peaches lit a cigarette.

"The dead can. But I'm not sure about those in the future."

"How long have you been able to do this?" Stoner asked.

"It started when I stopped taking the protein-vitamin injections. The first significant incident was after I snuck the kids into Avalon. I saw my parents and Chase, the little boy Morgan killed. Most of the time it feels more like a dream."

"Can you see anyone around us?" Claire pulled a chair over to sit.

"No, doll. It only works with those in the beyond connected directly to my life." He held up his left-hand and touched his pinky. "You see, there's this red thread wrapped around my pinky, and the strands are attached to all the people and things. Once a person dies, the red thread is cut. However, the frayed ends still flow between us, me and that person, but it's forever severed." He lowered his hand. "Some ancient Asian cultures believed in the 'red thread of fate,' which leads each of us to our future soulmate. But, in my case, it has connected me to everyone I've ever known and will know."

"That's some spooky shit." Snickers crunched a purple lollipop, rocking his chair.

"Okay. You see things. What did you just see in this room?"

Sloan glanced at his son, who seemed skeptical. "A vampire."

"The one they tracked?"

"No… Maybe. Shite, I don't know, son."

"Well, whatever it was, it gave you a good scare." Warrick cast his sapphire gaze at the others. "You're dismissed."

Without a word, everyone cleared the room, and the door shut, leaving them alone.

They've become a bit too obedient. Sloan ignored what his sixth sense was telling him, and he tried to sound upbeat. "Well, I suppose I should get a move on too." He went to stand, but Warrick gripped his shoulders.

"Stay." Warrick looked into his eyes. "I'm sorry about Raphael and Krista."

"There's no reason to apologize, son."

"You always say that, Dad, but I know you're broken up inside." Warrick grabbed a chair and sat in front of his father, knee to knee. "I heard you haven't been yourself lately."

"What is this? An interrogation or an intervention?" Now Sloan knew for certain his son had planned more than a hunt in his absence.

"You're *my* father, and I can do whatever I want."

"I have a right to my privacy." He folded his arms and glanced away, frowning.

"You're obstinate, but so am I." Warrick gripped his own knees. "If you just saw a vampire, that means it will manifest itself in the future, which puts you at risk."

Sloan's arms went slack as he finally made visual contact with his son. "Oh, I know exactly where this is leading…"

"Do you? Good. Then there's no need for me to get into a long-winded explanation. I'll send a unit to the island along with Snickers and Roddy. They can hunt down Raphael's phantom vamp—maybe even the females. Stoner, Yasmine, Claire, Peaches, and I will hunt down the vampire in the cave."

Phantom vamp? Does he think I made it all up because of my overly emotional state? "Right. And what about me?" he demanded gruffly.

Warrick got up and slid the chair to tuck it in against the table. "You're going to get some rest. I've already made arrangements with Elyse and Uncle Vince."

"*What?*" he thundered, leaping to his feet. "Not too fecking likely!"

"Somehow, I knew you were going to say that." Warrick sighed with profound dissatisfaction and turned to face his father. "You're retired, and your help is no longer required."

"Shite. I can't believe you're talking to me like this," he sneered. "I'm your father—have a little fecking respect—and there's no way I'll let you and my unit fight these things on my behalf. They are too powerful and dangerous, and—"

"I'm sorry, Dad, I really am. But you leave me no choice."

"Huh?"

The bunker flooded with APF, and his son strode to the only exit.

"*Please* don't do anything foolish." Warrick stared at him with seemingly painful remorse. "Just stay here. The bunker's been well stocked. There are books, a bed and whiskey."

Sloan felt deeply betrayed, and his baritone trembled in skepticism. "You think I've lost it…my own son."

"You've cried a lot, and you've had bouts of uncontrollable rage. And you just confessed to seeing things. The *dead*, Dad?"

"*My friend died.* I loved her," he bellowed. "It must be nice to be so perfect you never crack a fecking smile."

"You're wrong. I do feel. I'm doing this because I love you and I'm trying to protect you."

"No. You're just embarrassed." He sat hard with his back to his son, arms folded. "Leave, and take those fecking arseholes with you, before I do something we're both going to regret."

Warrick told his men to get out, and his eyes welled up. He silently gulped, shakily wiping his face on his jacket sleeve. He really didn't want to lock his father away, but it was for the best. If what Peaches said was true, and his father lost control, Sloan's safety—and the safety of anyone foolish enough to get caught in his crosshairs—was at risk. *I'm sorry, Dad.* He pulled the steel-clad door closed with a muted bang.

The soldiers slid a pair of metal bars into place, and then they stood in front of it.

"Lock the city down. Don't let anyone in or out. Got it?" Warrick said to colonels Vargas and Schulze. "No matter what happens, don't let my father out."

"Yes, sir," Schulze replied.

"What about the shapeshifters, sir?" Vargas asked.

"We've dealt with them on a few occasions now. The men aren't stupid."

"I realize, sir, but your father—"

"*Do not* let him out." Warrick repudiated the older man with a cool menacing stare, and he strode to the Jeep that was idling with Peaches in the driver's seat. He got in the passenger's side and shut the door.

"Not to bombard you. But permission to speak?"

Warrick groaned. "Go ahead."

Peaches put the shifter into drive, and they sped onto the road. "I didn't tell you that stuff so you could cage my friend like an animal."

"Then why did you tell me?"

"You're his child, and I was worried."

"And I've dealt with the situation."

Peaches glanced at him, on the verge of exploding. "Are you an imbecile? That wasn't dealing with it—that was like tightening the lid on a pressure cooker! And then you and the others made fun of him."

"I didn't mock him. No one did. We were stunned."

"Bullshit!"

"Don't tell me you actually believe he talks to the dead." Warrick glared at her, his mouth grim.

"What if I do? I've known your old man a lot longer than you, and he *doesn't lie*," Peaches barked, staring dead ahead, squeezing the steering wheel. "Do me a favour. The next time you decide to play your games, leave me out of it."

"You're scared." Warrick smirked, resting his head on his fist, watching the road.

"Damn right, I'm scared. He's gonna kill me. I broke his trust. But you broke mine!"

They rode the rest of the distance in uncomfortable silence.

The general was beside himself, bereft of rationality, and he kept wondering if he'd done what was best for his father. Nevertheless, even if he returned to the bunker, apologized profusely, and released Sloan, there was no telling how he'd react. Peaches was correct. He'd unintentionally humiliated his father in front of everyone, including his closest friends. "Crap," he muttered, pressing his fist to his mouth.

The Jeep came to a stop, and Peaches shoved the shifter into park. "If you're having second thoughts, I can go back and try to reason with him."

"It's too late for that." Warrick, very circumspect of her offer, glanced collectedly at her, got out and slammed the door.

The Independents and an additional unit of specifically trained elite soldiers were waiting at the designated starting point. They had their weapons, ammo, and survival supplies, and they were ready to go. Warrick gave each man a brief once-over, checking their gear and night camo uniforms. Considering the terrain, it could take up to ten hours to reach the cave.

"Okay. We get to the mountain range, locate the cave, and then rest for the night. Remember: stay downwind." Warrick wandered in a circle around everyone. "Fighting in darkness isn't ideal, but this vampire is nocturnal, so we have to be prepared. If we can stay under his radar, we may catch him off guard in the morning when he returns. But we'll see what happens."

Sloan lay on the cot with an arm draped over his eyes. "Bloody rotten kid. You deserve to have your arse tanned. You think you know it all, and you know fecking nothing," he grumbled. "Leona, I'm going to wring your scrawny neck when I get my hands on you." He heaved an annoyed sigh and switched to his side. The sagging cot creaked and groaned; he couldn't get comfortable. But, after a while, out of sheer boredom, his eyelids grew heavy, and his breathing took on a rough weightiness.

"Don't be too hard on him, sweetie. He thinks he's protecting you."

Sloan stared at his wife, who sat opposite him at a café style table surrounded by gardens. She looked beautiful, with the sun glistening in her hair. He ran his hand down her throat—hooked her blouse with his finger—and drew her close. "I want you, honey." He caressed her lips with a lengthy, impassioned kiss. *"I want you right now."*

She searched his eyes as their lips eased a part. "Me too."

He quickly removed his jacket, nuzzling her neck, and she giggled, unbuttoning her blouse.

"Dad, wake up."

"Shite. Not now!"

"Niisan."

Sloan all but toppled off the cot. With a thudding heart, he fought to upright himself, planting his hand on the cement floor. "You fecking eejit!" he snapped, looking back over his shoulder. "I was almost there."

Mystified, Vincent stared at him. "*There*?"

"Nothing. Forget it." He sat facing Vincent and Elyse, noting his brother had the ancient *katana* sheathed at his hip.

"Sorry, Dad."

He sighed, gripping the edge of the cot. "It's okay, baby doll."

"I didn't think he'd actually lock you in here. But his emotions get the better of him when he's upset. Don't be too hard on him."

That's exactly what your mother just said. Sloan noticed that beyond the quiet isolation of the bunker, there was a hell of a ruckus outside, including shouting, the sound of distant gunfire and the odd explosion. Vincent seemed anxious, an unusual state for him. His daughter was wearing camouflage, toting Petrov's AK-5000—a rifle three times too big for her—and carrying extra ammunition. He gestured to their gear before crossing his arms. "Do tell…" he said in a mordant tone. "Is there a problem?"

"Don't be a smartass, *niisan*. You can hear there's a problem."

"Hey, don't give me heck. I'm just a prisoner here."

"Oh, Dad, would you stop? You're acting like a petulant child. Forget about my stupid brother. Right now, we've got a bigger issue." She searched his expression. "We need your help."

He stuck his nose in the air and waved his index finger. "Nah-ah-ah. I'm sorry, but that'll never do. Who's asking?"

"We are, *niisan*," Vincent said with exasperation. "All the western districts have been invaded by shapeshifters and SA Bloc soldiers. Colonel Vargas is holding them off, but not for much longer."

"Granted, they are a fecking nuisance." Sloan rolled his eyes with a sigh; he couldn't bear it when his daughter batted her big sparkly sapphire-blues. He didn't know if it was merely her feminine wiles or the inherited traits of a female vampire, but the women in his life could pull his strings like puppeteers. "Fine. But if I help, you have to promise to deal with the general when he gets back, because I'm not having it."

"I promise." Elyse kissed his forehead, smiled, and stood back. "Was he that rude?"

"Yeah, and it really hurt, baby doll." Sloan rose from the cot, adjusting his belt, and strode past her.

Elyse and Vincent looked at one another. Vincent shrugged.

"Don't worry, I'll talk to him." She rushed out after her father.

EIGHTEEN
BATTLE ON THE MOUNTAIN

Dragging her crimson falx, a gift from Red that she'd only recently put to use again, Claire moved on her side to get under a narrow outcrop of shale. Her guts were leaking everywhere. The sounds of the men fighting and dying bounced in horrific waves off the mountainside. She swallowed a knot of saliva, pressing on her gaping wound. They'd acted foolhardy and had rushed in to capture the vampire, but he wasn't having any of their nonsense.

"Are you, all right?" Yasmine hunched over on her knees, reaching, and firmly grasped Claire's hand.

"It hurts like a bitch." Weepy-eyed, Claire rested her head on the rock, waiting as her body healed. "Sloan isn't some nut."

"You believed him too."

"What's he going to gain by lying?"

"Not a freakin' thing."

"Crackers, look out!"

Yasmine toppled down the slope, disoriented and bleeding. She grabbed a large rock as the enormous, male hybrid-vampire clung like a mountain goat to the ledge above, slanting over her. Dislodged dirt and gravel tumbled away. She exhaled, nervous, and slid her hand down her thigh and unsnapped her hunting knife. Snarling and hissing, the vampire slashed with massive black claws. Searing pain extended from her hip to her armpit, making it difficult for her to move. She madly tried to re-grip the rock. But the surface was slick with blood and, this time, she fell, screaming, into the darkness below.

"Crackers!" Claire grimaced, stabbing at the vampire's legs, the curved falx puncturing its albino flesh.

The vampire screeched and jumped to the lower ledge. It reached inside the stone cubbyhole, dragged her out kicking and yelling, and then flung her hundreds of metres in the air.

"Yasmine!" Stoner clambered through the rugged undergrowth of the centuries-old forest. "Yasmine!" Yards away, he spotted her broken body strewn at the mountain base. When he got to her, she was wheezing oxygen and frothing dark scarlet from a perforated lung; scarcely alive. He knelt beside her and carefully touched her soaked hair. Instantly, his vision burned to a blur, and he affectionately kissed her forehead. "Everything will be all right."

"I can't…feel anything," she murmured, staring dully at him, her cheek resting on the rocks and her hand involuntarily twitching.

Stoner quickly removed his coat and blanketed the gravel with it. "You're going to survive."

She wept, closing her eyes. "Help…me…"

"I am, baby." He sniffed, brushing his nose, and gently shifted her to lie on the coat.

The male vampire scaled the mountainside like a white robotic spider. Grenades sporadically lit the timberline with pockets of destruction, smoke, and raining debris. The elite troop attempted to drive the vampire into a submissive corner.

Warrick had lost track of Claire. But he'd seen her plummet somewhere within the evergreens. His men vanished amid the dense trunks and, seconds later, something odd happened. Just as fast as they'd entered the forest, they were spat back out as if regurgitated by some great sea monster. They landed in different spots on the slope, beaten, bruised and bloody.

"Get the men back to Avalon."

"Yes, sir." Peaches, who appeared unfazed, gave the order to retreat. The men helped one another descend the treacherous, lengthy slope. "Where do you think you're going?"

Warrick drew his broadsword, a gift from his father. The smoky-brown, double-edged blade had a dull shine at night. "To find Claire."

"Not that you'll listen… but I wouldn't advise it." Peaches drew her navy short sword. "I'll help you."

"As soon as you see it, don't hesitate. Go that way, and I'll head this way."

Peaches darted right into the thick undergrowth.

Shortly after, Warrick crept inside the belly of the rising plateaued forest. He knew Claire was close because he sensed her presence. Like the other Independents, her only saving grace was her parasite. As long as both her heart and head remained intact, she'd survive and heal. But he was determined to find her, because leaving anyone under his command behind wasn't an option he felt comfortable with.

He faltered through the pitch black until a subtle glow radiated in the near distance, a beckoning aura that illuminated the trees. He slid to the bottom of a ditch, waded into a waist-high river, and scrambled to the top of the opposite bank, feeling a ton heavier in his soaked camo uniform. Dripping, he entered the woods again and came to a stop. He rubbed his eyes, but his mother was still in front of him, as beautiful as he remembered. "Mom, is that really you?"

"I'm positive you aren't blind," Amanda said.

"How's this poss—"

"Hush, son. Talking to those who can't see us isn't permitted. So I don't have long, and I want you to listen."

He froze stiff as a board when Petrov and Tristan appeared on either side of his mother, sentries to the gate, accompanying the little sister he'd never known. "Uh... I'm listening."

"Release your father."

"This vampire's too powerful—"

"Trust him, son."

"I do trust him." Warrick heaved a despondent sigh, just like his father. "Okay, that's a lie… I really hurt him."

"Seeing is believing, and we are here." Amanda grasped his little sister's hand and as they faded, she cautioned, *"Apologize. Make amends. Do whatever it takes."*

Momentarily dumbfounded, he pinched his own face. *Yep, I'm awake.* He couldn't believe he'd just spoken to his mother. Her fleeting manifestation had done more than convince him. It had challenged everything he'd thought he understood about his father, even the things he'd doubted. *He really is sensitive to his surroundings. He really is an amazing vampire.* Switching direction, he raced back the way he'd come, stumbling through the swift-moving river.

Peaches was at the slope, looking worse for wear. Warrick wanted to tell her there *was* a spiritual realm—that the soul *did* continue on after death. He wanted to tell her that everything his father had ever claimed was the truth. But he put his thoughts on hold for the moment.

"I searched the entire side of the mountain." Peaches panted, scanning the lofty forested steps. "It's like that thing has vanished, sir."

"The cave."

"Maybe. We did disrupt its normal routine."

"Are the men out of harm's way?"

"Those who survived."

"What about the Independents?"

"Stoner carried Yasmine out a while ago. She was in pretty rough shape. I haven't seen Claire, though. And now with the lack of even moonlight and this terrain, searching will be tricky."

"I know what you're going to say, Leona."

Peaches stared at him. "Well, I know your old man isn't psychic—not yet anyway. Was your mom?"

"You're a mouthy woman."

"You're right. That was an asinine thing to say, sir. What did you want to tell me?"

Warrick thought better of sharing his experience, least of all with her, because it would be front page news by that afternoon. "Nothing. It's not important. I'll find Claire and you get the unit out of here."

Despite the concurrent invasions of various sections of the city, Colonel Vargas, Sloan, and the others still managed to pull Avalon back from the brink of subjugation, and with minimal casualties. The worst hit areas were Districts C, H, S and E. Sycamore Street was littered with bodies, and the recovery crews were hard at work. Vincent waited with Sloan and Colonel Vargas, who had successfully run the entire APF in the general's absence, defending the city.

Sloan squatted near a female shapeshifter. Rangy and humanoid, the shapeshifters were ugly creatures; their gaunt bodies, shaggy burnt-umber hair, and bronzed, scaly flesh gave them a scavenger like appearance, while, their misshapen teeth and beady coal eyes were menacing. Even in death, the shapeshifter's rank odour seemed to permeate any nearby absorbent material, similar to a skunk. He stood and moved away from the corpse.

"If it weren't for you, we'd never have caught them all." Colonel Vargas gave Sloan a firm pat on the back. "I'm grateful."

"No problem. And you didn't do half bad yourself."

The colonel grinned with a nod, then rejoined the crews working to collect the bodies from the street, shouting orders to his immediate lieutenants.

Sloan had located the shapeshifters blocks away, thanks to their revolting stench. The colonel had caught a whiff of the ammonia as well, but an insipid version, whereas to Sloan, the stink was unmistakable. Whenever a shapeshifter got close, especially a male, the ammonia was strong enough to make his eyes water as if he were chopping an onion. Now, his own shirt and jacket carried faint traces of ammonia.

"Dad, I got it," Elyse called out, holding the living atlas in the air. She placed the small globe on the palm of his hand. "Right now, it's off, so if you push the top, it will shrink enough to fit in your pocket. If you press it twice, it will awaken and expand to its normal size. You can also use verbal commands. Once it recognizes your voice, that is."

"Excellent. Thanks, baby doll. I think I can figure it out from here."

"Do you want us to go with you, *niisan*?"

"I'm good, Vince. I'm sure you've got a mess in District E to deal with." Without another word, he was gone, following Sycamore, then heading toward the library. And the closer he got, the faster he ran. Sloan didn't know why, but he felt a sense of urgency, and he was certain it had everything to do with his son. And, as he'd learned with Tristan's death, he couldn't ignore the parasite when she passed on a warning.

He raced at full speed through Chartreuse and, at the perimeter gate, he left the posted sentry reeling. The darkness didn't bother him. His pupils adjusted, absorbing every available speck of light, giving him a sort of orange-hued night vision. His blood was on fire and his instinct was guiding him as he tore north into the forest. While crossing a glade, he held up the globe, pressed the button inset on the top twice with his thumb like pressing a detonator and threw it up in the air. "Voice recognition required. Name: Sloan Whelan," he shouted, running. "Follow."

Lit neon blue, the globe flounced and replied in a rudimentary AI voice: "Voice identification acquired." Then it took off, flying just above his head at the same speed. "Guide me to the cave from the last activated map."

The globe illuminated a coloured 3D map just in front of his face. A neon-red arrow bounced over the cave. The globe perpetually adjusted, moving fluidly over the 3D terrain, using a solid neon-pink human icon to show which direction to take. Thirty kilometres into the wilds, he found Peaches leading the bedraggled elite unit, knocked down to half its original size. Stoner and Yasmine were at the rear.

"Sloan," Peaches said with trepidation. "You came…"

"Where's Warrick?" Sloan approached with the globe hovering from above.

"I was helping him search for Claire. Then he told me to get the unit home. He's still up there on the mountainside somewhere…but so is that thing."

"I'm going to borrow this." Sloan removed a military emergency torch strapped to the side of Peaches's knapsack. "Thanks."

"Yeah, sure." Peaches grabbed his arm and said quietly, "I'm sorry for spilling the beans."

"Don't worry. I'll break your neck later." Sloan smirked, cuffing her shoulder, and started running again.

"Good luck, big man." Leona watched until he disappeared.

Another thirty-odd kilometres deep, Sloan sped the rocky slope to snarls, growls and screeches. Either his son or Claire, or both of them, were engaged in a battle with the male vampire. He caught a whiff of that sickly-sweet decomp lingering in the air. "Off." The globe died, and he tucked it inside an interior jacket pocket.

Panting, Warrick sliced upward diagonally, cutting the vampire's ribs open. Screeching, the creature swiped, and his cry rebounded off the wall of trees. He dropped the sword and toppled backward, sliding down several metres through the gravel to land on a nest of exposed roots.

"General!" Claire sprang, thrusting her falx, and the blade sank between the vampire's busted ribs. She tore it out and struck again. However, the vampire sent her flying. Then it

263

screeched and charged Warrick. Claire hit a cedar and landed hard on the ground. "General, look out!" She clawed at the gravel, quickly getting up as a dark silhouette sailed past her and knocked the vampire into a boulder. "Papa bear…"

The vampire wriggled its' entire body like a dog flicking away water, then leapt in a cloud of dirt. Sloan jumped high and booted the creature in the chest. Skating backward, the vampire slashed. Sloan ducked, countering with a cross to its right cheek. He chopped both sides of its neck, drilled its left side and fractured its jaw. The vampire swiped. Sloan blocked with his forearm and jabbed its throat dead on. Bruised and pierced, its flesh instantaneously turned purplish-black, seeping dark fluid.

"Never touch my son!" Sloan roared, pounding the vamp's chest and diaphragm multiple times.

Warrick strained to see through the veil of blackness. He squeezed one of his amputated legs, the blood gushing, water from a faucet. He wept, briefly reaching for the image of his father, but collapsed.

Claire avoided the fight and dropped beside him, speedily unzipping her knapsack. "Don't move, sir."

"It hurts bad," he stammered.

She tore open several packages of new bandaging. "Breathe through your nose, sir, and exhale through your mouth." She glanced at Sloan, pulverizing the vampire as she dug out a pair of scissors and cut Warrick's pant legs. "That's it. Breathe in… Now breathe out. Deep breaths."

As Claire threw away the bloody sections of his pants, she noticed an eerie silence had settled over the mountainside. No echoes. No movement. The vampire had retreated, and Sloan was approaching them, healing from a minor wound. "Both legs have been sheared off," she mouthed. "Blood loss is significant."

Writhing in agony, Warrick chattered, "I'm sorry! I'm sorry, Dad!"

"Okay, shhh…" Sloan grabbed his son's head, forcing him to focus, and he searched his panicked, watery eyes. "I'm sorry too," he said with low softness. "You've got to calm down, son."

"Here." Claire passed him a roll of bandaging and held the general's left upper leg in place.

Sloan quickly wrapped and cinched his son's leg with the clean roll of fabric. He repeated the same with his right leg. He knew his children had the ability to heal as he did, but nowhere near as fast, and in the meantime, there was a good possibility his son might die from severe hemorrhaging if his genetics didn't get a grip.

"Dad, you were right." Warrick moaned in tears.

Claire eyed the Irishman, handed him another roll of bandaging, and dug in the main compartment of the knapsack again.

Sloan kept watch on the surrounding black backdrop as he wrapped both Warrick's legs with a second layer. If the creature was even half as resilient as the alpha female, he'd heal his wounds and return for a second round. "I was right about what?"

"I saw Mom and… she spoke to me."

He paused for a split second, then continued to pack the stumps, adding the final layers. "Did you?"

Claire didn't say a word. She loaded a vaccination gun with a large syringe of clear liquid and adjusted the dial to fifty milligrams.

"Petrov and Tristan were with her…and my unborn sister." Warrick moaned again, squirming a little. "She told me to make amends with you—that you are the only one who can fight the vampire."

"Okay. Will you let me help?"

Warrick nodded with a gasp, clenching his fists.

"It looks like his bleeding has slowed." Claire held Warrick's arm, pressing the muzzle of the vaccination gun into his flesh. "Sorry, but this is going to hurt, General."

The needle stabbed; he winced.

Sloan mopped the sweat from his pasty complexion. "Pack up, doll. We're getting out of here."

"Do you think it'll come back?"

"Guaranteed. That's why we have to hurry."

The large dose of rapid-release painkiller hit like a brick, and Warrick was silently dazed. Claire carried the knapsack, torch, her own weapons, and the general's while Sloan slung his huge son over his shoulder like a wet cape, then they slid and skidded down the slope.

"I'm sorry I can't help carry him."

"It's all right, doll. He weighs a ton."

She leaned sideways and examined the general's dull glazed eyes. "He's out cold and breathing normally."

"Good." Sloan glanced back at her. "What the feck happened?" ·

"Everything. But first, I need to say that we didn't want to imprison you."

"What's done is done. He was desperate to protect me." Sloan jumped sideways, hopping, and running with the tumbling rocks to the base of the mountainous escarpment. "Can you run?"

"Yes." Claire was directly behind him.

"I'll feel somewhat better when we're in a clearing."

They jogged side by side until they'd escaped the forest, and then they slowed to a brisk stride. Claire explained, and Sloan listened intently. Nothing came as a surprise anymore, not even the fact that his son seemed desperate to prove himself as a competent military leader.

"He's a good kid. Sometimes he just tries too hard," she remarked, keeping a steady pace with him. "But it's been difficult to step into your shoes."

"Yeah, but here's the thing, doll. He doesn't need to fill my shoes. He needs to wear his own." Sloan sighed and looked at her with concern. "Get my drift?"

"Sure. But you and I are old, Sloan. We've been around the block. He's young yet." She stretched, throwing her arms in the air and wiggling her fingers. "Maybe you should talk to him. Let him know he's a good leader in his own right."

"Nah, he'd never believe me. He'd think I was stroking his ego."

"Well, it's worth a shot. If his legendary father acknowledged him…" She paused. "By the way, was the vampire we fought tonight the same one you saw connected with the red thread?"

"No. Similar, though. Both are albinos. But the vamp here has gold eyes. The one I saw had mustard-yellow eyes, horns, and it was gigantic in comparison."

She sighed, gripping her knapsack straps. "Crap. I was afraid you might say that."

"The problem is, there's no time stamp when I see things."

"What do you mean?"

Sloan adjusted his son's weight but kept trudging the undulating terrain. "What I saw yesterday could happen in a minute or a year from now. I have no way of knowing."

"Then we'd best concentrate on our current situation."

NINETEEN

SATISFACTION GUARANTEED

From his usual perch, the cracked red-leather stool, Sloan watched his son peaceably slumber as Lucy and Wade worked their magic. Wade had added a sedative to the painkiller, and Warrick was out like a light, sporting an expression of childlike serenity.

Lucy carefully cut away the soaked bandaging, discarding it in a pail. She pressed an antiseptic pad to each stump, followed by fresh dressings. "His legs are several centimetres longer from the original wound," she said.

"Excellent. That means cellular regeneration is up to par." Wade scrutinized a glass slide under the microscope. "Aside from his damaged tissue being dead…it appears it was healthy."

"He doesn't have an infection." Lucy smiled at Sloan, tying off the new bandaging.

Internally, Sloan exhaled an enormous sigh of relief. He *was* extremely grateful. And now that he knew for certain his son would survive, he got up to leave.

"Oi." Wade folded his arms. "Where do you think you're going?"

"I've got important shite to do. Besides, my son's in good hands."

"Good hands or not, you need to rest and eat, and I haven't given you a physical."

"Oh, for feck's sake. I'm fine."

Lucy finished washing her hands in a stainless-steel bucket of hot sudsy water. "I could give you the physical." She grinned, drying her hands on a towel.

"Are you seriously flirting with me? I'm ancient enough to be your great-great-great grandad." He incredulously glared at the young woman.

"Of course not." Lucy covered Warrick with a blanket and rolled his gurney into the darkened corner nearest the row of refrigeration units. "Mind, I do have a thing for older men." She glanced at Wade, who completely ignored the comment.

The clinic was free of haphazardly scattered medical debris. Lucy had organized all the machines, even the cluttered open shelving units. Everything was tidy and had its designated spot, and certain items were tagged. Wade had never managed that. He lived in perpetual chaos. However, Lucy couldn't.

"Anyway, it wouldn't hurt to get some rest. And I'll make us all dinner." She grabbed both buckets.

"Not to mention we haven't talked in a long time," Wade said. "Don't you want to hear about my findings? I've got the test results from Doctor Avolare and Krista, and I've been working on something else, something to do with your blood."

Sloan didn't know why, but he complied with his childhood friend's wishes. He ate dinner with them, and they talked and drank for hours, and then he stayed the night. Not that another twenty-four hours would make a difference. His intentions remained the same: to remove the male vampire from existence, regardless of whether his family and friends agreed.

The sun had crested the horizon, painting the sky with soft hues of pink and orange; the pastel colours were visible through the clinic skylights.

Wade set a mug of steaming liquid on the steel table and paused. Near the far wall, beside the hospital bed, Sloan's bulky mass blended almost seamlessly with the melancholic light. "You're still here," he declared in shock. "I thought for sure you would've snuck off sometime during the night."

"His legs are nearly fully healed. I changed his bandages and administered another shot." Sloan got off the stool. "I'm leaving for sure, but not until Warrick's awake, unless you've got a better idea."

"Not really. Just be careful, Irish."

"If you don't mind, I'm going to have a nap." Sloan pointed to the broken-down couch on the other side of the clinic next to the entrance doors.

"Be my guest."

"Thanks." He lay down and bent an arm over his eyes.

Wade stared at the Irishman for a period before a disturbance from the ground-floor cafeteria roused him from his thoughts. He quietly darted into the kitchen, clicking the heavy fire door shut. Lucy was humming, shuffling around, opening and closing cupboard doors, and placing various food containers on the counter to prepare breakfast.

Lucy glanced in his direction and yelped with fright, and the kettle she'd been holding crashed in the stainless-steel sink. "I thought you were a ghost!" She shut off the faucet. "What are you doing?"

"Sorry, pet," he said in a malleable voice, drawing her into a warm embrace. "Sloan's asleep on the couch, and I didn't want to wake him."

"Oh." She kissed his lips and smiled. "Why's he sleeping in the clinic? I made a bed for him upstairs in an examination room."

"He wanted to stay with Warrick. I know this might sound odd but… have you noticed anything different with Sloan lately?"

She set the kettle on the stovetop and turned on the element before facing him. "What do you mean by different?"

He slouched with his rump on a long banquet table, folding his arms. "Last night, for example. You teased him, and instead of him giving you a sarcastic comeback, he was annoyed and serious."

She paused with the fridge door open. "Maybe his response was a bit strange. But nobody is going to be in a chipper mood every second of every day." She brought out a woven basket filled with eggs. "What's bothering you?"

He checked the kitchen door and leaned forward, whispering, "Everything, pet. I've known that big eejit my entire life, and I've never seen him like this. He's been too quiet. He hardly ever smiles anymore, and he snaps everyone's head off. I'm telling you, his behaviour's not normal. Either he isn't feeling well, or something else is bothering him."

"You don't think he could be dying, do you?" Lucy asked in a pained tone, clutching the basket of eggs.

"That's highly unlikely. But I could be wrong."

Lucy set the basket on the counter. "Oh, Wade, he can't be dying, he just can't!"

"Who's dying?"

Wade turned partway around, keeping his arms folded. "No one, Irish. I thought you were going to have a nap?"

"We were talking about you, Sloan. Wade just doesn't want to hurt your feelings."

Wade cringed.

Lucy dabbed under her eyes with a tea towel. "Both of us are concerned because you've been acting strange—out of character." She looked at him. "Are you ill?"

"No, doll." Sloan gazed darkly at his friend. At the very least, he'd thought Wade would give him an honest answer. Instead, it was Lucy who seemed to have the cahoonies.

"*Please*. Tell me what's eating you up inside."

He wanted to tell her, but he didn't know whether he could explain about the black mess swirling around inside his heart. Instead, he just stared at her for the longest time, before finding the nerve. "My glass used to be overflowing, but now there's only a drop left, and I don't know how much longer I can keep it from evaporating."

Lucy rushed over and hugged him tight. "Everything will be okay." She squeezed him. "Don't give up."

Wade stood beside the table as the pair embraced. Initially, he didn't have a clue what Sloan meant or why Lucy was distraught. When he noticed something genuinely troubling: his friend's eyes had a lifeless sheen, like the ancient matte-finish photos he'd found in a shoe box in the clinic office. *No way.* He had to be misinterpreting things. "I'll make us breakfast!" Wade slapped his hands together and completely disregarded what his gut was telling him. "Eggs, bacon dollars and toast—the whole shebang!"

"Everybody's in here," Warrick said, as the door slowly shut behind him. "I heard voices."

"Oh, you're awake." Lucy let go of Sloan and smiled. "How are you feeling?"

"Better, thanks."

"Just on time," Wade said, holding up a spatula. "I'm going to cook breakfast."

"Sounds great. I'm starved. Dad, can we talk in the other room?"

"Sure." Sloan followed his son out of the cafeteria. "How are your legs?"

"Good as new." Warrick looked down at his bare feet and wiggled his toes. "I just need pants, socks and shoes."

"Wade's got bins of excess clothing and footwear in this place. I'm sure he can fix you up." Sloan planted his backside on the cracked red-leather stool.

"Yeah, I'll ask him." Warrick rolled over a second stool and sat in front of his father. "I'm really sorry, Dad. What I did—"

"You've already apologized, son. No need to repeat yourself."

"Well, I wasn't sure if I had or not. When I woke, my memories were hazy. I also wanted to thank you for saving me and Claire." Warrick gripped his knees with a nervy smile. "I was an idiot to chase after that thing."

Sloan sighed, crossing his arms over his massive chest. "You're not an idiot. Right or wrong, you made a decision and stood by it, that's what being a leader is all about. Besides, you're a good leader. I think eventually that goodness will turn into greatness."

"Okay, now I know you're teasing me." Warrick's cheeks flushed a touch.

"No joke. You've got what it takes: patience and brains. The men respect you, son. Chiefly Vargas. I think he's your number one fan."

"Or he's an arse kisser." Warrick chuckled.

Sloan smirked, leaned forward, and gave his hand a pat. "Nah, he seems earnest." He glanced back at the kitchen. "I've got to leave. Do you mind if I take the Independents with me? I could use their help to bait the male."

Warrick searched his sombre expression. "I could assist…"

"Although I do appreciate the offer, not this time. I think you've seen enough action for at least a few months."

"That's fine, Dad. I've already promised to let you handle things. I just want you to promise me you'll come home in one piece."

"Nothing's for certain, but I'll do my best. How's that? Or are you going to fecking nag me some more?" Sloan flashed a wide, cheeky smile. "Relax. I like it when you nag, almost as much as I do when Peaches does it."

Warrick gazed at him with cool reserve and said flatly, "I wish you'd take what I say to heart."

"And I do, believe me." Sloan grinned and stood, adjusting his belt and jeans.

"Okay, then let's have breakfast together before you go."

"Aw, come on, son. It's getting late!"

"What's that? You want me to come with you?" Warrick got off the stool, his gaze fastened on his father.

"Right. Breakfast. Sounds *awesome*," he said wryly, trailing his son into the cafeteria. "Let's eat."

***

It took many sleepless nights. Nevertheless, after scouring the entire landscape that haloed Avalon, the Independents finally tracked the male vampire to a valley outside District N, in the southern deadlands.

Claire got into position on her belly. She propped the bipod, secured the sniper rifle butt at her shoulder, and fiddled with the scope; soon the Irishman came into focus. Stoner and Yasmine also found the best spots to hide and set up their rifles, while Snickers and Roddy were back at the perimeter fence in case things should go awry.

The sun had dipped below the highest summit, and the canyon was rapidly sinking into darkness. Fifteen hundred yards away from Claire's lofty bird's-eye view, Sloan entered the canyon alone. The landscape appeared as a strange, arid oasis far removed from Avalon. Wrapped in bands of sediment, mainly strips of iron ore, the valley snaked in disintegrating earth and falling columns of reddish sand. Boulders and eroded cement besieged the valley floor like splintered glass.

Sloan pressed the igniter, and the torch whooshed with a healthy flame. "I know you can hear me!" he called. "And I don't care anymore. It's you and me! No matter where you are, I'm coming for you." He held the torch high to make sure the vampires would see it. "Maybe I'll kill your females!"

He went to toss the torch but hesitated as three females slunk from the desert landscape on all fours. The female he'd fought on the island, who was still missing half her face and a chunk out of her arm, was among them. *That's it, bitches, come fecking closer.*

But Sloan hadn't anticipated that the male would readily show himself. And now that he had an unobstructed view, his opponent was huge. *No wonder Tristan never had a chance.* He ever-so-slowly lowered the torch, hypnotized; the male vampire's gold-ingot gaze seemed to dance in the light. It was him. The same vampire from the CCTV footage and the cave. The sinewy male moved with grace, his body rippling in lean muscle as he skulked around a boulder.

Sloan swallowed, taking a step back. He wasn't afraid of death. He'd lived his life. But Stoner was right: he feared what such a creature would do to the populace. Morgan's last words—*"Good luck"*—came to mind, an epitaph to the present. "It was you." He drove the torch in to the ground. "You took my son from me!"

The orange light cast the four creatures in a ruddy gothic glow, partially obfuscated in the darkness.

"I'm going to kill you if it's the last thing I do." He drew the Irish longsword and dropped the scabbard in the dust.

"Damn, papa bear, why'd you do that?" Claire attempted to get a clean shot at the vamps. However, with insufficient light and Sloan hampering her view…

Encroaching, the male snarled and snapped, his pupils glittering, and his eagle-like talons busting the dry, crusty soil. Once Sloan realized the sword had been knocked from his grasp, he just had the wherewithal to harden. Faster than a lightning strike, the attack was a million more times brutal than what the alpha female could dish out. Busted, bleeding and scarcely conscious, Sloan flung himself away.

"Argh, shite." He clambered to shield himself within a stone recess, trying to keep his torso together. He was healing, but the insidious pain was testing his resolve. Gasping, he wondered if the male had transmitted a contagion. Still holding his abdomen, he crouched and peered warily around the rock edge. "Feck!" He jerked back into the recess, and then he was gone.

The male vampire galloped, dragging him through the valley.

"Lousy fecker!" Sloan groaned, madly reaching for his ankle. But the vampire sped faster and flung him around like a wet towel, smashing him into the ground and against boulders until the very atmosphere was a dusty haze.

Sloan wrapped his head and nape with his arms, every centimetre smarting. *Shite!* He had numerous broken bones. *Harden, for feck's sake!* He knew the parasite was trying, but her efforts seemed in vain. *Have I contracted a disease? But that's impossible. I've been down that road. Come on, harden!*

I'm doing my best, the parasite admonished bitterly. *Whenever something goes wrong, you expect me to perform miracles. Why are you so rash?*

He choked, losing his breath. *Sometimes…impulse wins over logic. I'm sorry, doll.*

Claire cursed. *Warrick will kill me.* Collapsing the bipod, she shot to her feet and took the fastest way down into the canyon: the sheer cliff below. As soon as she began the descent, gunfire erupted. Stoner and Yasmine had joined the fight. "Crap!"

Sloan stretched for his ankle as his buttocks rode the rocky soil, the friction burning through his jeans. He was tossed high in the air, then savagely beaten for a second time. The vampire grabbed his busted arms and hurled him earthward.

He gasped loudly, lying supine; warm blood seeped from his nose. *I'm dying here...* he pleaded, near in tears with the parasite. *Hurry, do something.* Peering around, he sluggishly got onto all fours. He was healing quicker than he had minutes before. *Come on, faster!* The vampire was circling him. "What the hell are you waiting for?" He threw a handful of dirt. Snorting, it growled, pawing at its eyes. "If you're going to kill me, then do it!"

Scrambling to his feet, he took off at a mad-dash hobble, then a full-on sprint; it felt as if the creature were breathing down his neck, although it wasn't actually there. *Shite! Shite! Shite!* The hot evening air whipped his hair. He kept running. He leaped over concrete and dodged boulders. Carved from brilliant orange clay and sediment, the alien landscape zipped past.

But no sooner had he got away than he skated to a dusty stop, the ground crumbling beneath his boots. He stood at the precipice and nervously looked down. The chasm was so dark the bottom was indistinguishable. He looked behind. The male vampire, moving like a locomotive and dispersing a trail of dirt visible for kilometres around, headed straight for him. It ran on all fours, its snow-white body sleek, wiry and powerful.

Sloan didn't have time to think, and he didn't have the dexterity or speed to fight it. He'd known from the beginning this advanced hybrid was indestructible.

It's the monster. Not me. At least I have a fecking conscience!

The beast sprang, fangs and talons bared. Sloan protected his throat. But it clamped, gnawing greedily, biting off his fingers. He wailed. His flesh tore; fabric at the seams. Bones crunched. He was being eaten alive, and he knew their battle of genetic supremacy would soon be over.

He'd fought the good fight. Some souls had been lost. Amanda and their unborn child, Chase, Tristan, Mona, Petrov, and Raphael. He'd loved them all. But he'd also saved a few: the children, his brother, Warrick, and Elyse. His eyes welled up to the point of blindness. He let go of his throat and spread his arms, blood flying, and leaned backward as far as his spine allowed. And, with a loud cry, he soared off the cliff.

Their bodies entwined, they fell countless metres per second. The air thrashed Sloan's clothes and hair and whistled shrilly in his ears. He grappled the beast, squeezing with all his might.

The vampire writhed madly and growled, chomping and tearing out his throat. He couldn't breathe; the monster ripped out his heart. They continued to plummet. Sloan's eyes were dull as an unpolished stone, and his arms waffled. Then their combined mass struck the canyon floor with meteoric force, and a titanic expulsion of dust and debris shot up, filling the sky in a mushroom cloud.

All was quiet, and the world was at peace, as the beast and the Irishman lay beside one another.

TWENTY

VALE

Quilted in ruddy soil, an albino man watched with fascination as the Irishman's heart rapidly restructured. Muscle and fat, arteries, blood vessels, all organic tissue became whole once again as his bones then chest cavity, closed in.

The man clutched a squirming wasteland rabbit above Sloan's cracked, bleached lips. He slit its throat with a single swipe of his claw. Scarlet droplets fell and spattered Sloan's mouth and chin. One drop hit the back of his throat and slid down his esophagus.

The blood sent electrical shockwaves through Sloan's body. The first wave blasted his heart, which started to thump. The second awakened his brain, and the third blasted the interior of his eyelids with blinding light.

Disjointed thoughts—memories—surfaced: people and places, a rampage of emotions, and everything faded to white. He was floating in the middle of a void, weightless and free. The only other colour was red—the red thread.

He turned his left-hand palm side up, and instead of his pinky, his ring finger was bound in red thread. The thread, as it had so many times before, flowed from his finger into the distance, where the ethereal image of a person gradually materialized. The thread tightened, and tugged the person closer: a faceless woman floating and unconscious, in front of him.

He sensed she was important and something else, although he couldn't pinpoint it. Sloan frowned. She seemed familiar, but the name was lost to him. He touched her grey tinted cheek, caressing it with the back of his fingers. But there was something wicked behind the woman. An expanding, ominous presence and a pair of owl-like mustard-yellow eyes. Suddenly, the vampire charged, streaking the white with blood and driving its giant claws through her chest.

Don't touch her!

Sloan woke flailing in the warm night air to the clink of chains. The sky was the blackest fabric he'd ever seen, and the moon was a flawless orb of pure platinum. Feeling disoriented, he gasped lifting his arms; his wrists were shackled to heavy leads of chain. Cheeks wet, he sniffed, looking all around. He was half-naked, lying on a concrete slab like some sacrificial lamb in an ancient wrecking yard. Surrounded by mounds of rusted, decaying vehicles, appliances, androids, robots, computers, and a high, razor-wired fence. He had no inkling as to how he got there. His last recollection was falling over the cliff.

"Rebirth is painful."

Startled, Sloan turned his head on an angle. Seated on the roof of a broken-down crane was a lanky, albeit, thewy albino with tinsel-white hair to his shoulders and gold ingots for eyes. The man was nude, hugging his right knee whilst swinging his other leg.

"That is the price of immortality."

What the feck is going on? He looked at the strange man once again and this time, the pieces were slowly coming together. "You're the creature that attacked me."

"I am." Still hugging his knee, the man gazed at Sloan with curiosity.

"Do you have a name?"

"Just my name, or do you want my species too?"

"Both, then," he demanded, glancing around, trying to upright himself. "Where the hell am I?"

"My name's Vale—that's what the scientists' called me—and I'm a hybrid-human similar to you. This is a metals recycling yard."

"How did I survive?"

"I ingested your heart, and that's when the transformation occurred."

"Transformation?" Sloan frowned, giving the cumbersome chains a harder yank. They must have come from the crane, where they'd been used to hoist vehicles and androids. Both were impossible to lift with human strength alone.

"I was about to remove your head, but everything changed... And we landed on the earth together." Vale rambled on with childlike enthusiasm. "Then I was alive, but different…reborn. My thoughts became intelligible, connected. I have a purpose now. I feel human…somewhat. You did that for me."

"Great. I'm happy for you." Sloan could feel his temper intensifying. "Get me out of these."

"After what I've done, I fear you may kill me." Vale continued to hug his knee. "That's why you're bound."

"I'm going to kill you regardless, if you don't fecking take these off me!" Sloan exerted his strength, his arms pulling and vibrating, gradually stretching the globular metal links.

"Before you free yourself, listen to me."

Sloan fell flat on the slab, arms spread, and hands curled into fists. He sighed and examined the starry sky with disinterest. "Fine. Talk."

"There's something in your DNA… Your parasite shared with me, and that's why my mind is clear, and I can now understand and… explain in words. My emotions have returned to me. I am no longer the beast I was." Vale got up and gracefully hopped down from the backhoe, approaching the temporary altar. He pressed his hands on the slab, leaned over Sloan and studied his dark pumpkin gaze. "There are others like me: dangerous creatures with no thought other than to kill. But you can stop them."

Sloan closed his eyes, the defiance in him rising. "You've got a lot of nerve to ask for anything. You killed Petrov and the children—Tristan too!"

"I don't expect forgiveness…and I won't ask for it. But if you help the others as you did me, I'll make you a promise you won't be able to ignore."

"Feck off!" His mouth quivered with sorrow and tears crawled down the sides of his face.

"Whenever you need me, for whatever purpose, I'll come." Vale paused for a good minute, then said squarely, "You're wrong. I didn't kill Petrov or the children… it's the females who hunt. Tristan…your son…was my mistake."

"Right. And how do you know that?"

"One female has a deformed arm…and is missing part of her face. She had returned from a kill maimed."

"Then you can't regenerate."

"Not very well. But now I can, thanks to you."

"My parasite knew I had to survive," Sloan growled with resentment. "It spared you, so you'd save me. But considering the source of your initial genetic modification, our parasites are in all probability distant relations."

"Morgan."

Sloan stared at the strange man with consternation. "How did you—"

"Once I ingested your flesh, I received your memories. You can call it blood linking. You killed him. He's the person who created the secret lab… and me." Vale closed his eyes against the warm breeze and smiled as if he enjoyed it. "I was one of the first test subjects."

The guy's carefree, juvenile attitude was really beginning to rub Sloan the wrong way. As far as he was concerned, this creature had killed his loved ones in cold blood. So, they weren't friends. He considered them sworn enemies. He glowered, tugging on the chains again. "On second thought—I don't give a feck who you are. And you can stop chatting like we're old pals and you know everything about me, because you *know nothing*! Once I'm free, you're fecking dead, arsehole!"

Vale observed with attentive enthralment as he struggled. "You killed my children. My first-born outside the lab. After, I tried to keep a truce by eating the deer...but your colonel didn't care. Then you killed the rest of my children. They were just babies. All of them."

Shite. Great. Sloan turned his face to the side, jaw clenched. He'd suspected as much. "What do you want me to say? Huh? I was general of the Avalon Police Force. My men had been killed. I did what was expected of me. His brows furrowed. "There was a threat, and I wiped it out," he barked. "You would've done the same thing if you'd been in my position!"

"Then we are, how do you say? Even."

Dropping his head back, Sloan was quiet for an extended period. He didn't have an answer. They'd both slain others in the name of survival. *Maybe we're both animals*? "We're not even." He looked at the sickly-pale vampire again. "Killing each other's family and friends doesn't make any of it *okay*."

"We could fight to the death, or… you could help me. The choice is yours, *Irishman*."

"Fine. Get it over with," he said in an acquiescent tone.

Vale loudly clicked with his tongue, an odd, high-pitched sound that reverberated across the wrecking yard and outlying desert. The females jumped the chain-link fence from three sides.

"Ah, feck," Sloan muttered, as they encroached.

Sinking their razor-sharp incisors into his flesh, they ravished and consumed him. Sloan groaned, coughing up blood. *It hurts...* Eyes watering, he clenched making fists, fighting the pain, tugging with all his strength against the shackles.

"Enough." Vale gave the order, but blinded by bloodlust, the females kept feeding. "Enough!"

When he repeated it a third time and they still didn't listen, he brutally attacked. Grappling one after the other, he flung them away. Drenched in their thirst, the females snarled, glaring with rebuke, slowly retreating. He looked at Sloan, amazed at how quickly his flesh healed. "I will release you."

Sloan closed his eyes and lay still as Vale removed the weighty shackles and chains one by one. "Whenever I need you, and for whatever purpose, you'll come?"

Vale dumped the shackles in the ruddy dirt. "Yes."

***

Wade couldn't stop staring at the unusual man seated in the centre of his clinic, his pigment chalky and eyes as gold as sunflowers in a summer garden. He looked like a vampire out of a Victorian horror novel. "Can you explain one more time?" said Wade distractedly.

While Sloan reiterated his side of the story, Wade switched his attention back to Vale, who was examining his new clothes. He still couldn't get over the fact that he was looking at the vampire who, in the CCTV footage, had broken out of the glass-clad polycarbonate chamber and scaled the laboratory walls. He wondered about Vale's identity prior to the experiment. The vampire seemed clever, but he had an immature side Wade found puzzling. "Out of curiosity, how old are you, Vale?"

Sloan stopped talking.

Vale dissected Wade with his unnerving gold gaze in silence.

"Do you remember anything from the time before you consumed Sloan?"

"I remember it all."

"But not your age?"

Sloan remained observant, with his arms bent over his chest.

"I was fourteen when scavengers captured me and sold me to Morgan."

Both Sloan and Wade looked at each other, stunned.

"Fourteen?" Wade doubted his claim, but then nobody knew for certain what all Morgan had done, and to whom, or for how long.

"I hope everyone's hungry." Lucy set a platter of sandwiches on the steel table.

"Oh, thanks, doll." Sloan grinned appreciatively and took a cheese and an egg salad one.

"Thanks, pet." Wade picked a lettuce, cucumber, and tomato sandwich. Usually, tomatoes didn't agree with him, but he was willing to brave the acid reflux for his lover's sake.

"I've got tea too," Lucy said. "I'll be right back."

"Is that all you ever eat, Irish?" Wade griped, gesturing to the sandwich.

Sloan held the plate out to Vale, who took one of each. "I happen to love eggs." He set the platter back on the steel table.

"If it isn't whiskey, it's egg salad sandwiches, and if it isn't egg salad, it's fecking spearmint gum. Don't you own an imagination?"

"Are you looking for a fecking fight, arsehole? I eat all sorts of things, but this just happens to be my favourite. Okay?"

Vale bit into his vegetable sandwich while the men argued. He wasn't certain whether their heated words were sarcastic or a prelude to a confrontation, but he remained intrigued no less and munched in captivated silence. He bet the Irishman would win hands down, but the man who ran the clinic didn't look like a pushover. Vale knew Sloan had shared his parasite with Wade—an act of kindness that he couldn't fathom.

"Don't pay any attention to him. He's just full of hot air." Sloan finished his sandwich and brushed the crumbs from his lap. "If you don't mind, I want to go over a few things."

Vale nodded, taking a bite from one sandwich, then the other, swapping back and forth.

"If you were fourteen at the time, that would make you around thirty now. Right?"

"I suppose...as a human."

"Okay. Feel free to correct me at any time if I'm wrong."

Vale nodded, munching.

"Scavengers killed your parents and took you and your siblings' hostage. Then they sold you to Morgan. After that, I assume Morgan locked the four of you inside his secret laboratory outside District C."

"He did." Vale dropped his head slightly, holding the half-eaten sandwiches, one in each hand in his lap, his expression grave. "There were no windows... no daylight... I lost track of time."

Lucy entered the room with a tray of steaming mugs, and Wade gestured for her to be extra quiet. She carefully placed mugs by him and Sloan and set the last on the table in front of Vale, then she snuck away with the tray.

"He separated us, and my sisters got scared. They screamed and cried... I couldn't do anything because they'd locked me in the first chamber alone. I yelled at Morgan as loud as I could, banging my fists on the glass, but it did nothing. He just smiled. I was powerless." Vale continued to hang his head. "They gave us each an injection, but no matter what it did to me physically, I tried to keep my mind. But it was difficult. It was like... someone had draped a dark fog over my brain. I had only brief moments of clarity. The scientists were pleased with the results. They said I was a masterpiece of genetic splicing."

Although he felt uncomfortable sharing such information, Vale tried to set the depression and anxiety aside. They needed to hear the truth, and he needed to tell someone the brutality he'd suffered. He took a deep calming breath, then explained about the incubation tubes and how Morgan wanted his sisters to procreate. They attempted artificial insemination until his sisters were physically mature—then Morgan forced him to couple with his sisters by locking them in the same chamber together. Driven by rage and an animalistic urge, he did impregnate them. However, every attempt failed, and the same repeated for years. All the vampire babies were stillborn until the alpha female, his oldest sister, finally gave birth to a healthy mutant vampire.

The mutant grew rapidly and became too difficult to handle, attacking a scientist. Morgan disposed of the MV, and that's when Vale lost his temper and broke out of his chamber, killing every person in the laboratory. Morgan tried to stop him but realized he was no match, and he abandoned the facility. Vale remained at the facility, using the building as a nest, where his sisters gave birth to several hundred MVs. In time, he and the females moved on to roam the wilds, leaving their children behind. Ultimately, the MVs had children of their own.

"Eventually, my children had run-ins with the Independents, and they were killed," Vale said. "Then my sisters and I killed your friends and family in retaliation."

"Wait a minute." Sloan tapped his hands together, making a "time out" gesture like a referee. "Repeat what you said to me in the wrecking yard."

"Is it necessary?"

"Very."

Vale sighed. "The females, my sisters, killed your friend and the children on the island...but your son was killed by me."

"What about Doctor Raphael and Krista?"

"Krista?" Vale said with inquisitiveness, then he sported a gentle smile. "Ah, now I understand. The genetic engineer named my granddaughter... How nice."

"Who killed them?"

Vale was silent for a period, and Sloan knew he was rummaging through his memories at a snail's pace, as if accessing an ancient computer hard drive.

"Perhaps he doesn't know?" Wade offered.

"Be quiet," Vale snapped. "I have much to recall and analyze."

Wade frowned, resting his forearms on the steel table.

At long last, Vale's expression sank to disconcertedly confused. "It is...impossible," he murmured.

"What's impossible?" Perched on his usual stool, Sloan rolled over to him.

"I am the younger brother. My three sisters are the youngest. When we were captured in the northern wilds, Morgan ordered his men to kill my brother and my parents. We heard gunshots, and I assumed he died with my parents." Vale paused. "Wait... There was only my mom and dad."

"Are you trying to tell me, there's another male hybrid like you running around?"

Vale blinked, his expression sombre as usual. "He was many years older…in his mid-twenties. He was much bigger and more powerful than me. As I said, I was just a child at the time…fourteen."

"Shite. The *ideal* test subject." Now Sloan knew the truth. There was a much more heinous threat, and after what Raphael said the night she died, he believed Vale's older brother was the key. "Is there any way you can tell if he's still alive? And where he might be?"

"I don't have telepathy, Sloan."

"What about the blood linking?"

"I'd need to ingest some of his blood."

"Ah, shite!" Sloan pushed his chair and spun away from Vale, scratching his head in frustration. "This is so fecking annoying."

"Maybe we'll have to go back to basics," Wade said. "Start hunting."

"Take me to the cottage." Vale looked at Sloan. "Show me where they died."

295

Sloan stared at him absolutely spellbound for a moment; Vale had just read his memories; the blood linking was amazing. "You've got a deal."

TWENTY-ONE
DATA OVERLOAD

Vale wandered around the cottage, scrutinizing the unfamiliar surroundings and logging to memory, lightly dragging his fingertips over every surface. Each item he touched vibrated with life, sending information to his ultra-sensitive second sight. But, unlike that of a human seer, his clairvoyance wasn't restricted to future events. With the information he collected, he built images in his mind from both the past and present to the future. Blood linking wasn't his only psychic ability. He could link with any object, especially if it had survived a traumatic event. Every living thing, and even an inanimate object, held memories. "I desire a lover," he said in passing.

Sloan cringed, watching the tall, lithe albino. "That was unexpected."

"What was? The fact I need a lover or that I mentioned it?"

"Both, man. Shite. Some things are too personal to share."

"But you are the only person I can talk to. My sisters, although awakened like me, seem to hate it when I talk about other females."

"That's called jealousy."

"Do you think so?" Vale's expression was that of earnest perplexity. "When we were animals...I only impregnated them because I didn't know any better, and I felt a need to recreate my genetics. I can't possibly have sex with them now."

"I appreciate your frankness, Vale. But talking about the incestuous relationship you shared with your sisters makes me feel a tad uncomfortable." Sloan held his index finger and thumb a millimetre apart. "If you want a *lover*, do what everyone else does and go find one, and tell your sisters to do the same. Perhaps it would do you all good—help you adjust to your new lives."

"Maybe you're right." Vale stood in the middle of the cottage. The stained living room floorboards had caught his attention. *So much blood.* He got down on his hands and knees and sniffed, then licked. His toxic saliva moistened the dried blood enough that he was able to see Raphael's memories. "Fascinating," he mumbled, rising to his feet.

"What is?" Sloan said.

"Doctor Avolare was extremely intelligent." His eyes glazed over as the genetic engineer's entire life played like a first-person shooter game in his mind, snippets of a passionate person who truly cared about her work. Years were gone in a blink.

Suddenly, he was injecting Sloan. Time moved ahead; they were at the secret lab. More time, and he was back in the cottage, where he saw Krista, Petrov, and Sloan. Petrov was killed. More people vanished, and events flew by, and he was about to have sex with Sloan. Each memory evoked an intense emotional response.

Next, he was standing in the living room, shouting for Krista to come back as the little vampire rushed outside.

Vale's pulse rose, and he unconsciously backed away. With each thud against the front doors, the entire cottage shook down to the foundation. The creature burst through the wood, swiping wildly at the air. He stared, screaming, as it finally broke inside the house. But that's where his consciousness split from Raphael's and the fragmented 3D holographic image jammed and flickered like broken film, particles hanging semi-motionless in the air. Vale slowly walked around the enormous horned creature, with eyes that burned like dying stars, when he happened to see blood on the busted interior door. Not a lot, but certainly enough.

He touched the blood, got close and licked it as he had Raphael's. However, this time, the memories locked inside were far from nostalgic. His heart raced with flashes of disturbing images. The first was his parents' murders. His brother had lived years and years as a mindless doll, masked by darkness, tormented, and filled with raw energy, feeding on animals and people alike. There were images he couldn't unsee, and he wished he could shut off his mind and sever the connection. But the frightening abyss sucked him deeper in.

He knew that if he remained inside his brother's mind much longer, the experience would haunt him for the rest of his life every time he closed his eyes.

"Hey," Sloan barked, giving him a firm rattle. "Hey, snap out of it! Vale!"

Vale panted as the Irishman bled through his eyelashes. He lay pinned down on the sofa, but he was grateful to be back in the land of the living. "I'm fine now."

"Are you sure?" Sloan gradually released his arms. "You were screaming and freaking out pretty bad. I had to hold you down."

"I'll be fine." He nodded with a damp forehead, still a bit shaken from what he'd seen—not that he'd tell Sloan. He felt that, for the time being, he'd keep his fears to himself.

They departed from the cottage in silence, and Vale wandered ahead, swishing through the pretty wildflowers. Birds were chirping. The meadow was alive.

"I take it the second link was your brother," said Sloan.

"His brain is muddled, and the things he's done are horrid." He glanced back. "He's no longer in this area, but he *is* somewhere on the island."

"You're certain?" Sloan followed him, and said with blatant sarcasm, "I mean, we've only been here for like two seconds."

Vale squinted, observing the idyllic cottage and meadow from under the shade of his hand. Initially, it had seemed such an odd place for his brother to attack. But now he knew the reason. "My brother attacked Raphael and Krista because he smelled your scent. Vampires are territorial. No male vampire will tolerate another male, especially an alpha, wandering around his domain. I suspect that's why he allowed my sisters to live. They are female, so they posed no threat. But you did."

Sloan frowned and grabbed his arm. "Are you saying they died because of me?"

"He watched the cottage for several weeks prior to killing Doctor Avolare. But that was his normal routine. He'd always known she was living here, and he'd left her in peace. Then two trigger events happened. You fought my sister, a female, and nearly killed her. Then, at a later date, you had sex with Raphael, essentially marking her as your own. He viewed both incidents as territorial threats."

Instantly pissed, Sloan snapped, "You're serious. You blame me!"

"I'm not blaming you. There's no way you could've known. But you wanted answers, and now I've given them. In his mind, you are a threat, Sloan."

"Well, just so we're clear," Sloan pointed at his face, "she asked me to make love to her—not the other way around!"

"Be as angry as you want, but it doesn't change the facts."

Sloan glared at the albino, wishing they'd never met, wishing he could go back in time and kill Morgan long before anything had ever happened. The whole shitty chain of events hurt so much he wanted to run away and cry. Deep down, he'd suspected he'd brought on their deaths. But what could he do? The revenge that had encapsulated his heart with an unbreakable black barrier wouldn't allow it. That need for vengeance kept him grounded, focused, and at a safe emotional distance from everyone. "Fine. Then we've got to flush him out." He started to walk back to Fraochán Village.

"How much longer will you hate me?"

Sloan stopped and stood metres away from the albino and glanced coolly at him. "What the feck are you talking about?"

"I've apologized a hundred times, but you still despise my very existence." Vale frowned. "Are we not the same by no fault of our own?"

"We're nothing alike," Sloan retorted. Then he realized what he'd said was atrocious. He sighed, giving his head a rub. "Look, Vale—"

"It is your animosity that troubles me the most. You may have accepted your injection, but I did not accept mine." Vale strode past him. "I'm not asking to be your best friend… but I'd appreciate a little civility. It's *my* brother we're hunting. How do you think I feel?" He reached the end of the meadow and squeezed his chest between the wrought-iron entrance gates to the property. "If my being here is too much, my sisters and I will leave."

"Neither of us wanted the life we've been given, and we've both done things we aren't proud of…" Sloan followed him again, but with brisk steps. "You're absolutely right. I've been a rude prick, and I'm sorry."

The Norseman vanished, leaving Sloan alone on the narrow road. He cursed a blue streak, throwing his fist in the air. He really didn't mean to be such a cantankerous bastard, but lately he was finding it increasingly harder to cope with his own emotions.

Partner. Vale couldn't get the idea of finding a lover off his mind. *I'd like a partner. Everyone Sloan knows has a partner.* He drifted farther from the village to a good lookout spot. As promised, while they were on the island, he and his sisters would help keep watch over the people until they could locate his older brother.

Warrick tramped the lush grass, exiting the forest trail onto the main road. "I heard you dumped Ryouichi."

"Who told you? No, wait. Let me guess. Uncle Vince?" Elyse sneered.

"Masaki told me. He and Ryouichi are good friends. I thought it was love?"

"Love, my arse. I was just one of many women."

Warrick glanced at her. "Sorry to hear that, sis. If you want, I can have him roughed up."

"Who is *that*?" Elyse clutched her brother's arm and pointed to the lush rolling hummocks behind the village centre on the west side.

"Uh, that's Vale." Warrick grimaced.

"Vale?" She looked at her brother. "Who's Vale?"

"He's the hybrid-vampire that killed Tris."

"No way. Why's he here? Aren't we in danger?" She nervously studied the hummocks again, rushing to keep pace with Warrick, who could cross a football field in a few strides.

"It's fine. Not that I care for the idea, but…he's agreed to help watch over the village, while searching the island for the last mutant vampire."

"I don't understand."

"Neither do I, honestly." Warrick neared the garden gate. "But apparently, after he attacked Dad, he ingested some of Dad's blood. Somehow the parasite awakened his conscience—made him human again."

"That means he's one of those awful experiments from that lab Morgan ran."

Warrick nodded. "Dad told me Vale made a deal with him: he'd protect the island in penance for what he did. He didn't kill Petrov or the kids—that was one of the females."

"I remember. Dad mentioned there were multiple hybrids." Nervous, she kept glancing behind herself to see if they were being watched.

Warrick trod the flagstones in the front garden to the stoop. He banged the knocker on the cobalt-blue door, and his father answered. The cottage was already full of people. And by the sounds of things, the actual conversation—and the reason he and his sister had come—hadn't been addressed yet.

"Come on in, son." Sloan stood aside and Warrick entered the house, removing his jacket.

"Hi, Dad." Elyse gave her father a hug.

"What are you doing here, baby doll?" he asked with astonishment. "I thought you were staying with Ryouichi."

"We're not together anymore, so I thought I'd keep Warrick company."

"Okay." Sloan shut the door. He just knew that something had gone wrong, and he could practically guess what it was, because his fatherly instincts were tingling. However, Elyse was an adult, and it was none of his business unless she decided to tell him. And perhaps it was best he didn't have his assumptions confirmed. "Where are Peaches and Vince?"

"They'll be here any second," Warrick said, draping his jacket over an armchair in the small living room. "They wanted to talk in private while they finished their cigarettes."

Sloan had scarcely moved away from the door when it swung open, nearly bashing him in the face.

Vince gripped the knob. "Hello, *niisan*."

"Hey…"

"Hello, big man." Peaches grinned, brushing the soles of her boots on the welcome mat outside directly behind Vincent. "Sorry we're a bit late. Are Wade and Lucy here? We haven't seen them since disembarking the yacht."

"Yep, they're here. No problem. Take a seat."

Once everyone was settled and quiet, Sloan took his place at the head of the kitchen table. "The reason I asked you all here today is because I've come bearing gifts." He rummaged in a duffel bag near his feet, then placed a loaded vaccination gun in the middle of the embroidered tablecloth. The syringe held a tiny twenty-milligram injection. Benny, Jens, Akira, Rueben, Star and Ingalill stared at the viscous, coppery fluid. "I'm not going to lie to you: it's a risk, and you could die. On the other hand, my parasite knows I love each of you—knows that we've shared a special relationship through the years."

"Which means…?" Benny asked.

"Which means that if you survive, you'll have just won the immortality jackpot."

"In other words, we'll become hybrid-humans like you?" Ingalill said.

"Yes, doll."

"You don't have to decide right this minute," Wade said.

Rueben looked at Wade, and that was when it hit him. "You're one too, aren't you? And him." He nodded toward Vincent, seated in the corner, the silent and antagonistic observer with otherworldly emerald eyes.

Lucy held Wade's hand. "He is."

"Many, many years ago, I became extremely ill," Wade said. "So ill I lost control of my motor functions and couldn't walk for a time. The medical text said I had MS. Sloan offered me survival, and I took it."

"Has anyone else taken an injection?" Star asked.

"Peaches and Tristan." Sloan sat back, folding his arms. "Tristan was dying of cancer. My kids couldn't bear the loss, and neither could I."

"What about him?" Rueben asked.

"My transformation was more or less an act of booze-induced misadventure," Vincent answered point-blank.

"Once Wade survived the injection, I was envious. And since I was drunk, I demanded, 'What about me, *niisan*?' And Sloan actually cut his arm over my drink. Besides, we are brothers. We need each other."

Everyone laughed quietly except Benny, who appeared to be engrossed in deep thought.

"And what about you, Peaches?" Rueben asked.

"Go ahead, tell them." Peaches motioned to Sloan as she lit a cigarette.

"She was a young woman of twenty-three, alone in the world, who sold her body to survive," Sloan said. "One night a john slashed her face and all. She came to me, bleeding to death, and asked to be turned. I cared about her, so I gave her what she desired—my blood to drink. The parasite repaired her body and face."

"Is there anyone else who has willingly accepted your alleged immortality?" Benny stared at Sloan, nursing his glass of wine.

Sloan leaned back, clasping his hands behind his head. "There is one more, yes."

"I-I wanted to live as long as possible…" Everyone looked at Lucy, thunderstruck, and she blushed, searching Wade's smile. "Because he has many years left, and he couldn't bear the thought of losing me." She hugged his arm, glancing at each of them. "This will be the toughest choice of your lives. And if you choose the injection, you will watch those around you die, including your own children, if they turn out to be genetically normal humans."

"Will we live forever?" Rueben asked.

"Not necessarily," Sloan answered. "The parasite is a carbon-based organism, so it only stands to reason that it'll die eventually. Which means when she dies, you might die with her. Raphael stated there's no way to know for certain the parasite's life expectancy, and since you'd be hybrids like me, but copies of the original, you are still flawed to a point. A full-blooded vampire would live indefinitely. But the parasite does guarantee a longer-than-average life span—as well as immunity to disease, rejuvenation from injuries, improved senses, agility, speed, strength, *and* a thirst for blood." He glanced over their faces. "As Lucy said, there's a lot to consider. I didn't come here expecting anything."

"Why are you making the offer? That's what I want to know," Jens said. "You aren't doing this out of the goodness of your heart."

"He's right. We deserve the whole truth," Star added in her low, soft voice.

Sloan sighed, then rocked the chair, his copper eyes sparkling in the subdued daylight. "In the last fifteen years, Avalon has been invaded approximately twenty times, and only one of those adversaries were human. The other nineteen invaders were genetic freaks. The human population is growing, yes, but so are the numbers of genetic freaks—and the freaks are winning. Simply put, someone has to protect this island because I can't always be here. And if, God forbid, I do die, there will be no one. The other Independents are aging, and their genetics can't adapt like mine." He took note of their odd expressions but continued to rock his chair. "I'm not saying you have to do a thing. Honestly, for all my parasite offers, it is both a blessing and a curse."

"Then why are you here?" Benny accused gruffly. "Why even say anything?"

"Because I care, fecking eejit!" Sloan roared, and everyone jumped. He glared at Benny. "I care about you and everyone on this island! This was my fecking home. Hell, I'm related to half the islanders! Why else do you think I'd make such a dicey offer?" The chair dropped, and he leaned over the table, still glaring at Benny. "Don't you get it? We're at fecking war, Benjamin—"

"*Niisan*, calm yourself," Vincent barked, glaring him down.

Sloan shot a perturbed glance at his little brother and rose from the table, flicking the chair back into the wall. The cottage door nearly busted it hit the frame so hard. Vincent exhaled a weary sigh.

"He told us he was related to the villagers, but we did not know it was that many," Rueben said.

Vincent slid his fingertip around the lip of his wineglass, and the partly filled glass released an eerie howl. "After Sloan's grandfather Finn died, Sloan's father Patrick ran this village. Patrick had seven younger brothers and one sister. Patrick's only child was Sloan, but the brothers and sister had many children. And there's his mother's family. Ask around for surnames. Then you'll know."

"I just feel like he's making all the decisions again without telling us the whole truth." Benny frowned, rubbing his hands together. "Just like he did when we first met him. We aren't children. We have a right to know the details."

"Well, now you do." Vincent eyed him with revulsion. "Everything my brother has ever done has been to safeguard his loved ones—even at the price of his own happiness. To be honest, you should be thankful he's such a compassionate man. If it were left to me, I wouldn't care."

They all stared at him, flummoxed, as he set the wineglass on the windowsill to the right of the front door, then put a cigarette to his lips. For a split second, they couldn't believe he was Sloan's brother.

"Why so surprised? I feel no obligation to those who don't benefit me." Vincent blew smoke toward the ceiling. "The only people that matter is my family and a few I consider friends. I can separate charity from necessity." He leaned sideways and tapped ash inside the dead fireplace. "If you accept the injection, it will alter your lives. If you don't, then there's no need to worry."

"Such a typical Vincent Shiro response. When it comes to your brother, you're always selfishly overprotective." Rueben slid his chair back from the table. "I'm tired, and it's late. We have a lot to discuss."

Vincent wore the faintest grin, fiddling with his cigarette as they all rose from the table.

"Good night." Rueben escorted Ingalill out the door first.

Jens departed next, followed closely by Akira, and Benny sauntered after them.

However, Star lingered, and she placed a delicate hand on Vincent's shoulder. "We're grateful for the sacrifices you've both made on our behalf," she whispered near his ear. "But Benny cares too." She let him go and joined Benjamin, who was waiting in the front garden.

Sloan had no interest in forcing anyone to do anything. The choices he'd made in his life were his own. Nonetheless, he still felt apprehensive about the future. Bathed in moonlight, he stood in the middle of the village square. The evening breeze was cool. Every shop was exactly where it had been when he was a child, except for the butcher and baker, who had swapped premises because the butcher required the laneway access.

He thought about the injection. *What am I trying to accomplish? Will it actually protect them? I've struggled with my own identity for decades.* He stared as silver-drenched clouds passed overhead, and he lifted his hand, pretending to touch them. Curling his fingers, he quickly looked back; not six metres away was a hulking, dark humanoid figure with abnormal, noodle-like limbs, stringy shoulder-length hair, a hunched back and mustard eyes. Blackness stained any distinguishing features it might have had, and it seemed to absorb even the moonlight.

"What the..." Sloan swung around, and it dashed left, racing on all fours for the rolling hummocks on the west side of the village. *This is probably a trap.* He delayed only for a second. *Ah, feck it.* He bolted, taking the same direction.

With the deep grass and uneven rise and fall of the land, it proved a challenge to even track the creature, let alone keep up. And eventually, the village became a blip of lights in the far distance, and the creature stopped running. They were in a clearing. Panting, Sloan briefly scanned the forest, half expecting to find more of these misty creatures. But when nothing happened, he got closer to it. He still couldn't detect any physical outline. Hovering, it blinked.

"Fine. I'll play." Sloan lunged, throwing a punch, but his fist went through it. Confused, he jerked backward and examined his hand. "Let me guess... You're a figment of my imagination." He attacked a second time, and the creature dissolved in the air. He spun around, searching wildly. "What the fecking hell?" his frustration echoing throughout the clearing.

Elyse snuck outside through the back door, closed it, and sat on the worn slats of the rear porch. The injection dilemma didn't mean much to her. She already carried her father's genetics, and she appreciated what he'd given her. Facing the rear gardens, outbuildings, and forest, she tipped a glass of white wine to her lips.

"You have beautiful eyes."

She choked, spilling wine on her chest, and it dribbled down her chin. There was a strange man, the same strange man she'd seen on the village outskirts, staring at her from the fence line. He appeared now as a white spectre cloaked in moonlight. She quickly looked away, smearing her wet chin. Her cheeks were on fire, and her heart was banging. His expressionless gaze made her feel uneasy, like he was molesting her with his eyes. "Th-thanks I guess," she murmured, wiping her mouth. "So do you."

"Thank you." He placed his hands on the fence. "You are Sloan's offspring."

"That's right. And you're Vale?"

"I am." He gripped the top rung, leaped like a gazelle over the fence and strode toward her with determination.

Nervous, she leaned way back, clutching the glass, as he got too close and judiciously examined her entire face. "What do you want?" she squinted, recoiling.

He brought a curl of her soft hair to his nose and sniffed, then he gazed entranced at her thick, dark, pouty lips.

"*Please...*" Her lower lip quivered under his finger. "Don't hurt me..."

He immediately frowned with remorse and retreated. "Forgive me."

Elyse literally blinked, and he was gone. She exhaled with relief, then covered her mouth and broke down in tears, dropping the glass. Wine sloshed on the patio to drip between the slats. But once the initial shock wore off, the memory of his inscrutable countenance finally registered. She cupped her face and giggled like a fool. "Oh, my," she muttered. "He's attracted to me."

By morning, Vince, Wade and Lucy were on the yacht. Wade had left the locked metal container of injections and vaccination gun inside the cottage fridge just in case someone wanted to taste the Irishman's immortality.

"I'll return no later than tomorrow, *niisan*." Vince spun the steering wheel, and the yacht moved away from the island, cutting into the waves. "Don't do anything foolish!"

"Yep. Bye!" Sloan waved from the shoreline. "Get the feck out of here."

TWENTY-TWO
DADDY'S LITTLE GIRL

A MONTH LATER

The sun beat down, and the sound of rushing water was all around; the river was low but still swift flowing. Vale moved Elyse's hair and kissed her bare shoulder as they sat together in the grass near the riverbank. She shyly glanced back with a sweet smile, touching his cheek. He grasped her fingers, leaned in, and whispered, "I love you," in her ear.

Her complexion flushed to a bashful hot. "I love you too."

He watched her button her shirt, her large breasts disappearing under the airy floral fabric. Not seconds ago, she'd been lying in the grass, crying out with intense pleasure, her chin tilted skyward, and her nails raking his lower back. He'd never experienced such wanton gratification. But he also cared deeply for her. Now he understood the true meaning of love and knew why he couldn't live without her. She'd satiated his emotions and strengthened his mental wellbeing; she made him feel complete. As Sloan had stated, her affection had changed him, and he was unequivocally devoted to her.

White cotton clouds passed overhead, and the sunlit foliage swished in the breeze. It was an exceptionally beautiful day. Peaches heard splashing and a woman's laughter. She took a cautionary step, her boot crushing the dried leaves. She peered around, drawing her Magnum, and slunk through the undergrowth using the noise as her guide. Then, in shock, she lowered the gun. Elyse was at the river's edge, but that wasn't the problem. She was with a man, and the man looked directly at her.

Peaches scowled and quickly backed out of sight. "Shit." She drove the side of her fist into a tree. "This isn't good. *Really* not good."

"Don't tell him."

Peaches nearly jumped out of her own skin, and she aimed the Magnum at Vale. "Don't you ever sneak up on me like that. *Never ever!*"

"You snuck up on us."

"Are you a friggin' idiot?" Peaches glared, shaking from her boots up. "Do you wanna die?"

"Vale, where are you?" Elyse called from the distance.

Peaches ducked into the bushes, pulling down her hood to conceal her orangey-blonde hair. "You had sex with his daughter. You must have a death wish."

"Although it was sexual attraction at first, my feelings have grown, and I do truly love her now. If Sloan wishes to kill me, he may do so."

"Wow. Either you've got brass balls, or you're just plain stupid. You're supposed to be helping us find your brother and instead, you're shagging the boss's daughter." Overcome, she suddenly dropped to crouch with the pistol between her thighs; she gawked at the leafy ground, trying to come to grips with the situation. "Crap, I feel dizzy." She pressed her fingers in the dirt to stop from falling over. "While we've spent a freakin' month searching, you've been havin' a good old time."

"I will speak to Sloan."

"No, you won't." Peaches glared again, curling her mouth and she stabbed her finger at him. "You're gonna keep your friggin' mouth shut like a good boy and find your monstrous brother."

Vale crouched in front of her, hugging his knees, and they studied each other. "You're scared."

"Yeah, I am, and for good reason. And if you had any sense about you, you would be too."

"Vale, what are you doing?" Elyse gasped at the sight of Peaches, and she dropped to hide behind Vale. Her cheeks a mortified vermilion, and she squeezed her eyes shut. "Why are you here, Leona?" she demanded in a tremulous voice.

"My rounds. When I heard you giggling like a preschooler. If you don't want anyone to see, get a room at the local inn," she snipped, getting up to stand. "And I suggest you impress upon this idiot here that he's walkin' a very fine line."

Holstering the Magnum, Peaches rushed from the area, half running and half speed-walking. The last thing she wanted was to get caught with those two. She'd be bombarded with questions she didn't have the wherewithal to answer. Personally, she didn't give a shit who Elyse took to her bed. She was an adult. But it would matter to her father. Sloan acted like an overbearing tyrant when it came to his precious daughter.

Without even a glance back, Peaches raced through the fluctuation of brilliance and shadowy patches, only to come to an immediate unsteady stop moments later. Sloan was standing just yards away, fiddling with the living atlas. Even with sunlight raining down through the heavy foliage, the atlas glowed an eye-catching neon blue. Peaches swallowed, adjusting her jacket with her reclaimed composure, and sauntered over.

"How was your patrol?" Sloan kept his back to her.

"Good." She tried to sound upbeat; normal. "Whatcha doing?"

"We've tried everything, and we still haven't found Gunnar. I thought maybe this ingenious piece of ancient technology might help." He stared at a large 3D map of the island. "I've asked the atlas to keep track of all the locations we've searched with special markers, but unfortunately that's as far as it goes. It doesn't have heat-signature capabilities. I've requested a drone from the mainland."

"I thought drones only take photos."

"Most do, but there were a few military drones from World War III built with a wide variety of tracking options: heat, scent, biological, chemical. I'm not sure if they still work. Warrick's gone back to retrieve them."

She lit a cigarette. "Anything's worth a shot, I guess. Maybe he's escaped to the mainland?"

"That's doubtful. Vale claims he's still on the island."

"Are you sure he can read his brother's memories?"

"Yep. He proved it when we checked those caves. Someone had definitely been living there." Sloan angled the map. "The place was stockpiled with bones, and unfortunately not just animal."

"True. But doesn't that mean Gunnar can read his?"

"Gunnar would have to have the same blood linking ability, and in that case, he'd have to drink Vale's blood. They haven't seen one another since their initial imprisonment in the lab, so it's improbable. Besides, I think they received different parasitic injections." He paused and cast her a piercing glance. "Have you seen Elyse?"

The question, although anticipated, still gave her an internal jolt. She thought about Elyse and Vale, but remained calm. "Nope," she replied curtly. "She was in town last I saw her."

Sloan knew her answer was disingenuous, but he wasn't mad, only annoyed. Something was going on with his daughter. Despite tending the cottage and gardens, she always took off for extended periods during midday, when he was conveniently preoccupied. He wondered if he'd upset her. But they hadn't argued or even spoken much, and she was always in a cheerful enough mood when he got home at night.

"Well, if you don't need me, big man, I'm gonna head into town for a bite to eat." Peaches ground the smouldering cigarette butt under her boot heel. "I can't resist the baker's meat pies."

"Sure." He watched her walk away. Then he peered back to where his old friend had come from. *Something is definitely going on.*

***

Elyse cupped her mouth, her eyes wide, and she heaved into the flowerbed. Her body was telling her that her life was about to change, and not necessarily for the better. She tensely rubbed her abdomen, burst into tears, and pressed the back of her hand to her wet lips. She loved Vale, but she couldn't bring herself to tell her father. Getting up off her knees, she brushed her pant legs and went inside the cottage. She gently pressed the door shut, this time, with tears sliding down her face, and dashed to the bathroom.

It was an hour later when she re-emerged, feeling a lot better and emotionally stronger. She hung her bath towel to dry on the bathroom heating rack. She couldn't stop thinking about her father and Vale. She was up to her neck in hot water, and there really was no telling how her father would react.

She got dressed, exited the cottage through the front door, and walked to Canary Cottage via the back laneway. Despite the lurking danger, the village was bustling with activity as vendors and shoppers engaged with each other.

But it was the children who caught her eye as they ran around. They were high-spirited, so jovial, and their laughter abundant.

"Hello, Elyse!" Ingalill waved with a big smile from the garden, basket in hand. "Would you like to come in?"

"Oh, sure. I could use the company." Elyse feigned cheerfulness with a forced grin, closing the garden gate. The tall Norse woman was beautiful, like a Norse goddess, with her big blue eyes and white-blonde tresses, and she felt a tiny pang of jealousy; she'd always wanted to be taller.

"You look kind of down." Ingalill left the front door open.

"I'm, ah… I'm in big trouble," Elyse said softly, her eyes brimming with moisture.

Ingalill handed her a glass of iced tea and looked at her with caring sympathy. "Oh, don't cry, love. You're too pretty to be crying. Motherhood is as natural as breathing." She smiled soothingly. "You just have to tell him."

Elyse sniffed, staring. "How did you know?"

"Rueben and I have had three sons." Ingalill sighed, bent forward, and grasped her hand, giving it a reassuring squeeze. "And it's obvious. The fear is in your eyes, and your pasty vacant face. The question is, do you love him?"

"More than any man I've dated." She thought about Vale and a wonderful, amorous warmth filled her chest, a happiness she'd hadn't felt in a very long time. He was always bringing her flowers, and they'd talk for hours, and the intimacy… She blushed, making eye contact with Ingalill.

"Contrary to what everyone else may think, he respects me and treats me like a queen."

"Then you have to explain to your father. Help him understand for your sake and the sake of the baby."

"He'll think the worst. He always does. And if he hurt—" Elyse gulped, springing to her feet. The glass hit the table, spilling the iced mint tea to spread a stain, and Ingalill spun around.

Sloan's frown expressed more than sadness as he turned away from the open front entry.

"Oh crap! I'm so sorry, Elyse. I always leave the door open for air flow."

"It's fine. It's my fault." Elyse rushed out of the cottage into damp sunshine, through the garden gate and onto the dirt laneway. Her father was already a distance away. "Dad! Dad, wait!" she called, but he wouldn't acknowledge her. "I know you can hear me!"

Sloan stopped walking, and she caught up. She grappled his waist from behind. "All I ask is that you listen to what I have to say, before you lose your temper."

He didn't answer, and she pressed her face to his back; his lower spine was smooth, muscular, and slightly concave under his soft cotton T-shirt. Her face wrinkled, and she hugged him tighter, getting anxiously teary-eyed again. "I love you, Dad. And I'm sorry I didn't tell you first… but I was worried and scared. Sometimes you're difficult to talk to. But I really need you right now." She paused. "I'm pregnant."

When he still didn't respond, she released him and edged around to see his face. But who she saw made her light-headed: Vale was metres away, and Sloan was glaring at him. "Dad, *please* don't hurt him," she screamed in a blind panic. "*Please!*"

Sloan let the fury go and abruptly hugged her snugly to his chest as she bawled. "Hey, you've got to calm down. If you get too stressed, you could lose the baby." He sighed, holding her and kissed the top of her head. "I'm not going to hurt anyone." When it came to his daughter, he had the patience of a saint, and he waited until Elyse was quiet. Then he lifted her chin, leaned down and kissed her forehead. "We'll talk at home."

"But, Dad—"

"It's okay, baby doll. Honest. I promise I won't kill him."

She released her father, glanced at Vale with trepidation, and then, with reluctance, headed toward the family cottage.

Sloan waited until his daughter was well out of earshot. Then he went off like a bomb. "You just couldn't resist, could you?" he roared, flying at Vale only to stop short until their faces were millimetres apart. "Fecking arsehole. I just *knew* something was wrong! I never should've allowed her to stay here!"

Unflinching, Vale weathered his wrath. "I understand your anger."

"No, I don't think you do. Does she know about Tristan?"

"I explained."

He was rendered speechless; the guy had the biggest balls.

"I told her the truth. She did get upset at first. She is very much like her father when she loses her temper." He cracked a weak smile. "But in time, she forgave me. I did not intend to fall for your daughter, but she caught my eye the moment I saw her. She is genetically perfect and healthy, kind and loving." He looked at Sloan. "I will care for her."

"Shite, this is unbelievable." Sloan clasped the top of his head in exasperation, backing away from him. He couldn't believe what was happening. His only daughter had hooked up with a man who had more baggage than he did. Not to mention the complications that might arise with the pregnancy. A human had never given birth to a vampire. Gestation and birthing would be extremely dangerous for both the mother and child, and then there was the genetics to consider. His daughter could give birth to an abomination. "Now she's pregnant. Do you know what will happen to her?" he demanded with an acrimonious frown. "Do you even care?"

"I'm aware. I have lost children. The chances of a miscarriage are even greater because she's human." Vale stared at him, and a tear trickled down his stoic features.

They were at a stalemate again. No matter how much Sloan wanted to kick the living daylights out of the guy, he just couldn't muster enough resentment to do it. Either he'd become too soft in his old age, or he just didn't give a damn anymore. Nonetheless, he wasn't about to ruin his daughter's happiness. "Go," he muttered, gesturing limply toward the cottage. "Spend as much time as you can with her."

Vale was gone, expelling a tiny gust of wind, a blur of near-translucent movement. Sloan was envious of the man's ability. He looked in the direction of his family cottage and decided he'd take a long walk instead, to give his daughter and Vale space alone. He knew just the place. He backtracked half a dozen metres, glanced about, leaned over a chest-high stone wall, and plucked two large roses from Ingalill's front garden.

The cemetery was on a peaceful ten-acre parcel wreathed in greenery east of the village. He paused just long enough to leave a rose on Chase's grave, and he also took a moment to read the headstone for Petrov. Even without a body, he'd felt that the young Russian deserved to be remembered, and he placed another beautiful orange rose on the slab of sparkly polished granite.

Since he'd brought Vale to the island, no one else had been attacked. Whether it was coincidence or calculation, the insinuation that Gunnar may have recognized his brother and knew Vale was snooping around, bothered him. When he'd fought Vale in his previous form, he had sensed no malice or emotional presence of mind from him, only a natural predisposition. He also suspected the alpha female, akin to her brother and any predatory animal, had acted instinctually. Maybe Vale's hypothesis was correct? Maybe his older brother's actions had been *purely* instinctual. Maybe Gunnar had simply seen him as a territorial threat.

But he hadn't gathered enough intel yet, so his theory was merely speculative. Regardless, leaving the island wasn't an option in the near future. Sooner or later, Gunnar would make his move, and he had to be prepared.

***

Elyse spent the rest of the summer, winter, and spring bed-ridden. When she was too active, she bled, and the unborn child would give her fits, nausea, and cramping. Vale stayed with her day and night, and all the women from the village visited regularly to bring food and to help bathe her and wash her hair. Sloan checked in on her when he could; otherwise, he and the other men were out searching the island. In sunshine, rain, sleet, ice, and snow, they hiked the heavily forested landscape. But they found not a trace of Gunnar. It seemed the mysterious mutant vampire had disappeared.

It was mid spring, and there'd been heavy rainfall. The ground was water laden and everything else dripped in wet. Which meant the mornings were still chilly and there were many swamped by fog.

"Well, I'm stumped." Rueben leaned closer to the fire, briskly warming his hands.

"He's got to be travelling back and forth from the mainland." Benny nursed a bottle of beer on his chest.

Benjamin's cottage, which had lower ceilings and less living space than Rueben's cottage, always felt cramped when there was more than a couple of guests. And now, packed with Sloan's usual crew and men from the village, the old building was ready to burst. But no one seemed to mind. Everyone was drinking and staring at the fire.

"Migration." Sloan gawked as if star struck by the flames. "Vale mentioned he used to migrate with the herds of deer. Perhaps, Gunnar the illusionist, is migrating to the mainland and back."

"Or he could be dead, big man." Peaches downed a swig of beer.

"True." Sloan's eyebrows arched, and he pointed at her with his bottle. "Very true."

They burst with laughter, and the other men laughed too.

"I think we're all a little overtired," Jens said.

"Speaking of tired, I'm ready to pass out." Akira set his bottle in an empty crate beside the coffee table. "Good night."

Everybody mumbled their goodbyes. Jens quickly finished his beer, ditched the bottle, and followed Akira out of the cottage. Soon after the local men also departed for the evening. Which left Rueben, Benny, Sloan, Peaches, and Vincent.

Vincent flicked his cigarette butt into the fire and stretched, arms in the air. He rose and moved his chair to tuck snugly against the kitchen table. "If you don't mind, *niisan*, I'm tired as well."

"Wait. I'm coming with you." Sloan placed his empty bottle inside the crate. "And what about you?" He looked at Peaches, stifling a yawn.

"Star made up a room for me."

"Sounds good, sexpot. Thanks for the drinks, Benny. See you in the morning."

"Sure thing. Nighty-night, old man." Benny waved with a goofy grin.

Sloan smirked, shaking his head, and ducked the lintel to step outside. The knocker clanked as he shut the door. A hint of damp was in the cool air. He walked beside his brother on the road. "He's long gone... at least until the fall."

"The migration thing?"

"Yeah. Fall harvest is the best time to hunt."

"Spring's better for livestock."

"Not livestock, Vince: humans." Sloan pulled out a stick of gum and unwrapped it. "By the end of the summer there's the fall, and I think that's when he'll re-emerge."

"Let's say your hypothesis is correct, *niisan*—"

"Sloan!" Vale was suddenly standing in front of them.

Both Sloan and Vincent nearly had heart attacks. Sloan gulped, and Vincent exhaled a shaky breath, giving the albino the death glare.

"For feck's sake, man! How many times do I have to tell you—don't sneak up on us like that." Sloan pressed his fist to his chest. "Bloody eejit."

"Can I hit him?" Vince frowned.

Vale faintly grinned. "I'm sorry."

Sloan eyed him. *You're not fecking sorry.* "Right. What's wrong?"

"Nothing. Elyse is in labour. I'm excited."

"Well, why didn't you say?" Sloan waved him back toward the cottage. "Move, man!"

The three rushed inside the cottage to find the small house in an uproar. Elyse wailed in agony from the master bedroom while several older midwives from the village were preparing clean towels and boiling hot water in the kitchen.

Sloan shot to the rear of the house, but he didn't go in the room. He lurked just outside the door. Star was holding his daughter's knees and coaxing her to push. He glanced at the ceiling, then turned his head to the side and asked with a slight inflexion of sarcasm, "Is everything all right in there?"

"She's doing just fine," Star said.

"Bullshite I'm doing fine! Whose fecking idea was it that women should give birth? I'm going to die it hurts so bad." Elyse gasped, panting heavily, twisting the sheet in a fist. "Never again!"

"You're not going to die, Elyse," Star soothed in a calm voice. "Pain is a normal part of childbirth. Now, I want you to push."

Elyse strained. "Dad, you can tell that good-for-nothing man of mine he can have the next one!"

"Okay, baby doll." Sloan chuckled quietly, resting his head on the wall. "Whatever you say."

"Argh!"

"Push again—harder."

The other women brushed past Sloan with the water and towels, and that was his cue to leave. He wandered into the living room to find Vince and Vale seated respectively on the sofa and an armchair.

"How is she?" Vale briefly stopped rubbing his hands.

"Good. I think. If there are no complications, the baby should come soon." Sloan flopped into the armchair opposite him, dangling his arms with his head back.

"I want to be with her." He got up.

Sloan lifted his head and looked at the albino with mild interest. He was about to tell Vale to wait, but then he shrugged and put his head back down. "Go for it." He remained poker-faced. "Knock yourself out."

Vale hesitated in confusion, but then dashed to the rear of the cottage. The next thing they heard was Elyse barking with the viciousness of a guard dog.

"That really was an asshole move, *niisan*." Vince sniggered softly.

"Never." He chuckled with unreserved delight. "Vale's a grown man. I remember when Amanda went into labour. She nearly broke my fingers, and for a woman who never swore, she had no problem giving me an earful. However, two years later, she was begging me for one more child." He grinned and then exhaled a contented sigh. The memories were wonderful, and he missed his wife something fierce. "She said Elyse needed at least one sibling. She didn't want our daughter to grow up spoiled. Didn't matter, though. I spoiled her rotten any—"

A baby's cries filled the cottage. The brothers sat up and twisted around toward the rear of the house. Then both men looked at one another.

"Congratulation, *niisan*." Vince reclined again, wearing a huge smile. "You are an official *sofu*."

"Thanks. Now I do feel my age."

TWENTY-THREE

THE LAST BOSS

"Do you want to hold him, Dad?"

"Sure."

Elyse placed her son in his arms. "He's so little."

"That he is." Sloan gently cradled the tiny bundle against his chest, and smiled with affection. "Not every infant is born a *sumo* wrestler like your brother. He looks healthy, though."

"Star said the same thing, and she's delivered something like a hundred babies. Did you know that?" She sat on the sofa, tucking her legs in under her robe. The cottage was cozy warm with a fire lit. "The local seamstress mentioned there's been a significant population boom in the last decade."

The baby was considerably more alert and responsive than a normal human infant would be. He looked at Sloan with bright sapphire gems ringed in gold, the rich blue exactly like his mother but enhanced by his father.

"Yeah, that sounds about right." He chuckled, stroking his soft white-blond hair.

"Vale didn't know what to name him, so he left the choice to me. Last night I looked at that ancient baby-name book you and Mom used for us."

"Uh-huh, and what did you decide?"

"I really like Valerian. It means strong, healthy, and powerful." She yawned, resting her arms and head on the broad comfy armrest, watching her father kiss and cuddle her son. "I wanted him to have a memorable name. What do you think?"

"I think whatever you've chosen is just fine, baby doll." He fondly studied the tiny boy with wisps of fine hair and ashen flesh, gently rubbing his chubby jowls. "Well, Valerian, I'm your *seanathair*. Try to say that fast five times in a row." The infant flailed his fists stiffly with a lopsided smile, and Sloan laughed, shaking them both. "Don't worry. *Grandfather* is fine too."

The front door opened, circulating a cool draft throughout the house. Vale, Vincent, Peaches, and Warrick entered the main living area, out of breath and displaying different levels of anxiety via their facial expressions and body language.

"Dad, we found him," Warrick announced.

"Okay." Sloan slid forward in the chair and kissed the baby's forehead before placing him in his mother's arms.

Elyse stared nervously at Vale. But, as usual, he remained solemn. She watched her father tighten the buckles on his boots, don his old aviator bomber jacket and sling the Irish longsword over his back. "Please be careful, Dad."

"Shouldn't you be telling Vale that?"

"He already knows how I feel."

"We have to hurry, *niisan*."

"Right." He touched his daughter's shoulder. "Don't leave this house."

"I won't."

"Don't worry, big man. Ingalill and Star will be here shortly to keep her company," Peaches flicked her cigarette into the roaring fire. "We made sure to ask them."

"Excellent." Sloan ushered the men and Peaches out of the cottage and shut the door with a rattling clunk of the knocker. "Where is the bastard?"

"The north end of the island," Vale replied, striding ahead of the others.

Sloan's breath misted; there was still a spring chill in the damp air. The seasons were overlapping, and he wondered if summer would ever come. There were years where the weather made no sense. Thankfully, though, such incidents were becoming fewer and farther between as time went on.

A large group of armed men, the same bunch who assisted with patrols, was waiting in the village square with Benny at the helm. He and his strapping nephews, Rueben's two eldest sons, wore camo. Sloan wished they'd taken him up on his offer of immortality. Then he'd feel better when they were in the thick of it. The parasite would at the very least waylay their death. But it seemed the brothers were still undecided.

"The north end is two full days on foot," Benny said, "and that's with non-stop hiking. By the time we get there, everyone will be exhausted, and the vamp might move on. Does anyone have any suggestions?"

"We could go on horseback," Rueben said. "Most of the terrain is fairly flat."

"Horses are a priceless commodity. The villages can't function without them. I don't know if that's a good idea."

As they talked, the men congregated listening attentively.

Sloan gently pulled Vale aside. "Where are your sisters?" he whispered.

"They're waiting in the field east of the village."

"Are they willing to help?"

"Yes."

"Okay. Good." Sloan patted his shoulder, then more or less forced his way into the centre of the group. "I have a proposition…"

Everyone looked at him.

"Vale, his sisters, and I will go on ahead. That way you'll have a chance to get ready. We're faster and stronger, and we'll get there in no time."

"Whoa, wait a minute," Warrick interjected, searching his father's vibrant copper eyes. "You can't just take off on your own. Vale said, even he can't beat his brother."

"Warrick's correct, Sloan. There's strength in numbers, and we need all the numbers we can get." Rueben nudged his brother. "Tell him."

Calm as could be, Benny folded his bulky arms over his chest and looked at the Irishman for a while before exhaling a lengthy, grave sigh. "If the old man wants to go on ahead, we should let him. After all, he's the veteran."

"Thanks a lot," Warrick sneered, slicing the air with his arms. "Just because he's not your father!"

Rueben jumped to his brother's defence. "He didn't mean it that way."

Benny shifted his gaze to Warrick, and he said staidly, "No, he isn't, but he is my friend, and I trust his judgment. Whatever you want, Sloan, it's fine by me."

"Thanks, Benjamin."

"Dad, this is wrong. You need backup. I can get the other Independents."

"They've already got their hands full protecting the city in your absence. Which is where you should be, son. I'll have Vale and his sisters with me," Sloan said, studying the general's nervous expression. "We're the immortals."

As arranged, Sloan, Vale and Vale's younger siblings left that night before the rest. While the others were home, packing supplies, eating, and saying goodbye to their loved ones, Sloan was crossing the open, rolling grasslands and stony cliffs along the eastern shore.

"If you ask, I will fight him." Vale trudged beside him.

"My daughter loves you, and that means mistakes are a luxury we can't afford." Sloan kept a close eye on his sisters, who darted onward in the foreground. "You have to return to her in one piece, and I'm going to do everything possible to make certain you do. We have to work together, Vale."

"Thank you, Sloan. That's the nicest thing you've said to me." Vale's normally stern features softened at the edges, and he finally cracked a wide grin.

Sloan nearly tripped. "Shite… Is that a smile?" he said with exaggerated wonderment, poking the albino's cheek. "Well, hallelujah. He actually smiled."

Vale frowned. "You're laughing at my expense and, bullying me again."

"Relax. It was a joke." Sloan's laughter died, and he nudged him. "And don't you know bullying is a sign of affection? I don't waste my breath on anybody I can't stand."

Dumbfounded, Vale stared at the Irishman. He was such a strange man, literally a contradiction in terms. Old yet youthful, courageous yet lacking confidence, intelligent yet acting a fool, taciturn yet deeply compassionate. *Maybe it's true that humans only reach a certain level of maturity.* He looked at Sloan again, and this time he saw a nine-year-old boy lying in a pool of blood, reaching for his father. He was certain that moment was when the disconnect happened. Some tiny part of the man he saw now had remained as that nine-year-old, lost and continually searching for approval, and for forgiveness. He thought about his own life. When Morgan stabbed him with the needle, his own disconnect happened. He'd been only fourteen. Although Sloan would probably never acknowledge the similarities, Vale honestly believed, their upbringings were comparable; trauma had shaped their personalities and dictated their future lives.

"Earth to Vale." Sloan waved his hand in front of the albino's face.

"Sorry." Vale blinked.

"You were zoned out. What's wrong?"

"Nothing." Vale smiled. "Nothing at all."

They travelled the night, running or walking according to the landscape. By early afternoon the next day, they'd covered almost two-thirds of the calculated distance. There was no way they could have come so far if the human men had tagged along.

Sloan came to a weary stop and doubled over, gripping his knees. "I think I'm getting too old for this shite—running all over the fecking countryside."

"You're a big, heavy male. Agility isn't your speciality." Vale stayed close with him, scanning the open plain, the briny wind pummelling their clothes. "But you make a superb soldier."

Yards away was a stream. The rushing water wasn't loud enough to impair Vale's hearing, but it was a nuisance, no less. West, behind him and Sloan, was a low range of mountains. It began to spit. He hated wide open spaces. He motioned to his sisters, and they separated from one another, racing for the foothills on the hunt for anything unusual.

"Where are they going?"

"I feel uneasy," Vale replied.

The second he'd put his apprehension into words, the ground shuddered from deep below, as if a great serpent was slithering in the bowels of the earth. Sloan and Vale looked at their boots. They both swung around. Vale groaned, pressing his palm to his temple.

An enormous, long-limbed humanoid creature with the build of a silverback rose on its haunches, arms at its sides. When it blared, the sound shook the air. White hair flowing in the drizzly wind, it stepped closer and blared again.

"Sloan, he's mucking with my brain!" Vale grabbed his own head. Vibrating, thick red droplets fell from his right nostril. "Get out, Gunnar, get out!"

"Somehow, he must have found and ingested your blood. Run." Sloan stood in front of the albino. "Get the feck out of here!"

Vale wailed, faltering onto his hands and knees. He blinked, secreting blood from his eyes, the cold, hard ground under his hands rapidly going in and out of focus.

"Okay, two can play this game." Sloan concentrated. "I've seen you before." He stared into the creature's mustard-yellow owl eyes. He willed it, and his claws grew, his pupils expanded, and his fangs lengthened. "Hey, don't ignore me, arsehole! *Come on!*" he roared, spreading his arms. "It's you and me!"

The attack scarcely registered. Hit in the chest, Sloan was sent careening into the far-flung trees. Coming to, he shook his head and grasped blindly for anything that would help him get up. *Feck.* He clutched his ribs, rasping. The pain was unbelievable. *God, give me strength.* He stumbled from the tree line to see the grass peppered ruby-red. *Where are the others?*

They're in a battle for their lives, the parasite answered.

Vale was fighting his brother. But he couldn't inflict enough damage. The only thing that kept him alive was the fact that he stayed out of Gunnar's strike zone. Gunnar was huge, lean, and mindbogglingly fast. Moreover, he was a rapid healer. One female had already perished.

What can we do?

I don't know, Sloan. Your abilities are limited, as I still am.

You can't be serious, doll?

Sorry, but it's the truth. I am still a fledgling and learning, and I can only work with what we have.

Shite! Sloan drove his fist into a tree.

Don't get angry, please. You must focus, she whispered.

Sloan didn't know what to do. His mind raced through past conversations with Doctor Avolare. *What am I missing?* he thought frantically. *Think harder, think!* Clenching both his fists, he watched as the vampire sheared the head off another female and it sailed through the air, turning to dust.

Now it was down to Vale and the alpha female, his eldest sister. As he continued to watch them battle, he remembered...

"Did you ever consider mixing different parasites with mine?" he asked, looking about his great-grandad's cottage, touching the knickknacks.

Raphael laughed as if it was a preposterous notion but continued to stare into the firelight. "Did I consider it? Yes. My colleagues and I were always up to trying something new. Was I willing to muck with perfection? No. From a hypothetical standpoint, it could be possible if both hosts have pure matching bloodlines. But only if the parasites can mesh. That reminds me." She looked at him. "Did you know they're Norse?"

"Who?"

"The MVs' parents. DNA doesn't lie, and Krista is full-blooded Norse. After I got her test results, I watched the CCTV footage again, then reread all the notes collected from the lab. It's the only logical explanation, Sloan. The Norse, like yourself, were ideal test subjects. That means the genetic splicing altered the male's appearance—that's why his hair was white, and his eyes were gold, in the footage."

Sloan blinked; he heard the echo of gunfire. Warrick, Peaches, his brother, and the men had arrived much sooner than he'd expected and were shooting at the vampire. Vale was badly injured. But Sloan smiled. *Thanks, doll.* He started to run, then sprint, and just as he crossed the plain, he hardened, punching Gunnar in the stomach and sent him flying a kilometre away, obliterating the trees. He stopped on a dime, turned, and bolted back whence he came. He grabbed Vale and slung him over his shoulder. Cutting through the woods at lighting speed, he jumped a different section of the stream and took off again.

Inside the foothills was an entire network of caverns. He'd shown Petrov on several occasions when they'd gone fishing and trapping; they'd even used them as shelter. The dark cavern had a dry, earthy scent. He set Vale down, and then he collapsed against the wall, huffing and puffing at the stale air.

Vale gasped, scarcely able to move. He pressed his palms to the dry soil and hung his head, his hair sweeping the dirt. "What... are... you... doing?"

"I just saved your arse." Sloan gulped. "And now you're going to save everyone."

"He will find us."

"Probably." He licked his lips. "I give us a few minutes, tops."

Vale's eyebrows wrinkled into an arch, and he searched the compressed soil under his hands. It was hard and stained rust in spots. "Petrov... He died here?"

"No. It's a long story, and...I'll gladly tell you when we have more time." Sloan pushed away from the wall, staggered over to him, and dropped to his knees. "Vale, the key to ending this is in our blood."

Vale looked into his eyes and read the sincerity. "Tell me."

"Again, we don't have time. Do you trust me?"

"I do." Vale nodded. "You are my son's grandfather."

"Then I need to feed." Sloan waited until the implications of what he'd said sank in.

"But you have never fed before. And that type of thirst, once started, is nearly impossible to control. And ingesting tissue and ingesting blood are two different things."

"We're different genetically. I'm not talking eating your flesh. All I want is your blood. I need your speed and dexterity—and your second sight wouldn't hurt. I'm fast but not fast enough." Sloan sighed and confessed with shame and a contrite frown, "I've felt the thirst since the beginning. I've turned before, but I swore to myself if it ever happened again, I wouldn't lose control."

"My blood is not the same as a normal human's. It's probably poisonous. You could die. We both carry parasites. My parasite could kill yours, even though they're still somewhat the same."

"True. Or I could survive and become this awesome, kick-arse vampire." Sloan chuckled with a teasing grin.

Vale shifted and lay down on the dirt, raking the hair from his face. "Do it. Do it before I change my mind."

Sloan didn't have time to second-guess. He carefully slid a hand in under Vale's nape and examined his exposed throat. *Here goes nothing.* His fangs, this time as if on instinct, grew and sank into Vale's flesh as he bit down. Vale gasped, then automatically struggled, but Sloan's viselike grip was unbreakable. Sloan stared dead ahead, gulping down the blood, his lips drenched, his nostrils flared, inhaling the sickly-sweet scent of iron. He suddenly let go.

Vale, coughing and choking, grabbed his throat and skittered to the far side of the cavern. A howl echoed from the

343

adjoining tunnels. He tore his eyes away from Sloan and anxiously stared into the muted darkness.

Sloan lay supine, his arms in a stiff crescent as if he were clutching at someone, his eyes racing side to side under the lids, his breathing jackrabbit elevated. Vale's heart thumped as he neared him. Something had gone wrong, or something was very right. He couldn't choose, but they had to get out of the caves. "Sloan," he murmured, giving him a cautious shove, "he's here."

Another howl, followed by an ear-splitting screech, bounced off the stone walls, and Vale grabbed Sloan's jacket and began lugging him toward the mouth of the cavern; he was as heavy as a tank and just as awkward to move. "Wake up," he demanded through his teeth. "If you don't wake up, I'll kill you myself."

But the man didn't budge. Vale dragged him out of the cave and down a steep rocky escarpment into the bushes, and there he clutched Sloan's head and upper body against his chest, waiting and listening. The loss of blood had weakened him, and Sloan was unresponsive. The mutant vampire let off another string of bloodcurdling screeches and yowls, but they were amplified, a syncopated, terrorizing tune.

"Do not let the thirst control you," he said, closing his eyes. "You must control it."

Surrounded by white, Sloan noticed the red thread flowing from his pinky, multiple strands shooting in every direction.

There were people connected to each strand, some dead and some living, and some faceless individuals from the future.

And from out of the radiance, Petrov walked toward him, his boot heels clacking as if the ground were a glass platform. He had a pair of scissors in his hand. "Do you want me to cut it forever?" He angled the blades over the string, threatening to snip.

"No!" Sloan stared at him in tears. "No, don't."

"Then kill it for me. Kill it for Raphael and Krista."

"I don't know how. I thought Vale's speed would help me."

"That thirst you feel is only part of your power."

"Part? Vale said not to lose control."

Petrov got closer still and studied his eyes. "Do not fear it. Embrace it. It only takes a drop of blood."

"I'm confused, Mikhael. Embrace it…?"

"The blood of every opponent is your prize and your greatest weapon. But you have the ability to do much more than just steal their genetics. You need to learn how to manipulate the gift."

Sloan was gradually beginning to understand. "I should've told you more often… Thanks for always being there, Mikhael."

Petrov smiled and tucked the scissors in his back pocket. "That is what friends are for. Now, finish what Morgan started."

"Ahh!" Sloan shouted, holding his head, as Petrov's voice reverberated. He was alone, curled in the fetal position on the forest floor, with no idea how he got there. Scanning the gloom, he hastened to his feet, covered in pine needles and dirt. "Vale," he whispered. His brain was on fire, and everything around him sent an overabundance of information. He had to weed through what was trivial until he found what he needed.

Amazing, the parasite said. *I've never seen genetics like this...*

Great. But can you amalgamate the speed to my DNA, doll? Suddenly, the familiar barrier froze him, keeping the world out, and seconds after, he felt the pins and needles, then...

Done, she said. *The genetic editing is complete.*

There was a cry. His ears pricked, and he bolted through the trees onto a wide mountain ledge. Gunnar was thrashing Vale. His pupils expanded to saucers, his heart rate slowed, his incisors lengthened, and his muscles swelled in seconds, the thirst driving him. He took a step, and he was in front of the vampire, his movement fluid and smooth to him, but so fast it was invisible to Vale. He hardened and swung. The punch connected like stone, and Gunnar's bones crunched. The vampire wailed, falling backward away from them. Released, Vale retreated, shielding himself with his arms, but he didn't see Sloan.

The vampire regained its' footing and tackled Sloan to the ground. Brought its' fists up like an ape and smashed but missed, fracturing the rock ledge. Gunnar leaped to his feet, chased Sloan, and punched his chest and head, flinging him into the mountainside.

Normally, working through the pain was part of Sloan's condition. However, Vale's DNA kept the pain at a numbed distance, so it was no longer a hindrance. The DNA kept him more alert and able to concentrate. He got up, raced between the trees into a small clearing and jumped high in the air, clashing with the vampire.

Vale slid on his buttocks down the ledge, slipping over the gravel and loose soil. At the bottom, he jumped deadfall to find his sister slumped on frangible branches. Her right arm was missing, and she was hemorrhaging; she put up an agonizing fight for every breath. He touched her clammy forehead.

She lifted her sparkling ruby eyes, looking more human than he could remember. "He is… faster… now," she wheezed. "He will… win."

"Is there anything I can do?" He kept stroking her hair.

"Stay with me."

"I'm not going anywhere." Vale sensed her sorrow, and it was equal to his own; the blood link they'd shared with their younger sisters had been severed forever, and they missed them both.

Sloan charged and jabbed. The vampire copied his moves perfectly, throwing an identical jab. Sloan blocked the jab and punched him in the gut, chest, and throat in split-second succession. Gunnar screeched, slashing, and they clashed again. Sloan thumped his chest hard with both fists and jumped with a roundhouse, booting his head. He landed and side-kicked Gunnar in the ribs. The vampire hurtled into the trees, and Sloan yelled, racing after.

All the way down the slope, the soaring evergreens wobbled. Sloan landed with a tremendous thud at the base of the mountains, and he sped into the forest. The vampire's screeches luring him. "Come on, you fecking bastard!" he hollered, darting through the wet shadows, narrowly missing spruce, and cedars.

The vampire appeared and clotheslined Sloan, sending him flailing backward. He hit a pine, dropped to the ground, and barely raised his arms when Gunnar walloped him with a huge section of trunk. After the third swing, Sloan grabbed the tree trunk and groaned, flinging it, together with Gunnar, toward a crag. Both the trunk and Gunnar fell, crashing and tumbling backward over the escarpment. Sloan sped to the cliff edge and soared into the rainy air.

They fought everywhere in the forest and across the sodden valley, savagely beating each other time and time again, until Sloan got hold of Gunnar's arms and snapped them back to the sound of his bitter, snarling wail. In that fraction of a second, Sloan drove his fingers into Gunnar's chest. Ripped out his heart, sliced his throat and twisted off his head.

Standing in freezing rain, Sloan held the head in the air like a trophy, and he watched as it rapidly decomposed, eyeballs sinking and shrinking, skin falling away to dust, teeth crumbling. Then the skull collapsed to ash, pouring through his fingers.

Finally, he sighed. *It's over.*

Vale watched closely; Sloan's movements were hardly a blur. Apparently, he was already learning to manipulate his new ability. The Irish Independent had dodged almost every strike, pulverized the hybrid-vampire, and ultimately killed it. Even with the battle won, the fury remained inside Sloan. But for how long? Dependent on the type of parasite, whether by necessity or want, the exchange of DNA could last minutes, hours, days, or it could be permanent, the standard result. However, if the enchantment did last forever, Vale wondered if the old warrior had it in him to summon it at will.

Sloan reappeared beside Vale and helped him stand. "It's time to go home."

Vale's sister got up with him, and they both shambled alongside Sloan.

By the time they joined the others on the plain, Vale and his sister had healed and were able to walk unaided.

"I'm sorry about your brother."

"I saw it in his eyes. He was dead the moment they stuck the first needle in his arm." Vale glanced at him. "He let them take his soul. I refused to lose mine."

TWENTY-FOUR
EVERLASTING GRIEF

"How's Vale doing?" Elyse set a mug of coffee on the kitchen table in front of her brother.

"He's good," Warrick said. "He patrols the wilds, and none of the men want to be sent out there. So, I've got zero complaints."

"I'm glad. It's been hard on him to conform to my lifestyle, living in the apartment and dealing with the people in the city."

"Assimilation doesn't work for everyone. It's the way he was maltreated." Warrick took a slurp of the steaming brown-black liquid.

"You mean the lab."

"Well, it wasn't ideal, was it? Vale's had a shitty life. Have patience."

"Oh, I do. He always comes home unless he has a night patrol. But it's not him I'm worried about." She stared into her mug, turning it with her delicate fingers. "Ever since the incident with Gunnar, Dad's been travelling farther and farther from home. I don't know why but I've got this bad feeling... I'm scared that one day he might not come back."

"He'd never leave. Now that everything's over, he's probably just bored." Warrick sighed as his sister broke down in tears. "The last time I tried to help, I hurt him. I don't know if we should get involved."

"But his behaviour isn't normal." She sniffed, patting her eyes dry with a pale-blue handkerchief.

He looked over at Valerian, who was playing with a pile of ancient toys in the living room. The little boy had grown substantially in the last five months—infant to toddler, virtually overnight. A sign that told Warrick his nephew wasn't a typical human, and that reminded him that their entire existence wasn't typical. "Maybe this is our normal...the constant battle to survive. And maybe Dad's just had enough. Remember he's been to hell and back."

"What about us? We lost our mom and our brother, and Petrov was our friend." Her face wrinkled. "It isn't like I don't miss them too."

"I know." He felt empathy and patted her hand, then gave it a rub.

"Can you come home for a while? Help me look after Dad?"

"Sure, when time permits."

That same night, Elyse woke to thudding from the closet in the master bedroom. She got up on her elbows and stared at the opposing wall. Another thud. She flipped back the bedding, put on her housecoat, and snuck cautiously past her son's bassinet into the hallway. Dull lamplight filtered under the edge of her father's bedroom door. She pressed her ear to the wood. He was talking to someone. She bit her lower lip and took hold of the knob.

"What are you doing?"

She jumped, clutching her chest. When she saw her brother's ghostly mass, partly hidden in the darkness, she walloped him. "You jerk," she whispered. "Shouldn't you be at the base?"

He grabbed her wrist and dragged her into the living room. "I just got in a few hours ago," he whispered back. "I was sleeping on the couch. Besides, you're the one who asked me to come home."

"Sorry. But I thought you were busy… Oh, never mind."

"You were going to sneak in Dad's room. Why?"

"You mean to tell me you didn't hear all that racket?" She looked up at him.

"No. I was exhausted and crashed when I hit the sofa."

"Well, it woke me, and I thought something was wrong."

They both heard a loud thud. Warrick moved quickly through the hall, stopped, and grasped the master bedroom doorknob, but his sister grabbed his arm.

"I don't know if we should do this." She stared with nervous uncertainty at him.

"It's too late now." Warrick turned the knob and they entered the room.

Elyse clung like lint to his shirt and leaned sideways to see past his bulk.

Sloan was spread-eagle on his back, his forehead stippled in sweat, his brows arched as if he were confused, his eyes racing under the lids. And he was mumbling. He smashed his arm against the wall and rolled onto his side.

"Oh, Warrick. His knuckles are bleeding and bruised and look at the dents in the wall." Elyse didn't dare get close to her father because he was thrashing about, and she shied back near the door.

Warrick knelt on the bed and grabbed his father before he hit the wall again. "Dad, wake up." He used all his strength and pinioned Sloan's arms with a grunt. "Dad!"

Sloan woke with a fright. Initially, he stared enraged, but when he realized it was Warrick, he went limp. "*Son…*"

"It's okay, Dad." Warrick slowly peeled away his fingers and released his arms. "You must've had a nightmare. You were hitting the wall, and you woke us up. And you've hurt yourself."

Sloan examined his sore but healing hand, then dropped his head back on the pillows. He licked his lips. "Shite. I'm sorry, son. Did I injure you?"

"I'm fine. We're just worried about you."

"Can you get me a glass of water, baby doll?"

"Sure." Elyse returned moments later with the largest glass they had filled to the rim.

As usual, the water had a cloudy film, but Sloan didn't care. It was wet. He downed the entire glass, handed it back to her, and wiped the trickle that had escaped to glide down the side of his chin.

353

He studied his children's pained faces. In truth, he'd spoken little to Warrick since his imprisonment, and he'd ignored Elyse's carking doubts about his erratic behaviour. But he knew they couldn't keep avoiding one another. Propping himself against the pillows, Sloan rested his head on the wall above the headboard and stared at his son. He didn't have a clue how to explain his feelings, and the awkward silence mounting between them wasn't helping.

"Maybe I should leave." Warrick glanced uncomfortably at his older sister.

Sloan leaned forward and seized his arm. "You're not leaving."

"But you're staring at me like you hate me, Dad. I can't take it anymore," Warrick said with hoarseness, and his shoulders rose to conceal his neck as if he feared reprisal.

"Now you listen to me. No father could be prouder of his son than I am of you, Warrick. I don't care if we argue or make mistakes or if we have a difference of opinion. You will always be *my son*."

"I'm sorry… for the way I treated you."

"Me too." Sloan continued to hold his arm. "I'm truly sorry."

Warrick slumped down beside him, shaking the bed, and his chin quivered slightly.

Sloan sensed he was finding it difficult to express whatever was on his mind. He sighed and pulled the young man sideways into a powerful bear hug. "I love you and your sister, more than anyone or anything in the entire world."

After a minute, Warrick eased up and looked Sloan in the eyes. "I love you too, Dad."

The air raid warning went off with a loud, eerie howl, startling them. Warrick sprang into action and almost knocked Elyse into the bed. Sloan flung the covers back, getting up.

"What's going on?" She backed into the corner, twirling a lock of her hair, hugging her own chest. "I thought the mutants were dead."

"I don't know, sweetie. Get dressed and get Valerian ready. I'll escort you to the bomb shelter." Sloan pulled Petrov's scarlet T-shirt down over his head.

She dashed past Warrick, who was standing just outside the master bedroom. "I'm ready," he said. "I'll meet you downstairs."

"Don't worry about me, son. Get to the base. I'm going to help your sister."

"I'll see you later, then."

"Sure thing." Sloan grabbed the holstered pair of FN Five-seveNs that hung in the closet, and he flipped on his aviator. By the time he'd strung the Irish longsword over his back and stepped into his boots, his daughter was waiting at the apartment door with Valerian strapped to her chest, the baby carrier brown corduroy. The little boy gnawed on his fist, watching Sloan. Sloan couldn't resist. He kissed the boy's head. Valerian stopped gnawing and beamed.

"He sure loves his grandad." Elyse giggled. "And I think being a grandad suits you."

"Maybe it does." His lips creased into that famous crooked grin, and he opened the door. "After you, baby doll."

***

The South American shapeshifters invaded District B. And they'd returned in greater numbers, with a reserve of five hundred human soldiers in their midst. Warrick, directing APF units and the Independents, found himself caught in the thick of it. While Sloan joined the fight on the frontlines, he worked alone unless his brother or Peaches tagged along.

Days turned into weeks, and at the end of the conflict—a narrow win for the bedraggled Avalon—necessity forced the federal panel to reassess their military, and restructure the existing perimeter fence. Because, as it seemed, the SA Bloc's attacks were becoming more frequent.

Sloan steered clear of the politics. Still battling his inner demons, he once again drifted away from home. He used any excuse to leave the suffocating atmosphere of the apartment and all the memories it harboured. Ever since Vince had moved him back into his old suite, he couldn't seem to curb his emotions. Night after night, the second he shut his eyes, the trauma surfaced, a vivid mishmash of painful memories that were strangely exaggerated.

Then, in the late fall, scarcely two months after the first attack, as if by some sick twist of fate, the shifters returned. This time with an even larger army. A mix of both human and freak, they invaded Avalon with unrelenting force, pushing the great northern city into a full-scale war and toward the brink of collapse.

With no end to the war in sight, commanders sent additional scouts—any able-bodied man, or woman—to patrol the southern District N. Newberg, a farming region, was the easiest to infiltrate. Destroying Newberg storehouses and farms would prevent the people surviving the winter, and that, as the federal panel soon learned, was precisely the shifters' strategy.

Elyse glanced back at one of the many farms. The sprawling acreage had a silo, several barns with hay lofts, chicken coops, a pigsty, geodesic dome greenhouses, and a split-rail fence that separated the grazing land from the horse paddock and shelters. The farm was a logistical marker because of its size and proximity to the southern gates. She was wandering farther from where she felt the safest. "Where are you going?" She tramped the grass close behind her father.

"Anywhere that's away from here. And didn't I say this was no place for you? You should be at home with your son."

"I'm a scout, Dad. I have to do my part in order to get paid. New shifter sightings have been reported." She quickened her pace. "Dad, *I* need you. *Warrick* needs you." She tried to think of the right words, anything inspirational that would persuade him to return home with her. "Valerian needs his grandad."

Sloan came to a standstill and twisted around to look at her. The wind was as cold and acrimonious as his expression, and a couple of snowflakes floated earthward. Winter had arrived. "I know you do, but I'm incapable right now. I'm hanging on by a thread."

"Thread? What's wrong?" she begged. "Tell me. Maybe I can help you."

"It's me, baby doll. My heart's broken, and I can't seem to put the pieces back together." He motioned with somewhat interlocked fingers, as if he were trying to put together an invisible puzzle. "Ever since that night, I... I can't seem to focus. I drift... I just keep seeing Mikhael die over and over again. His death haunts every breath I take."

She stared at him, glassy-eyed. "You just need time, that's all," she said with sympathy. "You've done nothing but fight battle after battle since he died—even before that your life was rife with violence. You need time to heal and sort out your feelings."

"Heal... I don't think I know how anymore." Sloan choked with a tear sliding down his face. "When a person's mind goes... there's nothing left but a shell."

Elyse was about to respond, but she suddenly sensed they weren't alone. "Dad, don't move," she whispered, carefully scanning the terrain. "They're all around us."

"Shh, I know," he whispered back, with dead, dark eyes and a finger pressed to his lips. "But don't worry. Everything will be okay, sweetie, because I'll protect you."

Elyse detected an odd sensation from her father, and she intuitively knew he didn't intend to survive. This battle would be his last. She'd sensed his depression for a very long time, ever since her mother's death in fact, but no matter what she did, it only seemed to worsen. She had hoped he'd pull himself out. However, the depths of his despair were too deep even for her to reach. The shapeshifters had given him his out: his way to escape immortality. Now, she really wished she had possessed more foresight.

Blood sprayed the air. She flinched, and her father was gone. Fast, precise, and vicious, his movement was scarcely distinguishable as he flew between the trees and tore the shapeshifters to shreds.

"Dad, don't!" Elyse tightened her grip on the old AK-5000, Petrov's prized assault rifle, that was still in pristine condition even half a century after its manufacture date. She'd often wondered how many conflicts the gun had seen. Fearful, she watched a shapeshifter crush Sloan. And more came, smaller than the large one locked in combat with her father.

If she hadn't followed him, none of this would've happened. If she hadn't argued… But she knew Peaches, Claire and the other Independents would soon arrive. In the meantime, all she had to do was assist her father. She smeared her runny nose on her sleeve. Although shaken by the appearance of the hideous shifters, she managed to keep a level head.

She took aim. "*Please*, Petrov. Help me." The instant the words left her lips, it was as if the large Russian were holding her from behind and steadying her arms; tranquility washed through her.

"Do not be scared. Remember: short, controlled bursts," he said in her ear. *"The bullets will not harm your father, but they will hit the target."*

Gathering the courage, she squeezed the trigger. Her entire body juddered. The elephant-sized bullets blew apart whatever they hit: leaves, branches, tree trunks and the shapeshifter, that wailed in agony. From the corner of her eye, she glimpsed the Russian standing only a short distance away. *I don't believe it.* What her father had said was true. *The dead are among us.* She continued to shoot, and then she realized, with mounting anxiety, that Petrov wasn't alone. Her mother, Raphael, Tristan, and others were in the background. They all seemed to wait. "Don't take my dad, *please*," she implored in tears.

Then she froze and her watery gaze inched down. A shapeshifter's fist was sticking out from her gut with fingers sopping red. "Dad!" she screamed, walloping the creature with the rifle butt. "Dad, help me!" But quickly overcome, she staggered and fell, dropping Petrov's gun. "Dad…"

When Elyse reopened her eyes, the enemy was gone, ashy flakes were falling all around, and Sloan was hugging her securely to his chest. "Dad…" She feebly reached and brushed his grimy face with her bloodstained fingers. "Dad, I love you."

"Oh, God, no, no, no!" Sloan grasped her hand and kissed the palm, pressing it to his lips. "You're going to be okay, baby doll."

"I-I don't think so." She gulped, searching his woeful expression. "I feel very cold and heavy… and they're waiting for me…"

Sloan paused, and with great disinclination, he peered over his shoulder. The moment he saw his wife and Petrov, he burst into tears, clutching his daughter tighter. "Don't do this to me. Not again, *please!*" But, however much he willed it, Elyse was already standing in front of him without injury, wearing a heartbroken smile. He gritted his teeth. "I love you so much!"

"I know, Dad."

"If you leave…" His lashes fluttered languidly and all of a sudden, he felt exhausted, barely able to move. "I can't go on…"

Everybody he'd lost, that insufferable pain, had taken its toll, adding layer upon layer of grief. And now the pressure had become too great. Imploding with incredible destructive velocity, the most powerful emotive link was made: the parasite was crying with him.

He gently laid Elyse in the snow-sprinkled ferns and collapsed beside her. Arms at his sides, he turned his head, breath misting, and gazed at Petrov crouched next to him.

"Do not fall asleep," Petrov said sternly, touching his chest. "You must stay awake, Sloan."

"No more," Sloan mumbled, shutting his eyes. "I want to be with you all…"

Petrov stood and he, Amanda, Elyse, and Tristan circled the Irishman, watching with grave sorrow as in less than a minute, he hardened to solid stone.

***

A large group of solemn-faced Asian guards crowded near the clinic entrance doors and around the shelves of medical oddities, their clothes smelling musty. Vincent was on top of a lopsided school desk with his boots anchored on the attached chair. He gave his scalp a rub; his pained expression revealed the ache in his heart. For the first time in his life, he was truly scared—scared of what fate had in store.

"He won't wake up." Peaches paced the room, wringing her hands. "The big man won't wake up!"

Wade stared in disbelieving shock at his childhood friend, slowly manoeuvring around the Asian guards. Sloan's appearance was perfectly normal—his hair, even the maroon pigment of his lips—but he wasn't breathing. Wade put a nervous hand on Sloan's chest, hesitating. He was as cool and hard as rock, a porcelain corpse prepared for burial. "What the feck happened?"

"That's the thing," Peaches answered, her voice strained. "We just don't know!"

"When we got to where he was, south of Newberg," Vincent said quietly, "Elyse was dead, and he was in this condition."

"What do you mean, Elyse is dead?" Wade's panic doubled.

Vincent pointed behind to a body wrapped in a blanket on the gurney. "We brought her here for you to examine."

"We didn't know what else to do." Peaches shakily lit a cigarette.

He didn't want to unwrap the blanket. What if everything they'd said was true? As he gently separated the folds of grey wool, his heart thumped. Elyse's wilted, mummified corpse was curled in a ball like a napping cat, hugging her knees with her eyes closed. *This can't be happening.* He cast his blurred vision to Sloan, who was a statue. "Help me bring them into the operating theatre next door."

The small army of Asian guards lifted Sloan, and with grunts and groans, they carried him into the adjoining room. After one mightier heave, he was on the steel autopsy table under a bulbous, high-powered light fixture. A pair of guards rolled in the gurney with Elyse and brought it to a stop beside Sloan.

"I haven't told Warrick yet." Hands clasped together at his mouth, Vincent's miserable frown glistened in tears. His emerald eyes had lost their spark. "But he won't react well. Sloan is his hero... and Elyse is so special to him."

"That's to be expected."

After Vincent and Peaches departed, Wade sat on a stool beside Sloan. He didn't know where to begin. Should he run tests? *Could* he run tests?

"So, it is true..."

He held out his hand to Lucy. She grasped his fingers, instantly teary-eyed. Getting up, he drew her into a strong hug, as if to spare her the pain, and she clung to him, weeping. "I'm so very sorry, pet."

Eventually, she regained her composure but still clung to him. "He's like a father to me. You've got to do something."

"Not sure I can do anything."

"Maybe not." She patted her face with a kerchief. "But you're a brilliant man. I'm sure you'll find an explanation."

"I'm going to be busy for a while."

"That's fine. I'll bring your meals to you in here." Gripping his shirt, she rose on her tiptoes, and they kissed. "Don't stay up all night."

The inner door shut. Wade thought about what she'd said. He did need an explanation. It was the only way to come up with a solution if there was one to be had. Several ideas sprang to mind. He believed Sloan wasn't dead but in a coma like state, and as such, he required as much stimulus as possible. He touched Sloan's arm. "Hey, Irish. I don't know if you can hear me or not, but I'm going to talk to you from now on. And whenever you've had enough, you can wake up and deck me. How's that sound?" He grinned, then leaned over him and said evenly, "Because I ain't buying the act. I know you're in there—you just need to snap out of it."

At the crack of dawn, Warrick bashed through the clinic doors, waking Lucy and Wade. But his rampage died the second he saw his father. The sight of the general bawling like a little boy, hugging his father, broke Lucy's heart, and Wade wasn't far off. Wade couldn't imagine his life without

Sloan. He still didn't have a clue what to do, but he wasn't about to concede to defeat.

As for Vale, he was so emotionally wrecked by the loss of Elyse that he disappeared, never to be seen again, leaving his son Valerian in the joint care of Warrick and Vincent.

***

MONTHS LATER

The clinic was bright, clean, organized, and the aroma of steeped rose hip tea hung in the air along with freshly baked pumpkin spice cake. Lucy was in the cafeteria. She'd turned to cooking, baking, and cleaning, everything domestic, into a coping mechanism.

Wade watched her waddle to the large commercial sized refrigerators and bring out a basket of eggs and a jug of milk. After six months, the war finally ended, but because food was still rationed, she only had six eggs instead of a dozen. He'd really wanted Sloan to be present for the birth of their first child, but he was afraid that wouldn't happen.

The buzzer went, and he closed the cafeteria door. Next, Vincent and Peaches were inside the clinic; a confrontation he had desperately wanted to avoid. He sighed and motioned for them to take a seat. Sloan was lying on a hospital bed in the centre of the room.

"Any ideas yet?" Peaches asked, sitting on a stool at the stainless-steel table.

Vincent also pulled out a chair and sat, lighting a cigarette.

"He may be in a state of dormancy because he bit someone, and the genetics were too much to apply to his arsenal. However, I have another theory: perhaps this is some kind of self-defence mechanism."

"He was overwhelmed by the enemy and turned to stone?" Peaches said.

"But there's another factor involved."

"What's the other factor?" Vincent exhaled smoke.

"Elyse." Wade pressed on his knees, rose, then walked around Sloan as he talked. "It's just a guess… but I think they were ambushed. She was attacked, and he couldn't save her, and she died as a result. Then whatever killed her turned on him. And, either he realized he couldn't fight it, or he was too distraught and gave up." He paused and looked at them. "I've attempted dozens of tests. But obtaining tissue and blood samples is impossible. He has turned into a composite that is harder than rock."

"You're certain?" Vincent asked.

"I even tried smashing him with a hammer. Nothing happened. Bullets, arrows, extreme temperature change, even high-frequency sound waves: nothing breaks his body."

"What do we do, then?" Peaches lit a second cigarette.

"There's nothing we can do." Wade laid his hand on Sloan's arm. "It is up to him and, even then, I don't know if he's actually dead or alive. Near as I can tell, he isn't getting any worse. But he isn't improving. It could take days or years, or he may never regain an animated state."

Vincent stood, his gaze despondent. He touched Sloan's forehead. "Give me a few days to think this over."

"Take as much time as you need."

"Is that all you've got to say?" Peaches said, flicking the burning cigarette into a tin can full of water. "You're talking like he's dead. He isn't dead. He lost his daughter—he was hurt! You don't know what happened. He's *your brother*, damn it!"

Vincent grimaced, shooting Peaches an ominous glare, but didn't say a word.

"Oi. Calm down, woman." Wade frowned. "Why are your knickers in a knot?"

Peaches's eyes welled up. "Because I know him. I know how he thinks."

"*Arigato*." Vincent frowned with a bow, then he took one last look at Peaches before exiting the room.

Numb, he wandered away from the clinic into the street. Pedestrians bumped him. Each expressionless passerby wore a hooded cloak. It started to rain, a couple of droplets at first, but then it poured. His vision blurred, and he gritted his teeth. He didn't know how to survive alone. Sloan had been more than just his older brother—he was his substitute father, best friend, and conscience when needed. Everything in his life revolved around their relationship as siblings and business partners. His lower lip and chin quivered, and he gasped, hot tears falling. *What will I do?* He felt as if he'd lost his parents all over again.

Days later, Vincent followed through with the toughest decision of his life. It took ten of his strongest men to lift his brother's casket onto the back of a horse-drawn wagon. After they loaded Elyse's much smaller one, they exhumed Amanda's severely degraded casket and gently set it in the wagon together with her husband's.

Warrick was beside himself with grief, and he shuffled behind the cart in a tearful daze, holding Valerian's hand, with Vincent's wife Stephanie and their grown children accompanying them. A never-ending line of loved ones trailed behind Wade and Lucy; Peaches; Claire, Stoner, Yasmine, Roddy, and Snickers; Rueben and the other grown orphans and hundreds of islanders Sloan had saved.

The moonlit night was beautiful in stark contrast to the silent procession. After nine months in Wade's laboratory, Sloan was finally laid to rest beside his wife and daughter in a private family tomb. Vincent stepped back as his men shut, locked and bolted the interior and exterior doors of the mausoleum, after which they chained and locked the gates. Warrick was the first to leave. He trudged the cement pathway past his uncle and everyone else, carrying Valerian.

Vincent hadn't an inkling, but nothing would ever be the same. At that moment, fate snuffed out the life he'd once shared with Sloan like a candle.

To be continued…

NAME DEFINITIONS

Sloan (Irish Gaelic *Slaughan*): warrior; a man in the service of his country.

Patrick (Latin *Patricius*): noble one.

Whelan (Irish *Ó Faoláin*): wolf; clan of the wolf.

Morgan (Old Welsh *Morcan*): the white sea; dweller by the majestic foamy breakers.

Griffin (Irish *Ó Grifín*—spelling belongs to the Kerry family): descendant of the griffin-like; gryphon.

Vincent (Latin *Vincentius*): conquering one.

Tatsurō (Japanese): plural marker-bright, clear.

Shiro (Japanese—variant of *Shirou*): fourth son.

PARASITES

Very little is known about the first parasite created by Doctor Avolare, which she self-administered to combat her lung cancer, though it is assumed to be the precursor to DY51.

DY51 or *Diaemus youngi 51* (white-winged vampire bat) was a carbon-based parasitic injection Doctor Raphael Avolare created for human trials. This parasite was the forerunner to Sloan's *medicus* (DY51v), and the injection given to Sloan's nine co-workers, the Independents. The physician provided its host with a list of comprehensive physical enhancements: speed, dexterity, strength, stamina, heightened senses, a boosted immune system, rapid cell regeneration, and an extended lifespan, but also a thirst for blood (genetics).

The "physician" or *medicus* in Latin, labelled DY51v (*Diaemus youngi 51 Vlad*), was also a carbon-based parasitic injection Doctor Raphael Avolare created for human trials, a significant upgrade from its' progenitor. However, due to a raid on her laboratory, only one viable injection had been produced, which was later given to Sloan. *Medicus* is the only known sentient parasite that can reason, learn, steal genetics and perform genetic knockouts.

The "shield" was another carbon-based parasite strictly created to improve the Avalon Police Force's defence. Doctor Avolare combined superhuman strength, endurance, a resistance to sickness and disease, and the ultimate augmentation, an ability to harden flesh and muscle at will.

The "warrior," brainchild of Doctor Avolare's colleague W. Middleton, a fast-moving contagion type synthetic parasite, became the most effective North American counterattack to the AI/computer warfare. Embedded with a singular genetic desire to "eradicate all," the warrior became so successful, almost all worldwide technological knowledge was lost. After this, W. Middleton wanted to know if it would work the same against a biological threat. As a carbon-based parasite, the warrior unexpectedly morphed and killed every test subject. Deemed a biological "extermination level" threat, the government ordered it destroyed.

CHARACTER PROFILES

CURRENT STAT YEAR 2344

Name: Sloan Patrick Whelan
Race: Irish human/vampire hybrid
Age: 66
Hair: soot-black waves
Eyes: dark metallic copper
Height: 7'1"
Weight: 129 kg/285 lbs pounds prior to genetic modification; 163 kg/359 lbs pounds post-injection
Side effects of injection: increased muscle and bone density, heightened senses, copper glint in the irises, speed, strength, and agility
Blood type: AB- prior to injection
Life expectancy: unknown
Background: military and APF
Class: sniper
Tattoo: Irish (Celtic) longsword wrapped in vines over chest and neck to jaw
Personality: intelligent, sarcastic, dependable

Name: Claire Russo
Race: Italian human/vampire hybrid
Age: 44
Hair: golden-brown

Eyes: metallic blue
Height: 6'3"
Weight: 99 kg/219 lbs prior to genetic modification; no change post-injection
Side effects of injection: heightened senses, metallic glint in the irises, speed, strength and agility
Blood type: O prior to injection
Life expectancy: unknown
Background: APF
Class: sniper
Tattoo: Roman gods fighting for Mount Olympus; sleeves
Personality: short-fused, stubborn, passionate

Name: Mikhael Petrov
Race: Russian human/vampire hybrid
Age: 48
Hair: white-blond; clean shaven
Eyes: metallic pale mint-green
Height: 7'6"
Weight: 125 kg/276 lbs prior to genetic modification; 181 kg/400 lbs after injection
Side effects of injection: significant increase to muscle and bone density, heightened senses, metallic glint in the irises, speed, strength and agility
Blood type: B- prior to injection
Life expectancy: unknown
Background: APF

Class: military police (Russian KGB)
Tattoo: flag of the Tsar of Russia across underside of forearms
Personality: prideful, loyal, sociable

Name: Henry Stoner
Race: Eastern European human/vampire hybrid
Age: 47
Hair: dark
Eyes: metallic obsidian
Height: 5'10"
Weight: 77 kg/170 lbs prior to genetic modification; 82 kg/180 lbs after injection
Side effects of injection: slight increase to muscle and bone density, heightened senses, metallic glint in the irises, speed, strength and agility
Blood type: O prior to injection
Life expectancy: unknown
Background: APF
Class: military police, tracker
Tattoo: pair of interlocked stained-glass hoops around left eye
Personality: clever, calculating, reliable

Name: Huizhong Galicz, Snickers
Race: Chinese-Hungarian human/vampire hybrid
Age: 46
Hair: brown-black

Eyes: dark with silver metallic
Height: 5'7"
Weight: 66 kg/145 lbs prior to genetic modification; no change post-injection
Side effects of injection: sugar addiction, heightened senses, silver glint in the irises, speed, strength and agility
Blood type: B+ prior to injection
Life expectancy: unknown
Background: APF
Class: hand-to-hand combat, scout
Tattoo: yin and yang symbol on nape
Personality: quick-witted, mouthy, humorous

Name: Roddy Tetreault
Race: Acadian-French human/vampire hybrid
Age: 46
Hair: brown
Eyes: metallic brown
Height: 6'0"
Weight: 69 kg/153 lbs prior to genetic modification; 84 kg/185 lbs post-injection
Side effects of injection: slight increase to muscle and bone density, heightened senses, metallic glint in the irises, speed, strength and agility
Blood type: O- prior to injection
Life expectancy: unknown
Background: APF
Class: bomb technician

Tattoo: shipwreck on back
Personality: reserved, cautious, forthright

Name: Yasmine
Race: American human/vampire hybrid
Age: 47
Hair: ash blonde
Eyes: metallic slate blue
Height: 5'10"
Weight: 59 kg/130 lbs prior to genetic modification; 66 kg/145 lbs post-injection
Side effects of injection: slight increase to muscle and bone density, heightened senses, metallic glint in the irises, speed, strength and agility
Blood type: B- prior to injection
Life expectancy: unknown
Background: APF
Class: military police, assassin
Tattoo: sun rays from pierced navel to pelvic bone
Personality: vicious, tactless, brassy

Name: Mona Lisa Ramos (Adopted by Mexican family)
Race: Unknown human/vampire hybrid
Age: 50
Hair: chocolate
Eyes: metallic hazel-green with gold
Height: 5'4"

Weight: 46 kg/102 lbs prior to genetic modification; 48 kg/105 lbs post-injection
Side effects of injection: slight increase to muscle and bone density, heightened senses, gold glint in the irises, speed, strength and agility
Blood type: B+ prior to injection
Life expectancy: unknown
Background: APF
Class: military police
Tattoo: long, heavy steel chain around throat and between breasts
Personality: friendly, tenacious, trustworthy

ADDITIONAL STATS YEAR 2344
Name: Doctor Raphael Avolare
Race: Japanese
Age: 513
Hair: straight, waist-length black spun with silver
Eyes: metallic turquoise
Height: 5'11"
Weight: unknown
Blood type: unknown
Life expectancy: unknown
Background: medicine, genetics
Class: top of field
Personality: prodigy, shy, detail oriented

Name: Vincent Shirogatsu (aka Shiro)

Ethnicity: Japanese-Irish
Race: Hybrid-Human
Age: 55
Hair: thick, wispy ebony-brown
Eyes: metallic emerald-green
Height: 6'2"
Weight: 82 kg/180 lbs
Blood type: A-
Life expectancy: unknown
Background: yakuza boss, head of District E, black market
Class: swordsmanship, some martial arts
Tattoo: evolving, Japanese style that covers chest, arms and back
Personality: intellectual, laid-back, cruel

Name: Leona Carmichael, Peaches
Race: Greek-Scotch
Age: 57
Hair: slightly curled, orange-blonde
Eyes: metallic hazel-green
Height: 5'8"
Weight: 68 kg/150 lbs
Blood type: unknown
Life expectancy: unknown
Background: former prostitute, martial arts
Class: spy, reconnaissance
Personality: smart, aggressive, sassy

Name: Elyse Whelan
Race: Irish
Age: 22
Hair: long, wavy, ebony
Eyes: metallic sapphire-blue
Height: 5'2"
Weight: 49.90 kg/110 lbs
Blood type: AB-
Life expectancy: unknown
Class: sniper
Personality: smart, tenacious, spirited

Name: Warrick Whelan
Race: Irish
Age: 18
Hair: soot-black waves
Eyes: metallic sapphire-blue
Height: 7'1"
Weight: 146 kg/345 lbs
Blood type: A-
Life expectancy: unknown
Class: swordsman
Personality: laid-back, collected, intelligent

Name: Vale
Race: Norse
Age: 30

Hair: long, straight platinum-white
Eyes: metallic gold ingots
Height: 6'10"
Weight: unknown
Blood type: unknown
Life expectancy: unknown
Personality: mild-mannered, observant, candid

DISTRICTS OF AVALON

District A or Algreise: residential area. Landmarks: the Carlyle Hotel and the Royal Dragon Convention Centre.

District B or Bunting: salvage shops, ration stations and eateries. Landmarks: the Hunters Lounge, a private bar for mercenaries and the like; Bunting Fair, a black-market outlet.

District C or Chartreuse: the original artistic heart of the city. Landmarks: all government facilities including the library, looted museums, art galleries and high-end gift shops.

District D or Drixton: residential area and nightclubs. Landmarks: the Praying Mantis, the Pink Flamingo and the Kitten Shack.

District E or Eien no inochi: *Eternal Life* is a heavily populated residential area. Landmarks: the Asian Market, the Red Geisha, the Green Dragon brothel and the Metropolitan Centre.

District F or Fainsworth: sparse, rough residential area where minor gangs and a large population of homeless children live. Landmarks: Le Grand Hotel, the French Plaza restaurant, casinos and brothels.

District G or Garner: repair yards, restoration shops, abandoned industrial and commercial zones.

District H or Holisfield: commercial and industrial. Most buildings are used by the Avalon Police Force.

District I or Ingram: military training zone. Landmarks: Dalhousie Hotel.

District J or Junkyard: a no-go zone barricaded by a high fence topped with razor and barbed wire, this area cuts straight through Avalon. The architecture is collapsing and too degraded even for salvage crews.

District L or Limerick: residential and retail area. Landmarks: the Kilkenny Hotel, the Anglican Cathedral and Avalon Hospital, Wade's clinic.

District M or Manzanillo: residential, salvage shops, black-market auction house.

District N or Newberg: sparse residential. The majority of land has been converted to farmland.

District P or Pallenberg: salvage yards and incineration pits.

District R or Roma: Little Italy, a residential area with manufacturing.

District S or Surrey: military. Location of Raphael's original laboratory. Landmarks: centuries-old naval base.

GLOSSARY

AI: artificial intelligence
AIDF: artificial intelligence document format
APF: Avalon Police Force
arse (Irish): ass
baka (Japanese): idiot, fool, dumb
bento box (Japanese): boxed lunch
bonsai (Japanese): an ornamental tree grown in pot to mimic the shape and scale of a full-sized tree
CAB: Central Asian Bloc
cambiaformas (Spanish): shapeshifter
da (Irish): dad
EAB: East Asian Bloc
EB: European Bloc
eejit (Irish): foolish person
eien no inochi (Japanese): eternal life
feck (Irish): refer to author's note in book one
fraochán (Irish): blueberry
freak (world blocs): anyone born with fully modified genetics: vampires, werewolves, elves, dwarves, shapeshifters
freak "half-blood" (world blocs): anyone born half human half modified genetics
gaijin (Japanese): foreigner

gankona (Japanese): stubborn
geisha (Japanese): traditional female, Japanese escort
gobshite (Irish, very informal, pejorative): fool, contemptible person
gomenesai (Japanese): I'm sorry
grandad (Irish): grandfather
hei (Japanese): yes
hiragana (Japanese): the most standard form of Japanese writing used on its own or in conjunction with *kanji* (symbols that represent a thing or idea-taken from the Chinese language) to form words
hybrid-human (NAC Bloc specific): a human soldier injected with a carbon-based parasite (the physician), who performs a genetic knockout, adding primarily a strand of vampiric DNA
idaina sofu (Japanese): great-grandfather
Isojiman Shizuoka: a brand of Japanese *sake* (rice wine)
itadakimasu (Japanese): I receive this food; an expression of thanks to whoever prepared the meal
ito (Japanese): wrap on the hilt (*tsuka*)
jindachi-zukuri (Japanese): a decorated sword sheath worn for battle
kagema (Japanese): a young male prostitute
kanpai (Japanese): cheers
karate (Japanese): unarmed martial arts discipline
katana (Japanese): a backsword with a curved single-edge blade

kikyo (Japanese): for the Chinese bellflower, balloon flower or platycodon grandiflorus a species of herbaceous flowering perennial plant of the family Campanulaceae

kimono (Japanese): a robe worn by both Japanese men and women

kissaki (Japanese): the rounded edge between the flat side of the (*katana*) blade and the point

koi (Japanese): ornamental, domesticated, common carp (*nishikigoi*)

kumichō (Japanese): the head of a yakuza group, an *oyabun* or kumichō (組長, family head)

menuki (Japanese): decorations under the *ito* (wrap) on the *tsuka* (hilt), made to fit the palm for grip

NACB: North American Continental Bloc

Nihonjin (Japanese): a Japanese person

niisan (Japanese): older brother

nunchaku (Japanese): a martial arts weapon that consists of two hardwood sticks joined by rope, chain or thong

obi (Japanese): sash, belt

ojisan (Japanese): uncle, older uncle

oji (Japanese): uncle

okaasan (Japanese): mother

otōsan (Japanese): father

otōto (Japanese): younger brother

oyabun (Japanese): the head of a yakuza group, an *oyabun* or kumichō (組長, family head)

papa: dad, daddy

PTSD: post-traumatic stress disorder

ramen: quick-cooking Japanese noodles, generally used in broth

ricasso: blunt-edged portion of the blade above the sword guard

roiyarudoragon (Japanese): royal dragon

SAB: South American Bloc

sake (Japanese): rice wine

sakura (Japanese): cherry blossom

san (Japanese): mister

sashimi: a Japanese delicacy of primarily fresh raw seafood sliced into thin pieces and served only with a dipping sauce

saya: a Japanese katana scabbard

sayonara (Japanese): goodbye

SB: Saxon Bloc

seanathair (Irish): grandfather

seme (Japanese, gay slang): the attacker, top

senpai (Japanese): mentor, protégé

shite (Irish): shit

Slaughan (Irish): literal pronunciation of Sloan

sofu (Japanese): grandfather

Surōn (Japanese): Sloan

tsuka (Japanese): hilt of a Japanese sword

uke (Japanese, gay slang): the receiver, bottom

ume (Japanese): plum

vampiro (Spanish): vampire

VRB: virtual reality book

Vu~insento (Japanese): Vincent

WAB: West African Bloc

wagashira (Japanese): part of a yakuza group, first lieutenant under the *oyabun* or kumichō (Japanese): family head

WWIII, WWIV: World War III, World War IV

yakuza (Japanese, slang): member of a Japanese organized crime syndicate, Japanese mob (also known as *gokudō*)

TIMELINE

March 2272 Word War III ignites as the starving *New Age Vikings* or Nordic Alliance—Finland, Denmark, Sweden, Norway, Iceland, Greenland, the Faroe Islands and the Åland Islands—invade Russia, vying for control of their meagre food stores and polluted farmlands. The alliance wipes out the ailing Russian military, and Great Britain, fearing it will be next, launches a defensive strike against the Norsemen. The old Commonwealth nations, along with their European allies, attack. Canada supplies the allies with food and water, while the United States supplies arms.

May 2277 World War III ends, and almost thirteen billion people are lost. The remaining inhabited zones have greatly reduced populations and are scattered across the globe in small pockets: the Euro Bloc (EB), the East Asian Bloc (EAB), the Saxon Bloc (SB), the West African Bloc (WAB), the South American Bloc (SAB), the North American Continental Bloc (NACB), and the Central Asian Bloc (CAB). Sixty percent of the surviving races are gone, while others are extinct. During this period, world governments are re-established, and the city of Avalon is founded, becoming the only inhabited zone in North America.

November 2277 Still in its infancy, the NAC Bloc government's authority is challenged by gangs that had come into power during the war, and the Rebellion begins as they take over the streets and the black market. Scavengers and others who refuse to join the gangs retreat to the deadlands, uninhabitable zones outside Avalon.

September 2278 Sloan is born to parents Elyse Dillon and Patrick Finn Whelan.

May 2287 The NAC Bloc government, or federal panel, consists of three women and three men. The panel establishes paramilitary-type police, the Avalon Police Force (APF). The APF regains law and order, ending the Rebellion. Sloan is almost nine years old when his father Patrick is murdered by Patrick's younger brother Morven. Shortly after, Elyse escapes the island with Sloan to live in Avalon.

April 2288 Sloan's mother Elyse meets Tatsurō Shirogatsu (aka Shiro), eldest and only son of Hiroko Shirogatsu, who died in old Tokyo during World War III. Soon afterward, Tatsurō relocated to the NAC Bloc and established a branch of the family business, taking the title of *kumichō*. Elyse and Tatsurō marry that same year.

June 2289 Vincent Shiro is born.

March 2295 Sloan voluntarily joins the APF just after his seventeenth birthday. The Nordic Alliance once again sets its sights on a target: North America, due to its wealth of technology. World War IV breaks out in November that same year. Shortly after signing up, Sloan's stepfather is gunned down in the streets during a gang-related turf war. Sloan wants to stay home to help his mother but is sent to the front lines. Vincent is six when he loses both his father and brother. Not unlike the previous war, the Norsemen want what is left of the ancients' technology to rebuild their countries. Core industries such as agriculture begin to rapidly disappear, as do those with the knowledge to sustain them. While fighting, Sloan becomes romantically involved with his lieutenant-colonel. The lieutenant-colonel gives him the black card to unlock any of the old emergency bunkers scattered throughout the deadlands.

November 2295 World War IV begins.

October 31 2301 World War IV ends. At the onset of the conflict, the world population was 2,032,000,000 people. After the dust cleared, only thirty-three million remained, and most technology was destroyed or lost.

December 25 2301 Sloan returns to Avalon to find his twelve-year-old brother out of control. He takes on a fatherly role. By this point, he's become a professional boxer and accumulated wealth in money and goods, which he uses to help his family.

January 2302 Sloan takes over his dead stepfather's business, the Avalon yakuza, establishing control as the *kumichō* to safeguard the position for Vincent. He is feared and revered thanks to his "no-speak" policy and the lucrative business he creates via the black market.

April 2308 Sloan kills his Uncle Morven, saving the island inhabitants and indirectly those in District L (Limerick). He establishes a supply route and protection for the people on the island.

December 2311 Elyse dies from a heart attack. Vincent becomes the visible figurehead, and Sloan fades into the background, as the elusive but highly feared *kumichō* of the Shiro Group.

February 2312 With a seven-to-one ratio of men to women in Avalon, brothels that housed women also housed *kagema,* young male prostitutes. A young female hooker, Peaches, begs Sloan to help her and her friends at a brothel run by a rival gang. The abuse there is horrendous, and Sloan seizes control of the establishment by killing the rival gang leader.

June 2322 Sloan and Vincent control an empire. They also help street people, the homeless and poor. Their futuristic

Robin Hood ethos works as the Shiro Group reaches mythical status, a status that doesn't go unnoticed by the government. Sloan is approached by Morgan, an old war buddy, on behalf of the APF. Morgan chooses him to participate in a new government program, the Independent Initiative. After his completion of the program, Sloan meets Amanda, a government worker and they marry October of that same year.

August 2323 Elyse is born, named after her grandmother.

May 2326 Warrick is born.

November 2330 The story begins as Sloan crosses paths with a South American Bloc troop. Then through a series of odd events, he meets Chase.

December 2330 Chase is murdered, and then Sloan kills the Independent Captain Red in Ainsworth, a deserted town north of Avalon.

April 2331 Sloan kills General Morgan Griffin near the Ocean View Park, saving the other Independents.

June 2344 For her birthday, Lucy moves in with Wade at his clinic in Limerick.

ABOUT THE AUTHOR

D. G. Pearse is passionate about writing and has been creating stories since childhood. She's written web content articles, interviews, owned an online magazine and published with a small house under a different pseudonym. But she also enjoys tea, Japanese and Italian foods, baking, gardening, art, music, driving fast and the colour purple. Thanks to an entrepreneurial spirit and a lot of hard work, she's been successful in business. Her life, especially personal experiences from her youth have heavily influenced her writing. Currently, she resides on a farm in British Columbia, Canada with her husband, son, pets and a forever-expanding collection of art supplies, books and anime.

https://www.facebook.com/dgpearsecom/
https://www.x.com/dgpearsecom
https://www.instagram.com/dgpearsebooks/
www.dgpearse.com

www.ingramcontent.com/pod-product-compliance
Lightning Source LLC
Chambersburg PA
CBHW050025030726
47506CB00001B/122